# GOTCHA!

# Books by Fern Michaels

*The Blossom Sisters*
*Balancing Act*
*Tuesday's Child*
*Betrayal*
*Southern Comfort*
*To Taste the Wine*
*Sins of the Flesh*
*Sins of Omission*
*Return to Sender*
*Mr. and Miss Anonymous*
*Up Close and Personal*
*Fool Me Once*
*Picture Perfect*
*About Face*
*The Future Scrolls*
*Kentucky Sunrise*
*Kentucky Heat*
*Kentucky Rich*
*Plain Jane*
*Charming Lily*
*What You Wish For*
*The Guest List*
*Listen to Your Heart*
*Celebration*
*Yesterday*
*Finders Keepers*
*Annie's Rainbow*
*Sara's Song*
*Vegas Sunrise*
*Vegas Heat*
*Vegas Rich*
*Whitefire*
*Wish List*
*Dear Emily*
*Christmas at Timberwoods*

## The Godmothers Series
*Classified*
*Breaking News*
*Deadline*
*Late Edition*
*Exclusive*
*The Scoop*

## The Sisterhood Novels
*Gotcha!*
*Home Free*
*Déjà Vu*
*Cross Roads*
*Game Over*
*Deadly Deals*
*Vanishing Act*
*Razor Sharp*
*Under the Radar*
*Final Justice*
*Collateral Damage*
*Fast Track*
*Hokus Pokus*
*Hide and Seek*
*Free Fall*
*Lethal Justice*
*Sweet Revenge*
*The Jury*
*Vendetta*
*Payback*
*Weekend Warriors*

## eBook exclusives
*Fancy Dancer*
*Texas Heat*
*Texas Rich*
*Texas Fury*
*Texas Sunrise*

## Anthologies
*A Winter Wonderland*
*I'll Be Home for Christmas*
*Making Spirits Bright*
*Holiday Magic*
*Snow Angels*
*Silver Bells*
*Comfort and Joy*
*Sugar and Spice*
*Let It Snow*
*A Gift of Joy*
*Five Golden Rings*
*Deck the Halls*
*Jingle All the Way*

**Published by Kensington Publishing Corporation**

# FERN MICHAELS

# GOTCHA!

**ZEBRA BOOKS**
**KENSINGTON PUBLISHING CORP.**
http://www.kensingtonbooks.com

ZEBRA BOOKS are published by

Kensington Publishing Corp.
119 West 40th Street
New York, NY 10018

All Kensington titles, imprints and distributed lines are available at special quantity discounts for bulk purchases for sales promotion, premiums, fund-raising, educational or institutional use.

Special book excerpts or customized printings can also be created to fit specific needs. For details, write or phone the office of the Kensington Special Sales Manager. Attn.: Special Sales Department. Kensington Publishing Corp., 119 West 40th Street, New York, NY 10018. Phone: 1-800-221-2647.

Zebra and the Z logo Reg. U.S. Pat. & TM Off.

ISBN-13: 978-1-4201-2148-3
ISBN-10: 1-4201-2148-0

First Kensington Books Hardcover Printing: March 2013
First Zebra Books Mass-Market Paperback Printing: July 2013

eISBN-13: 978-1-4201-3199-4
eISBN-10: 1-4201-3199-0

First Zebra Books Electronic Edition: July 2013

10 9 8 7 6

Printed in the United States of America

# Prologue

*Late August*

Myra Rutledge sat alone at the kitchen table in her McLean, Virginia, farmhouse. The dogs were sleeping at her feet, giving her a comfortable feeling to be sure. Her husband, Charles, was down below in the dungeons of the old house, in what they called the War Room.

A pile of mail she'd just gone out to the road to pick up sat in front of her. Outside, it was raining the proverbial cats and dogs. A good day to be indoors and play catch-up on her weekly "to do" list. Reading mail was definitely not one of her favorite pastimes. Not many things these days were favorites of hers at all. When enough time had gone by, she attacked the mail with a vengeance. First, she separated the catalogs from the throwaway flyers, after which the "Occupant" and "Resident" mail went into another pile. Bills found their way into still another pile; then, finally, her personal mail, which was slim to none these days, went into the last pile. A good thing, too, she thought, because she had just run out of table space. Charles would handle the bills, so she moved them to the kitchen counter. One of these days, he had said, he was going to start paying online, an idea that Myra had nixed the moment the words were out of his mouth. She dumped the throwaway flyers, along with the "Resident" and "Occupant" mail, into the trash compactor and turned on the switch. The catalogs she added to the pile of catalogs already gracing the side of the fireplace. The stack was already almost two feet high. She either needed to look at them or toss them. Tomorrow would be time enough to think about that. She shrugged.

She was now down to the miniscule amount of personal mail. Three pieces. Two looked like invitations. She opened them and realized she'd gotten it right. One was an invitation to the wedding of the daughter of someone she barely knew. The second was a thank-you note from a charity to which she'd made a handsome donation. That left the long, legal-size letter with a return address in Rosemont, Alabama. Myra frowned. She didn't know a soul in Alabama, much less Rosemont. She ripped at the envelope, being careful to preserve the return address. The frown stayed on her face. It wasn't just a short letter; there were enclosures.

Myra reached for her glasses, but they weren't where she'd left them. They were on top of her head. She finally put them on and read the letter, then the enclosures. There were tear splatters on her glasses when she removed them. She got up, walked over to the old-fashioned phone attached to the wall, and called Annie. "I know it's raining hard, Annie, but do you think you could come over? I got something in the mail I'd like you to see. We can have lunch. Will that work for you?" Myra listened, then said, "Okay, how does tuna on rye sound? Hurry, Annie. This is really important. I think you'll agree when I show you what came in the mail today."

Myra swiped at her eyes as she opened the refrigerator. The tuna, thanks to Charles, was already made. All she had to do was slice the rye bread Charles had picked up earlier in the morning, peel off some lettuce leaves, slice a tomato that Charles had picked from the garden the night before, and lunch would be served.

Ten minutes later, the dogs were up and barking. Myra looked at the video feed above the door and saw Annie driving through the gates. Her luncheon guest had arrived.

The two women made a production out of hugging one another even before Annie could shrug out of her slicker and rain hat. She kicked off her shoes and padded barefoot to the table. Myra poured and handed Annie a cup of coffee. "It's actually kind of chilly outside," Annie said as she picked up Myra's reading glasses and perched them on her nose. "Now, is this what you want me to read?"

Myra, tomato in one hand, a wicked-looking knife in her other, just nodded. The tomato and knife were forgotten as she watched her friend read what had come in the mail. She waited until Annie was finished. She watched as Annie removed the glasses and looked across at her. "This is . . . beyond sad. We have to do something for this lady. That's why you called me over, right?" Annie brushed at her own eyes, her lips set in a grim, tight line.

"She said she wrote to me before . . . when . . . shortly after it happened. She said I didn't respond. Of course I didn't respond, because I never got the letter. We were on the run then, hiding out. I never did find out where the mail went or . . . it doesn't matter now. We can explain to her and, hopefully, she'll understand."

"We could call her," Annie said. "She included her phone number."

"Or we could go to Rosemont, Alabama, and explain why we never got in touch with her. You know, personal, face-to-face. Had I gotten this letter earlier, I would have moved whatever missions we had to the back burner and concentrated on her. Do you agree, Annie?"

"I do, Myra, one hundred percent. I think we should investigate this on our own before we call the others in.

"Now, are you *ever* going to make that sandwich? I think better when I eat, so get cracking, Myra."

Myra got cracking while Annie made a fresh pot of coffee. When lunch was ready, both women looked at one another and burst into tears. "I know *exactly* how she feels," Myra said as she reached for a paper towel to wipe at her eyes. She handed another towel to Annie.

"We could have helped her, Myra. We should have been there for her, and we didn't even know about what had happened. And now look at what she's facing. I say we call her after lunch. If I'm not mistaken, I think there's a one-hour time difference between Alabama and here. Not that time matters. You don't think she'll hang up on us if we call her after all this time, do you?"

"I wouldn't bet on it, Annie," Myra said, chomping down on the tuna sandwich she didn't even want. She did hate to waste food, though, so she would finish it even if it killed her. Annie ate just as fast as Myra, and they both finished at the same time.

"Who's going to make the call?" Myra asked fretfully.

"Well, the letter was addressed to you here at the farm, so I guess it's up to you to do the honors," Annie said.

Myra was reaching behind her for the phone just as Charles appeared in the kitchen. "I see lunch is ready. Did you forget about me? Nice to see you on such a rainy, miserable day, Annie."

"You, too, Charles," Annie mumbled.

"Am I interrupting something?" Charles asked as he eyed what he considered two guilty-looking women.

"No," Annie mumbled again.

"Yes," Myra said forcefully.

"Well then," Charles huffed, "I'll just make my own sandwich and take it back downstairs with me."

"That's fine, Charles, but would you hurry it up?"

Charles slapped together a sandwich and poured coffee into a thermal container, gave a sloppy salute, and was gone within minutes.

The two women looked at one another, and both shrugged at the same time. The shrug meant they didn't give two hoots if they had ruffled Charles's feathers or not.

"Well, what are you waiting for, Myra, a bus?"

"No, dear, for you to read me the number. I'm not a mind reader."

"Oh, okay." Annie rattled off the number, and Myra punched it in. She listened as the phone rang six times before it skipped over to an answering machine. She left what she hoped was a comforting message and ended by leaving her unlisted phone number for a return call.

What Myra didn't know was that, at the very moment she was leaving the message on Julie Wyatt's answering machine, lightning struck a transformer in front of Julie's house, and all power and phones went out. There would be no messages on Julie's machine when she checked it later after the power came back on.

"How long do you think it will take her to call us back, Annie?"

Annie started to make another fresh pot of coffee, since Charles had emptied it. "I think it might depend on how pissed off she is that we ignored her for five long years. If I were standing in her shoes, I'd be pissed to the teeth, wouldn't you, Myra?"

"Absolutely. Well then, let's plan a trip to Rosemont, Alabama, so we can plead our case if she doesn't return our call. Let's take your plane, Annie. That way we can leave on the spur of the moment and not have to worry about reservations. Fergus won't be a problem, will he?"

"Just as much of a problem as Charles will be. That means no problem," Annie said, picking up one of the articles that had come in Myra's letter. "You know what, Myra? I have the perfect punishment for that bitch." She leaned across the table and whispered her suggestion.

Myra's eyes popped wide. "Oh, Annie, I do like the way you think. That's just lovely. I can see it now, playing out right in front of our eyes. Do you think the others will have a problem with this? It will be the first mission of the second string. I know you and I are up to it, but the others . . . they haven't been around when we go into action."

"Are you kidding? They're going to love it. And, no, I don't think any of them will have a problem. But first we have to lay all the groundwork. How long are we going to give Julie Wyatt to call us back?"

"Tonight, eleven o'clock. No one ever calls anyone after that for fear of scaring them. It will be midnight our time if they are an hour behind us.

"If we don't hear by tonight, then I think we should plan on heading south late tomorrow afternoon. Earlier, if you can make it. Do they have to do any maintenance on the plane before we take off? Check that out, Annie."

Annie huffed. "My people always have the plane at the ready, so, no, it will not be a problem. Bear in mind that this is summertime, Myra. There's every possibility Ms. Wyatt could be on vacation. Have you thought of that?"

"No, I didn't think about that. It won't matter; we'll be able to find out where she is vacationing, and we'll just go there. We can't let that poor woman think we won't help her one minute longer than necessary. I'm certainly up for it, Annie. I can stay as long as it takes. How about you?"

"I'm with you, Myra. As long as it takes."

"Let's go into Charles's office and do some googling. We need as much information as we can get before we head to Rosemont, Alabama."

Walking down the hall, Myra called over her shoulder, "Do you really think that punishment will work?"

"Well, if it doesn't, I'll just plain old shoot the damned bitch," Annie drawled.

Myra laughed, knowing full well that Annie meant every word she had just uttered. She was still laughing when she booted up Charles's special computer.

"By the way, Annie, how are your *hacking* classes with Abner Tookus coming?"

"Abner said that maybe in twenty years I might be as good as Dwight something or other.

I told you about him, he's Abner's star pupil, and he looks like he was just hatched out of an egg."

"Should I be impressed, Annie?"

"Hell no, Myra, but I am getting there. One of these days, I will be just as good as Abner himself. And then think of all the money I'll save us. I work for free. If you have any doubts, think about that pole that I mastered."

Myra started to laugh and couldn't stop. She just loved Annie de Silva.

# Chapter 1

*Earlier that summer*

In Manhattan, Mace Carlisle stepped out of the door of the Dakota, where he lived, and looked at the new day. A perfect early summer day, the temperature just right, he thought. Perhaps not at six o'clock in the morning but certainly by nine o'clock, just three short hours away, the day would be bright and sunny, with marshmallow clouds moving lazily across the sky. The trees in Central Park would whisper and do their dance for all the tourists, dog walkers, and joggers trying to take advantage of the golden day.

Mace stood a few minutes more to savor the early morning air before he walked to the curb and hailed a taxi. He could have driven, but today was a secretive kind of day, a day when he didn't want to be followed or watched. A Mace Carlisle day.

He was headed to the office of his lawyer, Oliver Goldfeld. Oliver was the only other person he knew who arrived at his office by six thirty, just the way he, Mace, did. For over twenty years, the two men had convened for coffee and Danish at Oliver's office two days a week to discuss Mace's affairs. It was something Mace looked forward to, because he always seemed to have a good day after meeting with Oliver.

Oliver and Mace weren't just lawyer and client. They were friends in the true sense of the word. While Mace wasn't Oliver's only client, he was his biggest and richest client. In fact, most of Oliver's clients had signed on with Oliver because of Mace's endorsement of the lawyer. Goldfeld and Associates was an eight-man law firm whose specialty was corporate law.

It was six twenty-five when Mace stepped out of the elevator and walked to the plate-glass doors he knew would be open. No one else would be in the offices yet, so they would have the place to themselves.

The reception room was neither lavish nor shabby. There were shiny green plants and a lot of mahogany. The lighting was subdued and the carpeting soft. Once, years ago, Mace had told his friend that he needed to "slick up the place," and this was the result.

Mace looked up at the sound of footsteps coming down one of the halls. He fixed a smile he wasn't feeling onto his face and moved forward.

Some people meeting both men for the first time might take them for brothers, or at least close relatives. Both men were tall, six-two and -three. Both weighed in at one-seventy or thereabouts. Both liked to dress in custom-cut Savile Row suits. Both had gray hair, and both had summer blue eyes even at their age, which was, in both cases, sixty. Both had hawkish noses and strong chins. They had both been bachelors until three years ago, when Mace had gone off the rails and married his masseuse, a marriage he had regretted the moment he returned from his Hawaiian honeymoon.

Oliver led the way to his private conference room, where he already had two containers of Dunkin' Donuts coffee and a bag of sugary donuts sitting on the table. "Your turn next week, Mace," he said as he handed over napkins and paper plates.

"Shouldn't you be serving this on fine china, with all the money I pay you?" Mace grumbled.

Oliver laughed, a great, booming sound. "Mace, you say that every time we picnic here in the conference room. One of these days, I'm going to surprise you and haul in some *fine china* just for you. Spit it out, buddy. You look like hell, by the way."

"I feel like hell. Where's Andrew? I thought you said he wanted to sit in this morning, so he could do a hatchet job on me." Andrew was the firm's CPA and a lawyer in his own right.

"It's his turn to carpool this morning. I don't

know what more he can say except to say it in person. I faxed his report to your office. You need to get rid of her, Mace, before she does a number on you from which you cannot recover. Wall Street is already rumbling, but then you know that. I have the divorce papers drawn up; they just have to be filed and served on her. I did the restraining orders for her and her son. You hired that weasel, and he's biting you big-time. The eviction notice is prepared and ready to be served. The thing is, I want you out of here, far away, when all this goes down. Tell me you understand, Mace?"

"I understand. Did she really divert twenty-seven million dollars to her own bank? I almost lost my lunch when I read that. Yes, yes, I know I never should have put her son in charge of the legal department. Look, I was stupid, okay? I'm sorry I didn't listen to you. I admit to being the biggest fool to walk the face of the Earth. What more do you want me to say, Oliver?"

Oliver massaged his chin as he stared at his friend. "Do not worry about the money. We can freeze the money. I have a very good man who excels at such things. But I want her out of your apartment before I do that. At the proper moment, her credit cards will be canceled, right along with everything else. The minute she walks out of the building, it will get done. Everything has to be synchronized, and you have to be *gone*. The weasel will also be escorted from your corporate offices by your security. I need you to tell me you are okay with all of this, Mace."

"What about the prenup?" Mace asked.

"Ten million dollars if the marriage lasts five years. It's cut-and-dried. When I draw up a pre-nup, I draw up a prenup. No way on this Earth can it be broken. She gets nothing other than what you've given her in the way of jewelry and her own personal bank account, which, by the way, has over eight hundred thousand dollars in it. That, plus what you paid her son for doing nothing and screwing up your legal department, is more than fair for three years of marriage. I also took the liberty of canceling the lease on his apartment in Trump Towers that you're on the hook for. What I mean is, it will be canceled the moment your security walks him out of the building."

"Should I worry about any of this, Oliver?"

"Hell, yes, you should worry. Your wife is a greedy, vindictive woman. She's already saying you're over the edge and doing insane things to the detriment of the company. Your shareholders are not going to like that. As I said, the boys on the street are making rumbling noises. No matter how you look at it, Mace, it's a mess. Now, when are you planning on leaving?"

"As soon as I walk out of here. I can't go back to that place. The minute she's out, put it up for sale and be sure to get the locks changed. You have someone who can handle all of that, right? Oh, and have someone pack up my things and put them in storage. In the meantime, I can buy what I need when I get to where I'm going."

"Where *are* you going, Mace?"

"I don't know. When I arrive, I'll let you know. Here," he said, tossing his cell phone across the conference table. "I bought a new one. When I call you, you'll be able to see the number. Here are my credit cards. I've seen enough spy movies about people going on the run and the good guys tracking them by their cell phones and credit cards."

"Take mine, Mace. At least take my passport. The picture is bad enough that no one will look twice. We could pass for each other anytime, anyplace. You need cash, too."

"Yes, I know, but I didn't want to risk going to the bank and taking money out. I didn't want to tip my hand. Give me some cash out of one of my escrow funds. One last thing; I want you to have my power of attorney, Oliver."

"Not necessary. The old one is still good, Mace. How much cash do you want?"

Mace grimaced. "A wad. I can always call you if I run out. Okay, now what is my cover story?"

Oliver blinked. "You're asking me? You're the one taking it on the lam. I thought you had a plan."

"Well, if getting in the car and driving somewhere is a plan, then I have a plan. I'll just drive till I run out of gas, and that's where I'll end up. Can you come up with something better?"

Oliver shook his head. "No, actually, I can't. What car are you planning on driving, Mace?"

Mace slapped at his forehead. "Crap! My car will stand out like a daisy in a manure field. How about I take one of yours?"

"Mine are just as noticeable as yours. In case you forgot, we bought our cars at the same time. So take your own and don't worry about it. When whoever it is gets around to me, I will have all the answers. You better get going, Mace; it's almost seven o'clock. No matter which way you're going to go, you are going to hit rush-hour traffic. Let me get the cash for you, then you need to go. Check in from time to time, okay?"

"I will. So, from this moment on, I am going to be Oliver Goldfeld, right?"

"Just don't go practicing law and giving out advice. I don't relish being hauled before the bar. What about her and the kid's cars?"

"Take them," Mace snapped.

"And . . . ?"

"Sell them to the highest bidder. I really don't care what you do. Just get rid of them."

"I have this vision of the mother and son riding the subway. Now, there's something I would pay money to see."

In spite of himself, Mace laughed.

Five minutes later, Mace had a manila envelope full of cash.

Five minutes after that, the two old friends gave each other a manly hug.

"This is going to turn out okay, isn't it, Oliver?"

"Well, if it doesn't, it won't be for lack of trying. Everything is set to go. She won't even know you're missing until you fail to show up this evening. That puts you in a good position. Keep a low profile, and I'll take care of this end."

"Oliver, why hasn't either one of us used her name? We refer to her as *her* or *she*. We don't even call the boy by name."

"First of all, he isn't a boy, he's thirty-three

years old. His name is Eli. Her name is Eileen. There, does that make you feel better?"

"Not one bit. See ya when I see ya, Oliver."

"Go on, you big lug, get out of here before I go all mushy on you. Hey, on your way out, why don't you go to the SPCA and pick up a dog. Pick the ugliest one they have, the one no one else wants, and that dog will love you forever. You have enough time to do it."

"You know what, Oliver? That's the best advice you've given me since I got here. Do me a favor; call them and tell them I'll be by to pick her or him up in an hour. I'm going to do it. Thanks for the suggestion. Man and his dog. I like that. I really do."

When the door closed behind Mace Carlisle, Oliver Goldfeld picked up the phone to call the SPCA. While he waited for the call to go through, he muttered, "Good luck, Mace."

Ninety minutes later, Mace Carlisle roared into the SPCA parking lot. He climbed out and literally sprinted toward the door, to be greeted with barking and howling dogs. A frazzled attendant looked up and said, "You must be Mr. Goldfeld." Mace nodded, then looked around. He had a bad moment when he realized he was there just to rescue one dog. He blinked, and in that instant he knew if he wanted to, he could save every animal in the shelter. He blinked again and yanked out his brand-new cell phone and called Oliver. He turned away and spoke quickly and quietly. A huge smile split his features when he turned back to the attractive blond woman behind the counter.

"Here she is," the woman, whose name tag indicated that she was Connie Toulouse, said. "Her name is Lola. She's a mix of God only knows what. She's timid, and she needs some TLC. Actually, she needs a lot of TLC. Are you up to it, sir? Owning a dog is a huge responsibility. Lola is going to depend on you. I don't have any stats on her. Someone found her and brought her here, so I have to assume she's been on her own for a while. I cleaned her up, and she's had her shots. I'd have your own vet look her over. That will be seventy-five dollars."

Mace whipped out two one-hundred-dollar bills and laid them on the counter. "Give me one of everything she's going to need." Then he bent down to look at the skinny, trembling dog, who was trying desperately to be invisible to the huge man standing over her. Mace dropped to his knees. When he looked into Lola's eyes, it was love at first sight. He picked her up and held her close to his chest. He couldn't ever remember anything feeling this good, this right. He stroked her head and whispered words he would never remember later. Lola continued to shake, but, gradually, she seemed to calm down. Mace continued to croon soft words in her ear.

Mace looked at his $1.38 million Maybach Landaulet, which generated 543.1 horsepower. Lola was certainly going from rags to riches. He grinned, something he hadn't done in a very long time. He opened the door and set the dog down in the front seat. He threw her gear into the back and slid behind the wheel. He buckled up and set Lola on his lap. He babbled nonstop to the dog until she relaxed and curled into a ball on his lap. "Don't you worry, little lady, you're mine now. I'm going to take good care of you, and I'm not going to feed you those rabbit-poop pellets Connie Toulouse gave us. We're going to stop at the first place we come to when we get out of Manhattan and get you some real food. Later, we'll adjust your diet after the vet checks you out."

It was almost noon when Mace peeled into a fast-food stop in New Jersey and went through the drive-through. He ordered basically one of everything, then pulled the ultra-luxurious high-end car over to a shaded area. Lola sniffed at the bag of food but didn't move. In the end, Mace fed her by hand. She ate daintily and looked up at him with soulful brown eyes. She had completely stopped shaking by then. After eating as much as she wanted, Lola sat up, put her paws on Mace's shoulders, and licked at his face. Mace could feel his eyes mist over. After hugging the dog, he opened the car door.

Lola cringed. "No, no, we're just going to go over there under the tree. I'm going to carry you. It's okay, Lola. Shhh," Mace said as he cradled the dog against his chest.

Once they were under the tree, Mace sat down on a bench and lowered Lola to the ground. "I think this is where you pee or something since you just ate and drank. You have to do it."

Lola tilted her head to the side, listened to the words, and squatted. "Good girl! You . . .

ah . . . have to do anything else?" Lola tilted her head again and moved off to the base of the tree, where she proceeded to do the something else. Mace laughed. When she was finished, he scooped her up, and they were back in the car within minutes and on the way south to God only knew where.

By late afternoon, Mace and Lola had entered the state of Virginia. He stopped for the night at a roadside campground whose sign said that dogs were welcome. The cabin was a far cry from the Ritz, but not only was it clean, it even smelled clean.

In the lobby of the main cabin, Mace picked up a road map and took it with him back to his cabin. He spread it out on the floor and told his dog, "Pick a place, Lola." He never knew if Lola had understood him or not, but she obligingly planted a paw on the map. Mace looked down and laughed. "Okay, Lola, Alabama it is!"

# Chapter 2

Julie Wyatt looked down at her dogs and wagged her finger. "Listen up, you guys. I am just going to the market and bank, and I'll be back in an hour. You chew even one string, and you both get punished. Bark once if you understand me, twice if you plan on defying me."

The two Chesapeake Bay retrievers looked up at their mistress and barked. Once. Julie laughed. "Yeah, right! Listen to me, Cooper. I know you have separation anxiety when I leave, but I *am* coming back." Then she looked over at Gracie, who was swishing her tail importantly. "Bite his ear if he starts chewing, Gracie."

Normally, Julie took the dogs with her when

she ran her errands, but the A/C in her truck was on the sluggish side, and the big dogs had trouble with the high humidity. So she was leaving them behind.

Outside, on her flower-bedecked veranda, Julie looked at the golden day, then at her yard. Yep, with all the rain they'd had lately, her four-acre yard was beginning to look just like Jurassic Park. She groaned when she thought about how much extra she was going to have to pay the gardener just to trim everything up before it got out of control.

As she looked around at the different flower-pots and the comfortable furniture on the veranda, she found herself smiling. Once the sun went down, she loved sitting out with a frosty glass of iced tea and watching the paddle fans overhead whir softly, causing the luscious ferns hanging from the beams to stir in the light breeze. The dogs loved it, too, especially when she gave them bacon-flavored chew bones to chew on. Sometimes she even dozed off with the dogs.

Her domain in Rosemont, Alabama. She'd inherited it from an uncle she had barely known, but since she was his very last living relative, it had come to her. Living in the wilds of New England, the land of ice and snow and frigid temperatures, she hadn't thought twice about moving to the South when she heard that the property had been willed to her. Her children lived within walking distance. But inheriting the old plantation property wasn't the freebie she had thought it would be. She'd had to sink tons of money into the old house and the grounds, then she'd had to refurbish the guesthouse in the back that had originally been slave quarters. Her uncle had had the building rebuilt back in his day, and as far as she knew, he had never rented it out. Nor had she. When she had company, her guests had all the privacy they wanted. But the way her finances were of late, and with all her annual bills coming due, she might have to give some thought to renting it out.

Earlier in the day, it had been beautiful outside, with barely any humidity. But, now, in mid-afternoon, she could feel the sticky dampness washing over her. Time to get a move on, or she wouldn't make it back within the hour as she had promised the dogs. She needed to stop at Rosemont Produce to pick up some fresh fruits and vegetables so she could try out some new recipes for her job as a food-show hostess on the Food Network. She was even thinking about writing a cookbook, but she doubted she would ever get around to doing so—despite already having a title for the book, *Julie's Down-Home Cooking*. Not bad for a transplant from Vermont.

She also had to stop at the bank to deposit her final check from the series, which had wrapped up last week. The check would keep her afloat for another six months until the show started shooting again and she had a regular income stream.

Julie fished around in the pocket of her walking shorts for her car keys. She pulled them out, along with a slip of paper. She looked down at what she was holding in her hand. Her heart kicked up a beat, then another beat. She licked at her lips, knowing she was going to have to deal with the slip of paper, and soon. But not just then. It was the wrong time. Her gut said so. She had a bad moment when she thought maybe, just maybe, she should have talked to the kids about the slip of paper. No, she wasn't ready for that, either. Because she didn't want to look at the paper any longer, she jammed it back into her pocket. Maybe she'd lose it along the way. Well, tomorrow was another day, and the day after that still another day. She had plenty of time to make a decision one way or the other.

There were only a handful of customers at the market, most shoppers preferring to go out before the heat of the day. Julie, however, went whenever the mood struck her. She picked out her vegetables and fruit along with a basil plant in a little pot, which she would keep on the windowsill. She dearly loved basil.

A young boy carried her bags to the car and deposited them. She gave him two dollars, and he thanked her profusely. Next stop, the bank, where she would deposit her check to make sure she stayed solvent for another six months.

Like in most banks in small Southern towns, the people in the Sovereign Bank liked to chat, especially with a TV personality who was living in their midst. People would ask about the family and the dogs, so she stopped to talk to the tellers, the bank officers, and a few of the customers. In her hand, she had two dog bones for Gracie and Cooper that one of the tellers had handed her.

Julie waved good-bye and headed out the door to the parking lot. She was about to climb into her old Chevy Blazer when a man leaned out of his car window and said, "Excuse me! Can you tell me where I might find an apartment complex. I just got here, and I need to find someplace to rent quickly."

Julie tossed her handbag into the backseat of her truck and walked over to one of the most interesting, flashiest cars she'd ever seen in her life. "What exactly are you looking for?"

"Just a small place, and I only need it for a little while. I just don't want to go to a motel, and most places don't take dogs." He held Lola up for Julie to see. That was all Julie needed. The man was a dog lover, she could tell. Her kids were going to kill her when they found out what she was about to do.

"Actually, I do know of a place. I have a cottage I'd be willing to rent to you. It's about eight hundred square feet, has a loft, circular staircase, no bathtub but a full shower and a full kitchen, and it even has a fireplace. It's furnished."

"You do! I'll take it! Just tell me how to get there."

He looked nice, Julie thought. And the dog was cute. "Just follow me. That's some fancy set of wheels you have there, mister. Does it fly or skim over water?"

The man shook his head. "Sorry, no. Oliver Goldfeld," Mace said, holding out his hand.

"Julie Wyatt." They shook hands. "Don't you want to know how much the rent is?"

"Yes. How much is it?"

"You know what, Oliver? I don't know what to charge you. I've never rented out the cottage before. Actually, I was thinking about doing just that this very afternoon, and now here you are. Why don't we wait till you see it, then you can tell me what you think it's worth. Will that work for you?"

"It will. Are there restaurants around here?"

"All kinds, but it's all Southern cooking. I guess you can't cook, huh?"

"No, I can't cook."

"I could teach you. I host a cooking show for the Food Network and keep telling myself to write a cookbook, which I never seem to start. If you stay long enough, you could be my new guinea pig and allow me to test on you the recipes that I will probably never include in the book that I will probably never write," she called over her shoulder. Dear God, did I just say that? For sure, the kids are going to strangle me. She turned the engine on and backed out of her parking space. Mace Carlisle, aka Oliver Goldfeld, followed right behind her.

Seven minutes later, Julie pulled into her driveway, punched in the code to the electrified gate, and sailed through, her possible new tenant right behind her. She could hear Gracie and Cooper barking. They knew a strange vehicle was invading their territory.

Julie drove all the way around to the back of the house, parked her truck, and cut the engine. She waited until the man in the fancy car got out with his dog. "There it is!" she said, waving her arms at the guesthouse. "Everything is good to go. My day lady just cleaned it up and put fresh sheets on the beds, and there are clean towels in the bathroom. There is coffee and powdered creamer for the morning to hold you over until you can go to the store to get what you want. Take the tour. I'll go in and let my dogs out, then you can tell me what you've decided."

*You are crazy, Julie Wyatt. You don't know this man from Adam. He could be an ax murderer for all you know. The kids are going to blast me. Stupid, stupid, stupid.*

Her hand went into the pocket of her shorts. They closed around the paper she'd anguished over earlier. She withdrew her hand as if she'd touched a hot coal. She opened the back door, and the two retrievers raced out to run across the yard to where Oliver Goldfeld was waiting for her.

Julie watched as Oliver panicked when he saw Cooper and Gracie charging toward him. He scooped up his dog and held her in a vise grip. "She's nervous. I rescued her from the SPCA. They won't hurt her, will they? By the way, her name is Lola."

"Cooper and Gracie? They wouldn't hurt a fly! All they want to do is play. Put your dog down, and you'll see."

Reluctantly, Mace lowered Lola to the ground.

The retrievers sniffed her, circled her, then
barked. "That means they like her." Julie
laughed. "See, they're going to show her the
best bushes and trees to pee on, the place where
they hide their balls and toys and chew bones.
They'll be back in ten minutes. By the way, this
entire four acres is fenced in, so she won't get
lost. I have lights that come on at night, too. So,
have you decided whether to take it and, if so,
what do you think it's worth rental-wise."

"Is a thousand dollars a month acceptable? I
can pay for the utilities, too, if that will help."

Julie almost fainted. She hoped she didn't
look too eager when she said, "I can live with
that. When the utility bills come in, I'll show
them to you." Then her conscience attacked her.
"No, that's too much. How about seven-fifty, and
you still pay the utilities?"

"You drive a hard bargain, Julie Wyatt. I never
rented anything before, but I've seen television
shows where the owner asks for a deposit and
then first and last month's rent, so that makes it
twenty-two-fifty. If you let me get settled in, I can
bring the money over to you."

Julie literally swooned. Now she could get the
A/C in her truck fixed and pay off her new Wolf
stove. Not to mention updating and stocking
her pantry, something people involved with
cooking at a professional level had to do at least
once a month.

"That's fine, Oliver. And to welcome you into
your new home, I'm going to invite you for dinner. I'll send the dogs over when it's ready. They
know how to ring the doorbell. Well, at least

Gracie does. Cooper just paws at it. And you are welcome to bring Lola. Look! She's playing with the dogs. I need to warn you, if you let Cooper inside the cottage, he will chew things if you ignore him. He has separation anxiety."

Mace waved his arms about, suddenly shy. "I don't know how to thank you, Julie. You literally saved my life today. Lola's, too. I would be honored to have dinner with you. Does this come under the heading of Southern hospitality?"

"Nah. Sometimes I just like company. I can use the money, too, so I won't lie to you. Hey, it's win for you and win for me. By the way, I did notice you don't have any luggage, and I'm not being nosy here, but I don't think you want to hang out in that designer suit you're wearing. Upstairs in the closet are a lot of my son's clothes. You're about the same size. He has stuff in the drawers, too, and the bathroom is stocked with new toothbrushes and razors. Feel free to use it all. This is just a guess on my part, but do you know how to work a washing machine?"

Mace gave an embarrassed shake of his head. "Okay, when the dirty clothes pile up, I'll show you how to use it. It's behind the sliding door in the kitchen." Julie whistled for her dogs to follow her. They both ignored her. "Guess you're stuck with them. Send them home when you've had enough of them. Gracie will ring the doorbell. Now, is there anything else you can think of that you might need?"

"I can't think of anything. I think you covered it all. I'll bring the money over when I come for dinner, or do you want it now?"

"Later is fine. I think you'll be comfortable in the cottage, Oliver. The beds are really good ones. It's very peaceful here at night, with the crickets and the trees whispering in the breeze." She gave an airy wave as she sprinted across the yard and up the steps that led to the kitchen door.

Inside, Julie sat down on one of the bar stools at the counter and dropped her head into her hands. "God, please don't let that guy be some kind of mugger or ax murderer." Satisfied with her pep talk, she got up and started to prepare her dinner for two. Her digital camera was placed within easy reach as she got out her cooking utensils and the food she was going to prepare. Stuffed peppers, mashed potatoes, coleslaw, grilled corn she would shave off the cob when it was done. She would photograph all the steps for easy following for the readers of the book she would probably never write.

Today's menu highlighted what she called wraparound stuffed peppers, and what that meant was she would cut the bottoms off the peppers, as well as the tops, and set the peppers in a roasting pan. One filling mixture was ground turkey. The second set of peppers would have ground chuck. To both fillings, she would add finely chopped peppers from the cut-off tops along with some finely chopped onion and pars-ley, a smidgen of garlic, and, of course, salt and pepper. The sauce in both recipes would be a fire-roasted tomato sauce with a good-sized por-tion of chopped garlic. Cooking time—one hour and fifteen minutes. She spoke into her recorder, which was next to her digital camera, saying she would be using red, yellow, and orange peppers in both recipes, because the green peppers were too bitter in her opinion.

Julie worked silently and efficiently, her hands working in tandem with what she was saying into her recorder, even when she was snapping pictures of her culinary endeavor. Her ears were half tuned to the television on the counter, which she kept on all day and sometimes during the night. If she did say so herself, she excelled at multitasking, and put all thoughts of her new tenant on a mental shelf for the moment.

Julie pressed the button on the dishwasher to clean up her cooking utensils just as Cooper slammed his huge body against the kitchen door. A nanosecond later, Gracie hit the doorbell with a look that clearly said this is a woman's job. Cooper bounded into the house, sniffed at the oven, then planted his paws on Julie's shoulders, his plea for TLC, which she gave willingly. Gracie was next, nudging her leg, so Julie sat down on the kitchen floor and rolled around, Cooper's tennis ball, which he slept with, in her hand.

"Did he kick you out, or did you come home willingly?" Julie gasped when Cooper pinned her to the floor as he tried to get the ball. Gracie barked twice. Twice meant yes, they came home willingly because Cooper was anxious. At least, that's what she thought it meant.

"Okay, enough," Julie said, struggling to her feet. "We have to set the table since we're having a guest. C'mon, now, Coop, let me up." Gracie nipped Coop's ear, and he yelped, but then he moved. "Thank you, Gracie."

Within minutes, Julie had the kitchen table set with place mats and dishes she used when she wanted to impress. She loved the vivid blue violets on the plates, the mats, and the napkins. When she ate alone, she usually ate off hard plastic plates and used paper napkins so she wouldn't have to run the dishwasher a second time. She was into conserving everything on the planet, and that included water. She had a fat blue candle she sometimes used, but decided that might be overkill for such a casual dinner with someone she didn't even know and who might just be an ax murderer.

As she folded the napkins, she stopped to wonder what kind of palate Oliver Goldfeld had. Did he eat high-end food like lobster and filet mignon? Did he eat out all the time since he didn't cook? Was he married? She should have asked, but then, that was none of her business. A rental was a rental. Maybe his wife cooked, or maybe they had a housekeeper. She shrugged. If he didn't like her dinner, then he would simply not eat it, and she and the dogs would be the judge of whether her food would pass muster so she could include the recipe in her cookbook. Personally, she loved stuffed peppers, especially with the fire-roasted tomato sauce.

With an hour to kill before dinner, Julie went to the little built-in nook in the kitchen, where she kept her laptop. She uploaded the pictures she'd taken, then opened a new file and typed in both recipes. Such a lot of meticulous, painstaking work, she chided herself. *I really have to sit down and write that book one of these days.*

Done!

Just time enough to wash her face and comb her hair, which she promptly did.

"Okay, Gracie, go get our guest. You only have to ring the doorbell once," Julie said, opening the back door to let the big dog out. Cooper waited to see if he was to follow. When he didn't get his command, he trotted over to the sink and lay down on the rubber mat, his beloved red tennis ball between his paws.

While the beaters went to work on the mashed potatoes, Julie realized that she was nervous. Just as nervous as she was when she had to look at the paper she'd been carrying around in her pocket for over a month now. Her heart thumped in her chest. When it quieted down, she muttered to herself, "What will be will be."

# Chapter 3

**D**inner over, Julie suggested they head for the veranda with their second cup of coffee. Mace agreed, and they settled themselves in two of the five ancient—repainted a hundred times—rockers. The paddle fans overhead gave off a soft whisper of a breeze, while the mister sprayed the luscious ferns that hung from the overhang. Julie smiled when she heard Mace sigh.

"This is so . . . I don't know what the word is I want to use. Your dinner was beyond my expectations. I can't remember when I had a meal like that. Probably when I was a kid, and my mother cooked for me. I can't believe you cook for your dogs. Lola loved the beef meatballs you mixed with her dog food. I didn't know you couldn't give dogs turkey or tomato sauce. I never met anyone like you, Julie Wyatt," Mace said as he held his face up to the mist swirling over the ferns. "I just love all this," he added, waving his arms about.

"I guess I'll take that as a compliment, Oliver Goldfeld. Tell me about yourself. I probably should know something about my tenant. I'm not talking secrets here, just normal stuff."

Mace hated lying to his landlady, the same lady who had shared dinner with him, the dinner that she had cooked. Well, she did say not to share secrets.

"I'm a pretty boring person, Julie. I never married." *That was true, Oliver had never married.* "Corporate law is dull and time-consuming. I live in New York. There are times when I love it and times when I hate the frenzy of it. I liked this little town the minute I arrived. My original intent was to drive to Huntsville, but when I walked around your town square, and people— people I didn't know—said hello to me and smiled at me, I thought this might be a good place to hang my hat for a little while."

Julie digested the information. She didn't know why, but she thought Oliver was parsing his words very carefully. She decided it was the lawyer in him just being careful.

"The South, Rosemont in particular, is a wonderful place. I had a hard time adjusting to the slower pace down here, slower even than in Vermont, which is not particularly frenzied itself, but I acclimated fairly quickly. I wouldn't go back to the North for all the tea in China. And our winters are mild. The older I get, the more I appreciate the milder temperatures. How do you like living in New York?"

"I've never lived anywhere else. Never found a place that appealed to me. Until now." He laughed. "I might decide to retire here one of these days."

Julie chuckled. "That's pretty funny. Everyone who visits me says the same thing. Then they go back home to wherever it is they live and promptly forget about this place."

"This is really a big—how should I refer to it?—*spread*, for one person living alone. Don't you get lonely?" His stomach churning about the lies he'd told, with more to follow, he hoped Julie wouldn't ask him too many questions. He'd never been a liar, and it wasn't coming to him naturally, as it did to some people who just lied for the sake of lying.

Julie laughed again. "No, not really. I have the dogs. My kids live within walking distance. I keep busy. Friends, that kind of thing. You live alone, or do you have a significant other?"

Hah. There it was, tossed right back into his lap. "No significant other. To be honest, there aren't enough hours in the day to do everything I have to do. I'm rarely home, and when I am, all I do is sleep." That was true, too. Oliver didn't have anyone special in his life at the moment. A lie is a lie, he warned himself.

"And yet, here you are," Julie said lightly, almost playfully.

One more lie coming right up. "Yes, here I am. I needed some downtime to prepare for an upcoming trial. Away from interruptions and distractions. It's a very important trial." It wasn't *exactly* a lie; it was Oliver's life he was talking about. Somehow, though, he didn't think Julie Wyatt would look at it like that. To her, a lie would be a lie no matter what. Maybe he needed to quit while he was ahead and go back to the cottage he'd just rented. But he didn't want to leave. He couldn't remember the last time he'd felt this much at peace, so contented. The answer was probably never.

"Do you think you'll win?"

"Oh, absolutely. There is no doubt in my mind." Oliver always won when he went to court. Even though Oliver's specialty was corporate law, he also happened to be a superlative litigator. Before Julie could ask another question, Mace dived in with a question of his own. "What is it like to host a TV show? And what about the cookbook you say you will probably never write?"

"I used to do a little locally produced program on cooking for a PBS station in Vermont. It was pretty much of a hobby. I guess some people on the Food Network happened to see my show and asked if I would like to host one of their programs. I said I would, and here I am.

"When I was a teenager, I used to read romances and thought that maybe I would try my hand at that when I grew up. Never happened. Never actually wrote anything.

"But as I continue to host cooking shows on the Food Network, I keep thinking about different ways to present recipes in a cookbook. I keep meaning to start the book, but, somehow, it never happens.

"My life took a change when I started at the Food Network, and, no, it had nothing to do with the death of my husband. He passed away while we were living up in Vermont, a few years after I started hosting."

Julie got up off her chair to turn the misters off. When she sat back down, Mace should have been intuitive enough not to ask any more questions, but he didn't listen to the inner voice whispering in his ear that enough was enough.

"That's so interesting. You mentioned that your children live close by. Tell me about them. Do you have any grandchildren to dangle on your knee?"

Mace knew in an instant that he'd asked the wrong question. Even in the lavender twilight, he could see the pain in Julie Wyatt's eyes.

He tried to cover up his question with a statement. "Well, would you look at the time! I hope you won't think me rude, but I'm really tired, and I think Lola is, too. I know a guest should never eat and run. But all of a sudden, I just can't keep my eyes open. Hopefully, we can talk about kids and everything under the sun tomorrow or some other day when you have free time."

Mace was up and off his chair like he'd been shot in the tail with a load of buckshot. He scooped Lola up and waved wildly as he rushed down the steps to the footpath that would take him to the alpine cottage.

Julie barely noticed her guest's departure. She sat a while longer as the solar lights in the yard came on one by one. For some reason, she always thought of the solar lights as fairy lights, something to make her smile.

Cooper, always more sensitive to her emotions than Gracie, nuzzled her leg and whimpered. She stroked his silky head just as Gracie made her presence known. She hugged both dogs, and the tears she'd held in check were rolling down her cheeks.

"I don't think I handled that very well, guys. Even after all this time . . ." Her voice trailed off. "Come on, let's go in and empty the dishwasher. Then I'll give you some of that dog ice cream you hate so much." As both dogs tried to slink off on their bellies, Julie said, "Yeah, well, I'm not wasting my money, so you have to eat it until it's all gone." Gracie barked shrilly as Cooper nipped at her tail.

Her thoughts everywhere but on the brainless task of emptying the dishwasher, Julie finished, then ladled out the dog ice cream, which even smelled terrible. The dogs sniffed it, circled around it, then gulped at it. Both retrievers looked up at her as if to say, *Okay, we ate it. Now can we have a chew bone?* Julie obliged.

Julie looked at the clock on the stove. Too early to go to bed. She'd caught up on her notes and recipes. She didn't have a good book to read—not that she would have been able to concentrate—so that left television and reruns of something she'd probably seen at least a dozen times already.

Settled on the sofa, Cooper on one side, Gracie on the other side, Julie settled down to watch a rerun of *The Closer*. She loved the feisty chief of police. Within seconds, she was sound asleep.

Not so the two retrievers. They lay with their heads on their paws, their eyes and ears alert to any strange sounds that might wake their mistress. They knew the doors hadn't been locked or the alarm turned on.

Cooper looked at Gracie and tilted his head. Gracie hopped off the couch and went from door to door, turning the dead bolts just the way Julie had taught her, back in the days when Julie hadn't been able to function and barely knew what her name was. Satisfied with her task, she moved on to the alarm. All she had to do was press the blue button, and the house would be locked up tighter than a drum. She waited, her ear tuned to the three pings that told her she could go back to the sofa. Her tail swished with excitement as she stood in front of Cooper to see if he approved. He did, and showed it by tapping her lightly on the snout with one of his big paws.

Precisely at ten fifty-five, Cooper's internal clock kicked in. He leaned over and started licking Julie's face. Gracie let loose with an earsplitting bark, which meant, get up, it's time to go to bed. Julie obliged. She turned off the TV and looked over at Gracie. "Did you lock up, Gracie?" Gracie barked twice. "Good girl! Okay, quick in and out, then it's sack time. No visiting with our new tenants, just go pee and get right back in here." Both dogs ran to the sunroom and the oversize doggie door. They were in and out in five minutes.

In her bedroom, Julie's small television was on. More often than not, she left it on all night because she was a poor sleeper. She'd sleep an hour or so, wake up, watch television for a while, then doze off but never into a sound sleep. Once, she'd slept through the night and always woke refreshed. Those days were gone, never to return. As she brushed her teeth, she could hear the news anchor babbling over the sound of running water. Bank executives were still blaming everyone but themselves for the massive losses they had suffered when the housing market turned against them. Some sports giant not worth the money he was being paid was threatening to leave his current team. Last month's big lottery winner still hadn't claimed the prize. Two more movie stars were going into rehab. Again.

The euro kept falling, and the talking heads were wondering if the European Union was going to survive and what effect that might have on the barely recovering American economy. "Like the world really needs this before they go to bed," Julie mumbled as she emptied out her pockets and stripped down.

She swallowed hard when she stared down at the piece of paper she'd been carrying around in her pocket for so long. She shook her head to clear her thoughts as she pulled on a sleep shirt with a picture of Mustang Sally on the front. The picture was of herself and had been a long-ago gift from one of her sons, because "Mustang Sally" was her favorite song. She slept in the shirt every night and washed it every morning. It was threadbare. She wondered again, as she often did, if changing her sleep attire would allow her to sleep better. She never came up with an answer.

Julie was about to click off the TV with the remote and climb into bed when she did a double take at what she was seeing—and hearing— right in front of her eyes. In the time it took her heart to beat twice and to gasp in surprise, Cooper and Gracie were on her bed as they tried to snuggle into her lap, something they never did unless there was a thunderstorm. Her mouth wide open in shock, she stared at the picture on television of her new tenant. Only his name wasn't Oliver Goldfeld; it was Mace Carlisle. *Lawyer* Oliver Goldfeld was fielding questions from a persistent reporter right in front of a building in lower Manhattan that said CARLISLE PHARMACEUTICALS in huge brass letters next to the plate-glass doors.

When the anchor moved on to the weather, Julie finally closed her mouth and thought about what she'd just heard. Her brand-new tenant had lied to her. Her brand-new tenant and his drug company were being accused—by his soon-to-be-ex-wife, Eileen, and her son, Eli— of paying off the FDA for approval on a new drug for high cholesterol in children. Wall Street was in a tizzy, and shareholders were up in arms that the stock shares they owned were going to plummet. And if that wasn't bad enough, Mace

Carlisle had hightailed it out of town, leaving his lawyer, Oliver Goldfeld, to clean up the mess—including serving divorce papers and evicting the wife, Eileen, from their pricey apartment in the Dakota and firing the son, Eli, from the company and tossing him out of his digs in the Trump Towers.

That was the end of Julie Wyatt's sleep for the night. She recalled words her deceased husband used to say: Nothing is as it seems, and there are two sides to everything. Do not judge, do not assume, and do not presume. Words to take to heart.

# Chapter 4

Knowing that sleep was now out of the question, Julie made a pot of tea and booted up her computer. She didn't even bother to turn on the lights. The laptop and the night-light on the stove gave her all the light she needed. No sense alerting her new tenant—in case he wasn't sleeping—that she was a night owl, which she wasn't. What she was, was someone who hated to be lied to, someone who valued truth. And she damned well hated being made a fool of. Her husband's words kept ricocheting around and around in her head. She cautioned herself not to be hasty.

Julie plopped several tea bags into a red-and-white polka-dotted teapot, then poured the boiling water over it. While it steeped, she tapped into Google and typed the name Mace Carlisle. Nice name, she liked it. She blinked at the mile-long list of sites she could click on to get the skinny on her new tenant. She clicked and clicked and printed everything she thought would tell her all that she needed to know. Make that . . . *wanted* to know. When she had used up half a ream of printer paper, Julie switched up. She typed in the name of Oliver Goldfeld and did the same thing, using up the other half of the ream of paper.

Then she poured her tea, a blend of wild currant and blackberry. Carrying her mug of tea, which was as big as a soup bowl, and the stack of printouts, Julie trotted back to her bedroom, settled down in a deep, comfortable rocking chair, and proceeded to read about the lives of Mace Carlisle and Oliver Goldfeld.

Julie finished the last of her cold tea at three forty-five in the morning. She rubbed at her eyes, then stacked the papers neatly into a pile. She leaned back and closed her eyes. She sighed. From everything she'd read, Mace Carlisle was Mother Teresa's male counterpart. There was no hint, no breath of scandal attached to the man in all his sixty years. Until yesterday.

Mace Carlisle was born and raised in Hoboken, New Jersey. His father had been a pharmacist and owned the Carlisle Pharmacy in Hoboken; his mother was a schoolteacher. As a youngster, Mace had worked in the pharmacy after school, holidays, and summers. He gradu-

ated magna cum laude from Rutgers University
and went on to pharmacy school and again grad-
uated with honors. He joined his father at the
drugstore, whose name was then changed to
Carlisle & Carlisle Pharmacy. To this day, Mace
still owned the pharmacy. But other people ran
it for him because, as he said in more than one
interview, he just couldn't part with it, even
though it operated in the red. His policy was
that if a family couldn't afford the medicine it
needed, he gave it to them for free. He didn't
keep records of who owed what, either.

Mace's philanthropy was well known. He donated millions of dollars to every cause in the
book. He was a well-known animal-rights activist
even though he didn't own an animal himself
because, as he said, he was never home, and it
wouldn't be fair to the animal. He donated
handsomely to charities he thought his mother
would approve of, had she still been alive:
women's shelters, women's rights causes, free
clinics, and so many children's causes the reporters couldn't keep track of them all. He had
awards, plaques, citations, man-of-the-year awards
out the yin yang. The ones he was most proud of
were the awards from Little League coaches,
whose teams he funded far and wide because, as
a child, he'd never had a chance to get out and
play like the other kids. He funded thousands
and thousands of full-ride scholarships, and the
only thing he asked of the students was for them
to do their best. And they did. He and Oprah
Winfrey had set up a foundation to support aspiring young actors and actresses in their early

years, which everyone knew were especially tough ones.

He was modest, didn't like to give interviews, and was considered shy. To his employees, he was generous to a fault. While he ran a tight ship, he was always fair, and his people respected him and were loyal. It was said the only way to get a job at Carlisle Pharmaceuticals was to be on a waiting list in case someone went to that big drug company in the sky and, even then, more often than not, one of the deceased's relatives took over his or her job. One enamored reporter went so far as to say the company should be called Carlisle & Family Pharmaceuticals.

Mace Carlisle, with the help of his childhood friend Oliver Goldfeld, who had been fresh out of law school, started up Carlisle Pharmaceuticals. To this day, the two men were considered best buds. Obviously, Julie thought, since Mace had assumed his best friend's identity. Julie knew in her gut that Goldfeld had okayed the switch in identity. She heaved a huge sigh of relief that Mace Carlisle, aka Oliver Goldfeld, was an okay tenant, but one with personal problems.

Julie's thoughts rambled on. Both men had been bachelors up until three years ago, when Mace Carlisle took the plunge and married. Wall Street reacted, and CP stock took a tumble. The stock took a second tumble when Mace's stepson, Eli, was brought in to head the legal department and decided to revamp things. The stockholders pitched hissy fits. Dissension in the ranks was rampant, with Mace giving pep talks to his people almost on a daily basis.

Early in the marriage, reporters noticed that Mace was starting to look drawn and haggard and was taking time off, blocks of time. His new wife was looking better than she'd ever looked. She'd made some dentist extremely happy, not to mention assorted plastic surgeons. She was into daily spa treatments, and expensive three-hour lunches with her son. She single-handedly kept Saks and Bergdorf Goodman in the black. She decorated a five-room apartment in the Trump Towers for Eli and didn't once look at the price tag of anything she bought to furnish and decorate the place. Or so it was rumored. She demanded and got a chauffeur, then demanded a place in the Catskills. The reporter went on to say that while he couldn't prove it, he thought Mrs. Eileen Carlisle had carte blanche at Tiffany's.

Oliver Goldfeld was yet another pillar of the community; no taint of scandal anywhere near him. Excellent reputation in the legal field. Several years ago, he'd taken a case all the way to the Supreme Court and won. He was Mace's best friend, something both men shouted to the heavens. Oliver had never married but had been keeping company with federal judge Marion Odell for many years. Julie liked the old-fashioned term, *keeping company*. It was rumored that Mrs. Carlisle did not like Oliver Goldfeld and was jealous of the friendship the two men had. It was also said that her son worked long and hard behind the scenes to sabotage the legal and personal relationship between the two men, causing strife in the new marriage.

And then the latest report, dated just two weeks ago. CP stock tumbled again, and there were rumors of a hostile takeover just as the company was waiting for FDA approval of their new children's cholesterol drug.

The cherry on top of what she'd just finished reading was what she'd heard on the news this evening. Even an idiot could figure out why Mace Carlisle had cut and run. To get his head on straight. She would have done the same thing if she were walking in his shoes. Sometimes, as she'd found out the hard way, you had to distance yourself from a situation to get your bearings. God, had she learned that lesson. The hard way.

The big question for her at the moment was whether to let Mace know she knew his secret or to just go along with his charade. Always the first to champion the underdog, Julie finally decided to keep his secret and pretend she knew nothing. As long as the man paid his rent, she had no right to interfere in his private life. She felt sad that she couldn't help him in some way.

Julie Wyatt felt sorry for Mace Carlisle, so sorry she wanted to run across the yard, wake the man, and hug and comfort him the way mothers had done since the beginning of time. Of course, she wouldn't do any such thing.

Julie squinted without her reading glasses and tried to see the red numerals on her digital clock. Five o'clock! She looked at her bed and almost laughed out loud. Cooper was stretched out on her side of the bed, Gracie on the other, with no room for her because Cooper wouldn't

move until he was ready to move, and he was
out for the count. Oh, well, she might as well
shower and think about making breakfast for
her new tenant, since there was no food in the
cottage. When the dogs finally stirred themselves, she'd send them over to the cottage with
a note.

At five forty-five, Julie was in the kitchen, trying to decide what to make for breakfast. In the
summertime, she usually just had fruit, usually a
mango, some yogurt, or toast. In the winter, she
liked warm cereal. She wasn't sure, but she
thought Mace Carlisle might be a breakfast eater
like her sons, who early in the morning would
eat anything that wasn't nailed down.

Such a dilemma.

While Julie pondered her breakfast menu,
she turned on the small television sitting on the
counter. Maybe there would be fresh news, but
what that could possibly be, she had no idea. She
made coffee while she waited for the six o'clock
news to come on.

Her elbow propped up on the counter, her
chin in the palm of her hand, Julie stared at the
television. The face of the latest politician to be
caught with his hand in the till appeared, smug
and self-assured. She muttered a few choice words
and was glad there was no one within earshot to
hear them. The other news was just as stupid as
what she'd just heard. Nothing seemed to be
forthcoming about Mace Carlisle and his problems. One would think tampering with the FDA
and a new kids' drug would be the top news.
Maybe the seven o'clock news would have some-

thing. She rarely was up this early to watch the news. So she didn't know what the order of news stories was this early in the day. She switched to the Weather Channel—and wished she hadn't. Rain for the day starting midmorning. Well, sometimes the weatherman was wrong; she could hope.

The forecast meant that Cooper was going to be rolling in puddles, as water was his best friend. Not so Gracie, who liked to keep her nails dry. Gracie particularly liked the scarlet hibiscus polish the groomer had put on her nails last week. Gracie also liked the red bow the groomer tied around her neck with each visit. Cooper hated his blue bow, and Gracie always tugged it off him. And then they would tussle with it for hours on end until it was nothing but strings.

Julie continued to sit at the counter, woolgathering, as her mother used to say when she was deep in thought. She looked down when she felt Cooper nudge her leg. She got up, ruffled the place between his ears, turned off the alarm, and opened the door. The dogs were out and back within minutes, at which point she scribbled off a note and handed it to Gracie. She opened the door again, and both dogs sprinted off to the cottage.

Julie made a second pot of coffee, mixed batter for pancakes, and nuked some bacon. She fired up the electric griddle, and while it was heating up, she beat some eggs into a frothy foam. Breakfast would be served on hard plastic plates. Paper napkins were the order of the day. Fresh cantaloupe would finish off the meal.

She had a full day, and she had yet to decide what would be on her dinner menu. But she had plenty of time to come up with something that would be worthy of space in her dream cookbook. And if not, oh, well.

Thirty minutes later, everything was good to go for the minute her tenant showed up with the dogs. She was back on her perch at the counter, but now the television was tuned to the Shopping Channel. No sense alerting her tenant that she was an inveterate news watcher.

Hands jammed into her pockets, Julie felt the piece of paper she'd transferred so many times she'd lost count. She really had to make a decision. Maybe she should round up her kids and take them to lunch and talk it to death. Maybe she needed to call the New York lawyer who handled her business affairs first. Arnie Rosen had been her lawyer as well as a good and loyal friend for twenty-five years. She knew in her gut he was going to pitch a fit, but at least he would know what to do and offer up some sound advice, which she would either follow or not. Hopefully, he would understand what she was going through. Hopefully.

She heard the joyful barks of the dogs as they barreled up the steps that led to the kitchen door. She'd installed little platforms between the steps years ago when her old dog, Cyrus, an Australian herder, couldn't do steps anymore. She heard the light knock on the door. She

smiled at her tenant, who looked freshly showered and shaved. "Good morning, Oliver. How
did you sleep in your new digs?" she asked
cheerfully.

"Like a baby. I opened all the windows, and
crickets put me to sleep. This morning, the
birds and the sun woke me. It was wonderful. It
reminded me in many ways of where I used to
live as a child. It smells good in here."

"Don't get too excited about the sun. The
weatherman is predicting rain, but I think he's
wrong this time." Julie laughed as she poured
Mace coffee and cut him a huge wedge of
melon. "Go ahead and eat while I make the pancakes. I suppose I should have asked, are you a
breakfast eater?"

"Very much so. But sometimes I don't have
the time. To be more accurate, I don't *take* the
time, and I know breakfast is the most important meal of the day. If you're going to be cooking for me—and you haven't said you are—but
if you are, we need to discuss payment. I don't
have a clue what to pay you or what homemade
meals cost on the open market, so whatever you
decide is okay with me."

Julie pondered the question as she turned
the pancakes. "Well, I can't charge you full price,
whatever that would be, because I'm asking
your opinions of the dinners. Breakfasts are a
no-brainer. I'm going to be cooking the dinners
anyway, but then there is the shopping and prep
time involved. How does three dollars for breakfast sound and ten dollars for dinner and you
clean up? That would be ninety-one dollars a

week. Do you know how to load a dishwasher or work the garbage disposal?" Mace shook his head. "Well, I'll show you. So, do we have a deal?"

"Absolutely," Mace said as he pulled money out of his wallet to pay a month in advance. "I think you're cheating yourself, Julie. Are you sure this is enough?" Mace said, pointing to the money he put on the table.

"It's fair." Julie stacked the pancakes and the golden fluffy eggs onto a plate, the bacon on a separate dish, and set it in front of Mace. She proceeded to scramble more eggs, then crumpled tiny bits of bacon in them. She added dog food and set three plates down on the floor.

"My dogs eat what I eat. They even like vegetables and some fruits. My last two dogs lived to be twenty and twenty-one, so I know what I'm doing. There are people out there who wouldn't agree with my dogs' diets, but I really don't care. Oh, I'm taking Gracie and Cooper this week to the vet to have their teeth cleaned, and I can take Lola, too, if you want."

"Of course. These pancakes are delicious. What kind of syrup is this?"

"My own blend, banana and mango syrup with melted butter. I won a blue ribbon for it at a bake-off."

Julie sat down at the table with her cup of coffee. If her breakfast companion had seen the late-night news, it obviously wasn't bothering him. He smiled and asked if she shopped off television.

"I hate waking up to hearing the news; it's never anything good. I don't watch it before I go to bed, either," she fibbed, her fingers crossed in her lap. "I am not a television watcher; I prefer to read. When I do watch television, it's more for sound than anything else. Either the Discovery Channel or the Home Shopping Network and, yes, at times I do shop online because I hate going to the malls and standing in line. Been there, done that, when my kids were little. How about you? By the way, how did Lola do last night in her new home?"

"I read the *Times* online. Lola did very well. She slept on the bed with me. I hope that was okay."

"Of course it's okay. She obviously feels the need to be close to you. Dogs have feelings, you know. Cooper, as I mentioned, suffers from separation anxiety. He's getting better about it. You might want to think about getting another dog when you go back home; otherwise, Lola is going to be very lonely. Oh, look! Gracie just showed her the doggie door." Cooper threw back his head and howled, an ungodly sound. Mace bolted off his seat, a wild look of panic on his face. Julie laughed. "He's mad because Gracie went first, then Lola. It's that male thing. You see how bothered the two females are."

Mace sat back down, a sheepish look on his face. "Obviously, I have a lot to learn when it comes to animals. I'll take all instructions and criticism to heart."

Julie laughed again. "More coffee?" Mace shook his head. "I'll give you some to go in a hot pot. If you're done, then, let me show you how to work the dishwasher and how to clean up the kitchen. I have to go out now and run some errands. Is there anything I can get for you while I'm out?"

"No, not really. I'm going to . . . ah . . . *work* myself. Do you want me to keep Gracie and Cooper with me?"

"That would be nice. That way I can sneak out, and Cooper won't go ballistic. The A/C in my truck has to be fixed, and I don't like leaving them while I'm gone. Like I said, Coop chews anything in sight, so watch him. They'll know when I get back. Well, come on, Oliver, here is your first lesson in running a kitchen. Remember now, these plates are throwaways."

Ten minutes later, Julie's kitchen seminar was over. With an airy wave of her hand, she was gone, shoulder bag in place and a string shopping bag in one hand.

Mace Carlisle looked around the blue-and-white kitchen in a daze. He fixed his gaze on the dishwasher, which was as alien to him as a spaceship. It took him a good fifteen minutes to position everything to his satisfaction. He dropped in some orange squares, which said on the box that the dishes and pots would come out shiny bright if this product was used. Julie hadn't said anything about cleaning off the counters and the mess of drippings on the griddle. He wasn't sure, but he thought that part went along with the job. He went to work, but not before he turned up the volume on the television, where they were selling Birkenstock sandals for $59.95

a pair. He wasn't sure, but he thought that might be a tremendous bargain compared to buying them in New York.

Mace fell to his task, soaped up a sponge, and went to work. When he was done, the kitchen glistened. He was congratulating himself on a job well done when all three dogs bellied through the doggie door. Cooper again howled his displeasure when he realized Julie was nowhere to be seen. Gracie swatted him with her paw, and he quieted down. Lola watched these antics and let loose with a bark of her own as she nudged Mace's leg.

"Okay, let's go!" Mace felt like the Pied Piper as he led the three dogs out the door and down the steps and the mini platforms and across the yard to the cottage. Inside, he handed out chew bones he'd found on the counter. Now he had peace and quiet. Not that he didn't like the commotion—he did—but he needed to concentrate on the phone call he was going to make to Oliver.

He talked for over an hour on his untraceable phone. The first ten minutes of the phone call were devoted to the news and his current problems, the other fifty minutes were spent talking about Julie Wyatt and the dogs and his new rental, where he was wearing someone else's clothes and loving it. He went into great detail, even laughing at how he'd cleaned the kitchen and loaded the dishwasher. Mace listened to his friend, then said, "I want you to do something for me, and this is important, Oliver. I don't want any screwups, and I don't want it coming back on me in any way. Just take care of it for me, and I'd like the offer to go out today. Pull every string you have to get it done. By the way, I have to tell you, this lady *can cook*!" He listened to his attorney for another five minutes, then powered down.

Satisfied that there was nothing else for him to do, Mace picked up his laptop and a book he'd found on the bookshelf and started to read last evening. A page-turner; not that he was any authority on political thrillers, but he did like the intricate plotting on the one hand and the author's direct style on the other. He knew that if he stayed long enough, he would read more books by this author, of which there were a number on the shelf. He carried the book along with the hot pot of coffee out to the deck in the backyard, where he settled himself in a bright yellow Adirondack chair. He went back into the cottage to bring out a bowl of water, which he set down on the deck. The dogs started to romp and tussle with each other until Cooper spotted a squirrel, and off they went.

Mace read for well over two hours, eventually dozing in the shade a large oak created over the small deck. The dogs, exhausted, curled up at his feet.

While the life he'd left behind in New York was in turmoil, he consoled himself with the fact that he wasn't spinning in that turmoil. He was hundreds of miles away, enjoying his temporary new life, which he was loving more and more by the minute. And he had a dog that loved him and two other dogs that thought he was okay.

He wondered how much better life could be, considering his present circumstances.

The throwaway phone tinkled, the sound low enough that it didn't disturb the dogs. It had to be Oliver, since no one else had this particular number. He powered up and listened. "You did *what?* For God's sake, why? I can't believe you googled Julie Wyatt. No, Oliver, I don't want to know her business. Her business is not my business. I'm her tenant. End of story. That lady could have booted my ass out of here, but she didn't. Do not even think about telling me whatever it is you found out. No! What do you mean maybe I can help her? She doesn't look to me like she needs my help or anyone else's help. Julie Wyatt has it going on, I can tell you that. She has a family, children who live nearby. No, I don't want to know her life story. All right, all right, tell me."

Mace listened and didn't say a word. When Oliver finally wound down, all Mace said was, "Thanks for telling me."

# Chapter 5

Mace Carlisle bolted upright from the chair on the deck when he heard an earsplitting bark. He looked around in a daze until he remembered where he was. The three dogs clustered around his ankles as if to say, hey, it's raining, and we're afraid of thunder and lightning, so let's go. In a matter of seconds, they were all drenched.

Go they did, with Mace leading the way. Once inside, the dogs shook off the rain as Mace beelined for the stairs to change out of his wet clothes. When he came back downstairs, he had to turn on all the lights before he wiped the dogs down with the fluffy yellow towels stacked up on the washer. He eyed the wet towels and knew he had to wash them, but the washer was as much an alien entity to him as had been the dishwasher in the main house. He stared at the machine as if it were his worst enemy and suddenly felt incredibly stupid. His face grim, he opened the cabinets and there they were, instructions encased in a plastic bag. Ten minutes later, the machine was humming right along with Mace. Cooper pawed the tile floor, then barked his approval that Mace had mastered this little domestic chore. Mace bowed low to acknowledge the dog's approval. Gracie pranced off, Lola in her wake, as if to say, *a woman wouldn't have had to read the instructions.*

Outside, it had become totally dark as thunder roared overhead, and lightning danced across the darkened sky. Mace had a bad moment when he thought of all the ancient oak trees on the property. He hadn't seen any lightning rods anywhere, not that he had looked for them. Maybe people didn't use lightning rods anymore. He was so far behind the times, he couldn't believe it.

The power flickered, then went out. "Crap!" he muttered. The dogs, who were clustered in a tight knot on the deep, nubby sofa, started to howl. Mace made his way in the dark to the couch and sat down. A second later, all three dogs were draped over and around him. He spread his arms as wide as he could and whispered to them. In a million years, he never would have believed dogs could be frightened of thunder and lightning. He was certainly getting an education on the fly here.

As he was crooning to the dogs, he thought of Julie and wondered if she had gotten home before the storm. Insulated in New York in a highrise all these years, he hadn't experienced this kind of storm since he was a child and, even then, all he could recall were rainy days and the need to wear galoshes and carry an umbrella. He was sure that Julie, living here in the South, was used to storms like this one and had sought cover wherever she was.

The dogs had quieted down as he stroked first one, then another. His thoughts were suddenly all over the place. He thought about how lucky he was to have run into Julie Wyatt when he did. Someone must be watching over him. He thought he was even luckier that Julie Wyatt was not into watching the twenty-four-hour news channels. His conscience pricked at him for the way he was lying to her after she'd gone out of her way to be so nice to him. Julie with the haunted eyes. While she smiled and even laughed out loud, the smiles and the laughter didn't reach her eyes. And now he knew why.

Mace squeezed his eyes shut and wished with all his heart that Oliver hadn't shared what he'd learned on the Internet in regard to Julie Wyatt. Mace was out of his depth when it came to Julie Wyatt. He wished there was something he could do for her. He made a strange sound in his throat that the dogs didn't like. They stirred and pawed at his legs until he calmed them down.

He marveled at how astute animals were. Later, he would talk to Oliver about Julie Wyatt. Now, he needed to think about his own life, where it was going, if he would survive his immediate crisis, and the time he had left to either go forward, backward, or languish in some damned high-rise in New York. All alone.

As hard as he tried, Mace couldn't concentrate on his own problems. Problems that, except for one, were being taken care of by Oliver. In the end, he knew it would all be all right because Oliver would make it all right. His thoughts drifted to Julie again and the information Oliver said he'd downloaded and sent to him on his laptop. He wondered if he would have the willpower to ignore the e-mail that was waiting for him. Probably not, because, in the end, Mace Carlisle cared about people, and his greatest joy in life was helping the people he cared about the most. Right now, he had moved Julie Wyatt to the top of his list.

Forty-five minutes later, the rain stopped, the sun peeked out from the clouds to the west, and things began to dry. Fifteen minutes after that, the power flickered a few times and finally came back on. "And we have light, boy and girls!" Mace said dramatically. Cooper hopped off his lap and ran to the door, Gracie behind him. Lola waited until Gracie turned and offered up a sharp bark that meant Lola should get it in gear. She leaped to the floor and ran to the door. All three dogs waited for Mace to follow. He opened the door in time to see Julie park her truck. He hadn't heard a sound, and yet the dogs knew. He marveled again at how intuitive the animals were.

Julie waved as she made her way to the back steps that would take her up to the kitchen. "How did you like that storm?" she called out.

"It was awesome," Mace called out in return before he shut the door.

Totally alone, Mace didn't know what to do. He turned on the TV to Fox Cable News to see what they were saying about him. He got an earful. He turned it off and opened his laptop. He downloaded the material Oliver had sent to him. That's when he heard a pinging sound that he couldn't identify. He walked around listening until he realized it was the washer telling him the towels were done. Now he had to figure out how to work the damned dryer. Once again, he searched the cabinets and found the instructions in a plastic bag. What happened to OFF and ON switches? Why did appliances need all these bells and whistles? Were housewives rocket scientists these days? He finally came to the conclusion that all the bells and whistles were just something to drive up the prices of the machines.

Mace dumped the wet towels into the dryer and pressed six different buttons that the instructions told him would make the towels soft and fluffy. He didn't like soft and fluffy towels. He liked a coarse towel, one that would absorb the water. The instructions told him to set the timer to forty-five minutes. He did. The machine came to life with a little three-second tune he could have done without. He was back at the table and his laptop a few minutes later.

Mace tapped the touch pad and read steadily for over two hours. He was oblivious to the television playing, the sunshine that lit up the room like a stadium at night, and his own problems as he read just about everything there was to know about Julie Janson Wyatt. His eyes were burning when he closed his laptop. He meandered into the kitchen in time to hear the three musical notes signaling that the drying process was complete. Apparently, the machine had been trying to alert him that his laundry was dry for some time, but he'd been so engrossed in what he was reading that he'd tuned out the sound.

He folded the towels, then popped a Diet Dr Pepper and returned to the living room, where he clicked on Fox Cable News again. Since it was the middle of the news hour, the commentator was rehashing everything he'd said hours before. Mace stared off across the room to the huge fieldstone fireplace and wondered what it would be like to live in this little cottage in the winter. Would Lola lie by the hearth, or would she be near him on the deep, comfortable sofa, contentedly chewing on a rawhide bone?

Mace continued to look around at his cozy digs and wondered if it was Julie Wyatt who had decorated the place. The job was perfect, neither feminine nor masculine. Just a homey, comfortable, *woody* kind of place. He loved the fact that the cottage didn't have ceilings per se, just wood and beams and heavy black hardware. The circular oak staircase that led to the loft was a work of art. The windows were multipaned and glistened in the sunlight; just enough light for .

the hanging ferns and philodendrons suspending from the beams. They were so lush, he knew someone with a green thumb tended them. Julie? Maybe one of her children? She said she had a gardener. Maybe that was who watered them.

He looked down at the braided rugs, which were every color of the rainbow. His mother had hooked rugs like these in the wintertime back when he was a small boy. Who had hooked these? Julie? Maybe she'd done it during that tragic time in her life. Maybe it was cathartic for her to use her hands. The oak floor was beautiful—almost a shame to cover it up—but the rugs did make a difference, made the room come together somehow. And they seemed to warm up the room. The word *cozy* came to mind.

There were pictures on the walls, something he hadn't noticed before. Pictures of dogs. And the curio cabinet was full of dog figurines. Dogs in costumes. Sad-looking puppies. Happy-looking puppies. And dogs with no expressions. Over the fireplace was a huge framed collage of different scenes. Childhood drawings. Julie's children's endeavors? Obviously, and they were important enough to warrant the one-of-a-kind frame that surrounded them.

Mace got off the couch and walked around. His first stop was the bathroom, where he turned on the light. *Spotless* was the word that came to mind. No clutter, but tastefully decorated with seashells, obviously collected by Julie or her children. The linen closet was full, anything and everything a guest would need. Once again, there was a hooked rug by the shower and one by the sink, with bath mats to cover them when stepping out of the shower.

The kitchen had a garden window with pots of herbs and a few old glass bottles someone had found and thought important enough to save. The kitchen itself was small and compact, with gleaming appliances. For some reason, Mace had the feeling that someone had lived here at one time, that it wasn't always a guesthouse. It was just a gut feeling since there were no personal items or mementos to attest to that supposition. It was a sunny place, a cheerful place, with the yellow teapot on the stove and hand-painted yellow plates hanging on the walls.

Mace didn't need to go up to the loft to check it out as there was nothing there except two queen-size beds separated by a screen and, at the foot of each bed, an old-fashioned trunk with ancient black hardware. They were probably antiques handed down through the family. There were colorful quilts on each bed. Probably more heirlooms passed from generation to generation. He knew a thing or two about quilts as his mother had been an active participant in a quilting group. He still, to this day, had his boyhood quilt packed in one of his dresser drawers back at the Dakota. It was almost threadbare, but he'd sooner part with his right arm than the quilt.

A small, oak bookcase beckoned him. He squatted to look at the books and their colorful jackets. There were books by Robert Ludlum, Dean Koontz, John Irving, Helen MacInnes,

Isaac Asimov, and Andrew Greeley. On the kitty-corner, a small shelf held a well-worn white Bible. He struggled to his feet with the realization that he himself had never read any portion of the Bible. Somehow, he just knew that Julie Wyatt read it from cover to cover.

Julie Wyatt . . . his landlady.

Across the yard, in what Mace considered the main house, Julie Wyatt changed out of her wet clothes and put away her groceries. Then she put on water for hot tea because hot tea always made her feel better when she was stressed. While she moved about her kitchen, she listened to Fox News. To be on the safe side, she snapped the lock on the kitchen door so that her new tenant couldn't venture over and take her by surprise. She stopped what she was doing when the news at the top of the hour came on. Good at multitasking, she dipped her tea bag into the boiling water as she focused on the stern-faced commentator. She blinked when she realized that Mace Carlisle was the hour's headliner. She blinked again as she listened to someone named Shepherd say that Carlisle Pharmaceuticals donated millions of dollars' worth of drugs every year to Doctors Without Borders.

The scene changed, and a shaggy-looking doctor with a beard said he was somewhere in the Hindu Kush, and without the drugs the company donated, he and his colleagues wouldn't be able to help the thousands of people in life-and-death situations. Another doctor appeared, a woman who said that Mace Carlisle and his company were saints. Then a straggly group of people appeared, some with casts, some with bandages, all with smiles on their faces as they pointed to a picture of the man they said was their benefactor.

Julie knew this was PR as good as it got. Who in their right mind would believe anything Mace Carlisle's wife said after seeing this segment? Julie continued to watch as the scene changed from the Hindu Kush to a film clip from *GMA*, where one of the hosts had interviewed Mrs. Mace Carlisle earlier in the day.

Julie quickly calculated the cost of the woman's designer attire, the elaborate hairstyle, the winking diamonds in her ears, around her neck, on her wrists and fingers, and the porcelain veneers that had enabled some dentist to retire in style. She grimaced when she heard the woman say, "I did everything I could for that man! Then what does he do? I'll tell you what he did!" she shrilled. Realizing how her voice sounded, Mrs. Mace Carlisle dabbed at her eyes. "The man evicted me. My belongings were packed up and sent downstairs. The locks were changed, and if that wasn't bad enough, he had my son— who slaved night and day over that new drug with the FDC so Mace could make billions of dollars—evicted! My son, Eli, was the head attorney at Carlisle Pharmaceuticals, and how did Mace Carlisle show his gratitude for all his hard work and loyalty? He had him fired, and evicted also. His personal sleazy lawyer, Oliver Goldfeld, did all of Mace's dirty work while my husband cut and ran. No one even knows where he is. We're staying in a hotel. This isn't right. It just isn't right."

The screen split, and Shep was back, along with Doctors Without Borders. The ragtag group were smiling as Eileen Carlisle's diamonds winked under the studio lights.

"Bitch!" Julie mumbled under her breath. "My money's on you, Mace." Julie was more sure than ever that she'd made the right decision not to let Mace know she knew his real identity. She told herself things would sort themselves out at some point. And she again reminded herself that Mace Carlisle's personal life was none of her business.

# Chapter 6

Julie stood on the veranda and stared out across the yard. The dog days of summer had finally arrived. For the first time since moving to Alabama, she couldn't wait for autumn. She was thankful that so far the hurricane season had been mild, and she hoped it stayed that way. She looked toward the cottage and wondered, as she did every day, what her tenant did all day long. His tenancy was fast approaching the two-month mark, and it didn't look like he was in any hurry to leave. Yet. She had to admit that she enjoyed his company over breakfast and dinner, followed by the hour they spent after dinner with coffee on the veranda, making small talk, talking about everything and nothing.

Every day he left the cottage with Lola and was gone for three hours. She had no idea where he went or what he did, and she had not asked. He never returned carrying anything that she saw, but, then again, she didn't exactly spy on him, either. Every day she asked if he needed or wanted anything, and if he did, he would give her a list and make sure he paid her to the penny and even *tipped* her for her time and gas.

Julie jammed her hands into her pockets. She was still carrying around the slip of paper, and it had become so wrinkled and creased that it was hard to read. But that was okay since what she had in her pocket was only a copy. The original was in her lockbox.

It was Monday, and she always had lunch with her twin daughters, Connie and Carrie, on Mondays. They always went to the same place to eat because the twins were true vegans, and a friend owned the eatery. She hoped she could choke down the veggie burger she always ordered. Maybe the girls wouldn't notice if she left half the burger on her plate when she told them the news that had almost blown her out of the house yesterday—when her lawyer, Arnie, called to tell her the good news. She'd been in such a tizzy, she had packed up dinner for Oliver, aka Mace, and taken it over to the cottage, saying she had to go out unexpectedly. And she had gone out to the park, where she sat on a bench until it got dark, as she tried to come to terms with what Arnie had told her.

She hadn't slept a wink the night before, to the dogs' dismay, as she sat up drinking cup after cup of tea. Then, in the morning, she'd had coffee out the wazoo and was *wired,* a term the young people used today.

As Julie settled herself in her truck, she mentally chastised herself for not cooling it down. Only then did she remember that the A/C still wasn't working. "Damn," she muttered to herself, "why can't I ever remember to take the truck in and get it fixed?"

Eight minutes later, making every green light in town, Julie pulled into the parking lot of Davino's Eatery. Her daughters were sitting on a bench by the front door, surrounded by tubs of colorful flowers. Julie was tempted to take a picture of them, but she refrained.

They hugged because they always did that, then everyone started talking at once. Julie smiled. They were as pretty as pictures, but then, every mother thought that of her children. Tall, blond, blue-eyed, with beautiful smiles. They took after her husband's side of the family. Her twin sons, Peter and Philip, took after her side, with their dark hair and dark eyes. And then there was Larry. *Don't go there, Julie.*

Connie held the door for her mother, who headed for the booth they always sat in. She waved airily to the friend of the girls, who didn't even bother to take their order since they always ordered the same thing every Monday.

Carrie beamed from ear to ear. "I got an

e-mail from Peter this morning, Mom. He said he and Philip might get home for Christmas. He sounded as happy as a pig in a mudslide."

Connie laughed. "I got an e-mail from Philly last night. He loves India as much as Pete does. Who knew your sons would love living in a third-world country? Well, they always said they wanted to build bridges when they grew up. And that's what they're doing, and working for peanuts for the privilege. My brothers, the architects," she said, as if that explained Philip and Peter Wyatt and no more needed to be said.

Julie smiled. For years now, this was how they started off their Monday luncheons. Now it was time to ask about her daughters' business. "So, girls, how is business?"

"We're keeping our heads above water. You know business is always off in the summer. Art schools for gifted young artists, even ones as good as ours, just do not flourish when the sun is out and the beach beckons. We pick up by the end of September, and that's just around the corner. Hey, Mom, we're in the black, and what more could we ask for? We love working with the kids. So, what's up with you? How's that new tenant of yours doing? You got a thing going on there you aren't telling us about?" Carrie needled.

Julie rolled her eyes. "It's going well, and, no, there is no *thing* going on there. I do have news, though, and it's going to blow your socks off. So start guessing what it is. Actually, there are two things. One is even more awesome than the other."

Julie mashed at her veggie burger and listened to her twin daughters as they shot out one wild scenario after another. It was still a mystery to her why neither twin was interested in marriage. Each had a significant other in her life, but they still maintained separate residences. She consoled herself with the fact that marriage and motherhood were not for everyone, and Connie and Carrie dealt with children all day long, five days a week. Phil and Pete weren't interested in the marriage game, either, preferring to travel and do good in the world. Phil and Pete both, like their twin counterparts, had someone special in their lives, but those relationships never lasted longer than a year, because the boys were off traveling to better the world. She sighed.

"You're moving back to New York because your new tenant is leaving, and you want to be in the same state?" Connie said tightly, her expression showing her misery at the idea.

"Wrong," Julie drawled.

"You had another *vision,* and you're going to act on it?" Carrie said sadly.

"Wrong again," Julie drawled a second time.

"Okay, then, we give up already," the twins said in unison.

"Okay, listen up. Arnie called late yesterday and told me that Oprah's production company is interested in having me do a cooking show for Oprah Radio. Something like what I do for the Food Network, but for a lot more money. They will pay one point five million dollars up front and two million a season for every season after the first for as long as the show lasts. Arnie faxed me the contract this morning, and all I have to do is sign it, and the money will be in my account within ten days." Julie looked at her stunned daughters, then she looked down at the remains of her veggie burger. She winced inwardly. "I really think you should say something, girls."

"Well, damn," both girls said in the same breath. For some reason, probably because they were twins, they thought alike, spoke alike, and said the same thing at exactly the same time, especially at times like this.

"There's more," Julie said, a devilish twinkle in her eye. "No one knows this but me. I haven't even told Arnie because I don't want him to have a heart attack. I've known about this for . . . a long time. I just didn't act on it. You want to try guessing what the second thing is?"

"No!" The single word shot out from the twins at the same moment.

Julie reached into her pocket and pulled out the creased and tattered piece of paper. She made a production out of unfolding it, then spreading it out upside down so her daughters could read it. It took a moment before the twins realized what they were looking at. "My God, Mom, you won the lottery! The BIG lottery. How could you keep something like this a secret? That's three hundred and forty million dollars! Split in half, you keep one hundred and seventy million, pay taxes on it, but you end up with one hundred million or so. That means right now, sitting here smashing up that veggie burger, you are worth one hundred million. Oh, my God! Did you tell Philly and Petey?" Connie asked.

"No, I haven't told anyone but you."

"Mom, why haven't you claimed it? Why have you waited three months?"

"I have a year to claim it. It will change my life, and I'm just not ready for that right now. I'm not sure I want to go down that road even in the future. I don't do well with change, you should know that."

Stunned expressions on their faces, the twins stared across the table at their mother.

"Mom, think about what you can do with all that money! You can follow your dreams, whatever they may be. You can buy anything you want, go anywhere you want. You could buy a yacht, take sailing lessons, because you'd never trust anyone else at the helm. Hell, you could buy your own Gulfstream. You could get the A/C in your truck fixed or junk it and buy a new one. Buy new furniture. What am I saying? Mom, you could buy a whole new house!" Connie said.

"What's wrong with my house and my furniture?" Julie sniffed. "All those things you mentioned do not interest me at all. See! That's what I meant. This is all going to change my life. I like my life. I love my life. I did make one decision, though. I'm never going to write that cookbook I keep talking about but never get around to doing.

"I know exactly what you're going to say, so don't bother. No, I have no interest in hiring a cook or a housekeeper. Besides, no one with half a brain would work for me, what with Cooper and Gracie underfoot all the time."

"I'm getting all that, Mom. I'm just trying to say you can do whatever you want with all that money. Petey and Philly are going to go over the moon when you tell them," Connie said.

"You must have given *some* thought to what you would do with it, haven't you?" Carrie asked.

"Sometimes I thought about it in the middle of the night, when I couldn't sleep. One time, I actually made a list of how I'd spend the money."

"And . . . ?" the twins asked in unison.

"Well, I was going to pay off all your mortgages—on the art school, your houses—buy you all new cars, put money in a trust for the four of you. Take you all on a shopping spree. Have Arnie set up some kind of foundation where I could give money to the town to improve it. You know, the fire department, the police department, the sheriff's office—new equipment, state-of-the-art stuff for our hospital, things like that. Maybe build some new schools to help with the overcrowding; set up some scholarships. Make sure no more animals are put to sleep at our shelters. For sure I'd want to help all the women's and children's causes."

The twins stared at their mother, their jaws dropping.

"That's it?" the twins said at the same moment.

"No, there's one more thing."

"Say it, Mom. Out loud," both girls said.

"I'm going to go after that effing bitch, and I'm going to get justice for Larry. I'll hire the best damned legal team in this country. I'm going to make that monster wish she'd never been born. I'm going to drive a stake so far up her ass, I'll be able to pitch a tent up there. If I have to, I'm going to find those vigilantes we read about in the papers and have them as my backup. What do you think of *that*?"

"Yo, Sadie!" Carrie bellowed. "Fetch us the best bottle of wine you have in the house. Three chilled glasses." The twins all but leaped over the table to hug their mother. "Way to go, Mom!" they both said.

Julie laughed. "Do you think the boys will approve?"

"Mom, the minute you put the wheels in motion, your sons will be here so fast you'll think they were shot out of a cannon. Hey, you could charter a plane to bring them home. Boy, would they get off on that," Carrie said.

Connie poured the wine into the chilled glasses when the waitress set it down on the table. "We need to get serious here, Mom. Turn it all over to Arnie and let him handle everything. When the smoke clears, we'll all meet and . . . and do what needs to be done for Larry. Let's agree and drink to that!"

Julie smiled, her eyes glistening with tears as she held her glass up. The twins did the same. There was no turning back. She could see her life starting to change right in front of her eyes. She finished the wine in one long gulp. The twins did the same. Like mother, like daughters.

While Julie paid the bill, Carrie carried the remainder of the wine over to a couple she knew sitting at another table. She joined her mother and twin outside. She loved the wicked grins she was seeing on Connie's and her mother's faces.

They hugged and kissed the way they always did when they parted company, with Julie saying, "Drive carefully, girls," to which they both replied, "You, too, Mom."

Julie drove home, her thoughts all over the map. The sky opened up just as she climbed out of the car. She was soaked to the skin before she could climb the steps to the veranda. She hated these afternoon pop-up showers that were like monsoons. Thank God there was no thunder or lightning to upset Cooper, who was already barking his head off just knowing she was outside the door, and he was inside the house. The moment she stepped inside, he threw himself at her and didn't calm down until she squatted on the floor and rolled around with him. Gracie let her disapproval show as she pranced ahead to the bedroom, where she knew Julie would head to shed her clothes. Then she'd get her hugs and smooches and not get wet. Her tail swung importantly as she made her way. Inside Julie's bedroom, Gracie hopped up on the bed and waited like the lady she was.

Julie knew the drill and followed it to the letter until everyone was happy. She kept up a running monologue with the dogs and knew without a doubt that both retrievers understood every word she said.

Dressed in a light summer dress and sandals, she made her way to the kitchen, where she pulled out a bottle of wine and a glass, and stuffed some dog chews in her pocket. "Ladies and gentlemen, we are going to retire to the veranda because I need to *THINK*."

And that's where Mace found her four hours later. With her internal dinner clock working to the max, Gracie had gone out through the doggie door, across the yard to the cottage, and rang the bell. When Mace had opened the door for her, she backed up and barked. She backed up again, tail swishing, her head jerking to indicate that he was to follow her. He did.

At the big house, Gracie again scooted through the doggie door, then raced to the kitchen door to undo the dead bolt. Mace entered, his heart pounding as he followed the retriever out to the veranda, where Cooper was guarding Julie. *Please God, don't let there be anything wrong.*

Cooper reared up and showed his teeth. Gracie smacked him with her paw. He barked, a sharp, be-very-careful kind of bark that Gracie approved of.

"Julie! It's me, Oliver. Are you all right?"

Julie reared up, her eyes glazed. "Oh, Oliver, it's you. Hell, no, I'm not all right. I'm pie-eyed. I drank this whole bottle of wine. And . . . and . . . I had a glass of wine at lunch with the twins. I'm schnockered. We're not going to be having dinner this evening unless you want to try your hand at making something. I tried eating that shitty veggie burger at lunch, but I just couldn't get it down. The wine was good, though. The twins are vegans, so we have to eat there every Monday. They love it. Then I told them my news, and my life started to change right in front of me. I'll refund your dinner allowance tomorrow. I never get drunk. Well, I did when I was eighteen. I puked my guts out for three days. Then I got drunk one other time . . . that was the pits. I'm not a drinker, but I did drink today. I am so ashamed. You have a drunk land-lady, Oliver. I also made the decision that I am never going to write that cookbook for which I kept testing recipes out on you. In fact, I might not ever even cook again, but I'm not about to hire a cook or a housekeeper," Julie babbled, her arms flapping all over the place.

Mace smiled, looking at the dogs as though they should have an answer for him as to what he should do. They stared back at him with such intensity that he felt himself cringe. Even Lola was eyeing him with suspicion.

"I have a great idea, Julie. I'll feed the dogs, then heat up some soup or something. I think I can handle that while you . . . ah . . . recline on the sofa and maybe take a nap. How does that sound?"

Julie tried to get up, then flopped back on the rocker, her head spinning. "I think that sounds like you think I am . . . incapacitated . . . which I am. I am also going to be sick, so if you could just . . . you know . . . help me inside. Did I say I am so ashamed for you to see me like this? There's nothing worse than a drunk landlady. My kids would be appalled. They would, you know. Even *I'm* appalled. I'm talking too much, right? That's so I won't throw up. Oh, God, all I wanted to do was come out here and *THINK*."

Mace picked Julie up like she were a feather and carried her into the house. He headed down the hall to the bathroom, got her situated, and closed the door behind him.

He winced at the horrible sounds he was hearing. The dogs howled, and he did his best to quiet them. But Cooper was having none of it. He kept slamming up against the bathroom door until Mace finally gave in and opened it. The big retriever whimpered at seeing his mistress on her knees hanging over the john, and he did his best to get his head under her armpit. Julie's arm flopped over the dog to reassure him that she was okay. Mace backed out of the doorway, shut the door again, and leaned up against the wall until he was sure all of Julie's retching was over.

Mace cautiously opened the door. Julie was curled up in a fetal position on a colorful hooked rug, like the rugs in the cottage. Cooper was stretched out next to her, one of his big paws draped across Julie's chest. In spite of himself, Mace smiled. He walked back into the bedroom and looked around for a blanket to cover his landlady. That was when he saw the family picture of Julie, her husband, and their five children. He stared at it. Two sets of look-alike twins and a handsome young man. He peered closer at the picture and frowned as he tried to figure out how long ago it was taken. The best he could come up with was ten years ago, based on the way Julie looked when the picture was taken and how she looked now.

Mace felt guilty, like a sneak. He shouldn't

even be in Julie Wyatt's bedroom. He quickly picked up a light blanket from the foot of the bed, brought it to the bathroom, and covered Julie. He left the door to the bathroom open and headed for the kitchen. Gracie stretched out in the open doorway, Lola at her side.

"Guess that means I am on my own," Mace muttered as he made his way to the kitchen. Now it was his turn to sit down and *THINK*.

# Chapter 7

Mace Carlisle was dripping sweat from every pore in his body when he let himself into the cottage. He must have walked over ten miles already. Lola was panting badly. He soaked a towel in cold water and wiped her down, holding the towel around her whole body for a good ten minutes to cool her down before he offered her some ice water. She drank daintily, then lay down on the cold, wet towel, her breathing once again normal, as was Mace's. He waited a while, chugging on a bottle of iced tea, to make sure his dog was fine before he headed for the shower.

Mace realized that he loved this little town of Rosemont. Especially the drugstore, which was so like his father's store back in Hoboken. He loved the old-fashioned wooden cabinets with the shelves, the smell of powder. It even smelled like their old store. He loved that you could buy a hot dog or an ice-cream cone, then sit at a little spindly table to eat both.

During his stay and on his many walks, he made a point of buying something from the local shop owners. He was obsessed with Burns Hardware. He checked every tool in the store, stared for hours at the garden hoses, the leaf blowers, the big sit-on lawn mowers. He wanted one of everything. Buying locally was the only way small towns could survive, with the Walmarts and Targets taking over everything.

What he put into the town was a drop in the bucket, but if he moved to Rosemont, he'd help the community. *If he moved.* Perhaps he would move on a limited basis. He could come down three or four times a year. Ah, the eternal optimist. It wouldn't happen, but for now, he could dream. He had to think positively, even Jonesy told him that was half the battle. He could take a break, or he could retire altogether and let the company be run by those bright young buttoned-up MBAs he had on his payroll. All he had to do was make a decision to step down as CEO. That decision was off in the future—if there was a future—not something he had to think about immediately.

Satisfied that Lola wasn't overheated and was sleeping peacefully, Mace headed to the bathroom and started to strip down. His phone rang just as he put his hand on the showerhead to fix it the way he liked. He grimaced as he wrapped a towel around his midsection and took the call. He listened for the most part to Oliver Goldfeld giving him the good news, without saying anything. Carlisle Pharmaceuticals had gotten a clean bill of health from the FDA. Eileen and Eli were still spouting vitriol, but no one was listening. Oliver assured him they were out of his life for good. And, he said, it had all been done legally.

"You need to come back, Mace, and tie up the loose ends. I did my part; now the rest is up to you. I found you a place to live that I think you'll like. And you can have a dog. We have a buyer on your apartment in the Dakota if his financing goes through. I'd like you here in my office bright and early Monday morning, Mace. Take care of business here, and if you want to go back, then you go back. That's up to you."

All Mace really heard were the words *if you want to go back, you can go back.* "Okay, Oliver, I'll leave on Saturday, make the trip in two days. I'll see you Monday morning, and be sure to bring the donuts. It's your turn. Thanks, Oliver."

"Don't mention it, you big galoot."

Standing under the stinging cold shower, Mace mumbled to himself. He didn't want to leave, but he understood why he had to return to New York. He wanted to stay here. He really did. He wanted to join the community, wanted to make friends, and he goddamned well wanted to buy one of everything from Burns Hardware. And he sure as hell wanted Julie Wyatt to invite him to dinner once a week. And he wanted to get another dog.

As Mace lathered up his hair, he thought about Julie's question of what it felt like to be rich. Well, right now, this very minute, he knew what it felt like to be rich. Being rich meant he could do whatever the damned hell he pleased. And it was going to please him to come back here and join the community of Rosemont. Hell, he might even take up golf.

Mace started to whistle in the shower, then he started to laugh until his mouth filled up with soap from the shampoo. He kept laughing.

Life was good.


Julie looked over at her tenant and smiled in the twilight. "Normally, I love a nice rainy day, but four days of it is a bit much, especially when the power keeps going in and out. I am such a creature of convenience. I'm just glad I had the good sense to have natural gas put in the house when I moved in; otherwise, we would be eating cold sandwiches and drinking warm drinks as opposed to drinking hot coffee. It's supposed to be clear and sunny tomorrow. The dogs will love being able to romp around. They hate being cooped up."

Mace sipped at his coffee, wondering where all this was going. Or was Julie just making after-dinner conversation? He looked around. He was going to miss his daily dinners and sitting out here afterward, talking about everything and nothing.

His stomach crunched into a knot as he tried to come up with a way to tell his landlady he was leaving and would be canceling his short-term lease.

"I got some good news the other day. I still don't believe it, and I didn't say anything because I wanted to be sure . . . to be sure I wanted the deal. My daughters think I'm off the rails because I even thought about saying no. People from Oprah's production company showed up at my lawyer's office, contract in one hand, check in the other. They want me to do a show on her Sirius radio station. Arnie—that's my lawyer—said he had his best contract people at the firm go over the contract with a fine-tooth comb, and there was nothing awry. He advised me to sign it. I did today, and my stomach has not been the same since. My life is going to change. I saw it changing the minute Arnie told me about it." Julie jammed her hands in the pocket of her shorts and felt the wrinkled paper. Beyond telling her daughters, she still hadn't dealt with *that*.

Mace tried not to smile. "Congratulations! Sometimes, change is a good thing, Julie."

Julie shrugged. Her coffee was cold, but she didn't care. She wrapped both hands around the cup as though warming her hands. "What's it like being rich, Oliver? I know I asked you that question once before, but I need to ask you again."

The question caught Mace off guard. He grappled in his mind for an answer. "I suppose it's pleasant. That's probably the wrong word."

He had to remember he was supposed to be Oliver Goldfeld, who did not consider himself rich, just comfortable and well-off. "Having enough money in the bank so you don't have to worry about anything is very comforting. Taking days off just because is a perk. Being able to help those who need help and not worrying if you're going to come up short is a rewarding feeling. I just never gave it that much thought, Julie."

"I'm going to be rich," Julie said flatly. "Actually, I think I am already rich since Arnie said he wired the money into my very lean brokerage account today."

Mace was frowning and was glad Julie couldn't see his face clearly. "And this does not make you happy? Is that what you're saying?"

"I don't think money can make a person happy. I'm sure most people wouldn't agree with that. What . . . what's your feeling on vengeance, Oliver? You know, like if you had a score to settle, and you couldn't settle that score because money was the problem? And then, all of a sudden, you have enough money to . . . to . . . settle that score. Would you do it? You know, pull out all the stops and get even?"

*Aha.* Mace chose his words carefully. "I suppose it would depend on how important settling that score is or was. I suppose if I was wronged somehow, taken advantage of, then I'd pull out all the stops. That's just me, but I think I'd do it all legally if humanly possible. Do *you* have a score you want to settle, Julie?"

Julie set the cup down on the little table next

to her chair. "It's more like a promise, Oliver. I made a promise, and I couldn't follow through because I ran out of money and . . . and a whole lot of other things."

Mace did not miss the catch, the break in Julie's voice. "And now you have the money to follow through. Do you want to talk about it? I'm a good listener."

"No. Yes. No; maybe some other time. No offense, Oliver."

"None taken, Julie. It was a wonderful dinner. I can't remember the last time I had rice pudding with raisins in it. My mother used to make it like that when I was a kid. You cook old-fashioned. I mean that as a compliment," Mace added hastily.

"I know what you mean. I'm not going to be writing any cookbook. I made up my mind the other day that my plan was a fantasy; to write one was just a pipe dream. The only thing I regret about not doing it is that now I can't dedicate it to you, my guinea-pig recipe taster. About that, I am sorry."

Mace felt a lump in his throat. "I'm flattered as well as honored that you even thought about doing that. I suppose you will be quite busy with your new show for Oprah."

"I guess so. But I think I also have another project I'm going to start on. I should be good to go on that by September. It's long overdue. But now that I have all the money I could ever need, and enough time, that's all the incentive I need."

"I wish you all the luck in the world, Julie. If there's anything I can do, all you have to do is ask."

"I appreciate that, Oliver, because I know you mean it from your heart. I'll be fine. I think I have some very impressive people—not that you aren't impressive—who will help me do what needs to be done. But you know Murphy's Law. I never discount that."

Mace laughed. He should tell her now, get it over with. He wondered if he was flattering himself that Julie Wyatt would be crushed when he left. Just do it!

"Ah, Julie, I need to tell you that I'll be leaving at the end of the week." There, he'd said it, right out loud, and he felt sick to his stomach. He wished he could see her face.

"Really! I thought you said you would be here three months. I understand. I'll have your refund monies for you tomorrow."

"No, no. Absolutely not. I'm leaving early, so you get to keep the money."

"That's not the way I do business, Mr. Goldfeld. I'm going to tell you what I've always told my kids when I get the last word: 'Don't even think of sassing me.' I will give you the refund. I hope you enjoyed your stay. I'm going to miss you, Oliver. I mean that. It won't be the same sitting out here in the evening, Of course, I can get a dialogue going with the dogs, but they can't talk back."

"I'd like to come back for a visit from time to time. And to call you or e-mail you if that's all right."

"Of course it is. But, Oliver, don't make promises you can't keep."

"Don't you worry about my promises. I have

never broken one yet, and I won't break this one, either. I'm really going to miss this little town. I think I've walked it from one end to the other. I bet I've seen places you haven't seen even though you live here. Everyone knows Lola now. She gets so many treats along the way, she's spoiled rotten."

Julie laughed. "That's a good thing, Oliver. When you get back to New York, will you still walk her?"

"Absolutely. I'm . . . ah . . . making changes in my life. Actually, they're already in effect. I'm going to semiretire. I'm going to do a lot of things I never had the time to do, and they all include Lola."

"I still think you should get Lola a mate. Cooper and Gracie are going to be devastated when you take Lola away."

"Lola is going to be devastated, too. Maybe when I get back to New York, I can call you, and you can hit the speakerphone, and they can bark at each other."

Julie burst out laughing. "I can't wait."

"Julie, these last weeks have been extra special to me. I'll never forget your generosity, your friendship, and your cooking. I don't know what I would have done without you. Thanks seems hardly adequate."

*And let's not forget that deal with Oprah and Sirius you arranged for me behind the scenes,* Julie thought to herself.

"Oliver, I'd like to invite you for the holidays. You can meet my family. The boys are coming home for Christmas. I tend to go all out during the holidays. Well, that's not quite true, for years now I haven't done that . . . but just the other day, the girls asked me to make an old-fashioned Christmas this year. I said yes. Think about it. You don't have to give me your answer now. You might even get a better offer, like from the White House. I'm inviting you for Thanksgiving, too."

Mace chuckled. "I accept both dates. I will be here, count on it. Thanks for inviting me. I look forward to meeting all your children."

"All but one," Julie whispered so softly, Mace had to strain to hear what she said, though he pretended he hadn't heard her.

"I think I'll call it a night now. Thanks again for a wonderful dinner and the pleasure of your company."

"My pleasure," Julie said, picking up both coffee cups. She motioned for Cooper and Gracie to follow Mace. "Ten minutes, guys!"

Gracie barked. She would be back in exactly ten minutes. Cooper usually took fifteen before he crawled through the doggie door.

Inside, Julie put the cups in the dishwasher and turned on the kitchen TV. She turned on Fox News in time to hear Sean Hannity say that Mace Carlisle had been cleared of any and all wrongdoing, and that his children's cholesterol drug was ready for market. Julie's closed fist shot high in the air. The camera switched to an interview Eileen Carlisle was giving. She looked mean and hateful when she said, "What did you expect? He paid them off." Julie turned off the television and sat there thinking and wondering how soon she would get a response to the letter she'd sent out a few days ago. Probably never, since they hadn't answered her first one years ago. She felt like crying, but hope springs eternal.

It wasn't until she laid her head on her pillow that tears formed in her eyes. She was going to miss Mace Carlisle. Really miss him. Not romantically, just his friendship. Years ago, she had forsaken all her friends because she didn't want to burden them with her problems. She missed talking to people. She'd been so insulated these last years, with just her children and the dogs. And now she was going to lose Mace, too. Only this time, it was through no fault of her own. When her pillow became too wet, she turned it over, punched it a few times, and once again tried to go to sleep.

# Chapter 8

Mace Carlisle looked around the little alpine cottage in which he'd been living the past two months. His bag, a canvas sports bag he'd bought from a local shop, was bulging with the things he'd purchased during his stay. Maybe he should leave all of it behind so when he returned, his things would be waiting for him. Because, he *was* going to return. Of that there was no doubt in his mind. And if he was lucky, Julie Wyatt would give him a long-term lease. On the other hand, maybe on his return, he would think about purchasing a house of his own, one that would be close by.

Lola was rubbing up against his legs, sensing

all was not right. He hated that he was leaving and taking her to another unknown situation, but Julie said that as long as he was in Lola's life, the dog would adapt to any environment. Julie, in his opinion, was an expert in all things pertaining to dogs. He smiled when he thought about how she'd trained Gracie, who she said was the brains of the outfit, to lock and unlock the doors, to set the alarm, and to always be vigilant. The smile stayed with him when his thoughts turned to Cooper and his neediness and how she handled it. There was no doubt, not one shred of doubt, that should Julie Wyatt ever find herself in trouble, Cooper and Gracie would tear to shreds anyone intending her harm.

Mace felt a lump in his throat. He didn't want to leave, that was the bottom line. He gave the canvas bag at his feet a vicious kick. Lola whimpered, sensing her master's distress. Mace was quick to drop to his knees to hug the dog. He crooned to her. "It's okay, Lola. We are coming back. I have some things to take care of, then we're going to come back here so fast your head will spin. That's a promise, and I never break a promise. Now, let's get ready to go on that picnic out at the lake Julie planned for us."

Mace looked at the expensive watch on his wrist, wondering why he'd ever bought it in the first place. Why in the hell he needed to know about sea level and all the other things the watch told him was beyond him. When he got back here, he would go to the drugstore in town and buy a plain old watch with a leather strap, the kind everyone else in town, including Julie, wore. Julie said nine thirty, and it was already nine thirty.

Mace opened the door. Lola ran to Cooper and Gracie, who were waiting for the command to hop into the back of the Blazer.

It was a beautiful day, and the humidity hadn't kicked in yet; but it would. The sun was golden, the sky clear blue, the clouds, those he could see, were like puffy cotton balls. A light breeze fluttered through the trees. A picture postcard-perfect day. When he came back, he was going to bring a camera and take pictures of every tree, every person, every house, every blade of grass, and put them all in an album the way his mother used to.

He watched Julie as she slid a wicker hamper into the back of the Blazer. She looked like a young girl in her khaki shorts, yellow tank top, and sneakers, the kind he'd seen in the shoe store in town that sold for $5.98 a pair. Her hair was tied up in a ponytail with a yellow ribbon. She looked like she was thirty, not the fifty-eight she said she was.

Julie Wyatt, his landlady, his friend, his savior. That's how he thought of Julie Wyatt.

"Good morning, Oliver! Are you ready to go picnicking? The dogs are, that's for sure!"

"I'm ready. How far is the lake?"

"An hour as the crow flies. You'll like it there. It's so peaceful. Just three cabins, and I didn't rent them out this year, so we'll have the place to ourselves. The kids have a canoe and two Jet Skis. The lake is just big enough to have some fun, and with no one on the water but us, we won't have a problem. It's very rustic, so don't go expecting anything fancy. The kids used to love going there. I'm the only one who goes these days. I guess they outgrew it."

"Lakefront property is a luxury. How did you come by it?"

"Long story. The short version is that shortly after I moved here, my neighbor, an elderly man who I cooked for, passed away. He had a son who wanted no part of Alabama in any way, so he sold it to me dirt cheap just to get rid of it. He really didn't care about the financing, either; he just let me pay what I could afford. Actually, I only paid it off two years ago. I rent out the other two cabins from time to time, but for the most part, they stay empty because it's way too rustic. When the kids were teenagers, we would go up there, take their friends, and have some wonderful times, cooking over campfires, that kind of thing. Have you ever been on a Jet Ski, Oliver?"

"No, but you make it sound exciting, so I'm looking forward to it."

Hands on her hips, Julie turned to Mace and said, "Do you ever have fun?"

Mace thought about the question. "No!" he said. Julie threw back her head and laughed until she had to hold her sides. Mace joined in as he ushered Lola into the back of the Blazer.

"There's no A/C in this truck. For some reason, I seem to have a mental block about getting it fixed, so we're going to have to roll down the windows. That's the bad news. The good news is it's always at least ten degrees cooler at the lake."

Mace settled into the passenger seat of the truck, rolled down the windows, and leaned back after he buckled up. The dogs loved the breeze and chewed contentedly on their chew bones as the Blazer hit the interstate. Julie drove at sixty-five miles an hour, and in Mace's estimation, she was an excellent driver.

"Do you want to do a sing-along, Oliver? I used to do it with the kids when we would make the trip to the lake, to make the time go faster. Of course, the songs back then were kind of hokey compared to what they're playing these days, which, by the way, just sounds like a bunch of noise to me. This young generation to me will always be a mystery. I'm a dyed-in-the-wool Sinatra fan. I like smooth and mellow."

"Let's skip the sing-along," Mace suggested, laughing. He was just loving every minute so far. He could hardly wait to get to the lake.

It was seven o'clock, the sun starting to set, when the dogs piled into the back of the Blazer for the trip back. Julie shoved the empty picnic basket over to the side catchall that she said came with the Blazer when she'd bought it years and years ago. The dogs lay down and went to sleep, their hours of chasing and retrieving sticks all day, as well as frolicking in the cool lake water to cool off, now just memories to dream about.

Exhausted, sunburned within an inch of his life, Mace realized that this day had been one of the happiest of his life. He stood looking around at the rough, rustic cabins, the last of the sun glinting off the lake, and the covered canoe and Jet Skis they'd anchored to a monster pine tree. He sniffed at the pine resin that was all around him. It reminded him of Christmas, for some reason. He said so.

"We used to come up here and cut down our Christmas tree when we first moved down. The man I cooked for insisted. We might do it again this year, but I have to talk to the kids about that. You are going to be one hurting ballplayer tomorrow, Oliver. Even with the sunblock, you got a good burn going there."

Mace sighed. "Believe it or not, it was worth it. I'd do it again, too. I had a wonderful day, Julie. I can't thank you enough for thinking of this and taking me along. It's a memory that will stay with me for a long time, maybe forever."

"That's nice of you to say, Oliver. I had a great time myself. How many times did you fall off the Jet Ski?"

"I lost count. And before you can say it, yes, I know tomorrow I will be stiff and sore for that long drive back to New York."

They made the rest of the trip home in silence, both busy with their own thoughts.

The dogs woke the moment Julie pressed the code to the gate. "I'll make you a poultice for that sunburn. You aren't going to be able to sleep tonight." Mace nodded. He knew that the minute he showered, he was going to be in a

world of hurt. But he'd still do it all over again—
though, next time, he'd wear a long-sleeved
shirt. He thanked Julie again for a wonderful
day.

Inside, the dogs ran to their beds and lay down.
Julie boiled some tea bags and eucalyptus leaves
and let it steep after it came to a boil. While it
cooled down, she took her own shower and
threw on a sundress that showed off her glorious tan. She tied her wet hair into a bun on the
top of her head, slipped her feet into sandals,
and made her way back to the kitchen. She eye-
balled the concoction she'd made and hoped it
would work for Mace. She dumped it all into a
jar and carried it across the yard, along with a
bag of cotton balls and a tube of Lanacane.

She was back home and in bed by ten. She
locked up herself, not wanting to disturb Gracie
or Coop, who were both out for the count.

Julie was up the next morning at five and in
the kitchen, the dogs outside. This was the last
meal she would be cooking for Mace, and she
wanted to make it special. Banana pecan pancakes—the pecans from her tree in the yard—
her own homemade banana butter, crushed
pecan syrup. Mace would love it. A side of scrambled eggs, some crisp bacon, freshly squeezed
orange juice, and a gallon of coffee. She was so
depressed, she didn't think she'd be able to eat.
And she still hadn't gotten a response to the letter she'd sent to Virginia, something else to de-
press her.

Was she really going to let Mace Carlisle, aka
Oliver Goldfeld, leave and not tell him she knew

who he really was? She'd started to tell him a
dozen times but just couldn't bring herself to
say the words out loud. She hated the lie she'd
been living, just absolutely hated it.

It wasn't quite light out when Mace came in
through the kitchen door. These days, he didn't
bother to knock. These days.

Julie whirled around. "Ooooh, does it hurt?"

"You have no idea how it hurts. That stuff you
brought over did help. I look like a boiled lobster."

"You do. Maybe you should delay your departure a few days."

"I can't, Julie, I have to be back on Monday."
He should have chartered a plane. Maybe it wasn't
too late. Mace asked Julie what she thought of
the idea.

"If you can afford it, why not?"

"Is something wrong? You look out of sorts.
You really didn't have to make this magnificent
breakfast this morning. My plan was to be up
and out and on my way as soon as it got light
out. Since this is Saturday, I'm thinking I won't
hit any rush-hour traffic on the way. I'm going
to drive. It's a good way to get all your thinking
done at one time."

"There is that," Julie said, picking at her pancakes. Mace wolfed his down and went for seconds.

And then it was time to say good-bye. Julie
fought the urge to cry, and she followed Mace and
Lola out to the veranda, where Mace's fancy car
was parked. "At least you'll have air-conditioning

for the trip." She handed over a bowl of dog food she'd made up for Lola and a container of ice cubes. "They'll melt soon enough, and she likes cold water."

"Okay," Mace said, shuffling his feet.

"Have a safe trip. Drive with the angels, *Mace Carlisle*. My mother always used to say that."

"You know? And you never said anything? Why?" There was such total disbelief on Mace's face, Julie laughed.

"I was flipping the television channels before I went to bed the day you got here, and I saw you on the news. It was your business, not mine. I understood why, and I'm not upset. I'm just glad you are going to get your life back. It pleases me that I could help."

"I don't know what to say," Mace mumbled.

"I've always found it's best that when I don't know what to say, I don't say anything. Everything happens for a reason, and ours is not to reason why. Does that work for you?" Julie asked lightly.

"I want to hear you say out loud again that you aren't upset with me."

Julie smiled. Mace almost blacked out when he saw the smile reflected in her eyes. He stepped forward, his intent to kiss her cheek and give her a hug, but Lola moved, his leg went farther than it should have, and he was a hair from her face. He did then what he'd wanted to do since setting eyes on Julie Wyatt. He kissed her. Long and hard, until neither one of them could breathe.

Flustered, Julie said, "Oh, my! I . . . ah . . . I wasn't expecting that. Do you want to do it again?"

He did, so he did. Cooper howled. Gracie pawed the ground, then started to howl herself. Lola did her best to get into the act, but no one paid any attention. When the couple came up for air, the dogs howled in unison.

"I think this is a sendoff to end all sendoffs," Mace managed to say when he could get his tongue to work.

"I'd say so," Julie said, shock written all over her face. "I thought you were just going to kiss me on the cheek and say good-bye," she finally managed to say. "Now we have *this.*"

"Yes, now we have *this.* It was my intention to kiss you on the cheek and give you a hug. I don't know what happened, but whatever it was, I'm glad it happened. What about you?"

Still in a daze, Julie struggled to come up with something to say, and when she couldn't, she just bobbed her head up and down.

"I think I'll leave now. I'll call you this evening wherever I end up for the night. Will that be okay?"

Julie's head bobbed up and down again.

"Okay, I'm going to leave now. We can shake hands if you want."

Julie finally found her voice. "*Shake hands,* is that what you said? Shake hands after you kissed me like that and almost sucked out my tonsils and swallowed the caps on my back molars. I-don't-think-so!" One arm snaked out, and she grabbed Mace's T-shirt in her fist and yanked him forward. She kissed him until his eyeballs rolled back in his head, and he almost fell over the veranda railing. When Julie finally relinquished her hold on the man in front of her, she said, "Now you can go! And, yes, you can call me this evening. Drive with the angels." She turned and walked into the house, the dogs behind her. She slammed the door and locked it.

"I'll be damned," was all Mace Carlisle could think of to say. Lola whimpered all the way down the steps and into the car. Mace whistled.

"I'll be double damned," he said again, as the 543.1-horsepower engine turned over. He waved, even though he knew no one could see him. Then he shouted, "I'll be back before you know it! That's a promise!"

# Chapter 9

Charles gave Myra a quick squeeze, then kissed her lightly. "Fly safe, call me when you land, and if you need me, just let me know. Any idea when you'll be back?"

Myra sighed. "We're not sure, dear. My best answer right now would be we'll be back when there's nothing else for us to do for that poor lady. Can you handle that?"

"I can. Don't get into any trouble," Charles teased lightly. He picked up Myra's small suitcase and carried it out to Annie's car. He popped it into the trunk, closed it, then leaned over to kiss Annie lightly on the cheek. He stepped back and waved until both his ladies were out of sight.

"He handled that well." Annie laughed.

"He did, didn't he?" Myra smiled. "And how is dear Fergus this morning after his operation?"

"Myra, you would not believe what a horrible patient he was and still is. You would have thought he was the only man in the world to ever have his appendix removed. He milked it for four days. He ran me ragged. I was ready to kick him all the way to Scotland. Men make the worst patients. It's a good thing men can't have babies. Civilization would have died out long ago if that were the case. Whatever. He's on his own now. The doctor said he could go back to work tomorrow as long as he doesn't do any lifting. I arranged for a driver to take him back and forth. Nellie said she would cook for him until we got back. Win-win." Annie chortled happily.

"A four-day delay is how I look at it, and, no, I am not complaining, Annie. Fergus needed you. I just wish he'd had his attack earlier. There we were at the airport, ready to board the plane, and—bingo!—you get the call that Fergus had been rushed to the hospital. Like I said, I'm not complaining; it's just weird how that happened. But we both know everything happens for a reason. Four days is not that long a delay. I am worried about Julie Wyatt, though. Why do you think she didn't call us back?"

"I don't know, Myra. Maybe she had second thoughts. Maybe she didn't get our message. I wanted us to call her back again, but you said no, so I deferred to you. We're going to have a beautiful day for flying. Should we start thinking about what we'll do if Julie Wyatt has had a change of heart and doesn't want our help? Do we just turn around and go home?"

"I don't think that's going to happen, Annie. In her letter, she said she had tried to get in touch with us a few years ago. Evidently, her situation is worse now than it was then, or she wouldn't have contacted us a second time. I'm thinking some unseen force is at work here."

"Always the optimist," Annie said as she blasted her horn to pass a sedan that was going too slow for her liking. "I love this time of day, when it's just turning light outside. The beginning of a new day and the mystery that it will unfold. I love sundown, too, because at sundown we know what the mystery of the day was."

Myra laughed. "What's your feeling about night, especially midnight?"

"Actually, Myra, I don't have a feeling one way or the other about midnight because I'm usually asleep by then. Unless I'm doing *other things*."

Myra didn't need a road map to know what the other things were. She changed the subject. "I'm feeling a little guilty that we didn't tell the others, with the exception of Nellie, what we're doing. We had to tell her because of Fergus."

Annie blasted her horn again, then turned on her signal light to move over to the right lane. "Really? Why is that, Myra? Martine Connor is in Copenhagen at some ex-president summit. Pearl is on a camping trip with her daughter and granddaughter. Nellie has been suffering with her new hips, with all the rain and dampness we've had the last two weeks. None of them could have

come with us. What would be the point of calling any of them, when you and I can scout out
the problem and see if we all need to act on it?
For all we know, Julie Wyatt might just want to
*talk* to us. She picked *you* to write to for a reason,
Myra. That tells me she knows about your
daughter. And you are listed in *Who's Who* as well
as the phone book. Does that all make sense?"

"Yes, it does. We'll make our decision about
whether to involve the others or handle it ourselves, after we talk to Julie Wyatt."

"Ah, we're right on schedule. I do like it
when things work out the way I plan for them.
All we have to do is park this buggy, sprint across
the tarmac, and board our waiting chariot. Ah, I
see it now. She's a beauty, isn't she, Myra?"
Annie said, pointing to the sleek Gulfstream
that was her very own private jet.

"That she is." Myra giggled. "I'm not sure
about that sprinting part, though."

"How about a fast trot, then?" Annie said,
swerving into a private parking space reserved
for people who were rich enough to own private
jets.

Twenty minutes later, the Gulfstream was air-
borne, and ten minutes after that they were at a
cruising altitude of twenty-five thousand feet,
and both women were being served eggs Bene-
dict on fine china by a steward good-looking
enough to pose for *GQ* magazine.

"I could get used to traveling like this very
quickly," Myra said. She raised her eyebrows
when the steward set down two mimosas.

"They're virgin mimosas, Myra. We can't

show up at Julie Wyatt's house smelling of alcohol. How would that look?"

"Like we drink on the job, is how it would look. What do you think she's like, Annie?"

"Well, I googled her and showed you everything that came up on her. She's a pretty lady, not yet sixty, so younger than us. She has two sets of twins, which is a feat in itself. She's a dog person, and that's definitely a plus. She's had success in her life—she hosts a cooking show on the Food Channel. She's had tragedy, as you know, just as you and I have. My personal opinion is she *needs* help, our help, more than she wants it. Which means she's smart, Myra. She knows she has to resolve her problem before she can move forward and heal."

"She sounds to me like she'd be a good candidate to join our . . . second string."

Annie burst out laughing. "I was wondering when you were going to get around to mentioning that."

"You were ahead of me on that one, weren't you, Annie?"

Annie just laughed.


Annie fixed her eyes on the rental-car employee, and asked, "Does this rig have a GPS navigation system?"

"It does," the curly-haired youth responded. "This . . . ah . . . *rig* is fully loaded."

"Hmmm. Well, this is where we want to go, so will you please program it into that . . . that *thing* so we can be on our way," Annie said, shoving a slip of paper into the youth's hand.

The boy laughed as he programmed *the thing*. He had it done in seconds. Myra tipped him $20 before she settled herself into the passenger seat. Annie huffed and puffed as she slid behind the wheel.

"Don't look so damned smug, Myra; you don't know how to do it, either. They say ten-year-olds can do it."

"Well, guess what, Annie, we aren't ten years old, and furthermore, I do not want to learn how to do that. You don't, either, so don't pretend you do. Now, pay attention to what that damned thing is telling us so we don't get lost. Tell me again why we didn't hire a car service."

"Because you said we needed to economize."

Myra started to sputter, then they were off and running, their way of relieving the stress both of them were feeling.

Thirty minutes later, the computerized voice on the GPS navigation system alerted the women that they were three miles from their destination.

"This is a nice little town. Do you want to stop for some lunch, Myra? We need to get our wits together."

Before Myra could respond, Annie turned left and parked in a slanted slot on what she thought was the town square. "See, it says *Eats*. Soup and sandwiches. I'm not that hungry, but I could eat something. A cold glass of sweet tea would be greatly appreciated."

"You made your point, Annie. Let's take a table outside. It will give us a chance to get a feel for this little town. I like what I've seen so far. I just love towns with big old trees that shade the sidewalks. I wonder if children still roller-skate and ride their bicycles on the sidewalks." Her voice was so fretful-sounding that Annie flinched.

"Don't go there, Myra," Annie said, a catch in her own voice.

"Small-town America," Myra said, after they gave the waitress their order. One tuna sandwich to be split between the two of them, two cups of something called wedding bell soup, and two tall glasses of sweet tea with lots of ice.

The women made small talk; mostly it consisted of neither of them ever having been in Alabama. "I think they get a lot of hurricanes and tornados here," was Annie's contribution.

Suddenly, Annie poked Myra in the arm. "I think that answers your question, Myra." Myra turned to look at four young girls, bike helmets on their heads, as they parked their bicycles outside Penny's Ice Cream Parlor. They were laughing and giggling as they marched into the store, and they came out ten minutes later with ice-cream cones. They continued to laugh and giggle as they sat on a bench under the awning in front of the store. Both women looked away.

"Were we ever that young, Annie?"

"We were, Myra, but it was so long ago, it's hard to remember."

The moment the giggling girls pedaled away,

Myra got up, placed some bills under the salt-shaker, and they were back in the car and headed down Main Street on their way to Julie Wyatt's house.

Ten minutes later, the navigation system came to life, saying they would arrive at their destination within three minutes. Annie slowed the rental car and turned on her signal light but was prevented from making the turn into Julie Wyatt's driveway as a dark green pickup truck loaded with gardening supplies turned into the same driveway. They watched as the driver of the pickup punched in a set of numbers on the keypad. Their car was so close behind, it made it through the gate right behind the pickup. "Whew, that was close. We wouldn't have been able to get in if that guy wasn't ahead of us."

"We could have called Ms. Wyatt's number to ask her to let us in," Myra replied.

"You always have to have the last word, don't you, Myra?" Annie sniped.

Myra ignored her and got out of the car. "Oh, Annie, look at that glorious front porch. I wonder if they still call them verandas. Look at all the plants and ferns! And those wonderful rocking chairs. This is just too pretty for words. Shhh. Listen! Her dogs know we're here! Well, come on. Why are you standing there like that?"

"Because . . . because, this house, this veranda looks just the way Mama's did back when I was a little girl. Don't you remember, Myra? We used to sit on the veranda and have tea parties. We were so young and innocent back then."

"Annie, stop it right now. Tripping down memory lane isn't going to help us. This isn't about us or our memories. This is about Julie Wyatt. Now, come on, put one foot in front of the other, and let's go up on the veranda and ring the bell before those dogs come through the door."

They stepped up onto the veranda. Annie rang the doorbell, then stepped back. From inside they could hear a pleasant voice admonishing the dogs. The instant silence was deafening. The door opened, and a woman brushed back her hair as she stared through the screen door. She didn't say hello. What she said was, "How did you get in here?"

"We followed a green pickup truck. Ms. Wyatt, I'm Myra Rutledge, and this is Anna de Silva. You wrote me a letter. We called you and left a message, but you didn't return our call, so we came to see you. You have a lovely front porch."

"Dear God! I am so sorry. Is it really you? You came all this way? I didn't get any message, but we've had problems with power surges. When that happens, the answering machine goes haywire. I know I should get voice mail, but I hate all things electronic. Oh, my, I can't believe you're here!

"I'm babbling, and where are my manners? Please, come in. The dogs won't bother you. They love people, especially Cooper. I can't believe you came all the way down here from Virginia. I didn't know what else to do. I did write you once before, but you didn't respond, so I thought I'd try one more time."

"We're sorry we didn't come when you first wrote, but the fact of the matter is that we never got your letter. We weren't exactly easy to reach in those days. But we're here now," Annie said brightly.

"Yes, we're here now," Myra echoed, looking around at the cozy house. It was a woman's house, for sure. Everything about it was spick-and-span, colorful and comfortable, and it smelled like the house of a woman who did a lot of cooking.

"Coffee? Tea? Something cold to drink?" Julie asked as she ushered the two women visitors into the kitchen. "I always conduct business in the kitchen. I hope you don't mind."

"Not one little bit, dear. Annie and I are both kitchen people. Coffee would be nice."

"I just made it. I was going to take a break and sit down and think. I always think best with coffee."

"Us, too," Annie said, sitting down on a captain's chair with bright blue-checkered cushions.

"Oh, I am so nervous," Julie blurted.

"Don't be," Myra said softly. "Think of us as your two new best friends. You can tell us anything. Actually, you will have to tell us everything if you want us to help you. You can't hold anything back. In other words, full disclosure."

"Okay, full disclosure," Julie said, pouring coffee into blue-checkered cups that matched the cushions on the chairs. She returned the coffeepot to the machine and brought a sugar bowl and creamer that matched the cups and set them in the middle of the table, along with spoons.

Julie sat down at the table and folded her hands.

"Talk to us," Annie said.

# Chapter 10

Julie took a deep breath, the air *swooshing* out of her lungs. She clasped her hands and looked straight at the other two women. "Just so you know, I'm not good at this. I'm just way too emotional when it comes to the needless death of my son. So if I cry, just bear with me." Myra and Annie nodded.

"I pretty much told you everything in my letters, but since you didn't get the first one, I'll start from there. Larry was the baby of the family. He was always strong-willed, independent, and the kindest, gentlest person to walk the Earth. He loved animals and was always bringing strays home and nursing them. He really wasn't that good a student, but he made it through college, then got his CPA license. But, just like the twins, he didn't want to work with numbers, so he set up a catering business and did very well at it. He did all his cooking in the little cottage behind my house here. It was all certified by our board of health. We all pitched in to help if he had a large wedding or some other function that was too big to handle alone. It worked.

"Larry got married to a wonderful young woman named Audrey. They were so very happy. Even happier when Audrey gave birth to Olivia, my only grandchild. One stormy day, Audrey went to Olivia's play school to pick her up and on the way back, there was a car crash. Olivia survived but . . . Audrey didn't. Larry took it terribly hard, as we all did. We all worked overtime to make sure Ollie . . . well, you know. Larry threw himself into his business, and it thrived. He was mom and dad to Ollie. He tried to do it all. Then one day, some of his friends decided to take him out to celebrate something or other and he met this . . . this woman, Darlene Jimson, in some karaoke bar. Her tacky friends called her Jimmy, but the family always called her Darlene.

"She smelled money from day one. She was impressed with Larry's sports car, that he had his own business, and that he owned a house of his own. Well, he had a mortgage on it, but still, Larry did have a house, something Darlene had probably never had in her entire life. Darlene was working in some factory making eight dollars an hour. That's okay, it was honest work, and she did work. But she drank a lot.

"Did the family like her? Yes and no. In the beginning, she seemed to be good for Larry. He talked her into going for her degree, so she did, and she worked and went to school, and I know it wasn't easy, but she did it. That's the good part. Then, as Larry's business continued to grow, and he was making some really serious money, she changed. They weren't married at that point. She wanted to move in and Larry wanted her to move in. But he said he wouldn't do that with Olivia in the house, so he proposed, and they got married. She appeared to love Ollie, but we found out that was just a show for Larry's benefit.

"Eventually, Larry insisted Darlene adopt Olivia, and she did, but we all knew that was the last thing she wanted to do. But, she did do it. Eventually, Darlene finished school and got a job, but was making nowhere near the money that Larry was. We could all see problems developing. Some of them serious. She liked dressing like a streetwalker and going out at night with her friends and not telling Larry where she was going. She fell in love with credit cards and maxed them all out. The girls, Connie and Carrie, wanted to take her out behind the woodshed and go at it with her, but Larry said no, he was working through it.

"The signs were there that she was cheating on him. None of us said anything until finally he told me and the girls. Larry set traps for her, but she was just a shade too slick.

"Larry'd had a prenup drawn up before they

got married. When things started going south, he made a will, with his twin sisters as executors. Darlene signed off on the prenup because Larry said, no prenup, no wedding. But that's when she really turned into a conniving bitch. She wanted this, she wanted that. It was all about, *hey, look at me, look what I have!* All of Larry's friends took a step backward; none of them liked Darlene. And, of course, they told this to Larry, who then told us. They pretty much led separate lives, slept in separate bedrooms a year or so into the marriage. Darlene was not mother material. Half the time, she couldn't even remember Ollie's name. In short, she never bonded with the child, and Ollie didn't want to be around her.

"Darlene started working late, telling Larry she had to meet with people, et cetera. The girls and I played detective and staked out the place where she said she was working. She left at five, when everyone else left. At first, Larry refused to believe it.

"Time went on, and Larry tried to be super-mom and superdad. He continued with his business, Darlene did her thing, and we all took care of Ollie. And when she was five, Larry got sick a few days before the Fourth of July. A month or so before that, late May, we hired a private detective to follow Darlene. We didn't tell Larry. When we finally got the goods on her, we did tell him. He reverted back to the old feisty Larry we all knew and loved. He said he was going to make an appointment with a top-notch lawyer in Huntsville. Larry didn't want to hire one here in Rosemont.

"As I said, Larry came down with some kind of summer flulike condition, and he had all these big catering jobs over the Fourth. We all pitched in and even hired some help to take the pressure off him. Darlene never lifted a finger. Ollie was so excited because she was going to ride in one of the floats in the parade. Larry said he was moving out, and would be moving back in with me the day after the Fourth. He said he just wanted to get through the Fourth for Olivia's sake, so she could ride in the float. We didn't like that and tried to talk him out of it. He said he didn't want Darlene to know that he was leaving until the very last minute. We had to accept it because Larry was so headstrong, and his mind was made up. All he could think about was Ollie riding in the big parade and not wanting to disappoint her.

"Long story short, we managed to get all the catering done, and Ollie had a great day. Larry was too sick even to make it to the parade, so the boys took Ollie. It worked. I went by the house around two o'clock on the Fourth just to check on Larry, and Darlene wasn't there. He looked terrible and complained his back was hurting him—from a high school football injury that left him in pain from time to time. Sometimes, he'd sleep on the floor for relief.

"Larry said he had told Darlene he was leaving in the morning, and she had started to cry. He said he didn't mince words and told her to get the hell out. Those were his exact words to me. She took her golf clubs and left. Darlene liked to pretend to play golf, thinking she might meet up with a really rich man on the links. As she was leaving, she asked Larry to promise that they would talk about his decision later.

"I don't know if that happened or not. That was the last time I spoke to my son. He died early the next morning. The EMS people called me the next morning to tell me Larry was dead. I called everyone, and we rushed over there, but he was . . . gone. I took one look at that evil bitch, and I knew, the way a mother knows, that she had done something. As God is my judge, I just knew it.

"You have the rest in the letters I wrote. I made copies for you. Connie, my daughter, took Olivia home with her that day.

"Things turned ugly really, really fast. All of a sudden, Darlene's relatives and skanky friends swooped in and took over the house, and Darlene was calling around to see what Larry owned, wanting his bank records, everything. I had all that; the girls had some things, too. Larry didn't keep any financial stuff in the house where they lived because he said Darlene was always going through his things. He'd set little traps so he'd know. He said she'd go through his pants at night and take money out of his wallet; not a lot, but she did take money. Carrie told me that.

"Darlene was livid when she found out Larry had made a will. He never told her because he didn't trust her, and he knew his sisters would do the right thing, and that's why he appointed them as his personal representatives. And they tried and tried, but we had to go legal. The good news is Darlene never got a penny, and the will is still in probate. The girls filed lawsuits. This all went on for years until we ran out of money. We haven't seen Olivia in four years. I'm sure that baby thinks we abandoned her.

"Darlene moved some man and his kids into the house. People, friends who live in the area, tell us things about the mistreatment of Olivia and what a sad little creature she is. We did everything we could do legally, but the legal bills were astronomical, and we just had to call it quits. I don't know where Darlene got the money to pay her lawyers or if she even paid them. All I know is, we paid ours and called it quits.

"Just recently, within the last two weeks, God finally smiled on me, and I got an offer to do an Oprah cooking show for next season at really good money. Now I have the money to go back to court and fight, but having been through it once, I know the court system and how futile it is for cases like mine. As far as I'm concerned, there is no point in going back to court. I want . . . I want vengeance and real justice for my son, and I want that evil bitch to pay for his death."

"Are you saying Darlene killed your son?" Myra asked.

"No, that's not what I'm saying. What I am saying—based on the police report of what she said—is that when she came home that night from wherever she was, Larry was lying on the floor. She said she thought his back was acting up again and she just called to him and he didn't

answer her so she went to bed. She admitted she
had too much to drink that night and she couldn't
wait to go to bed. She said she called out to him
to go to bed, and that she was going to go to
bed, too. She knew he was sick, but she didn't
care enough about him to even check on him. If
your husband is sick, you don't go out and party.
At least, no one I know does that. If she had just
checked on him then or called nine-one-one,
Larry could still be alive today. We had expert
witnesses who would have testified to that at fifty
thousand dollars a witness. We didn't have that
kind of money and nowhere to get it. I mort-
gaged my house to the hilt just to pay for the
lawyers over the years. We all strapped ourselves
to the bone. There was nowhere else to borrow
money. We just had to call it quits."

Myra, a wicked gleam in her eye, leaned forward. "What do you want us to do, Julie?"

"Make that bitch pay for what she did. I want
a confession from her. I want my granddaughter
out of that house. I want her and those skanky
people she moved in there out of my son's—no,
my granddaughter's—house. I want her stripped
to the bone, made to suffer the way she has made
all of us suffer. I just want to honor the promise
I made to my dead son that I would make her
pay and I would see that Ollie had a good life."

"I think we can do that, Julie," Annie said,
getting up and heading for the coffeepot like
she was in her own kitchen. "Don't you agree,
Myra?"

Myra's head bobbed up and down.

"I want to help," Julie said. "My kids will also want to help."

Annie poured coffee, her eyes glistening with tears.

"How did you ladies survive the deaths of your children?" Julie asked, tears streaming down her cheeks.

"It wasn't easy," Myra said in a harsh whisper she barely recognized as her own voice.

"A parent is never supposed to bury a child," Annie said. "And yet, the three of us sitting here right now had to do that. In my case, there was no one to blame except for the elements. Myra saved my life and, at the time, she said something to me that I will never forget. She told me someday I might be called on to help someone go through what I had gone through, and she was right. I joined the vigilantes. It was before I joined up that Myra and the others found the man who had caused her daughter's death—and took care of him. Myra got her vengeance, which just goes to show payback is a bitch." There was such hatred and bitterness in Annie's voice that Julie winced.

"Listen to me, Julie," Myra said. "This kind of thing is not for the squeamish. I was the only one of the vigilantes who had to deal with a death. When it was my turn, the others agreed to help, but, in the end, while I got even with my daughter's killer, I didn't sleep any better. My daughter is still gone. I'm never, ever going to see her again. I speak only for myself when I say we will get even for you, but we will not kill any-

one. That's not to say that when we're done with
your daughter-in-law, she won't wish she were
dead. If we commit to you and your mission,
there will be no turning back. If you have a
change of heart, it won't make a difference."

"Are you comfortable with that, Julie?" Annie
asked.

"I am very comfortable with that."

"We can either stay on here and map out our
plan, or we can return home to Virginia and
map out our plan there. This time around, it will
just be Annie and me doing the . . . ah . . . wet
work. Are you comfortable with that, or do you
want the whole second string?"

Julie more or less laughed. "I see in your eyes
what I see in my own eyes every time I look in
the mirror. I would be honored to work with the
two of you. I promise not to get in your way, but
I have to be in on it. You understand that, don't
you?"

"We do," Myra and Annie said in unison.

Annie slapped her hand, palm down, on the
table. Myra placed her hand on top of Annie's.
Julie followed suit. "We're in business, ladies,"
Annie said cheerfully.

"We need paper and pens," Myra said.

Julie made them appear as if by magic. She
waited expectantly.

"Tell us what you know of Darlene's current
finances. Where does she bank? Where does she
get her money? Does the boyfriend live off her,
or does he have money? If you know."

"I do know. She has a checking account, no
savings account or money market fund. It's at

Alabama Federal. She gets money every month for Olivia, and it's an automatic deposit. Supposedly, she works for some fly-by-night company that organizes home shopping events and gets paid a commission. About six months ago, I heard she was one step away from filing for bankruptcy. They have four high-end cars, all with payments. She buys top-of-the-line of everything, and he is always buying something. She does have a poor credit score, that much I know for certain. I have her Social Security number as well as Ollie's if that will help you.

"I've lived in this town long enough to join all the citizen groups. I'm well known, and the people here are my friends and my kids' friends. I'm telling you that so you understand why people come to me or the kids when they find out something about Darlene. It's that small-town stick-together thing. I keep all those little confidences in a separate book. I don't want anything any of them tells me to get back and bite them, as Darlene is vicious. If you look at her crossways, she threatens to sue you. People do not want to get sued, and I can't blame them."

"Understood," Annie said. "But we aren't like those other people, are we, Myra?" Annie twinkled.

"No, we are not like those other people. We kick ass and take names later."

Julie burst out laughing. "I sense we are about to get down to business. Shall I make us a fresh pot of coffee? By the way, would you like to stay here? I have a lovely cottage with two bedrooms in a loft. They aren't actually separate bedrooms; there's a decorative screen separating the space. I'll even cook for you."

"Sold!" Annie cackled as she slapped her hand on the table. "More coffee would be wonderful. I have to call my pilot and send him back home. No sense in keeping him here. He can come back for us when we wrap this up, or we can fly home commercial."

"Myra, do you trust me to do the hacking, or should I call Abner to do it for us?"

"For this, dear, no offense, but I think we should use Abner. I think you need a little more practice."

"No offense taken, Myra. I agree with you. Hacking isn't like safecracking, but I do want to remind you that I excelled at that, along with the stripper pole."

Julie's eyes popped wide.

"Another time, dear, and we'll tell you things that will curl your hair. For now, we need to focus on our mission and not get sidetracked," Annie said.

"How much do you hate your daughter-in-law?"

"How deep is the ocean, how vast is the universe, how far is the desert? Combine all three, and that's my answer."

"That much, eh? It'll do," Annie said happily as she punched in numbers on her cell phone.

The plane situation was taken care of in sec-

onds. It was the call to Abner Tookus that made
the hair on the back of Julie Wyatt's neck stand
straight up. She listened to one of her new best
friends, her eyes as round as saucers.

"Abner, dear, this is what I need. Tell me if
you can have it done in the next few hours. Yes,
yes, I know who I am talking to. We need you to
erase two identities. Adam Fortune and Darlene
Jimson Wyatt. We want a full court on this. I'm
going to read off the credit-card numbers and
give you both their Social Security numbers. I
want their identities totally destroyed. I want
there to be no record of them anywhere at all.
Make them disappear from the face of the
Earth. ASAP. There's also a child involved, and I
will give you her Social as well. I can't be sure,
but I think Adam Fortune or Darlene set up a
credit line for her somehow. Ditto for Darlene's
dead husband. I have the child's Social, too. I
want her to disappear from the Social Security
database and have the funds that were being deposited for her redirected elsewhere under a
different name and number. So, what are we
looking at here, Abner, time-wise?" Annie listened, her eyes as bright and shiny as a squirrel's. She smiled and said, "And, as they say, the
check is in the mail. Give my love to Isabelle."

Annie powered down, then dusted her hands
together. "He said he'd be done by midnight,
his time. That means we'll know it's all been
taken care of when the news comes on at eleven
this evening. Tomorrow morning, the dark stuff
will hit the fan for Darlene Jimson Wyatt."

Julie was shocked speechless. "And you did all of that with *one* phone call!"

Myra laughed. "It's not what you know, it's *who* you know. Abner is the best of the best, and he's been training Annie."

"I read something in one of these papers that says Darlene practically lives at the ATM machines. That she doesn't carry cash as a rule and uses a debit card. Even pays for her groceries with a credit card. Is that true, or did I misread something?"

"No, you read it right," Julie said, her voice full of awe. "She even uses a debit card when she goes to Starbucks. She goes every morning for her daily fix. I used to stake her out."

Myra and Annie burst out laughing.

"Not anymore she doesn't. Myra and I can be there in the morning to watch firsthand if she has a certain time she goes there. She doesn't know us, so we can follow her. She might even go to the bank, and we can follow her there and take her picture when she pitches her first fit," Annie said.

Julie joined in the laughter. "She usually hits it around nine or a few minutes after nine." Finally, she was going to see some action. She was so excited, she could barely talk. *Please, God, don't make this a bad dream.*

"What does Darlene do for a living?"

"She was selling real estate after Larry died. Then she moved Adam and his kids into the house. When the townspeople got wind of that, no one would list or buy through her. I heard she worked in Huntsville in a department store for a while but got fired. The rumor around town, mostly beauty-parlor gossip, is that she's a sociopath. I don't think she does anything now except bail Adam's kids out of jail. Or Adam does. She dyes her own hair these days, too. Seems Betsy Kenyon mixed the wrong colors, then Darlene's hair started falling out. Darlene tried to sue Betsy, but no lawyer would take the case."

"They sound like pariahs," Myra said.

"I guess you could say that. Among other things."

"I have an idea," Annie said. "Let's go sit on your front porch, Julie. I want to hear everything there is to know about Larry, your other children, and, of course, Olivia. Will it bother you to talk to us about them?"

"No. I love talking about Larry, but everyone is tired of hearing me, so I don't do it anymore. I suppose in some ways, I'm obsessed."

"I was like that for a long time," Myra said, picking up her coffee cup.

"Me, too, but longer than Myra was," Annie said.

"Will you tell me about your children when I'm done?" Julie asked.

"Just try and stop us," Annie said, reaching for Julie's hand to pull her to her feet. "Just you try and stop us."

"I don't know how to thank you both."

"Glad to help," Myra said, leading the small parade out to the veranda. The dogs looked up and decided it wasn't worth the effort to get up and go out on the veranda in the hot weather.

"Watch the house," Julie said. Gracie barked in response. It was something she always said to the dogs when she went out the door, even if it was just to take the trash out.

# Chapter 11

A long with the dogs, Julie walked her guests over to the little cottage and opened the door. "Everything you need is already in there. You can make coffee when you get up, then walk over to the house for breakfast. I'll send the dogs to get you. Gracie knows how to ring the doorbell. I usually make breakfast around seven. Or is that too early for you?"

"No, that's fine. Myra and I don't sleep much, especially when we're planning a mission. We're going to spend most of what's left of this night reading through your legal papers. Do you want us to call you when our . . . *source* calls us later on?"

"I would dearly love that. Falling asleep knowing that evil bitch is finally going to get her due should make for a good night's sleep. Do you still want to go to Starbucks in the morning? She goes at nine. If you beat her to the shop, there is a wonderful spot where you can park and observe her going through the drive-through. She has her windows tinted very dark, so the only way to actually see her is head-on. You need to see what you're going to be dealing with."

"We'll do it as soon as breakfast is over. Annie and I are good at stakeouts. You're sure, now, that this is what you want?"

"I'm sure. No second thoughts at all. I think you'll be more than comfortable over here. I'll say good night now and thank you again for coming, and for believing in me."

The three women hugged one another, then Myra and Annie proceeded to settle down in their new digs.

Annie turned on lights while Myra dropped the bags she'd been carrying at the top of the steps. Annie, who had two boxes in her arms, placed them side by side.

"This is very pretty," Myra said, walking around. "I really like the oak floors and the ceiling-to-floor windows. I bet it's nice and sunny in here during the day. I just love all this wood. The kitchen is perfect—not too big, not too small. I could see how Julie's son Larry would have been happy in here with his little daughter. Yes, any young person would be happy here, don't you agree, Annie? And the little girl would be just across the yard from her grandma. This is just so sad."

"I do agree. I'm going to take a shower and change into my nightclothes. You make the coffee and get the stuff ready to read; then, when you hit the shower, I'll parcel it out to what I think we need to deal with first. I like Julie, Myra. I really like her. I'm wondering if maybe she wouldn't be an asset to our second string. I saw the way you were looking at her, and I'm thinking you are of the same mind-set."

"You're right, but how would that work for us when she lives here in Alabama? We can worry about that later. Take your shower, and I'll have the coffee ready when you get out. Just think, Annie, two more hours, and if Abner wasn't being overly optimistic, Ms. Darlene Wyatt will be floating down the tubes by early light. I can't wait!"

Annie laughed all the way into the bathroom and was still smiling when she stood under the warm water. She was chuckling to herself when she donned one of her old flannel nightgowns. She found true comfort in familiarity. She just loved it when things were on a roll. Just loved, loved, loved it! She sniffed at the fresh scent of coffee. It was going to be a very long evening.

Ninety minutes later, their coffee cups empty, their eyes on their watches, Myra looked up and over at Annie. "I never met this woman, and I already hate her guts!"

"Whoa there, Myra!" Annie said, rearing back. "What kind of mother would put her boyfriend and *his children* ahead of her own, even if her own is adopted? What kind of mother would spend her adopted child's money on her boy-friend and *his* children? What kind of mother would allow her boyfriend to slap, browbeat, and verbally abuse her child?"

"Not any mother I ever heard of. Okay, Myra, we both hate her guts! But we have a chance now to go after the evil bitch and make it right for little Ollie. She's a cutie, isn't she, with those blond curls and big blue eyes? So sad, though. Other than the pictures taken before her daddy died, there's not a single one of her smiling."

Myra's face was grim. "We're going to change that real quick, Annie. I can't wait to get my hands on that woman and her boyfriend." Myra looked down at her watch. "Ten more minutes, if Abner is on the money. You don't think there will be any glitches, do you?"

"God, I hope not. Abner is the best of the best. If he said he could do it, and he did say he could, then I think we should just consider it done. More coffee?"

"Sure, why not? My nerves are twanging all over the place as it is. One more cup isn't going to make a difference. You do realize we are not going to be sleeping tonight, don't you?"

"Of course. Why else do you think I didn't turn down the beds?"

"Then why did we put our nightgowns on?" Myra fretted.

"Because that's what we do every night, and we're creatures of comfort and habit," Annie said tartly.

"I suppose that makes sense in some cocka-mamie way," Myra observed, just as Annie's cell phone chirped to life. Annie had the cell to her ear in a nanosecond. She listened, her fist shooting in the air. "Yes, yes, Abner, I realize you are three and one-half minutes ahead of schedule." She listened again, her eyes sparkling like diamonds. When she finally broke the connection, she leaned over to hug Myra.

"He did it. The whole ball of wax. Darlene Wyatt no longer exists. Anywhere. She's in no databases. Her Social Security number now belongs to someone who died years ago. Her credit cards have been erased. She no longer has a credit report. Her cars will be repossessed in the next twenty-four hours, all traces of ownership erased. Ollie's monthly Social Security payments, under a different name and Social Security number—which can be changed back once this is all taken care of—have been routed to an account in a new bank. No one at the bank even knows about the account, but will at nine o'clock in the morning. All Darlene's bank accounts are now closed, as well as Adam Fortune's accounts, with no record that they ever existed. Both of them became paupers three and one-half minutes ago—unless they have some cash money in their pockets. I wonder how she's going to pay for her Starbucks coffee in the morning."

Myra clapped her hands in glee. "This is just too delicious for words. Hurry, call Julie and tell her. Ask her what she thinks Darlene will do when it hits the fan. She's made studying that wormy woman her life's work, so she might have an opinion as to where Darlene will go or what she will do to get money."

Myra brewed a fresh pot of coffee and made up a plate of cheese and crackers, which she carried back to the living room. She sat down in the middle of a pile of papers and started to munch on the snacks, the moment Annie hung up the phone.

"We just made that woman one happy lady. She said she thinks she will sleep like a baby tonight. I hope she's right."

"What did she say about Darlene?"

"Nothing good. She said she's been pretty much out of the loop this past year and a half and isn't sure what she's doing or not doing. As to where she could borrow money, she said possibly her family, who live in Upstate New York, but she said they are of modest means and don't have the kind of money she's going to need. Plus, according to gossip, they—the family—distanced themselves from Darlene once she moved her boyfriend and his kids into the house. She thinks that is a total dead end. There are no friends with money that she knows of. Adam was seen pawning stuff at a local pawnshop. She said Larry's jewelry—a Rolex watch, a gold ring, and a gold chain with a cross on it—never came back to the family. She said most of the boyfriend's friends are biker dudes who follow the road and work jobs on the fly. Darlene has no friends that Julie is aware of, because the bitch is so mean and nasty."

"Now that is music to my ears," Myra said, a

big smile lighting up her face. "Which brings me back to what I said earlier. How is she going to pay for that Starbucks coffee in the morning?" Annie was rolling around on the floor laughing at the visual Myra had just created for her.

"We did good tonight, Myra. Let's try and get some sleep. Right here on the floor with these pillows. We can pretend we're having a slumber party." When Annie punched in her pillow, she was dismayed to see that Myra was already asleep and snoring lightly.

Gracie rang the doorbell at six fifty. Myra and Annie were sitting on the steps, waiting to see if Gracie could really ring the bell. When she did, both women burst out laughing. "I guess I'm going to have to teach Lady how to do that." They followed the beautiful dog across the lawn and up the steps and the little platforms to the main house. The scent of bacon, home-fried potatoes—the old-fashioned kind, with onions and peppers—and coffee wafted about them.

The women smiled at one another. "How did you sleep, Julie?"

"I didn't sleep a wink. I was too excited. I wish I could go with you to Starbucks, but even I know that is not a wise move. But I want you to call me if you think you might need my help. How did you sleep?"

"We didn't close our eyes, either," Myra fibbed. "So you don't think there's anyplace she can borrow money, is that it?"

Julie filled both their plates with fluffy scrambled eggs, bacon, and potatoes. The toast was warm and buttered. Homemade strawberry jam sat on the table, along with a bowl of cut-up melon. The coffee was hot and freshly ground. "Not to my knowledge, but I guess we'll know soon enough if we see her scrambling."

"This looks wonderful, and it smells the way breakfast should," Annie said. "I just had a thought. Do you have a car-rental agency here in town? I think we should rent several different cars, so if Darlene or Adam get suspicious of us, at least they won't be sure."

"We do, actually. Enterprise, and they will deliver. I know they open at seven because last year I had to rent a car. I can call them now. How many do we want?"

"Let's go with three. I'll use my credit card to pay when they deliver the cars. We should also think about some reasonable disguises. My gut is telling me Darlene is going to be way too busy to pay attention to old ladies in different cars. But you never know, so let's be prepared."

"And I know just the place to get everything we need. In fact, as soon as I make the arrangements for the cars to be brought here, I will scoot over to the girls' art school and bring back what we need. Carrie and Connie have everything under the sun—wigs, hats, stuff that will change a look but not be overpowering. The kids put on a performance once a year to show off their artwork, and they do it in costume. It won't take but twenty minutes to go, scoop it up, and get back here."

"I just love it when a plan comes together. Remember how George Peppard used to say that on the *A-Team*, Myra?"

"He's dead, Annie, but, yes, I do remember how he always used to say that. That was one of Charles's favorite television shows."

"Okay, Enterprise will have three cars here by eight thirty. A Mustang, a Taurus, and a Ford pickup. I'm going to leave you now, and I won't be gone long. You can clean up if you want. I cooked. That's fair, right?"

"Absolutely," Myra said.

"I like that lady more and more each time we talk to her. She's like us, Myra; she has grease on her sneakers. No grass is growing under her feet, that's for sure. I also like the idea that now that she has money coming out her ears, she doesn't want to go the legal route, and wants us to do what we do best, get justice for Larry and pound that ex-daughter-in-law of hers into the ground."

"Have you given any thought to what will happen to us if we get caught?" Myra asked curiously.

"About as much as you have, Myra. I don't really care, do you?"

"Not one little bit, Annie. Let's clear the table and fill the dishwasher. Do you think these two bowls of food are for the dogs?"

"Why don't you ask them, Myra?"

"Smart-ass! Gracie, is this your food?" Cooper barked twice. Gracie just looked at Myra as if to say, *whose food do you think it is, since my name is on the bowl*? Myra, chagrined, set the bowls on the floor. The two dogs wolfed down their breakfast, then scooted out their doggie door.

Julie was as good as her word; she was back in twenty minutes. She made fresh coffee, and while it was dripping into the pot, she showed them what she had brought back with her in a big cardboard box. "I got in and out before the girls showed up. I'm not ready to own up to what we're doing just yet."

"Well, this isn't exactly Alexis's red bag, but I think it will do. But we'll need to pick up some latex and some stuff for padding. Maybe you can do that today, Julie. I'll make a list. If we work in unison, we'll make more progress," Myra said. Annie and Julie both nodded in agreement.

Outside, a horn blew. "I think our cars are here. I have to open the gates. I'm going to have them drive around to the back so the cars can't be seen from the street. I don't trust anyone these days, even though the shrubbery and trees are so dense. Darlene is going to be desperate, and the first person she's going to blame will be me. Do you want to come with me?"

The three women walked out the front door, and Julie directed the fleet of cars to the back part of the house. Annie signed her name, of-fered up her American Express Black Card, and accepted the receipt and keys. The drivers of the rentals climbed into the back of a fourth car as Julie explained how they were to exit the grounds. When the car was out of sight, the three women smacked their hands together as the dogs romped around, smelling the cars. Cooper lifted his leg on all three cars.

"He always does that. He has to claim everything if it's new. Gracie couldn't care less."

"Let's finish off the coffee before we get ready to leave," Annie said.

"I've had enough," Myra said. Julie agreed. Annie just shrugged as she perused the directions Julie had written out for her.

"Starbucks is pretty much a straight run from here, with just two left-hand turns. You can't miss it. See this big tree on the diagram I made for you? It's in the far end of the parking lot by Target. Target doesn't open till ten, so you'll get this parking space with no trouble, and it will give you a full frontal view of Darlene when she pulls up to the window. It would be nice if we could have an open phone line working for us. Just call me when you're in position and report in to me. I'll be sitting right here, waiting."

"That's a plan. Are you ready, Annie?"

"Raring to go. I have to tell you, I'm really excited. I hadn't realized how much I missed this kind of action."

"*Excited* is hardly the word. I'm downright giddy," Julie said. "What about you, Myra?"

Myra thought about the question for a few seconds. Those seconds took her back to another time, when Nikki Quinn had told her she was on board to go after the man responsible for Myra's daughter's death. She clearly remembered the overwhelming sense of relief that someone was finally going to help her, the way she and Annie were going to help Julie Wyatt. "I'm overwhelmed with relief that we can make this happen for you, Julie. I want you to trust us. We *will* take care of Ms. Darlene Wyatt."

"Then let's get on it, Myra. Who's driving this time?"

"I will. You drove here from the airport yesterday."

Outside, Myra climbed behind the wheel, offered up an airy wave, and sailed down the driveway to the open gate. She could hear Cooper and Gracie barking their send-off.

At precisely eight forty-eight, Myra swerved into the parking space Julie had drawn on the map. "I do like wholly accurate directions," Myra said. "I think I should cut the engine, and we'll roll down the windows. It's not too hot out yet. Have your phone ready to call Julie. In the meantime, we can talk. What should we talk about, Annie?"

"I'd say the little girl, Olivia. But if we do that, we'll both end up crying. This is a nice little town—not too big, not too small. I like it that people know one another and actually stop and talk to you. Julie said she knows most everyone in town. I have to believe she does because the townspeople certainly keep her up to date on what's going on, even though, as she says, she is no longer in Darlene's loop. Well, that is really going to change. Look, Myra, there's her car. The third one back. I saw the first few letters on her license plate when she turned in. I'll call Julie. I have to say, this is like having front-row seats at a movie or play. Okay, she's two behind now."

The two women continued to watch as a

black sedan in front took their coffees and peeled out of the drive-through.

"Okay, she's up. Lordy, is she one sleazy-looking woman. What's with all that frizzy hair? Looks like she's trying to cover up a bald spot or maybe her hair is thinning out. It is definitely an ugly hairstyle, in my opinion. She's ordered. She's handing over either a credit or debit card. The card is coming back. She's not taking possession of her coffee. She's handing over another card; this is probably a regular credit card. The first one must have been a debit card that was declined. Oh, oh, the young man at the window won't give back the second card. Darlene is opening her door. The young man is shaking his head. Oooh, looks like maybe the manager is at the window now. They're arguing. Darlene is livid. Looks like she's demanding something, and the two men are shaking their heads. They aren't giving her the coffee, either. She's shouting so loud we can hear her. She's demanding they call the credit-card company so she can speak to them. The cars behind her are blowing their horns. The manager is looking flustered, but she's holding her ground. Ooooh, he just slammed the window shut. Darlene is driving off. She's burning rubber, too. We're on her.

"We're two cars behind her. She's on her cell phone, and she's waving her arms, no hands on the wheel," Annie said into the phone, as they followed a very irate Darlene Wyatt down the street. Myra followed as close as she dared and was right behind her when she pulled into the Alabama Federal Bank parking lot.

"There is no drive-through here. You have to get out of the car and walk up to the ATM window. Go, Annie, pretend you're in line."

Annie was out of the car in a flash and walking as fast as her legs could carry her up to the ATM window. She stood back a distance, looking bored and just waiting her turn. Myra watched from the car.

It was all Annie could do not to laugh when Darlene bent down to peer at the slot where she'd popped her ATM card. Then she started shouting and shaking her fist. She turned around and stomped her way around the corner and into the bank. Annie ran after her. "Did that stupid thing eat your card?" she bellowed. "That's what happened to me the last two times, and I'm sick of it." Darlene ignored her as she yanked at the door and stomped her way to where one of the bank officers was sitting in the main part of the bank's lobby.

Annie stood by the desk where customers who didn't bank online filled out their deposit and withdrawal slips. She could hear Darlene's tirade clearly. She had to strain to hear the bank officer's reply since he was trying to be discreet. "I'm sorry, ma'am, we have no record of your ever having had an account at this bank. See for yourself. This is the Social Security number you just gave me, correct? Obviously, you are in the wrong bank."

"I am not in the wrong goddamned bank. I've been banking here for twelve years. My daughter's Social Security monies are automatically deposited into my account."

The bank officer sighed as he copied down the child's name and Social Security number. "I'm sure you're in the wrong bank, Ms. Wyatt. There is no record of your daughter's money coming in from Social Security online or otherwise. As you can see, I cross-referenced it with Social Security. I suggest you call them, and maybe they can help you. There is nothing more I can do for you. And may I say, I do not appreciate either your tone of voice or your choice of words."

"Oh yeah, well, I don't appreciate this asshole bank stealing my three thousand dollars, either. That's how much I had in this bank. I want to know where it is, and I want to know right now."

"If you don't leave, ma'am, I'm going to have to call the police. You have no money in this bank. I just showed you that neither your daughter nor you have ever been customers of this bank. Ever."

Annie made her move then, sensing that Darlene was going to give up the fight and leave. And she was right. She hit the door just as Darlene did. Annie held it for her as Darlene brought her cell phone to her ear. Annie trailed behind her and knew in her gut that Darlene wasn't paying the least bit of attention to her. Her strident voice was so hateful, Annie actually cringed. However, what she heard pleased her no end.

"Goddammit, Adam, what part of 'the money is gone' don't you understand? Call your bank and see if *your* account is still open. I couldn't even pay for the Starbucks coffee. The debit card doesn't work, the ATM doesn't work, and the bank says I don't bank here. They kept my credit card at Starbucks because when they called, they were told it was a stolen card. There is no record of Olivia's money going into my account because I don't have a goddamned account for it to go into. I have thirty-seven cents in my pocket, Adam. Call me back."

Annie knew she couldn't stay around any longer. She walked over to the car and got in. "The bitch is in a world of hurt right now. She only has thirty-seven cents to her name. She told Adam to call the bank and see about his account. He's supposed to call her back. Oooh, look, he must have called her, and she is *not* liking what he's saying to her. She just kicked her tire. Looks like she's cussing up a storm. If ever a woman needed a cup of coffee right now, it's her. She's getting in her car right now. Julie, where is the nearest Social Security Administration Office? I can't be sure, but I bet that's where she's going right now. Tell us how to get there in case we lose her in traffic. Okay, okay, I'm writing it down. I know, I know, but I don't know how to program the navigational system. This will work. I'm going to hang up, Julie, and I'll call you back when we get to the Social Security Administration Office."

Julie laughed on the other end of the line. Annie thought it was a sound of pure joy.

Myra gave her a snappy thumbs-up and said, "Let the games begin!"

# Chapter 12

Myra parked the car two spaces behind Darlene Wyatt's car. They could see her almost running to the door of the redbrick building that housed the local Social Security Administration Office. Myra cut the engine and hopped out of the car. "Don't look at me like that, Annie. I am more than capable of doing this. Besides, Darlene saw you at the bank, so you can't go into these offices. I can do this. Keep the engine running and call Julie to tell her what we're doing. Ooooh, this is so exciting," Myra gurgled.

The inside of the Social Security Administration Office looked just like any other government office. There were desks, wilted plants, and tired, frustrated-looking agents sitting at desks piled high with folders. Computers hummed, and fax machines whirred. Overhead, paddle fans buzzed. It was exceptionally cold for a government office. Myra shivered.

What Myra loved was that there were no people sitting in the wooden chairs waiting to see an agent. Probably because it was lunchtime. A good thing. She stopped at a desk and pretended to rummage through her purse as Darlene stomped her way to where a rosy-cheeked, bespectacled grandmother type sat at her desk. It was all Myra could do not to laugh at Darlene's appearance—pointy-toed six-inch stiletto heels, and stovepipe-tight jeans covering her skinny legs. A sleazy sleeveless muscle shirt completed her outfit.

Myra hustled over to a desk directly across from the rosy-cheeked grandmother and sat down in front of a middle-aged man with a deeply receding hairline. She pretended to rummage in her purse again as the agent waited patiently. She was close enough to hear everything Darlene was saying. She listened and watched as Darlene slapped two Social Security cards down on the desk and went into her spiel. Myra thought she looked menacing. The rosy-cheeked agent started to type. She reached for the two cards and looked at them closely, then up at her computer. "Neither you nor your daughter are in the system, Ms. Wyatt, or whatever your name is. Come around here and look at the screen."

Darlene came around the desk, her beady, heavily made-up eyes narrowing to slits as she stared at the screen. "This is fucking bullshit," she screamed. "Look at me. I'm standing here in front of you. I just gave you my Social Security card and my daughter's card. You've been paying me for years. I pay into this goddamned system, so where are my records?"

Myra did her best to pretend she wasn't listening to the exchange going on around her. Her agent waited expectantly, then prodded her by asking how he could help her on such a bright summer day.

Myra's mind went blank. Annie was going to kill her. "Well ... ah ... I, what I want to do is ... I want to give back my Social Security money. I don't need it!" Ah, that should work. She had his attention now, which was what she didn't want. Stupid. Myra fumbled for her billfold, where she kept her Social Security card, knowing full well she shouldn't even be carrying it. "I know you need proof, and I have it, but it will just take me a minute," she babbled. What kind of fool would give back her Social Security money? Then she remembered she hadn't changed her name to Sutcliff when she married Charles. Even more stupid. Across from her, Darlene was going on a rant. She kicked at the rosy-cheeked agent's desk and was shaking her fist. "I want answers, and I want them right now! Call someone over here who has a brain, because obviously you don't have one!" she shrilled as she shook her clenched fist at the cowering little grandmotherly agent.

Myra looked at the man across from her and said, "I think you need to do something and do it now! *If you don't, I will!*" The agent, whose nameplate said he was Donald Jonas, took one look at Myra and knew she would act on his response or lack thereof.

Darlene turned and looked at Myra. "Butt out, lady, this doesn't concern you!"

Donald Jonas got up and stepped over to the rosy-cheeked lady, careful to keep some distance between himself and Darlene. "You need to calm down, ma'am. Whatever your problem is, we'll handle it. Now sit down, and I'll call the manager." He looked at the rosy-cheeked woman and said, "Take your break now, Frances." The little lady scurried off.

"Don't tell me to sit down. According to that dim-witted woman, I don't exist. If I don't exist, that means I'm invisible," Darlene snarled.

Myra watched as three men came from three different directions. All of them wore suits with what Myra considered snappy ties. All three men looked determined. Myra had her cell phone in her hand and had already pressed 9-1-1. All she had to do was hit SEND if things got out of hand. She waited, hardly daring to breathe.

Darlene went through her spiel again. The three men looked skeptical, but a portly man who seemed to be in charge started to type. He looked up at Darlene, his expression grim. "Listen to me very carefully, Ms. Whoever-You-Are. You-are-not-in-the-Social-Security-database. Nor-is-your-so-called-daughter. The numbers on these two cards belong, or did belong, to a father and daughter who are deceased as of twenty years ago. In other words, these cards are fraudulent."

Myra was so giddy, she felt light-headed as her agent returned to his desk and looked at her while he, too, tried to pay attention to what was going on at the next desk. "You were saying . . . Ms. . . ."

"Martin. Mrs. Charles Martin. My name is Lynn." Well, that part was true. Her middle name was Lynn, and Charles was named Martin.

Off to the side, Darlene kicked one of her pointy-toed stilettos at the desk again. "Don't give me that bullshit again. I'm forty-five years old. I'm a citizen, and if you even think I'm not, then think again. Now, find my goddamned records and be quick about it. Wait a minute. Plug in Larry Matthew Wyatt and see what comes up. I was married to him before he died. He was Olivia's father. That should be all the proof you need."

The portly man did as instructed. "There is indeed a Larry Matthew Wyatt in the system. He pays into Social Security regularly. According to our records, he is alive and working somewhere that is none of your business. Can you prove you were married to him, *ma'am*?"

"I don't have my marriage license or his death certificate with me if that's what you mean. No one carries stuff like that around with them. Type in the Bureau of Vital Statistics, and it should come up. We were married on August 3, 2001."

"Not according to these records. Larry

Matthew Wyatt was married to a woman named Audrey Altman who died sometime I am not at liberty to reveal to you. He has not applied for a marriage license since then; nor has he remarried. According to our records, nor is he deceased." There was such venom and hostility in the portly man's voice, Myra found herself shivering. *How did Abner do all that,* she wondered.

Myra's index finger trembled over the SEND key on her cell phone. She jerked her head upright.

"Did I understand you right when you said you wanted to give back your monthly Social Security monies?"

"Well . . . ah, yes . . . I did say that, but considering what is going on with that . . . that person over there, I think I just changed my mind. You might decide to give my money to someone like her and, according to you people, she doesn't exist. Explain that, please."

Darlene Wyatt wasn't about to give up. "He's dead! D-E-A-D! Okay, okay, call my mother-in-law. She'll tell you I was married to her son. This is probably all that bitch's fault anyway." She rattled off Julie's phone number. One of the taller men who flanked the portly man dialed the number. He turned away and spoke softly. When he turned back to Darlene, he said, "Mrs. Wyatt said she never heard of you. And she also said she does not care to discuss her personal business or her family members with strangers, which is her right."

"That lying bitch! Let me talk to her! She's

my goddamned mother-in-law, and she's behind this. She paid you all off, I know it!"

"Mrs. Wyatt hung up. Mrs. Wyatt said she is not your mother-in-law and that she never heard of you even though you claim to have the same last name as she does. Now, either you leave here, or I'll be forced to call the police."

Darlene then went into such a tirade that Myra's jittery finger hit SEND. She looked at the agent across from her, and said, "I think I'll just keep my Social Security money and donate it to the SPCA."

Darlene went into threatening mode as she started pushing and shoving at the three men, who looked like they didn't want to get their fancy suits wrinkled. The rosy-cheeked lady was peeping out from a cracked door in the back. Myra hustled as fast as her legs would carry her to the front door just as a police car and ambulance, sirens blaring, pulled into the parking lot. She walked sedately toward the rental car as if she didn't have a care in the world. Once inside, she hissed to Annie, who was now behind the wheel, "I think our work here is done. Burn rubber, Annie."

Annie burned rubber.

Back on the highway, Myra repeated for Annie's benefit everything that had gone on inside the office. "That woman is a slimeball weasel, Annie. Julie was right. And we need to give Mr. Tookus a raise. A *BIG* raise, Annie. In a million years, I will never understand how he was able to do all he did. There isn't even a record that Darlene was ever married to Julie's son or that Larry Wyatt is dead. That's how detailed he was. No matter what that bitch threw out, Abner had it covered. I hope I did the right thing when I sent that nine-one-one call through. And then she had the nerve to demand they call Julie after all she's done to her. What do you think will happen now, Annie?"

Annie started to laugh and couldn't stop. "Since she doesn't exist, I have no clue. She can say whatever she wants, but if there's no paperwork to back it up, what good is it? I think that about now, she's starting to get the message."

"She had the message back in the office. She called Julie a bitch and said she was behind all this and that she had paid everyone off. Of course, those men didn't believe a word she said. The best part was when Julie said she had never heard of her, and wasn't her mother-in-law. I just loved that."

"I'm going to stop at that fast-food place up ahead. We can go through the drive-through and get some coffee, park in the lot, and call Julie. She's probably beside herself by now. You seriously said you wanted to give back your Social Security money? That was so clever, Myra. I have to say, I don't think I could have come up with that."

"My mind went totally blank, Annie. It was the only thing I could think of."

"You rock, Myra. Now, I need five bucks for the coffee."

Myra dug in her pocket for the money and handed it over.

The next twenty minutes were spent laughing like lunatics on the phone with Julie, who, as Annie later said, was happier than a pig in a mudslide at what they had accomplished.

"I have an idea," Annie said as she prepared to drive out of the parking lot. "Call Julie back and tell her to come up with some excuse to go to the police station and hang out to see if they haul Darlene in there. Tell her to make sure Darlene doesn't see her."

In a few minutes, Myra reported, "She said okay," and powered down.

"It's all in the paperwork, Myra," Annie said gleefully as she tooled along at a nice eighty miles an hour on the interstate. "As you said, a very *BIG* raise is going to go out to Mr. Tookus. ASAP."

"And we did it all by ourselves, Annie. We made this happen. How cool is that?"

Annie laughed again. "I think we both rock, Myra."

"That we do, Annie, that we do. I think I'll call Charles and give him an update."

"I called Fergus, and he's doing fine, but he said he's loaded with gas."

"Too much information, Annie."

Annie laughed again. "I'm having fun. Are you having fun, Myra?"

"You know it," Myra cackled, as Annie swerved to pass what she called a Sunday driver, who was only driving seventy-eight miles an hour.

\*    \*    \*

Darlene Wyatt roared into the driveway and skidded to a stop, her tires smoking. She bolted from the vehicle and slammed her way into the house. She saw it all at one glance, Adam drinking a beer and smoking a cigarette, his two derelict kids shoveling food into their mouths— food she paid for—the kitchen a mess. There was no sign of her adopted daughter. She asked where she was.

"Where do you think the little snot is? She's up in her room being punished because she wouldn't clean off the table."

Darlene looked at the slovenly mess in the kitchen, then at her boyfriend, with the cigarette hanging out of his mouth. She closed her eyes for a second as she remembered how neat and tidy everything was when she lived here with Larry. This place was a pigsty, and she said so.

"Then clean it up yourself," Adam snarled.

"That's not going to happen. You kids, clean up this mess or get the hell out of my house. I hope you enjoyed the food, because there is no money to buy more. You should think about re-joining your mother, wherever she is, if she'll have you. Let me be even more specific, and you, Adam, pay attention. Someone deleted my identity, wiped out every record there was of me in every database in the country. I think the same thing happened to you, so I'd get cracking on that right now. To you reject kids, that means no gas money, no beer money, no weed money, no food, *PERIOD*."

Adam's chest puffed out, he slammed his beer bottle down on the counter, and he bellowed,

"No, that's not what it means. What it means is you take your sorry ass out and get a job, even if it means flipping burgers somewhere. I told you what I would do if you messed with me, and I mean it. I'm tired of paying for everything."

Darlene clenched her jaw. She thought about the Botox she'd paid for, the breast implants, the liposuction, all with Olivia's money, and she felt sick to her stomach. "Do whatever the hell you want, Adam, but with no identity, how do you think I'm going to get any kind of job. I tried calling my old boss, and he won't take my calls. The party is fucking over. What part of this aren't you getting?"

"The part where you have no money—I'm getting that. So now is when you make a deal with that bitch. Give her the snotty kid; that's what this is all about. She'll pay you for her. We'll take the money and start over someplace. Without your kid. We're in this mess because of her."

"Shut up, Adam. If Julie Wyatt was smart enough to pull something like this off, she's smart enough to know I'll want to barter, and I'm not giving up Olivia even for you. That's two thousand bucks a month till she's eighteen. Do the math, you bastard! Right now, I hate your guts and your kids' guts. Get the hell out of my house. I mean it."

Adam laughed, an evil sound. "Whose house, Darlene? This is Olivia's house, not yours. She's just two thousand dollars a month to you. I'd like to see you try, and the key word here is *try*, to make me and my kids move out."

"Yeah," the son said, "try and make us." The daughter sneered, then laughed, the same evil sound as her father had made.

Darlene was so full of rage, she couldn't think straight. She opened the refrigerator and saw there was no more beer. In fact, with the exception of condiments, there was no food at all in the refrigerator, not even cheese. Tomorrow was grocery-shopping day, when they loaded up because Adam got paid every two weeks and tomorrow was the day his paycheck found its way to his bank account. An account the bank said he no longer had. She had thirty-seven cents in her pocket, not even enough to buy a White Castle burger. She slammed the refrigerator door shut and looked in the cabinet. Even the Ramen Noodles were gone, and she always bought a case on grocery-shopping day. Flour, sugar, brown sugar, dry oatmeal; but there was no milk. The cupboard was bare. Jesus. What the hell was she supposed to do now?

Once upon a time, the refrigerator was always full, and so was the freezer. The pantry had held enough food for an army, because Larry used her money to buy groceries, and they didn't have to wait for his clients to pay him. And, back then, there weren't two extra mouths to feed and support.

Darlene started to pace the kitchen. She looked into the laundry room, where three giant stacks of dirty clothes were piled up. Adam followed her gaze. He shrugged. "We ran out of soap." She couldn't remember ever running out of detergent back in the day. Who the hell ran out of detergent?

So now she didn't even have any clean clothes. Son of a bitch! She whirled around. "Did you do what I said? Did you check your identity, your bank account, Adam?"

Darlene started to cry, the heavy mascara running down her cheeks. She looked like a skinny, ugly raccoon. Adam said so. She hauled off and whacked him, and they went at it, with the two kids getting into it, too. "I'm calling the police," the daughter shouted. "I'll have your ass in jail in two minutes. I'll say you molested me," she screamed at her father. "And I'll say you helped him, Darlene!"

Adam reached for the cell phone in the girl's hand and slammed it down on the tile floor. He stomped on it. The girl attacked him. He shrugged her off his shoulders just as the boy came at him full bore. He stiff-armed the young punk, then banged the kid's head on the kitchen table. "Now get your shit and get out of this house. *NOW!*"

The two kids looked at their father to see if he meant what he said. Whatever they saw in his eyes, they headed for the door.

"Go on, do what he says; he's crazy. Go to your mother's and do not say one word about what goes on in this house. And do not ever come back here. Do you hear me?"

The doorbell rang. Darlene stopped crying long enough to run to the window. "Oh, my God! They're stealing our cars! Adam, do something!"

Adam flopped down at the table and dropped his head into his hands. "They aren't stealing our cars, they're repossessing them. I don't fucking believe this. That bitch didn't miss a trick."

"Do something!" Darlene screamed at the top of her lungs.

"How in the damn hell are we supposed to get to Mom's house if they take all our cars?" the boy bellowed.

"Try walking," Adam bellowed in return. Both kids slammed out of the house, every dirty word they knew spewing from their mouths.

"You happy now that you drove the kids out of the house!"

"Yes!" Darlene snarled.

Darlene raised her hand to lash out, but Adam grabbed her arm and twisted it behind her back. "I want you to shut up right now. Do not say one more word. In fact, get out of my sight immediately. Otherwise, I *will* hurt you."

Darlene looked up to see Olivia standing in the doorway to the kitchen. "Mommy, I'm hungry."

Darlene's eyes grew wild as Adam started to laugh like a hyena. She went outside, hopped the fence, which wasn't easy with the tight stovepipe jeans and stilettos, and walked through her neighbor's garden. She picked a few tomatoes, some small cucumbers, and some pears that were lying on the ground. She pulled out her shirt and dumped the produce onto her shirt. She cursed up a storm when she realized she couldn't climb the fence with the produce bundled up in her shirt. She walked over to the gate, which locked from the inside, and walked through it and around to her own back door.

Inside, she cut the tomato and cucumber into a bowl, then diced up the pear for her daughter.

Jesus, God Almighty, how had it come to this?

# Chapter 13

While Julie, Myra, and Annie were sipping wine on the veranda, and Darlene was slowly going off the deep end as she tried to plot and scheme revenge against the mother of her dead husband, Mace Carlisle was watching a legal secretary at the offices of Silverman, Rodner, and Weinblatt, the law firm recommended by Oliver Goldfeld to prepare Mace's will, witness the document, making it officially his last will and testament. Oliver and Mace had made it to the building where the law firm was located on the fifth floor, only fifteen minutes late. The torrential rain pelting the city had made traffic a nightmare and still showed no sign of stopping. Mace heaved a sigh of relief. It was done, finally.

Back outside, Mace looked at Oliver Goldfeld and laughed. "And here we are without an umbrella. What do you want to do, Oliver?"

"No matter what we do, we're going to get soaked. I say we head over to that bar on the corner and have a drink. I'm not going back to the office, and you said you aren't, either, so we could consider this a boys' night out starting now. Or we can split up and go home. I think I could use a drink, though. You look like you could use one yourself."

"I hired a dog sitter for Lola, so let's go get that drink. I know you have ten thousand questions you want to ask me, and since we have all night, let's just get them out of the way."

"I hope to hell you know what you're doing, Mace. You always listened to my advice in the past, but this time . . . you're being deaf, dumb, and blind. What is it with you?"

"I'm sick and tired of taking advice from you, from anyone. I've gotten to this stage in my life, and now I'm going to do what I want to do, not what seems right to someone else. You don't walk in my shoes, Oliver. I do respect your advice, but I just arrived at the Rubicon. And I do thank you for getting me out of that mess with Eileen."

Oliver held the door to O'Malley's Bar and Grill. Mace shrugged out of his wet jacket and carried it over his arm. Oliver did the same thing as he led the way to the back of the bar, where tables and booths waited for customers. It was still early, so they had the place almost to themselves. A young waitress dressed in cowgirl boots, tattered Daisy Duke shorts, and an off-the-shoulder peasant blouse handed each man a soft white towel. They both wiped at their hair and faces, then dropped the towels on the plastic tray the waitress was holding.

"We'll each have a double Scotch on the rocks," Oliver said as he slid into the booth.

"Coming right up."

Neither man spoke until their drinks arrived. Oliver held up his squat glass and clinked it against Mace's. He waited to see if Mace would make a toast, and he did. "To Burns Hardware and buying one of everything!" Mace laughed as he took a healthy slug from the glass.

"You want to explain that, Mace?"

"There's this hardware store on Main Street in Rosemont. They put Weed Whackers and all kinds of lawn equipment out front. They have a bench for customers to sit on, and on each end of the bench are big tubs of bright red flowers. They have brooms and rakes and all kinds of neat things. Inside, they have power tools and even coffeepots, camping equipment, peat moss, bags of manure. When I go back, I'm going to buy one of everything.

"I even found a house, if you can believe that! I was up all night taking virtual tours on the Net. If I buy it, I'll be able to walk to Julie's house, that's how close it is. Big yard. It's an old house, needs repairs, but it has a glorious front porch. I like porches. They call them verandas in Rosemont. It has paddle fans in all the rooms and even on the porch. Oh, and the hardware store also sells rocking chairs. I used to sit on them when I took Lola for a walk. On the way back, that is. Right next door, you can buy an ice-cream cone. Lola would get tired, so we'd stop for ice cream. What do you think of that, Oliver?"

"I don't know what to think, Mace. It's not like you made this decision overnight. You were there for two months. But are you sure this is what you want?"

"I'm sure, Oliver. I did not make this decision lightly. I want to have a life. I want to be happy. *At least, for the time I have left.* I'm not getting any younger, and neither are you. I smelled the roses, and I liked the way they smelled."

"I understand all that, Mace. But you left everything in your will to Julie Wyatt. She'll be a billionaire many times over if you pass on."

"Uh-huh."

"Are you in love with her?"

Mace pondered the question, the way he always pondered a question. "I think so. Maybe. Hell, I don't really know. I'm not exactly *in* love with her. Yet. But I feel something I think is love. Whatever it is, I definitely like the feeling. No, I never slept with her, but I did kiss her the day I left. And then she kissed me back. I felt . . . corny as this may sound to you, Oliver, I think she is my destiny. There is something definitely there; she felt it, too. If nothing comes of it, I'll have the most beautiful friendship in the world, and I can handle that. She's special in so many ways. She's forthright, she's honest to the bone, she cares about so many things, and she's had tragedy in her life that neither one of us can imagine. She loves animals, and her dogs in particular. People just love her. I never met her children, but I feel like I already know them because of the way she talks about them. She's a wonderful mother. She reminds me in some ways of my own mother. I hope she thinks of me the way I think of her. And, boy, can she cook. She said she would dedicate her cookbook to me since I approved all the recipes."

"Sounds to me like you're in love. That's not a bad thing, Mace. In fact, it's a good thing. I just wish you wouldn't jump into things so quickly. Leaving your estate to someone you just met . . . I'm having trouble wrapping my mind around that."

"Think about it, Oliver. Who else would I leave it to? You have your own fortune. I made you rich. If you want a slice of it, say the word, and it's yours. You certainly don't need my money. I have no heirs. I made sure all my charities are taken care of. I pensioned off my old housekeeper and my driver. They'll never have to worry about their advancing years. The foundations you set up will remain intact. Julie has a heart and a soul. She'll know what to do with it. But if my gut is right, she won't want to accept it. I know the lady, Oliver."

Oliver finished his drink and held up his empty glass, so the waitress would bring fresh drinks. "No thanks. Leaving me money would just give me tax problems. But thanks, anyway. Well, if things go south, you can always make a new will."

"That's not going to happen, Oliver. I'm going to miss you, old man."

"Yeah, me, too," Oliver mumbled. "When are you going back?"

"This weekend, if I can tie up all my loose ends. Don't look so shocked. Maybe my move will give you some incentive to get out and smell the roses. I'll fix up a bedroom for you in my new house. You can come as often as you want. I'll even give you your own key."

Oliver stared across the table at his old friend, his best friend, and suddenly wanted to cry his eyes out. "That's one of the nicest things you ever said to me, Mace."

"See, Oliver, that's our problem. Julie says people never say the things that are in their hearts, they just assume the other person knows what they're thinking and feeling. She says people are quick to criticize and don't take the time to compliment people when they do something nice, and she's right. You can't take anything for granted. You have to be out in front even if it means you wear your heart on your sleeve. I learned so much from that lady in two months, I could write a book. I might even do that someday."

"Okay, okay, but what are you going to do when you buy up one of everything at Burns Hardware? What are you going to do with all the hours in the day?"

"I'm going to fix my house. It's officially a fixer-upper. I'm going to join everything in town. I want to put down roots and belong. It's important to me, Oliver, that I belong. I can't explain it any better than that. I might stick my nose into the local politics. I plan to make friends, get to know my neighbors. I'm going to volunteer at the SPCA. I plan to get another dog or two, so Lola has companions. I'm going to ask Julie to teach me how to cook, so I can survive on my own without having to eat out all the time. There won't be enough hours in the day to do all I want to do."

"I think I might be just a little bit jealous," Oliver said.

Mace leaned across the table. "Oliver, they have sidewalks in town with humongous shade trees. All the stores have benches outside and the garden club hangs flowering baskets from the streetlights and there are tubs and barrels full of flowers all along the town square. They have parades, and Santa comes to the square on Thanksgiving. They have a YMCA, and all the kids go there for everything under the sun; potluck dinners, town barbecues, and picnics to raise money. Julie said she and her kids always enter the sack race. I want that, Oliver. Oh, you're going to love this. They have a daily newspaper, and they have paperboys and -girls who deliver the papers on their bicycles. Small-town America, just the way it was when we were growing up."

"Okay, okay, you sold me. You want to order something to eat, or are we just going to keep on drinking?"

"Let's do both. We can talk about your retirement next, unless you plan on hanging around in the hopes that someone will make you a judge of something or other. Then you and Marion can have his-and-hers monogrammed bath towels if you ever decide to take the plunge."

Oliver laughed. "Suddenly, you're an authority on everything. It doesn't work that way. I wouldn't know what to do with myself if I retired. The law is my life."

"That's just wrong, Oliver. No one thing should be one's life. It should be *part of* your life. You've been consumed with the law. It's time to kick back a little. I'm going to worry about you when I leave. Tell me you'll at least think about winding down a little."

Oliver stared at his friend and knew he was right. He couldn't ever remember Mace looking as happy and contented as he did right that minute, and it had nothing to do with the two double Scotches he'd consumed.

Dinner progressed with tenderloins, baked potatoes, and garden salads. The conversation drifted to Oliver's clients and where and how he'd transfer them to other attorneys in the firm if he did retire.

"I'd keep you, Mace, and maybe three others, and that would be it. I could give up my office, hire a paralegal on a part-time basis, and wing it from home. Then, I suppose I'd play squash a couple of afternoons a week, spend mornings at the club, get a dog like you did, and walk it four or five times a day. Explain to Marion it's time to commit or move on. All sounds kind of deadly to me. I just don't see hardware stores on my horizon."

Mace leaned back in the booth and looked

his best friend in the eye. "First of all, you jack-ass, you have to *want* to do it. You have to find your own path. And then you actually have to *step* onto the path. I don't even think you're in love with Marion. She's a convenience and a sexual partner. Where is all that going? What are your long-range plans, hopes, desires? If you don't reach for the brass ring, it's going to be too late for you."

"Now, why does that sound so ominous? You're sounding more and more like the kiss of death tonight."

Mace shrugged. "When you go home tonight, go into your study and sit down in that special chair you had made for yourself and think. When we were young, we used to have all kinds of hopes and dreams. We got so caught up in that money thing, we lost sight of what we wanted, and we lost part of ourselves. You know I'm right, Oliver."

"And all of this insight came to you because you met some woman named Julie Wyatt, who was nice to you, has had tragedy in her life, and is a good cook who was plugging along on the Food Network—until you decided to make her a very rich woman whose show is going to end up on Oprah, thanks to you. And because of that, she is not going to write that cookbook she was going to dedicate to you. Is that about right?"

"You know what, Oliver? Kiss my ass, okay? Do whatever the hell you want. I'm leaving at the end of the week, and when I get to where I'm going, that brass ring is going to be in my hand.

Put that in your pipe and smoke it, you . . . you . . . curmudgeon. And you can pay for dinner!" Mace said, reaching for his wet jacket and putting it on.

"Hey, hold on! I'm sorry, Mace. I'll do what you say. That's a promise. I don't guarantee you'll like the results, but I will do it." One look at Mace's grim face told Oliver his best friend wasn't buying his line of bullshit. "Okay, okay! Look, I'm happy for you, and at the same time, I'm jealous that you have the guts to do what you're doing. And, you're right, I'd love to meet someone like your Julie Wyatt. There, now are you happy? One more thing. Where the hell do you get off calling me a curmudgeon?"

In spite of himself, Mace laughed. He held out his hand and pulled Oliver up and out of the booth. "Leave a nice tip for that waitress; she could use some decent clothes."

Outside, it was still drizzling rain, but it was a warm rain. "You want to walk, Mace? I think we both had a little too much to drink. Do you want to stay the night at my place, since it isn't that far?"

"No, I have to get home to Lola. She's waiting for me."

"Yeah, right, Lola. Maybe I'll get a cat; you don't have to walk cats."

"Let's walk, at least part of the way." Mace linked his arm with Oliver's as they started down the street.

"Watch that stuff, or people will think we're gay," Oliver mumbled.

"What's wrong with that? I have a lot of gay people working for me. Nice people, too."

"So do I. I just meant . . . I didn't mean . . ."

"Just shut up, Oliver, and pay attention to where you're walking. You want to sing our old frat song? Julie says it makes the time go faster."

"I-do-not!"

"Sometimes, I don't even like you, Oliver. You always rain on my parade. You know that, right?"

"I know, and I'm sorry. C'mon, let's take a cab. By the way, did I give you my card with that phone number I scribbled on the back? Eileen's son called today and gave me his new phone number. He wants you to call him. My advice is, don't do it. You severed all those ties, so let it be."

"It's in my pocket. I won't call him, so don't worry about it. If he calls you again, tell him I have relocated, but don't tell him where."

A cab slid to the curb, and both men piled in. Nine blocks later, the cab slid to the curb again, and Oliver got out.

"Thanks for dinner, Oliver. I have the cab fare. I'll call you in the morning."

"Okay. Mace?"

"Yeah."

"I'll do what you said. We'll talk about it in the morning."

The cab pulled away. Mace leaned back in the seat for the thirty-minute drive to his temporary digs. It was raining harder by then, lightning dancing across the sky, the thunder booming all around him. Drivers, frustrated with the crawling traffic, leaned on their horns in the hopes it would make the traffic move faster. Mace actually thought about getting out and walking the rest of the way. He craned his neck to see if he could read a street sign, but it was raining too hard. Up front, the cab driver was mumbling and muttering to himself in some language Mace couldn't understand.

Mace's earlier happy, contented mood was suddenly gone, and he felt only stress and anxiety and didn't know why. Maybe it was the driver, who had some beads in his hand and appeared to be praying as he muttered and mumbled. Praying in traffic?

The night lit up at the same time that a roll of thunder sounded across the sky. For seconds, it looked brighter than daylight. Mace was able to see a street sign. Four blocks to go. He dug in his pocket for some bills. He leaned forward and handed them to the driver, telling him he would walk the rest of the way.

The driver turned to face him, shaking his head and saying, "You no go. Stay. One little minute, and you be safe."

"It's okay," Mace said. "Be careful. Drive safely."

It was the biggest mistake Mace would ever make in his life. He stepped out of the cab into water that came over his ankles. He could see lines and lines of cars, their headlights blurred in the driving rain. Deciding that the driver was right, he turned to get back into the cab but couldn't find the handle. Water rushed at him as he struggled to move, his hands outstretched in front of him. Lightning flashed, and thunder roared, as he squeezed himself between two cars to get to the sidewalk. He reached for the lamp-post and hauled himself to the curb. The last thing Mace Carlisle saw before he died was a bolt of lightning streaking to the streetlight he was hanging on to for support.

# Chapter 14

The police arrived at Oliver Goldfeld's suite of offices at the same time he did. Oliver took a moment to wonder how they had missed one another, but then he remembered that he'd come up the back way, huffing and puffing on the steps. His one concession to exercise other than his once-a-year squash game with his roly-poly internist. He squinted down at his fancy watch, a gift from Mace, which did everything but cook meals and take a shower for him—six eleven. The watch had to weigh at least half a pound, and he hated it, but because Mace had given it to him, he faithfully wore it every day. He looked at New York's finest, his eyebrows raised in question. He thought both officers looked tired and were about to go off their shift. He waited, his gut telling him he wasn't going to like whatever it was they were going to tell him.

The taller of the two officers held out a business card. Oliver sucked in his breath when he realized he was looking down at his own business card, the one on which he'd written Eli's number on the back, which was now nothing more than just a smear of blue ink. "Where . . . where did you get this?" he finally managed to croak, his tongue thick in his mouth.

The second officer licked at his lips. "From the dead body of a man. He was struck by lightning around eight o'clock last evening. The M.E. gave us this card and his personal effects. We went to the address on his driver's license, but that location is empty and for sale. His company's offices weren't open yet, so we came here. We didn't have your home address, just this address on the card. Are you Mr. Carlisle's attorney?"

Oliver thought he was going to black out. All he heard were the words, *dead body*. He tried to calculate how many hours had passed since he'd parted company with Mace, but his frozen brain wouldn't cooperate. "I am . . . was . . ." Suddenly, it was all important that these officers know he was more than Mace's attorney. "I consider . . . considered Mace my oldest, closest, and dearest friend in the whole world." His voice cracked, and he had to sit down. Again, he thought he was going to black out.

"If you're up to it, Mr. Goldfeld, we'd like you to come with us to identify Mr. Carlisle's body, unless you think someone from his company would be the better choice. Is there any family that you know of?"

"No family. I'm all the family Mace has. Of course I'll come with you," Oliver said, his voice cracking all over again. "But first I want to call Mace's physician to meet us there. His name is Jonah Levin." Oliver hit the number four on his speed dial, then spoke in a harsh whisper.

The city was alive and already going at full throttle when Oliver and the two police officers climbed into the squad car. The driver hit his siren and turned on his flashing lights as he whizzed into the teeming traffic. Oliver had never ridden in a police car before. He didn't like the way it smelled.

Oliver's thoughts were chaotic as he tried to come to terms with what had happened and what was going on at that exact moment in time. His eyes were wet as the fingers on his right hand caressed the watch he was wearing. Suddenly, he loved this watch and vowed at that moment never, ever to take it off.

Oliver was stunned to see Jonah, whom he and Mace called Jonesy, already in the hospital morgue. He wrapped his arms around his doctor and let the tears flow.

"I don't want you to see him, Oliver. I made the identification and signed off." The doctor's eyes were just as wet as Oliver's.

"No, Jonesy, I want to see him."

"No, you don't. Trust me on that."

The two officers mumbled something that sounded like they were sorry for their loss, and left the morgue room.

"Why?" Oliver asked.

Jonesy told him. This time Oliver did black out, but Jonesy managed to catch him before he hit the floor.

"Okay, you're coming back with me to my office. I need to check you out. You're white as a sheet." Oliver didn't protest, as he struggled to put one foot in front of the other.

"We have to . . . to make arrangements. We need to tell . . ."

"And we will, but not right this second. Harsh as this may sound, Mace isn't going anywhere."

Oliver knew that Jonesy was right, so he kept quiet.

Ninety minutes later, blood drawn, blood pressure taken, Oliver waited for Jonesy to say something.

"Your blood pressure is off the charts. I want you to go into my office and lie down on the sofa. It's not a request, Oliver, it's an order. The tech who drew your blood took the sample to the lab, and we should have the results later today. That means you are not going anywhere until I say you are. Consider this a wake-up call. I mean it, Oliver."

Oliver looked up into the doctor's kindly eyes and nodded. He obediently trotted into Jonesy's office and did as instructed. He thought his heart was going to punch right out of his chest. He talked himself down until his breathing returned to normal. The moment he was feeling clear-headed, he called his secretary, issued orders, and ended the call saying, "No, I am not going to change my mind. Be sure to call Marion. Start the ball rolling." And then he dozed off, because he had to escape the horror that his life had become since he had first seen those two policemen at his door.

When Oliver woke several hours later, Jonesy was sitting in a chair across from him. "I canceled all my appointments for the day. How are you feeling, Oliver?"

"Like shit! How do you think I feel? Want to take my BP again?"

Jonesy did. He smiled. "It's still a little high, but I think you're out of the crash-and-burn state, and I want it to stay that way. A shock of this nature will do that to a person's blood pressure. I took the liberty of making calls and taking care of things. Closed coffin for obvious reasons; we're doing the one-day thing. They actually tried to talk me out of the coffin, but I was insistent. People need to see one. I don't know why that is, it just is. Then it's St. Barnabas and cremation. I know for a fact that was Mace's wish, because we talked about it once not too long ago. Just a service. I assume you'll want to take possession of the ashes." Oliver nodded. "The service is at five tomorrow afternoon."

Oliver struggled to sit up against a pile of cushions. "You want to hear a crazy-ass story, Jonesy? Mace had a new will made just yesterday. He was hell on wheels about doing it yesterday. He was leaving to go back to Alabama this weekend. Oh, God! Where is Lola?"

Jonesy smiled. "She's with my staff. I sent them over to pick her up. Right now, she's in the conference room and loving all the attention. She's yours now, Oliver."

"Yeah, I guess so. I don't believe this."

Jonesy licked at his lips, and it looked to Oliver like he was trying to make up his mind if he should say something or not. "Mace was in here yesterday morning. I probably shouldn't be telling you this, but I'm going to tell you anyway. If you tell anyone I broke my Hippocratic oath, I'll deny it. Before Mace left to go to Alabama, before the dark stuff hit the fan with the eviction and divorce, we ran some tests. They weren't good, Oliver. Mace had both colon and prostate cancer. I was sending him his drugs. Hell, he could have gotten them himself or even written his own prescriptions because he was a pharmacist, but he didn't do that. He rejected chemo and radiation. That was one of the reasons he wanted out of his marriage so badly. He wanted it all over and done with before he . . . passed."

Oliver reared up, his feet thumping on the floor. "What the hell are you saying, Jonesy? Mace would have told me if he was that sick. He never said a word."

Jonesy sighed. "Mace said you wouldn't be able to handle it. He knew you as well as he knew himself. You were the brother he never had. He wanted to spare you, that's the bottom line. As sick as he was, all he could think about was you, Oliver."

Oliver was so choked up, he had to do battle

with his tongue and vocal cords to speak. "He kept talking about smelling the roses. Just yesterday, he tried to talk me into buying a getaway house close to where he was going to buy a house in Alabama. He said he would fix up a room in his house that would be just for me. He met a lady while he was there. Actually, she was his landlady. He thought the world of her. Since you broke your oath, I'm going to break mine and tell you he left everything to that lady, Julie Wyatt. I tried to get him to wait, not to rush into things, but he was adamant. I guess it all makes sense now," Oliver said brokenly. "I have to call and give her the news. I'll need Mace's cell phone to do that, though."

"It got fried along with the body, Oliver. I have his belongings out in the clinic. Maybe you can get her number from the information operator."

"I seem to recall Mace saying she had an unlisted number because of her ex-daughter-in-law, who harassed her. I'll try. If I can't reach her, I'll make a trip there to tell her in person. Is it okay for me to go home now, Jonesy?"

"How are you feeling?"

"Sad. All I want to do is cry my eyes out. I don't know what I'll do without Mace in my life. We weren't attached at the hip, but it was damn close."

"Crying is very cathartic. Don't hold it in. Let it all out. There are no rules when someone passes on. If something works for you, then go with whatever it is."

"How long did Mace have?"

"If he was lucky, a year, maybe a little longer. The last few months would have been hell for him."

Oliver struggled to his feet. He wrapped his arms around his doctor and patted him on the back. "Thanks, Jonesy. For everything. I'll see you in the . . . at the service."

"Call me, no matter what the hour, if you need me, Oliver. And do not drink any alcohol this evening. Promise me. And don't forget to pick up Lola on your way out."

Oliver nodded as he shuffled out the door.

Four days later, Oliver loaded up his car in the underground garage where he lived. Mace's ashes in the somber-looking urn were nestled in the corner of the SUV, with Styrofoam packed all around it. His eyes were wet, his nose dripping, as he packed his bags and all of Lola's gear. He swiped at his eyes as he ran off his mental list of things he had done and the things he still had to do. He'd retired his housekeeper, stopped all personal deliveries, and had his personal mail forwarded to the office. They would send it to him once he had a permanent address. All his cases had been assigned to other lawyers.

The office would remain open to tidy up all loose ends, then close down permanently within three months. He had arranged for his partners and associates to join another law firm. The only things he was taking from the office were Mace's files, at least the immediate ones. The other files would be sent on along with his mail in the next few weeks.

Oliver stared out and over the concrete wall to the day outside. He had one more call to make, to *Her Judgeness.* Mace had always called Marion *Her Judgeness,* and that's how Oliver thought of Judge Marion Odell these days. He knew he wouldn't get her personally, but at this point, he really didn't give a hoot in hell. She hadn't even shown up for Mace's service. No one was more surprised than he when she answered the phone. "Oliver, how nice of you to call so early in the morning. How are things?"

"What *things* are you referring to, Marion? I'm just calling to say good-bye and to wish you a good life. I've retired, and I'm leaving this morning. I thought I would give you the courtesy of a personal phone call, and tell you what I think of you for not attending Mace's service. That was a despicable thing for you to do."

"But, Oliver, I had my clerk call and explain that I had a meeting I had to attend. What do you mean, you're retiring? Where are you going? Does this mean you're terminating our relationship?"

Oliver sighed. "I am. South. Yes. Oh, one last thing. You sucked in bed, Your Honor." He could hear the judge sputtering as he clicked off.

Oliver swore at that moment he could hear Mace laughing somewhere overhead. Then he burst out laughing. "Damn, that felt good, Mace!"

Lola, who was dancing around at his feet, barked, a high-pitched sound that made the hair on the back of Oliver's neck stand on end.

He looked over in the direction where Lola was staring and saw a glob of vapor swirling about. He thought his heart was going to burst right out of his chest. Lola barked again, then one more time, as the vapor rose higher and sailed out over the concrete wall.

Oliver's hands were trembling so badly he could barely open the car door for Lola to hop in. But he managed somehow. He slid behind the wheel, taking great gulps of air into his lungs. "You're here, aren't you, Mace? Lola knows it, too, I can tell."

Oliver felt a poke to his shoulder, the way Mace always used to poke him. He closed his eyes, willing Mace to appear and, when he didn't, Oliver's eyes misted over. In a voice he hardly recognized, Oliver started to mumble, "I did what you said. I'm going to Rosemont, and I'll pick up the pieces. I promise to smell all the roses. I will, Mace. I got your laptop, took the virtual-realty tour, and bought the house you planned on buying. I wired the money yesterday. I'm going to do it all. That's the promise I made to you and to myself. So, if you want to ride shotgun, it's okay with me, buddy. Hey, did you like the way I blew off *Her Judgeness*? And now I'm ready for that sing-along. Hit it, Mace!"

# Chapter 15

It was barely eight o'clock in the morning, but the Darlene Wyatt household was wide-awake. Olivia was sitting in the family room, eating cooked oatmeal with no milk but loaded with sugar to make it more palatable for the little girl, and watching cartoons on television while her mother and her live-in boyfriend were screaming at each other in the kitchen. It was obvious to Olivia that neither one of them had gone to bed, because they were wearing the same clothes they'd had on when she herself went to bed. It was hard to hear the cartoon characters on the television with all the screaming.

"I told you, we're doing it, and that's final. She's behind all this, and you know it."

"No, I don't know that, Adam, and neither do you. For all we know, it could be that asshole ex-wife of yours doing it. She hates me, but she hates you more. And Julie isn't smart enough to steal my identity."

"You are so stupid you make me sick. My asshole ex-wife, as you put it, couldn't be bothered with either one of us. I'm telling you, it's that bitch. You should go over there to her house right now and kill her. I'll even help you. Well?"

Adam Fortune stared at the woman sitting across from him at the table, drinking coffee and smoking a cigarette. At that moment, he hated her. Really hated her.

"I am not going to Julie Wyatt's house, and neither are you. And no one is killing anyone. If you don't like the way things are here, leave. Go back to Kansas and live with your drunken mother."

"You bitch! I left my wife for you! You lied to me. You said you were *rich*. You don't have a pot to piss in. You own nothing. It was all lies. And I fell for it. You promised to buy me a boat and a fancy car, and what did I get? I get to move into your dead husband's house, with his snot-nosed kid. What's even worse is that it's the snot-nosed kid who owns the damned house, not you. Where's that fancy car, where's the boat, huh? Huh, Darlene? And another thing, my ex is laughing her ass off, along with that goody-two-shoes new husband of hers. They have it made.

They have fucking *money*. That new husband goes to a tony gym twice a week, they belong to the country club, they both have Cadillac Escalades. They eat out, they have good jobs, he buys her diamonds."

"If you don't shut up, I'm going to put you through the wall, and don't think I can't or won't. Now, I am going to the police station and file a complaint. Even though it won't do any good, I'm still going to do it. When they ask me who I think is responsible, I am going to say either your ex-wife or my former mother-in-law. The next step in this drama, in case your feeble brain still isn't working, is we will be evicted from this house. I don't know how that's going to happen, but it's sure as hell going to. We'll be living in a tent, or a run-down trailer park. The money I don't have is on the tent because I don't have money to pay for a rental trailer. Now, what's it going to be, Adam?"

"What about the snot? Are we taking her?"

"No, it's too far for her to walk. We are walking. I'm not taking the motorcycle out, because they'll just repo it. And it's almost out of gas, even though I have half a can for the lawn mower. It might help if you fixed yourself up a little, like shave or take a shower."

Darlene took the punch high on the cheekbone. She cursed, and whacked her beloved along the side of his face. In the family room, Olivia covered her ears and started to cry. She cowered into the corner when she saw her mother coming toward her. "I want you to go upstairs,

Olivia. We have to go out. I'll lock the doors, and we won't be that long. Do not open the door to anyone. Do you understand me?"

"I don't want to be by myself, Mommy. I'm afraid to stay alone. I want my daddy. I hate you, and I hate him, too. I want Grandma and Connie and Carrie. I hate this oatmeal, and I'm still hungry. I want my grandma. Please, Mommy, take me there. She loves me. Connie and Carrie love me, and so do Philly and Pete. I miss them, Mommy. Please take me there."

Adam started to unbuckle his belt. Olivia fled up the steps and into her room. She ran to the closet and crawled as far back into the corner as she could go. She cried for her father, grandmother, and aunts and uncles, begging and pleading for someone to help her.

Always when she did this, she felt something hovering over her. She thought it was angel wings, and that pleased her, because she knew it was her daddy who was an angel in heaven. Sometimes she thought she could actually feel the feathers, and one time she found a feather when she woke up. It was her dearest possession in the whole world, and she kept it in her Crayola box. But she had to take the brown and orange crayon out to make room for the feather. She thought she could feel the feathers brushing against her face. How soft they were. She closed her eyes and hoped she would dream about her father. "Please help me, Daddy," she whimpered.

*  *  *

"You should feel right at home here, Adam," Darlene said as she opened the door to the police station. "How many times have you been here for those kids of yours? Six? Seven?"

"Shut up, Darlene. If you keep this up, I'm going to tell these cops you molested my son. I'll tell them how you left your husband to die so you could inherit all his money. I'll tell them how you lusted after me and how you almost raped me that first time. I'll do it, too, and my son will back me up. They'll toss your skinny ass in jail, and you'll never see the light of day again. I don't have anything to lose, so make my day, you sorry-assed reject. I warned you not to mess with me, and I meant it. You are messing with me, Darlene."

Darlene knew he meant it. She broke out in a cold sweat the way she always did when he threatened her. She clamped her lips shut and walked over to the window, where she told the office girl she needed to file a report. She was told to take a seat, and one of the detectives would be right out.

Forty minutes later, Darlene was on her feet screeching her head off. Adam was blustering and cursing. Two police officers approached, and Adam sat down. Darlene stopped her cater-wauling and sat down next to him.

"You need a lawyer, Ms. Wyatt, or whoever you are, not the police. I'm filing your report, but you have no credentials to back up your identity. We can't go around harassing our up-standing citizens with complaints like this. My suggestion is the same as I told you when you first sat down. Hire a lawyer to investigate your case."

"I can't do that, since I have no money. Everything was taken away. We've been robbed of our money, our credit, and our identities."

"You are not in the system anywhere, that's all I can tell you," the detective said patiently.

Adam got up and kicked at the chair. "You're probably in on this, too. No one is that good to pull off something like this without help from the authorities. If you were any kind of a police department, you'd be trying to help us."

"Yeah," Darlene said, sliding off her chair. "Thanks for nothing."

Outside in the boiling sun, Darlene started to wail about the long walk home in the hot sun. She was thirsty, and she was hungry. Adam ignored her as he headed toward home. Jesus, God Almighty, how had her life gotten to this point?

She knew exactly how it had gotten to this point. The moment she cheated on Larry was when it had all started. Her dreams of a rich, lust-filled, wonderful life with Adam were nothing but pipe dreams. There hadn't been a single thing wonderful about it at all. And, to this day, she had not seen one penny of her husband's money. Not one penny.

Olivia was set for life—maybe for two lifetimes—but thanks to that bitch Julie Wyatt, Larry's sisters controlled his daughter's funds, and she would have to be at death's door before those two would give up a dime. She couldn't even petition the court, because she didn't have any money to hire a lawyer. And, in the end, what lawyer would represent her? She'd stiffed everyone she'd hired to represent her back in the beginning when Julie went after her following Larry's death. What the hell was she supposed to do now?

"Look, birdbrain, there's your mother-in-law's house," Adam said, thirty minutes later. "A house you'll never see the inside of again," Adam sneered. "Ah, look, she's just pulling out of her driveway. Aren't you going to say hello, Darlene?"

"Shut up, Adam." She'd loved Julie's house and the big dinners and the family parties. Julie had always had a birthday party for her, even though Julie didn't really like her. Julie tolerated her because of Larry and Olivia. She'd never been unkind to Darlene, though, until Larry died. Deep in her gut, she couldn't blame Julie; she should have called 9-1-1, but she would never admit to it.

Darlene was close enough to the truck to actually see the freckles on Julie's face. How nice she looked, how calm and serene. Back in the day, she'd liked that about her, that nothing ever ruffled her. Darlene stopped, because she had nowhere else to walk; she waited for the on-coming traffic to abate so Julie could pull out onto the road. The windows were down in the truck, probably so Julie could see traffic better. She looked right through Darlene like she was invisible.

Darlene pushed past Adam and was about to

put her face in the truck when Adam pulled her back. "You did it, you bitch! You happy now? I hope you rot in hell, you piece of shit!"

Julie looked at Darlene and smiled just as a break in traffic came. "Do I know you?" She was still smiling as she whizzed down the road.

"Do I know you? Do I know you?" Adam snarled. "She looked just like the cat that ate the canary. She did it, all right! Did you see that smile? She's got you right where she wants you now. What are you going to do about it, Darlene? When are you going to wise up and do something to get back at her?"

"Will you just shut up? I can't stand all your yacking. You're making me sick."

"I can't stand you, either, so maybe we should just call it a day," Adam snarled again.

Darlene hated the words she'd just heard. If Adam left her, she'd have no one but Olivia. She hated being alone. She needed people, she needed the chaos in her life. She didn't mean to say it, but she said it anyway. "Whatever you want, Adam. I hope you are going to like living with that crazy-ass mother of yours in Kansas. You better hope they send you enough money for a bus ticket."

Then she shut up as a vision of herself in an orange jumpsuit, being some convict's prison bitch, flashed in front of her eyes. She thought she was going to puke her guts out right there on the side of the road. Darlene started to wail and snivel again, sweat covering her body as she trudged along beside Adam.

Darlene's steps quickened the moment she

set foot on her street. She looked all around, knowing that the neighbors, who hated the two of them, were watching her every move. They were probably all cheering that all the cars had been repoed and the kids had moved out. She knew the neighbors reported her every move to Julie Wyatt. She hated them as much as they hated her, because they let her know she didn't belong and they didn't want her in their pristine neighborhood. Darlene's nude sunbathing and Adam's kids' drunken parties didn't help matters, either, what with the police on the street at least twice a week.

Those same neighbors had loved Larry, though. When Larry was alive, they'd been invited to all the neighborhood Christmas parties, the backyard barbecues, the block parties. The kids in the neighborhood played with Ollie, and Darlene had even played golf and tennis with a few of them. They knew early on about her infidelity, because Larry had told them. The minute they set eyes on Darlene—with her bleached hair, the makeup she put on with a trowel, the sleazy outfits—it was all over. Ollie, not really understanding what was going on, told her that one of the neighbors had said Darlene had to go through a car wash to remove her makeup. Well, she had Botox now, and in her opinion, she looked fabulous.

Inside the house, Adam went right to the coffeepot. "Look, Darlene, give me your ring; we have to pawn it. Even as stupid as you are, you have to know it's all we have going for us right now. Later, when this is all over, and we pin it on Julie, we'll sue her ass off, and I'll buy you an even bigger ring. Don't fight me on this because, if you do, I will kill you right here and now."

For the first time in her life, Darlene didn't put up a fight, and she didn't say a word. She removed the engagement ring Adam had bought her on credit back in the beginning and slapped it into the palm of his hand.

"You'll be lucky if you get two thousand," she sneered. "I told you I wanted a bigger diamond, but oh, no, you said this measly two-carat piece of shit was good enough for me. I bet you wish you had listened to me back then."

"Why don't you hock Larry's rings, huh?"

"We've been over this before, Adam. One more time: because they go to Olivia when she's old enough to appreciate them. It's the least I can do for her."

"Get the rest of your jewelry, the stuff you said Julie gave you. We need to sell it all or starve. I won't tell you twice, Darlene."

Darlene scurried away. Adam could hear her clomping up the steps in her designer shoes. When she returned with a small plastic bag full of jewelry, she said, "This is pathetic. This shit is all crap, and to think I thought it meant something. Go on, take it, you bastard!"

Adam took it, but he wasn't finished yet. "While I'm gone, get together all those designer handbags and fancy shoes and the clothes you said you needed but never wore, and we'll take them to a consignment shop."

Darlene screamed her outrage. "What about

all your junk—those fishing poles, your golf clubs, all that crap in the garage?"

"That's going to go, too. How much do you think I can carry at one time on my motorcycle? Get it all together in the garage. I'll take one load at a time. But first we have to get some food."

"Don't forget the cigarettes and beer."

"Those aren't necessities, Darlene. You are so stupid, I can't believe I am actually standing here talking to you. When are you going to *get it?* And don't start with the threats, either. This might be a good time for you to call your own mother or maybe your ex-mother-in-law to see if either one of them will take you in, because right now I've had enough of you and your shit. I rue the day I ever set eyes on you."

Darlene slid down to the floor and started to howl her unhappiness. Adam ignored her as he whirled through the door like a tornado.

No one bothered to check on Olivia. The little ten-year-old simply was not important enough in their lives to care about.

Two hours later, Adam was back in the house with two meager bags of groceries and money in his pocket. Darlene's greedy eyes sparkled. Adam couldn't remember how much he'd paid for the special contact lenses that allowed Darlene's eyes to turn various shades of green. He'd been so happy to have a green-eyed blonde on his arm, he would have paid any amount for people to look at him and envy him. It never occurred to him that the looks those people were giving him were not envy but pity.

"How much did you get?"

"Twenty-eight hundred. Did you do what I told you?"

Darlene shot him a look that could have killed him. "It's all piled up in the garage."

"Make us some lunch and fresh coffee. I got pizza for Olivia. Since the landline is still working, start calling around to used-furniture stores. We're going to have to sell off the furniture, starting with my kids' stuff since they are not ever coming back here, according to you. Do not open your mouth, Darlene. We need money to hire a lawyer. After you fix lunch, do the laundry. Give me any lip, and I'll stick your head down the toilet and flush till you turn blue. Then I'll dump your body in the well in the back. Then, again, maybe I won't do that since those artificial tits of yours will just make you float to the top. I'll bury you instead."

"Do you have any idea how much I hate you, Adam Fortune?" Darlene spit.

"Only half as much as I hate you, you bitch!"

# Chapter 16

"Watching and listening to that was really terrible," Annie said as she turned off the television in the guesthouse. That poor man was just cleared by the FDA, and now he's dead. It's sad because he was so generous, such a great philanthropist. I don't mean to sound flip or uncaring, but it just goes to show: here today, gone tomorrow, so live right because you don't know what's around the corner."

Myra nodded. She wasn't in the mood to talk about dead people. "Let's take a walk around the yard, Annie. I'm starting to get homesick."

"I hear you, Myra. A walk sounds nice. Maybe the dogs will join us when they hear us outside.

Julie isn't back yet—unless she parked up front. This is really a gorgeous piece of property, with all the azaleas and camellia bushes. And I love that two-hundred-year-old Japanese maple tree. Everything is pruned so nicely. It's like a very private oasis in the middle of town. You can't see beyond the shrubbery. I like that," Annie said.

"I do, too. Julie values her privacy just the way we do. I think I hear her truck, and here come the dogs!" Myra laughed as Julie stopped her truck just inches from where they were standing.

"I have news, ladies. Boy, do I have news!" A second later, she was out of the truck and standing, hands on hips, and about to explode.

"Tell us," both women said in unison, as Julie threw Cooper's ball for him to catch.

"I saw Darlene! Right there at the end of my driveway. She was walking with that greasy boyfriend of hers. Ooooh, she looks awful. So does he. She was screaming I did it, it was all my fault. Adam told her to shut up. I was *this* close to that . . . *that person,*" she said, holding up her thumb and index finger so that they were almost touching. "I even said, 'Do I know you?' or something like that. They were walking, and they were sweaty and cranky. I loved every minute of it. But that isn't the best part. I got four phone calls while I was out. One of the secretaries at the police station called to tell me both Darlene and her boyfriend were there to file a report. They did file it, but it won't do them any good. Darlene pitched a fit, to no avail. They told her to get a lawyer. Then Helen Masterson called and told me Adam went to Dollar Sam's pawnshop and pawned a ring and some other tacky jewelry. She was getting gas next door at the station, and when she saw him, she beelined to the pawnshop and learned that he got twenty-eight hundred dollars.

"Then Sadie Wilkerson called to say Adam bought forty dollars' worth of groceries at Food Lion and took off on his motorcycle. I no sooner hung up from Sadie than Hank Marshall called to say that Darlene called and asked him to come to the house to look at some furniture they wanted to sell. He told her they had too much inventory, then called two other shops like his and spread the word. They won't be selling Larry's furniture anytime soon. What do you think?" Julie asked, falling into step with Myra and Annie as they walked around the yard.

"I think we have her on the run," Myra answered. "Now all we have to do is fine-tune our plan and set it in motion. We need to get the snatch-and-grab down pat, so nothing goes wrong. And we have to be ever mindful of young Ollie. But I think we need to let Ms. Darlene and her boyfriend sweat for a few more days."

Julie agreed. "So what did you ladies do while I was off running my errands?"

"Not much; watched some TV," Annie said.

"I haven't turned on my television in days, or read the newspapers. The only thing they're talking about is the nuclear power plant they want to build in Hollywood. Hollywood, Alabama, that is, just ten miles from here; and the hurricane that seems to be headed our way. Everyone is up in arms with meetings and petitions. I signed two of them when I was in town this morning. I don't object to the plant, but it's just a little too close to Rosemont for my liking. There are all kinds of places they could build it away from our little town. It will be years before anything is decided, so I'm not going to worry about it today, or even tomorrow.

"There's nothing I can do about the hurricane other than to be prepared, and that I am. I just close the hurricane shutters, crank up my two generators, and I'm good to go," Julie explained.

Both women nodded. "I love this little alpine cottage. Did anyone ever live in it, or is it just for guests?" Myra asked.

"I lived in it for well over a year. Actually, almost two years, after Larry died. For some reason, I couldn't stay in my own house. In the cottage, I felt safe and insulated, for some reason. Sometimes even now, when things pile up on me or I get stressed, I go over there and just sit. Larry and Ollie loved it. Did you see her little playhouse in the back?"

"We did see it the other day. It's wonderful. Just what any little girl could want," Myra said.

"Larry . . . Larry had so much fun fixing it up. My daughters made those checkered pink curtains. We used to let Ollie nap in there, with Cooper and Gracie guarding her. But only in the summertime, and Larry and I were right outside drinking iced tea under that big old angel oak in the middle of the yard. She's too old for it now, though," Julie said sadly. "I'm never going to forgive Darlene for denying Ollie her childhood. Every day, I think about her and wonder what Darlene has told her. I hope she remembers us and knows in her heart that we fought for her and that we did everything we could. You don't think she believes all the lies Darlene tells her, do you?" Julie's voice was so fretful, so full of angst, the two women wanted to cry for her.

"Not for one minute!" Myra said forcefully. "Children—I don't care what age they are— know what love is. They feel it, and that's the one thing you can't drive out of a person's heart; I don't care what age that person is."

"Myra is right, Julie. I'm certain that little girl is pining for you just the way you and your family pine for her. I know in my heart she remembers everything just the way you remember. We're going to get her back for you, but we have to make sure we do this right. We have to make sure that nothing bounces back at you and that DSS doesn't take Olivia away from you. But then, we have Abner, our hacker friend, who will make absolutely sure nothing like that happens. We still have to be extra careful, though," Annie warned.

"I understand. Impatience is my middle name these days. I never used to be like this. I just went with the flow. That's not to say I didn't rear up every so often." Julie laughed, but it wasn't a happy sound.

The tour of the yard complete, Annie and Myra followed their hostess to the house. Julie whistled for the dogs, both of whom came on the run.

"I think it's time to take a break from today and everything going on for some iced tea and a visit on the veranda," Julie said. "We're having an easy dinner this evening. I bought everything in the supermarket already cooked. All we have to do is set the table. A picnic of sorts indoors, without the flies and ants."

"Works for us," Annie said.

Julie's veranda was especially nice at that time of day, with the sun at the back of the house. The paddle fans whirled as the misters sprayed the opulent ferns hanging from the beams. The overall effect was that it was at least fifteen degrees cooler out there than anyplace else on the property.

The three women rocked contentedly, conversation at a minimum.

Julie broke the silence by asking Myra and Annie what they thought Adam and Darlene would use the $2800 for.

"A lawyer," Annie said.

"Definitely a lawyer," Myra agreed.

Julie laughed. "Well, then, that isn't going to work. Every lawyer in town will turn them down. They'll have to go to Huntsville, and the retainers will be five thousand and up. I am an authority on lawyers from back when I had to find one to represent me where Darlene was concerned. Five thousand dollars was a rock-bottom retainer. If the used-furniture stores won't take her furniture, she might be forced to hold a yard sale and sell the stuff for pennies on the dollar. God, how I despise that woman! It breaks my heart that she's going to sell Larry's things."

"I wonder what she's doing right now," Myra mused.

What Darlene Wyatt was doing at that moment was speaking on the phone and trying her best, to no avail, to cajole a lawyer into taking her case. She had gone through a list of ten lawyers in Huntsville. When she called, they informed her that their retainers were at least $7500. In three cases, they wanted $10,000.

Darlene cursed and smashed the table with her bare fist until she thought she had broken her hand.

"So we're right back where we started," Adam said. "This is all your mother-in-law's fault, and you know it. I know you don't want to hear it, Darlene, but it is. That's where you have to start—with her. Take the bull by the horns and wrestle it to the ground. Otherwise, we don't have a chance. We can pile the furniture out front and hope someone buys it, and if they do, the money is going to go to a lawyer. Your mother-in-law can make this all go away. We can get back everything if you just hand over that snot-nosed kid. Why can't you see that?"

"Why can't you see that this isn't about Olivia; it's about you and me. Julie knows I cheated on Larry. She's blaming me for his death, and rightly so. I should have called nine-one-one, and I didn't. She blames you as much as she blames me. What we've been through is just step one in Julie's plan. Step two is something I don't even want to think about. Step three will be the big finale, the very bitter end! By the time it's all over, Olivia will find her way to Julie, and that you can take to the bank. This is *Julie versus Us,* and we are losing, big-time. In fact, we are getting our asses kicked all the way to Timbuktu." Darlene shuddered to make her point.

"What . . . what do you think step two is?" Adam asked, a catch in his voice. It did not go unnoticed by Darlene that Adam was now in real time, and the fun and games, the threats and the belligerence, were things of the past.

"Do you really want to know, or are you just asking to hear yourself talk?"

"I want to know what we're up against, so just tell me," Adam snarled.

"I think she's going to go after us until we are convinced that we'd be better off dead. Oh, she won't do the job herself. No, she'll find someone to do it for her. In fact, I think that she'll find a lot of someones to do it for her. And, guess what, Adam. We don't exist, so who can we get help from when she and her minions come a callin'?"

"Then make a deal with her. Do whatever it takes. I don't want to live like this."

"For your information, Adam, Julie Wyatt does not make deals. Her son is dead. That means she will never see, speak to, or hear from her son ever again. She holds me responsible. She called me a slut to my face. The fact that I cheated on her baby son with a known loser like you is something she will never forgive. She wants us both as good as dead."

Adam leaned across the table to stare into

Darlene's green contact lenses. "Do you understand what you just said, Darlene? The police
will not help us. We are on our own. And we are
no match for your mother-in-law. Right now,
she's got money coming out her ears. Didn't
you see that segment on the evening news last
week about our local food guru, meaning Julie
Wyatt, hitting the big time with that Oprah
deal? Sure you did, you mentioned it. Actually,
you almost put your foot through the television.

"She's going to hire the best of the best, drag
your ass back into court every day of the week,
then she's going to buy off all the judges and
just sit back while you and I wear orange jumpsuits. Then she'll cruise on by and pick up
Olivia and live happily ever after. The orange
jumpsuits are step three, I think. There is no
forgiveness in that woman's heart. Trust me on
that."

"There has to be something we can do. Think,
Adam. Maybe we can *kill* her. If we do that, it will
all be over."

"That's crazy talk, and you know it. I'd love it
if she dropped dead, but that isn't going to happen, so we're sitting ducks. She'll be making her
next move very shortly; that, you can count on.

"Why don't you cook those pork chops I
bought. I'm starving. While you're cooking, I
can take another run to the pawnshop and see
what I can get for the fishing poles and golf
clubs."

Darlene sulked, but she got up and walked to
the refrigerator.

Adam stopped midway to the door, turned,

and headed up the steps. Time to check on Darlene's daughter. She was sitting on the floor coloring in a coloring book. Adam dropped to his
knees and tried to hug her, but she wiggled out
of his grasp. He remembered how she'd said
she hated him and Darlene. His lips tightened.
"Be like that, then."

The little girl looked up. "I had a dream about
my daddy. He told me that you and Darlene are
going to jail, and you're going to die like he
died, and he's waiting for you. My daddy said
you aren't going to heaven where he is. He said
he's going to watch you and Darlene go to hell.
You and Darlene won't be angels like my real
daddy is. If you and Darlene die, who is going to
take care of me?"

Adam blinked, then blinked again. He slammed
out of the room without answering the little girl.
He didn't see Olivia pull the white feather out
of her Crayola box and hold it close to her heart.
"I told him about the dream, Daddy," Ollie whispered as she went back to coloring a squirrel
climbing a tree.

Outside in the hall, Adam leaned up against
the wall as he fought to catch his breath. A kid's
dream. What the hell did a ten-year-old know
about life and the shit he was going through? It
was just a stupid kid's dream, and he didn't
need to pay attention to it.

Or did he?

# Chapter 17

It was midday when Julie looked at Myra and Annie, her eyes full of questions, but she didn't say anything.

The dining-room table was covered with papers, blueprints, and drawings, along with local road maps. Annie rubbed at her aching eyes. Myra removed her glasses and proceeded to polish them with the hem of her shirt. Outside, to Cooper's dismay, the wind whistled through the trees. Cooper started to bark until Gracie smacked him with her paw.

"What's wrong with Cooper?" Annie asked.

"He doesn't like storms, and dogs know when the weather is going to turn." Julie got up and walked over to the television in the kitchen. She turned it so Myra and Annie could see and hear what was going on in regard to the hurricane that was, as of four hours ago, headed their way. "They're saying it's a category three, and that's not good. You girls continue while I bring out the generators and lower the hurricane shutters."

"Do you need any help?" Myra asked.

"No, but thanks for the offer. I just press buttons to lower the hurricane shutters, and the generators are on wheels. They're full of gas. I just want to put them in place in case the power goes out. I have a generator hooked up to the gas line. It will come on automatically after five seconds if the power goes out. The other two are for this end of the house."

"What about your daughters? Do they come here to be with you?" Annie asked.

"Nope, we all stay in our own houses. It's just the way it is. We've been through hurricanes that were fours and fives and survived. Our houses are built to withstand hurricanes. The girls' houses are built to hurricane code. Connie told me early this morning that they locked down Phil's and Pete's houses late last night. We're good to go, ladies."

Annie and Myra shrugged as they went back to what they were doing, while Julie set about preparing for the soon-to-be-arriving hurricane.

A mile away as the crow flies, Oliver Goldfeld was listening to his new neighbor, who had just introduced himself to Oliver and told him about the approaching hurricane, to which Oliver could only say, "What hurricane?"

Thirty minutes later, Oliver knew everything there was to know about hurricanes that had hit Rosemont, those that had skirted the town, and those that had veered off course. He also understood that his newly acquired property did not have one scintilla of protection against any kind of real storm, much less a category three hurricane. He was told to head to the nearest Hampton Inn but that they didn't take dogs.

Faced with his first dilemma, Oliver got into his car and programmed his GPS to take him to Julie Wyatt's house. He was confident she would take Lola, and he, in turn, would go to the Hampton Inn and wait out the storm. He really hadn't planned on meeting Julie Wyatt until he had gotten things in order, but with things the way they were, he didn't see that he had much choice.

Lola cowered in the front seat, not liking the sound of the ferocious wind into which they were driving. Oliver didn't like it, either, but he kept going, surprised at the amount of traffic on the road. He had to get Lola to safety; that was paramount.

Oliver turned on the radio, but it was hard to hear through the static and the wind howling outside the car. Lola started to shake. He wanted to pat her, to rub her belly, but he needed both hands on the wheel. He turned off the radio and hoped for the best. When the metallic-sounding voice on the GPS warned him that he was fast approaching his destination, he slowed and crawled along the highway until the voice announced that he had *arrived* at his destination.

Oliver turned right and was faced with an electronic gate and keypad. Lola barked. She was on her hind legs, pawing at the car window. "I know, I know, you remember this place, don't you, girl?" Lola barked happily.

Now what was he supposed to do? Without a code, he couldn't drive through the gates. "Ahhh, stupid is as stupid does," Oliver muttered as he pressed a button that would allow him to announce himself.

It was Myra who ran to the monitor and spoke. "Who are you?" she asked as she peered at the grainy video of a man in a dark SUV with a dog clawing at the car window.

"My name is Oliver Goldfeld. I was Mace Carlisle's lawyer. I have his dog here. Can you please open the gate, Ms. Wyatt? I need to talk to you about Mace."

Myra and Annie huddled. Both women shrugged when Annie hissed that they should let him in. And how, they both wondered, did sweet little Julie Wyatt know Mace Carlisle and his high-powered attorney?

"Julie is outside somewhere," Myra whispered, her finger on the button that would open the gate. "I think it's okay, Annie, don't you?"

"Well, if it isn't, we'll have to *take him out*."

Myra gasped but pressed the button, and the house moved as Cooper and Gracie raced to the front door. Both dogs clawed at it, and both dogs barked, the sound so harsh and shrill, both women clapped their hands over their ears.

"I think that means the dogs approve; their tails are going ninety miles an hour. You let him in, Myra, while I clear up the table. We don't need some high-octane lawyer seeing what we're all about, now, do we?"

"No, we certainly do not need that. I'll stall him by the front door. Be quick, Annie, so he doesn't get suspicious."

Myra stood by the open door, the wind buffeting her through the screen. She noticed that Julie had removed the ferns from the beams before she saw a tall man walk up the steps and across the veranda. Myra couldn't hear a word he said by way of introduction, as all three dogs were clamoring to be together. She opened the door, and Lola raced through the house, Cooper and Gracie hot on her heels. All Myra could hear was playful barking and growling as the dogs tussled and ran around each other.

Oliver Goldfeld held out his hand and introduced himself. He tried not to look surprised at the older woman standing in front of him. Either he was crazy, or Mace was half-blind. "Ms. Wyatt?"

"Sorry, no, she's outside battening down for the hurricane. I'm Myra Rutledge. I saw you on television just the other day. Come in."

Something teased at Oliver. Myra Rutledge. He knew the name from somewhere, but it wouldn't surface. All in good time. He looked around as he trailed behind Myra. The house was everything Mace said it was. The dogs were everything Mace said they were. He looked at the kitchen and smiled as he pictured Mace dining at the kitchen table with Julie Wyatt. He felt a lump in his throat.

"This is Anna de Silva, Mr. Goldfeld. We're just visiting Julie. She should be in soon. Can I get you something cold to drink, or would you like some coffee? We just made it."

"I would love some coffee, thank you." Anna de Silva. He knew that name, too. Maybe Mace had mentioned the names to him. Not that it mattered. It would come to him sooner or later; it always did when he couldn't remember something on the spot.

"How do you take your coffee, Mr. Goldfeld?"

"Dark, strong, and black."

The threesome looked at each other across the table. What to talk about until Julie came in? Myra brought up the hurricane, and said it was the first time either she or Annie had even been close to one.

"I'm with you on that. It will be my first time, too. I just bought a property down the road, and a neighbor told me to hightail it to the Hampton Inn because my house could blow away. It's a fixer-upper," he said. Myra and Annie nodded, knowing what a fixer-upper was.

"The Hampton Inn doesn't take dogs, so I brought Lola here, hoping that Ms. Wyatt would care for her until the hurricane passes. Lola knows Gracie and Cooper, but I guess you figured that out already."

"Ah, yes, we did. I'm sure Julie will be glad to

watch Lola. Is your fixer-upper your vacation home, or are you relocating here? You live in New York, don't you?"

"I'm relocating. If my house stays intact. Yes, I used to live in New York. I semiretired this past week."

The front door banged shut, and all they could hear was Julie's excited squeal of, "Lola! Oh my gosh, Lola, how good to see you! Where's Mace? Is he in the kitchen? Boy, this is sure a surprise. You guys arrived just in time for the hurricane! Mace!"

Oliver Goldfeld turned white. Annie and Myra just looked at one another. Myra got up and nodded for Annie to follow her. "It was nice meeting you, Mr. Goldfeld. Julie will be right here." A minute later, both women were out the door and going down the ramp to cross the yard to their temporary home.

"Oh, my," was all Myra could think of to say.

"Oh, my is right. Seems our little Julie knows some very wealthy people. Who knew?"

Inside, Julie walked into the kitchen to see Oliver Goldfeld standing with his hand outstretched. "I'm Oliver Goldfeld. I brought Lola to stay with you because they don't allow dogs at the Hampton Inn."

"Julie Wyatt," Julie said, shaking his hand and looking confused. "Of course I'll keep Lola. Where's Mace? Did he go over to the cottage? What's wrong? Why are you looking at me like that, Mr. Goldfeld? Where's Mace?"

Oliver cleared his throat. Christ on a crutch, she didn't know. Mace's death was national news. How could she not know? He motioned for Julie to sit down. She perched on the edge of the chair, waiting for him to say something.

"Is it okay to call you Julie?" She nodded. "Look, there's no other way to tell you this other than to come right out and say it. Mace is dead."

Julie's eyes rolled back in her head at the news. Oliver was on his feet and standing over her chair in a nanosecond. She looked sickly white with her dark tan. She blinked, then blinked again. She struggled to say something, but the words wouldn't come.

Oliver took it as a sign that he should tell her everything. He did, but he didn't mention the will. There was time for that later.

"As you know, Mace had no family. I was the closest thing to family he had. I took Lola because I didn't want to take her to a shelter. Mace had such wonderful plans for her. It was on all the newscasts. I'm surprised you didn't see it."

Julie finally found her voice. "I haven't had the news on for days. I didn't want to hear any more about the nuclear power plant they want to build here, and when they weren't talking about that, they were talking about the hurricane. I didn't know. If I had known, I would have gone to New York. He was a good friend. I only knew him a short while, so I can only imagine how you feel. Death is . . . it's just awful and all-consuming. I'm sorry for your loss, Mr. Goldfeld, and for mine as well."

"I . . . ah . . . brought Mace's ashes. I wasn't sure if you would want them or not, so I brought them. I bought the house Mace planned on buying. He was . . . his plan was to come down here this past weekend and start his new life. I was so devastated, I packed it in and came here instead. I'm going to try to do everything he planned on doing. He had some huge plans in place.

"There is one thing I need to tell you, Julie. Mace was ill. At best, he had a year, possibly a little more or possibly a little less time. I didn't know that until his death, after which his doctor told me."

Julie gasped. "I didn't know. He looked so . . . healthy. He never alluded to being ill."

"He fooled me, too."

"I feel like I should do something, say something, but I don't know what it is. I just can't . . . can't wrap my mind around the fact that he's gone."

"If it's any consolation to you, you made Mace happier during the two months he was here than I've ever seen him. When he got back, you were all he could talk about. He could not wait to get back in the car with Lola to return here. He loved this little town."

"I know he did. When he left here, he knew the entire history of the town. He walked it from one end to the other every day. He liked the people, liked buying an ice-cream cone, going to the hardware store, the barbershop. He said the people made him feel like he could belong here. Is there *anything* I can do? And, yes, I would like Mace's ashes. I'd like to bury them behind the cottage, if it's all right with you."

"I don't have a problem with that. As a matter

of fact, I think Mace would like that. Lola can visit. I'll help you after the hurricane."

Julie nodded, her mind going back in time to the day Mace kissed her on the veranda before he left. She was afraid that her heart was going to break into a million pieces.

"There is something else I have to tell you. Mace left his entire estate to you. His controlling interest in Carlisle Pharmaceuticals, the pharmacy he still owned in Hoboken, every worldly possession, and, of course, Lola."

Julie was mentally still on the veranda, saying good-bye to Mace. "I'm sorry, what did you say?" Oliver repeated the words he'd just spoken.

Julie shook her head. "No. That's not right. I don't want Mace's estate. I will take Lola and the ashes, but that's it. No. There is no way I could ever. . . . No! Give it to someone else. I don't want it." She started to cry then and couldn't stop. Great gulping sobs shook her slender frame.

"It doesn't work that way. There is a will; this is what Mace wanted. I was his lawyer. We can't undo a will. Mace trusted me to do what he wanted, and this is what he wanted. When probate is over and done with, then you can decide to give it all away. That's your choice, but for now, we have to do what Mace wanted."

Oliver was at a loss. *Her Judgeness* never cried. He seriously doubted she had tear ducts. He'd never been around a woman who cried like her heart was broken. He simply did not know what to do or say. He backed into his chair when the three dogs came on the run and tried to wrap Julie into a bundle. All he could see was copper-

colored fur and long legs trying to cocoon her.
Cooper, who didn't have a mean bone in his
body, was the first to back away and pounce on
Oliver. He showed his teeth, the fur on his neck
standing on end. Then Gracie moved to one
side of the chair and Lola to the other until they
penned him in. He had 250 total pounds of dog
snarling at him for making their mistress utter
such distressing sounds, sounds they'd never
heard before.

Oliver Goldfeld, for the first time ever, actually feared for his life. He wondered crazily
which way the blood would spurt when Cooper
sank his teeth into his jugular vein.

"No, Cooper, it's okay. Gracie, down. Lola,
come here," Julie cried as she tried to gather all
three dogs closer to her. "Shhh, it's okay. I'm
okay. I'm okay."

Oliver Goldfeld took that moment to black
out and slide off the chair onto the floor. The
dogs ignored him. Julie just stared at him.

# Chapter 18

It wasn't quite dusk yet at Pinewood as Charles and the boys set about clearing away their boys'-night-out dinner. Dinner that would be followed by the boys'-night-out weekly poker game.

Charles was busy lowering the awning and setting out the citronella candles to drive away the pesky mosquitoes that decided to invade the terrace as soon as the sun went down. Former director of the FBI Bert Navarro waited impatiently for ace newspaperman and current editor in chief of the *Washington Post,* Ted Robinson, to spread out the green felt tablecloth so he could line up the cigars and ashtrays. Photographer Joe Espinosa was in charge of the tub of ice and of replenishing both ice and beer. Former Assistant DA Jack Emery and world-renowned martial-arts expert Harry Wong were busy loading the dishwasher and tidying up the kitchen, something at which Harry most certainly did not excel. Elias Cummings, who had preceded Bert as director of the FBI, and Fergus Duffy sat in comfortable chairs watching the proceedings under the awning. Jack thought they looked like two stuffed slugs.

"Even though we're all here, and there's noise, it doesn't seem real without Myra or at least some of the girls being around," Harry grumbled.

Hands on his hips, Jack glared at his best friend. "What? Do I have to bop you over the head, Harry? That's why they call it boys' night out! Boys' night out means no women. We can be as messy as we want, drink as much as we want, smoke those ugly cigars Bert said came all the way from Cuba—which means they're illegal. Just so you know, Harry, we're breaking the law." Harry offered up his middle finger for Jack's inspection. Jack ignored Harry's statement.

"This is supposed to be a fun night. We can stay over, and we will if we drink, and we'll get up before dawn and head back to the city. Why aren't you getting it, Harry?"

"I get it! I get it! Shut the hell up, Jack. All I said was it seems strange without a female here, not that Myra ever made an appearance. It was just that she was here, that kind of thing."

Jack folded the dish towel the way Nikki had taught him, hanging it over the handle on the oven. "Harry, Harry, you're just pissed because you never win. If you'd pay attention to the cards, you might make a good move once in a while. Gambling is an art. If you don't believe me, just ask Annie. Man, if ever there was a card shark, it's Countess Anna de Silva. Guess you weren't paying attention as usual when she shared her expertise with us. Shame on you, Harry Wong! You know what else? This is just my opinion now, but we could run it up the flagpole for a vote. I think if you decided to give it a shot, you could have an illustrious career as a motivational speaker."

"Eat shit, Jack. Charles was pretty cagey about telling us where Myra is, don't you think?"

"Now that you mention it, yeah," Jack said, making sure he was a safe distance from good old Harry in case his buddy decided to swing his leg and knock Jack silly. "Why do you think that is, oh Wise One?"

"You are so stupid, I can't believe I'm standing here talking to you. Because he does not want us to know where she is. But . . . Annie is with her, wherever she is. I know this because . . ."

"You know, Harry, you are a real shit sometimes. Just spit it out! Because . . ."

Harry looked so evil at that moment, Jack edged toward the laundry room as he waited for Harry's response.

"Because Yoko told me Fergus went by the nursery to pick up some bales of pine straw and fertilizer. He told her Annie and Myra ordered up Annie's private jet and took off, and the jet came back sans Myra and Annie. If *he* knows where they are, he did not share it with Yoko. So there!"

"I know how we can find out!" Jack said dramatically.

Harry bit. "How?"

"We just ask Charles point-blank. If he doesn't tell us, you can kill him. Howzat?"

"Before or after I kill you?" Harry snarled.

Jack was out the door before Harry could swing either his legs or arms. "You're such an asshole, Jack," Harry mumbled as he mentally prepared to begin the process of losing the $50 Yoko had said he could gamble with.

Cigar clamped between his teeth, Charles talked around it. "Is my kitchen nice and tidy? No crumbs, no stains, everything in its place?"

"Harry excels at neat and tidy. The answer to your question is an unequivocal yes," Jack said as he fired up his own cigar. The air under the awning was already thick with blue-gray smoke.

"When is Myra coming back, Charles?" Charles shrugged as he watched Bert deal out the cards. "Where did she go, or is it a secret?" Jack asked, a definite edge to his voice.

"Alabama," Fergus chirped from his seat. "They took Annie's Gulfstream, then sent it back." He shrugged as if to say that was all he knew.

"Your turn, Charles, unless you're trying to avoid the question. I don't recall Myra—or Annie for that matter—ever saying they knew anyone in Alabama. What's up, Charles, or are you going to make us virile young men drag it out of you? We *will*, you know, if you don't tell us."

Suddenly, Jack had the attention of everyone

at the table. Ted's head shot up. Espinosa dropped the ash from his cigar on the felt tablecloth and ignored it. Bert blew a perfect smoke ring and put his fist through it. Elias pretended to stare at his cards, deep in thought, while Fergus leaned down to tie his shoe.

Charles looked flustered, something the boys had never seen before. "I'm not allowed to tell."

"What?" Jack bellowed. "That's what we used to say when we were in the fifth grade and swore on each other's blood, then told anyway. So cough it up, Charles!"

"There isn't one of you sitting here at this table, on this terrace, who knows the first thing about keeping a secret. Or do you want me to run down the list of disasters, starting with—"

"You're right, but so what?" Jack interrupted before Charles could enumerate. "Tell us anyway."

So Charles told them. The boys listened, their jaws dropping. "They went alone! You let those two go by themselves? Do you have any idea the trouble they can get into without us there to . . . help?"

Charles threw his hands up in the air. "Did any of you ever try to stop them from doing anything? Ah, I see, you are with me here. I had no say in the matter. They didn't *ask* me if they could go, they *told* me they were going. And they're right in the middle of a hurricane and loving every minute of it. Abner Tookus has their back, and Annie can shoot like a pro. Not that anyone is expecting any gunplay. At least, that I know of," Charles added nervously.

Harry decided to voice an opinion, knowing that if he could keep the dialogue going, they might never get around to playing poker, and he could take his $50 home with him and tell Yoko he broke even. "Why does Tookus have their backs?" It sounded like a brilliant question to him until Jack sent him a withering glance.

Charles went on to explain in excruciating detail all that Abner Tookus had done to start the ball rolling on Myra and Annie's mission. "This Adam Fortune is just one guy, 'a nasty little pip-squeak,' as Myra put it. She said they could work him over with one hand tied behind their backs. She believes it. The ex-daughter-in-law is something else."

Bert clenched his teeth. "Do you have any idea what desperate people will do when provoked in desperate circumstances, Charles? I could recite chapter and verse till this time tomorrow and not totally fill you in. Do you think for one minute that guy, pip-squeak or not, or the ex-daughter-in-law are going to stand still for having their very lives snatched away from them? I-don't-think-so! We need to go there yesterday."

Charles looked like he was going to burst into tears at any moment. "Then Myra will know I told you. Think just for a second how miserable she will make my life. Just think about *that*! I'm glad you want to go, though. I'm worried sick about the two of them. Aren't you worried, Fergus?"

"No!"

Jack blinked at Fergus's explosive comeback. "We'll tell them we beat it out of you, Charles. They might believe that."

"You're delusional," Ted said. "I get this story. Doesn't matter if I'm EIC or not. I want the story. It's got everything newspaper readers are looking for. So, does this mean we're going?" he asked hopefully.

"As sure as I'm sitting here, Annie will fire you," Charles warned him.

Ted grimaced. "There is that to think about. Hey, I can get a job anywhere. You in, Espinosa?"

"Yeah, I'm in."

Harry was ecstatic as he fingered the $50 in his pocket. It didn't look like they were going to be playing poker anytime soon.

"Jack, Harry, Bert, you guys in or out?"

"In," the three shouted in unison.

"Then, gentlemen, let's get down to what we're here for, *playing poker.*"

Harry groaned as he yanked the $50 out of his pocket and slammed it down on the table. He looked over at Jack, and if looks could kill, Jack would have died on the spot. Jack winked at him, and Harry burst out laughing.

The poker game wound down shortly before midnight, with the young guns, as Elias called them, deciding they would sleep over and head out at first light and be ready to leave for Alabama by noon. At least, that was the plan when they all fell into bed. The old guns, meaning Charles, Elias, and Fergus, cleaned up the terrace. And then Charles made coffee. "We need to talk, gentlemen," he said as he folded up the green felt tablecloth.

"Our ladies are not going to like the boys descending on them," Fergus grumbled. "That means there will be hell to pay on their return. And another thing, did Myra or Annie say anything about . . . being seen publicly? Surely there are people who will recognize them as the vigilantes, and that might cause a problem. Five strange men showing up in a small town like Rosemont might raise some eyebrows and, sooner or later, someone is going to put it all together."

Charles frowned. "I agree. Myra said they are staying in a guesthouse and just hanging out with Julie Wyatt as they firm up their plans. She didn't indicate any worries to me. Myra and Annie are *not* stupid, Fergus. You of all people should know that."

"I do know that. I also know they think they can do anything. I love self-confidence but am ever mindful of the age problem. Annie and Myra are not youngsters even though sometimes they pretend to be. I'm not sure they know their limitations, Charles."

Charles's frown stayed in place. He looked over at Elias, who grinned. "You two are spinning your wheels over nothing. Age, experience, payback, vengeance are what those two live for. They are not going to screw up. That's a given. In my not-so-humble opinion." Seeing the concern on Charles's and Fergus's faces, he hastened to add, "You both need to remember why they are there in the first place. First rule is, you never, as in *never*, fuck with motherhood. What

we have here is a dead son, a child being mis-
treated, a woman and her boyfriend who do not
deserve to walk the Earth. And you think those
two are going to screw up? It will never happen.
Annie and Myra will pull this off and laugh all
the way home. I'm up for a wager if either one
of you wants to go for it." There were no takers.

Charles continued to frown as he sipped his
special blend of coffee. "I don't see how we can
prevent the boys from going. Speaking strictly
for myself, I would just feel a whole lot safer if
they do go. Any number of things can go wrong,
we all know that. You always need backup and a
Plan B. And, worst of all, the minute they show
up, Myra will know I blabbed. She will never
trust me again, and don't think for one minute
either she or Annie will believe that the boys tor-
tured me to give it up. Myra knows me too well."

"He has a point," Fergus said as he fired up
the stub of his cigar. Smoke sailed upward. "I
suppose the boys could try to stay on the fringe
of things, but if push comes to shove, then there
they are, in everyone's face."

"In that case, Myra and Annie will be glad
they're there," Elias said.

"You can give that up right now, Elias," Charles
retorted. "Annie will shoot them first and take
names later. This is their gig, and they are loving
it. I mean *loving* it. That is precisely what Myra
said."

"So where does that leave us?" Fergus asked.
Charles was glad to see the worry on his friend's
face.

"Behind the proverbial eight ball, that's where,"

Elias shot back. "I'm just glad Nellie didn't go with them. She'd just out and out kill me." He shivered to make his point.

"So what do you esteemed gentlemen think our game plan should be?" Charles asked. His question was met with total silence, which meant there was no game plan to be had, and there would be none available anytime soon.

Charles sighed as he once again tried Myra's cell phone. The call went straight to voice mail. He looked over at his friends and said, "They're in the middle of a hurricane, so I really didn't expect an answer. The last news report I heard was it should all be over in the next few hours. I'm going to check the Weather Channel and head off to bed. Five o'clock will be here before you know it."

Elias and Fergus got to their feet. They gave Charles clumsy pats on the shoulder as they trundled off to the staircase that would take them to the second floor and dreamland.

Charles, left alone to fret, walked into the kitchen, locked the doors, turned on the television to the Weather Channel, and waited for the latest hurricane news in Alabama. News of hurricanes, and Myra and Annie.

# Chapter 19

Myra and Annie trailed behind Julie and the dogs as they walked around her property to inspect the damage from the hurricane, which turned out to be minimal. Downed limbs, bushes that were waterlogged, soggy ground from the torrential rain, and a few overturned trash cans.

"We lucked out," Julie said as she pointed to an oak limb as thick as a barrel. "That's the worst of it. The gardener will have it all back to normal in a few days, and I'll have enough wood to last me through the winter from just that one limb. I'm just glad the girls had no damage, either. Connie called to say the boys' houses are fine. You just never know with hurricanes and tropical storms. They hype these storms, get people all riled up, and for the most part that's a good thing. But when they fizzle out, people tend to get lackadaisical about it all. Other times, it's just words to fill up the news hour."

Annie stepped over a puddle in the driveway. "Do you think Ollie is all right?"

"I'm sure she is. Larry's house is sturdy and brick. He didn't have the hurricane shutters, but there are areas in the house that have no windows. I'm sure Darlene kept her safe. At least, I want to believe that. Come along, let's go inside before the dogs take it into their heads to roll around in the mini-lakes on the property."

Myra stared at her new friend, hating the redness around her eyes and the grim set to her jaw. All the while they'd been hunkered down inside the house, the ferocious winds whipping about outside, Julie had pretended to sleep. Even in the dim light of the family room, both she and Annie had seen her wiping at the tears in the corners of her eyes.

Both women had been surprised but had remained quiet when Julie had not asked the New York lawyer to stay at the house after he dropped Lola off. It was so unlike Julie that they had whispered back and forth about it far into the night.

Back inside the house, the dogs went off to the den, where their toys were scattered about, and Julie prepared the coffeepot. When she was done, she stood in the center of the kitchen and said, "I know you're wondering what's going on.

I'm sorry I didn't . . . it was just that . . . it was all such . . . I guess I'm still in shock. I do need to talk about this, though. I know that. Maybe you can help me make sense of . . . of . . . what's going on."

"We're good listeners, Julie," Myra said gently. "Tell us only what you're comfortable telling us."

Annie poured the coffee. "I talk and think best when I'm moving about. It all started a few months back. I was at the bank one day, and when I came out to get in my truck, this man leaned out the window of his car. It was a real fancy one, high dollar if you know what I mean. He asked me if I knew where he could find a short-term rental. He looked nice, and he had Lola, and without even stopping to think, I said I had a rental, meaning the cottage. I looked at it as extra money, and I could get my truck fixed and have some money left over. Foodies don't make a lot of money, and we only get paid while the programs are shooting and we had just done a wrap for six months. He took me up on my offer. He followed me home. We struck a deal, and Lola made friends with my dogs. That was the clincher for me. I judge people by the way they treat their animals. Anyway, he said his name was Oliver Goldfeld, and he was a lawyer from New York. Of course, that wasn't really his name. That night on the news, I saw how Mace Carlisle's wife was accusing him of all kinds of things.

"I stayed up all night googling and printing out information on Mace and on Oliver Goldfeld. I opted to keep what I knew to myself. I never let Mace know I knew about his deception until the day he left.

"I have to say, I grew to like the man during the time he was here. He was kind, generous, considerate. I used him as a guinea pig to test recipes for a cookbook I had convinced myself I was going to write. I charged him for breakfast and gave him a cut-rate fee on the dinners. After dinner, we would sit on the veranda with the dogs and have coffee and talk until it got dark.

"There was nothing romantic about our relationship at all. We became really good friends, and he loved it here in Rosemont. I have to admit that the months he was here were the happiest I've been since . . . since Larry died. That's the other thing; we never talked about Larry, but that was by my choice. But we talked about everything else under the sun. I think he knew about Larry. I'm sure he googled me the same way I googled him. And if he didn't, I bet that the real Oliver Goldfeld did.

"Then one day my lawyer in New York called to tell me Oprah's company had seen my food show and was offering me a spot on Oprah Radio for an astronomical sum of money. I was so stupid, I didn't put two and two together until later. I think Mace was behind it. But, I have to say, he never let on. When I told him, he was so happy for me. It was all just pleasant, and I looked forward to cooking for him, hearing whether he liked my recipes. And, of course, being a woman, I basked in his praise. And there was never any hint that whatever we had

going on would ever go to another level. None!"
Julie said emphatically.

"Then, one day, he said he was leaving. I felt . . .
sad. Not devastated, just sad. He said he was
coming back and was going to semiretire or
something like that. He was profuse in his
thanks, I was just as profuse in mine. Then I told
him I knew who he was. And then he kissed me.
I . . . liked it. So I kissed him back. I . . . ah . . . I
felt something. Not that bell-and-whistle stuff;
something more gut-satisfying. *Contentment* would
be my word of choice. Then he got in his car
with Lola and left. I never saw him again."

"Did he call you when he got back to New
York?" Myra asked.

Julie drew a deep breath. "He did. He said he
would be back soon. Mr. Goldfeld said Mace was
going to return last weekend. I guess being who
he was, his death made the national news, but I
didn't . . . I didn't have my television on for days
because of the nuclear power plant news and
the hurricane hype. I didn't know. My God! How
could I not have known? I should have felt
something, but I didn't. Not a thing. Nothing.
What does that say about me?"

Myra and Annie had Julie in their arms within seconds, murmuring words of comfort the
way only women can.

"And now he's gone. I'll never see him again.
Mr. Goldfeld said I could keep Lola if I wanted
to. I want to keep her. It's the rest of what he
said that has my mind spinning. Mace left everything he owns to me—his controlling interest in

his company, the pharmacy in Hoboken that he never sold, all his personal things, everything. Even Mace's ashes in an urn. Do either of you have any idea of what that means? His company is a multibillion-dollar company. I told him I didn't want it. I just want the dog. He said it doesn't work that way. Mace, it seems, was ill, and no one knew. I certainly didn't know. According to Mr. Goldfeld, he had a year, possibly a little more, possibly a little less time left. Why didn't I see that, either? I must be incredibly stupid. Or I was so wrapped up in my own personal woes with Darlene and Ollie, my mind was closed off to anything else, which sure doesn't say much about me."

"On the contrary, Julie, it says everything there is to say. You said it yourself, he was a friend, a good friend. A friendship that might or might not have gone on to another level. Based on whatever it was Mr. Carlisle was feeling, he wanted you to have his estate because he cared about you, trusted you. And it was his way of saying thank you for the wonderful two months he had with you, and knowing the time he had left would be just as wonderful. If you think of it that way, it might be easier for you to accept," Annie said softly.

"It's the money. Just a few short months ago, I was worried about where I was going to get the money to have the air-conditioning fixed in my truck. Then, suddenly, I'm a multimillionaire with the Oprah food show. On top of that—can you believe this?—it's like something out of a romance—I won the damned lottery, and that's another hundred million. And now this. I'm a billionaire. That's with a *B*, not an M."

Myra handed Julie a wad of tissues while Annie poured more coffee. "Join the club," Annie quipped.

"Money can be a curse, I suppose," Myra said. "But you can also do worlds of good with it. Ask yourself what you think Mr. Carlisle would want you to do with it. Then you act on that. You have your own children to provide for. Trust accounts. Then there's Olivia. Annie and I can help you with the best financial people out there. When you're ready."

"People are going to look at me differently now. There will be those who want something and those who won't want to come near me. I've seen it happen. My life is going to be turned upside down again. I don't know if I can handle that. I was just getting my life back, a little at a time, and now this. In case you haven't figured it out, ladies, I am a pretty simple person with simple wants and needs. I won't be allowed to be that person anymore. Mace's will is going to probate. And then the financial world will find out that I own a controlling interest in Carlisle Pharmaceuticals. That alone will be a circus. Then, when I claim that damned lottery money, it will be even worse. My privacy will be gone. My kids' privacy will be gone. The media will make us financial freaks."

Annie leaned across the table to cup Julie's face in her hands. "You, Julie Wyatt, are a very strong woman. You survived the worst possible event in any parent's life. If you could do that, you can handle this. You set the rules. Nothing has to change unless you want it to change. The worst-case scenario is you hire someone in PR to be your spokesperson. The only thing you have to concern yourself with is saying, 'No comment.' Eventually, the media and even the locals will get it and leave you alone."

"Annie's right, dear. The first few months will be stressful, but things will level off after that. The company will run itself with the capable people Mr. Carlisle has in place, and I'm sure Mr. Goldfeld will be overseeing that end of things," Myra said. "Did I hear him correctly when he said he bought the house Mace was going to buy and that he plans to live here now?"

"That's what he said. He's a New York lawyer, and for some reason, I can't see someone like him wanting to live in the sleepy little town of Rosemont. He said he was retiring. Even *I* know he was in shock about Mace. It sounds good at the time, when you think you can handle it. Then, as time goes on, you realize you made a mistake. I'm not saying that's going to happen, but I just don't . . . never mind, it's not important," Julie said.

"Yes, dear, it is important. I think the man is—as is to be expected, of course—in shock, and he's trying to do what he thinks Mace would expect of him. He's of an age when retirement should look good. I'm sure he'll keep his hand in the pot, so to speak. No one actually walks away without leaving a few options open. Right now, he's more or less in the same position you're in. I'm thinking the two of you will need each other to get through Mr. Carlisle's death and move on," Myra said.

"I agree with Myra, Julie. Please be open to cooperating with Mr. Goldfeld, and things will fall into place just the way they should."

Julie nodded as she swiped at her eyes. "I hope you're right," she mumbled.

Annie twinkled. "I'm never wrong, am I, Myra?"

"Hardly ever." Myra laughed. "Now, I think it's time to get back to work on Ms. Darlene and on getting Olivia back to Julie, where she belongs. I suggest we retire to the dining room, where all our maps and papers are. Oh, Julie, think of the wonderful life you can give that little girl. And a lot of other little boys and girls just like her in the same position. Think about what you can do for grandparents' rights. The possibilities are absolutely endless. Endless, my dear!"

Julie smiled from ear to ear. "Okay, let's do it!"

# Chapter 20

Julie Wyatt's twins, Connie and Carrie, finished picking up the debris that littered the walkway leading to the door of their art school for aspiring young artists.

Connie leaned on the rake and looked at her sister. "I have an idea."

"I hope it isn't one that has me doing all the work while you supervise," Carrie grumbled as she snapped a tie on the trash bag and carried it to the curb.

"Let's call Darlene. School starts on Monday, and we both know she hasn't taken Ollie for school clothes or her school supplies. Let's volunteer to take her. All she can say is no."

Hands on her hips, Carrie contemplated her sister. Connie was always considered the impetuous one of the twin sisters. Carrie was the more thoughtful, the planner, the one who saw a project through to the end. Unlike Connie, who, if things didn't work out right first shot out of the cannon, went on to other things without looking back. "And she would let us do this . . . why?"

Connie grinned. "She's destitute, if what Mom said is true. There's no extra money, I'm thinking, for Ollie. She's always come last with Darlene and her boyfriend. We make it a package deal, we take Ollie with us, or it's no deal. If she says no, then it's no. She's not going to want to send Ollie to school looking like a homeless waif and without her school supplies. Darlene is all about image."

"Oh, God, Connie, wouldn't that be great if she agreed? It's been so long since we've seen Ollie. She'll remember us, won't she?" Carrie asked, her eyes filling with tears.

"Of course she'll remember us," Connie said, but her voice carried no real conviction. "Let's do it. A call from us is the last thing she's expecting, and we'll catch her flat-footed, so to speak."

Carrie reached for the rake and leaned it up against the building while Connie tapped out Darlene's number on her cell phone. The time was ten forty. Darlene picked up on the third ring. "Darlene, it's Connie Wyatt. I'm calling to ask if Carrie and I can take Olivia school shopping. I think we could get everything done in a

few hours and have her back to you by, say, five
o'clock. We'll take her to lunch, too. School
starts on Monday, right?"

Both twins squeezed their eyes shut and crossed
their fingers as they waited for Darlene's response.

On the other end of the line, Darlene was
staring at the calendar on the refrigerator. Connie was right, school started on Monday. How
could she have forgotten that? Shit! Olivia
needed new shoes, and she'd grown like a weed
since school let out in May. School supplies
would run her around forty bucks. Forty bucks
she didn't have to spare. Plus sixty bucks for
shoes and a hundred or so for clothes. It was a
no-brainer. Still, what gave those bitches the
right to call her and . . . Olivia was the only control she had left. She could agree, but that didn't
mean she had to make it easy for them. "Give
me one good reason why I should let you see
Olivia after the way your family has treated me?"

Connie sucked in her breath. "I'm not going
down that road, Darlene. If you want Olivia to
go to school looking like a raggedy homeless
child, it's fine with me. I'm offering, and that's
it. It's what Larry would expect Carrie and me
to do. This isn't about you or me, my mother, or
your boyfriend; this is about Olivia. So is it yes or
no? Make up your mind right now while the
offer is still on the table."

Darlene's mind whirled. Adam was practically
crawling inside her ear as he tried to hear Connie's voice. "Say no," he hissed.

Darlene shrugged him off and lasered a look
in his direction that could have fried a rock.

"Okay," she said. "Have her home by five, not one minute later."

On the other end of the line, Connie almost fainted. "Okay! We'll be there in ten minutes to pick her up. Meet us in the driveway!" She broke the connection and reached for her sister, who had tears streaming down her cheeks. They hugged one another until neither one of them could breathe. "Quick, get our purses, Carrie, and lock up while I put this stuff away."

Carrie drove and burned rubber. They were parked at the edge of Darlene's driveway in seven minutes. The twins leaped out of the car and ran to the little girl, who was so breathless she could hardly talk. They all cried, as Connie ushered Ollie into the backseat, where she hugged her so hard the little girl squealed. "Guess where we're going," Connie said.

"To see Grandma?" Ollie asked tearfully. "I didn't forget you guys. Darlene took away all my pictures, and Adam wouldn't give them back. I drew pictures of all of you. Daddy said they were good. He always tells me they're good even when they aren't."

Neither twin knew how to respond to that statement, so they kept quiet.

"Can't you go any faster, Carrie? Mom is going to go over the moon. Boy, did we miss you, Ollie. Grandma missed you even more."

Ollie was still hanging on to Connie for dear life, crying and sobbing into her shoulder. The minute the car sailed through the gates, Ollie was perched on the edge of the seat. "Stop, Carrie! I want to run the rest of the way! I *have to* run the rest of the way! Please! Please, Carrie, stop!" Carrie slammed on the brakes, and Ollie hopped out. She ran, shrieking and hollering like a banshee. "Grandma! Grandma! I'm home! It's me, Grandma! I'm here, Grandma! Carrie and Connie brought me here!" Ollie bellowed as she ran up the steps to the veranda. Inside, the dogs howled as Julie, Myra, and Annie ran to the door.

Breathless, Connie and Carrie reached the top of the steps just as Julie opened the door and held out her arms. Ollie literally flew into those waiting arms, her legs wrapped around Julie's waist and her arms around her neck. She burrowed her head into her grandmother's neck and cried, "You feel just like Daddy, Grandma! I dream about you all the time. I love you, Grandma! Do you still love me? Am I still your special little girl? Darlene said you don't love me anymore, that you forgot about me. You didn't forget about me, did you, Grandma? Am I still your little butter cookie?"

Myra, her eyes bigger than Frisbees, poked Annie. "That bitch is *mine*. I'm going to kill her and *him*."

Annie reared back and hissed, "You'll have to go through me for that honor, Myra. We don't want to kill him. We just want him to wish he were dead."

Both women focused on Julie. All they could hear was Julie saying over and over, "Oh, my God! Oh, my God! You finally answered my prayers.

Thank You, thank you, thank you! Yes, yes, Ollie, you are still my special little girl, and I love you more than all the stars in the sky. I dream about you every night, little one."

"Daddy said I had to be patient. Even when Darlene and Adam were mean to me, Daddy said you would make it right for me. Can I live with you, Grandma? Can you get me, Grandma? Please."

All Julie could do was hug the little girl and make promises she hoped she could keep.

"We just called Darlene on the spur of the moment, Mom. School starts on Monday, and we offered to take Ollie school shopping. She said yes after she blustered a bit. We have to have her back by five."

"Do you want to come with us?" Connie and Carrie said in unison.

"If I do that, I'll be defying the court order," Julie mumbled against Ollie's blond curls.

"She'll be happy to go with you," Annie said. "And we will take care of that court order. In just about five minutes," she said, looking at her watch. "So, ladies, *GO!*"

Ollie lifted her head and looked at Myra and Annie. "Are you grandmothers?"

Myra had great difficulty finding her voice, but she managed. "In a manner of speaking. We would be honored if you would allow us to be your honorary grandmothers. Like a—an extra one and a spare one. A little girl can never have too many grandmothers."

"I like that. I don't know anyone who has three grandmothers. Daddy said something good was going to happen today. Daddy's never wrong, is he, Grandma?"

"Never!" Julie looked over at Annie and Myra. "Go already! We'll be fine here. Take your time, girls, and don't hurry back."

When the car was out of sight, Myra sat down on the steps next to Annie. "Now, that has to be a miracle of sorts. I don't know when I've ever felt this bad and good at the same time. She's a beautiful little girl, isn't she, Annie?"

Annie's voice was so choked up, she could barely speak. "All those golden curls, those big blue eyes. She looks like the pictures of Larry on the mantel. Myra, do you think Larry knows about this little miracle we helped bring about?"

"I certainly hope so. I know you didn't miss those . . . those strange things that child said. The spirits come to the innocent, we both know that. I think it's safe to say Larry comforts that child when she needs it most."

"Come along, dear, let's contact Abner and have him make that court order go away. Then we should put the finishing touches on whatever it is we're going to do to make what just happened permanent." Myra was up off the steps and heading straight for the dining room, where they would continue to plot and scheme to get Olivia back into Julie Wyatt's household after they called Abner.


Back at Darlene's house, Darlene started to bang pots and pans as she emptied out the dishwasher on Adam's orders. "And you have the nerve to call me stupid! You played right into their hands. You just turned that kid over to them like nothing ever happened. You might just as well give her to them now and be done with it. You're such a waste. I don't know why I ever got mixed up with you to begin with. Now I have to worry about where my next meal is going to come from." Adam's arm shot out.

Darlene took the blow full on her cheek, splitting the skin. She howled her outrage as she reached for a knife in the butcher block. Adam's foot shot out, and she crumpled to the floor, the knife sailing across the tiles.

"Damn you, Adam, get the hell out of my house! There's the door. Leave. No one is forcing you to stay. Olivia has to go to school. She needs things. Things I don't have the money to pay for right now. I had no other choice. Just because your kids are dropouts doesn't mean Olivia is going that route. Hit me one more time, you bastard, and I'll kill you! I mean it!"

Adam blustered, but they both knew he was in over his head. "Get your ass up and clean this kitchen. I'm going to make another run to the pawnshop. When you're done cleaning up the kitchen, go outside and clean up the yard. It looks like a war zone."

Darlene's eyes spewed hatred as she inched her way to the stove, where she grabbed the oven door and pulled herself to her feet. For the first time in her life, she was afraid of Adam Fortune.

"Tell me you heard what I just said, Darlene."

"I heard you, okay? The whole damned neighborhood heard you."

"I don't care about the whole damned neighborhood hearing me. You are the one with selective hearing. If you fuck with me one more time, Darlene, you will live to regret it."

Not knowing when to leave well enough alone, Adam added, "You do know those bitches took that kid straight to your mother-in-law's house, don't you? Now there will be no living with the little snot. You know that, too, right?"

Adam balled his hand into a tight fist. Darlene ran to the bathroom and locked the door. She stayed inside until she heard the garage door going up, then down, then Adam's motorcycle roaring out of the driveway. She'd lost whatever control over him she'd had, and she knew it. She opened the door and crept out. *One way or another, I'll make that son of a bitch pay for the way he treats me. And I'll make that snot-nosed kid pay, too,* she promised herself.

Darlene made short work out of tidying up the kitchen. She took a package of chopped meat out of the freezer and dropped it into the sink to thaw out. Adam hated meat loaf, but that's what they were having for dinner. She looked around the kitchen to make sure Adam could find no fault with it, then ran upstairs to Olivia's room. It always amazed her that a little girl could keep her room so neat and tidy. Adam's kids were natural-born slobs.

She started to rummage through everything.

She cursed as she pawed through Olivia's meager belongings. Nothing. She looked in the closet and found Olivia's "nest" way in the back. She dropped to her knees, knowing instantly that this spot was where the little girl went to hide. She ripped and gouged at the foam in the pillows, shredding the pillowcases. She tore and sliced the pictures Olivia had drawn of her *other family* and her *real mother* until they were nothing more than confetti. Satisfied, she backed out of the closet and headed back downstairs, where she gathered up trash bags from the garage. She reached for a rake that was minus a few prongs and proceeded to sweep up the driveway.

As she worked, Darlene cursed up a storm, wishing there was someone she could call to vent. A friend. But she didn't have any friends. Adam didn't really have any friends, either. There was no one. She couldn't even call Adam's kids—not that she would have—because Adam had smashed their cell phones. She wondered where they were, but then decided she didn't really care. Adam was right about one thing, at least. They really were nothing but trouble.

She continued to sweep and rake as her mind tore loose. She thought about all the damned money she'd squandered on the breast implants, the dental veneers, the Botox, the cut-rate designer clothes. She wished she had the money in her hand. She'd split from the city of Rosemont so quick, Adam's head would spin.

She started to cry then, because she realized the futility of her situation. Julie Wyatt was going to win. She'd be homeless, on the street, begging for food. And that little snot Olivia would be living in the lap of luxury just the way her dear old dad wanted her to live. "Well, screw you, Larry Wyatt. You're fucking dead. *D-E-A-D!* And I'm alive! That makes me the winner." Darlene nearly choked on her own laughter.

# Chapter 21

Charles Martin lowered the awning on the terrace and plopped down on one of the padded chairs. He felt so alone, even though the dogs were with him. He rarely, if ever, took a break like this, a sure sign that something was troubling him and he needed to think it through. He was worried about Myra and Annie, and that was the bottom line.

He knew he was going to be in a boatload of trouble once the boys arrived in Rosemont, Alabama, in the morning. He didn't even want to think about the tales they were going to be telling their wives and girlfriends about where they were going. He had been insistent on that little detail, knowing the Sisters would want to rush to Myra and Annie's side to *help,* something he knew Myra and Annie didn't want. Well, he'd just have to soak up the punishing silence Myra would dole out on her return. He cringed when he thought about the cold shoulder his wife would give him. Once, she'd gone *weeks* without speaking to him. And then it had been months before she would allow him back into their bed. His wonderful, lovely, independent wife was so good at holding a grudge. He shivered in the warm sunshine.

Charles wished he'd made coffee instead of iced tea as he shivered despite the warmth of the day. With nothing else to do at the moment, he went back into the house to make coffee. He nibbled on a sugar cookie while he waited for the coffee to drip into the pot. He purposely made his mind a blank as he waited. That was the whole reason for going out to the terrace to think. Terraces were for thinking, not kitchens.

The moment he heard the last little gurgle from the pot, he poured and walked back out to the terrace so fast, he spilled half the coffee. A loud sigh, so loud the dogs raised their heads, escaped his lips. He'd clean up the spill later. He needed to *think* about all the things Myra had told him yesterday afternoon. There had been so much he wanted to say, but he'd kept quiet. When it came to children, especially little girls, Myra wouldn't have listened anyway. Not that he had any words of wisdom at that point.

He had to admit, though, so far those two ladies had it going on. A smile tugged at the cor-

ners of his mouth as he pictured Darlene Wyatt
finally realizing she didn't exist, thanks to Abner
Tookus. The man was a pure genius. And now it
was coming down to the wire. He couldn't decide if he was angry, miffed, or plain old pissed
off that his two ladies wouldn't give him details
of their plan to, as Myra said, *take out* Darlene.
In the covert world, he knew what the term
meant, but with Annie and Myra, that same
term could have a whole other meaning. That's
why he was sending the boys to Rosemont, and
now he had to call Avery Snowden so he would
be at the ready for *disposal purposes*. There was
no way on Earth that Darlene Wyatt and her
boyfriend could be left behind when Myra and
Annie were through with them.

Charles gulped at the hot coffee and burned
his tongue. He barely noticed. His mind wan-
dered to the little girl and all the things Myra
had told him. His eyes burned at the memory.
Then he started to think about Julie Wyatt and
the bond Myra and Annie had forged with her.
He smiled at the way Myra had described all the
money she had suddenly come into. According
to Myra, the amazing part was that Julie Wyatt
was totally not interested in the money. All she
wanted was that little girl, peace, and contentment. The money was just that, money. Myra
had said she felt confident that Julie was going
to give it all away. Myra was usually on the money—
no pun intended—when it came to things like
that. It was Annie who had suggested Julie start
up a movement for grandparents' rights and
take it all the way to Capitol Hill. There was not

one shred of doubt in Charles's mind that it was exactly what Julie Wyatt would do, with Annie and Myra leading the charge.

The phone in his breast pocket chirped. The dogs didn't stir as he flipped it open and listened to Avery Snowden say his ETA in Rosemont, Alabama, would be in three hours. He went on to say he had everything in place, and that nighttime was best to do reconnaissance work. They spoke for a few more minutes. When Charles ended the call, he felt much better, so much better that he poured the ice-cold tea into his glass and scrapped the hot coffee. He'd stopped shivering somewhere along the way. He gulped at the tart drink until it was gone.

Then it was time to go out into the yard and throw sticks for the dogs so they would get their daily exercise. He whistled for the dogs. A moment later, they were all in the yard, whooping and barking, as Charles did what he did best. He laughed out loud when he remembered how Myra had said she was going to start throwing sticks for him so he could run and lose some weight. She'd added insult to injury and poked at his midsection to make her point. Then, she'd added a further insult and said that she was still the same size eight she'd been when he'd first met her all those years ago.

Ted Robinson marched up to the Avis car-rental kiosk and gave his name to a chipper young woman with flaming red hair. He handed over a credit card from the *Post* and signed his name.

The pert young thing smiled up at Ted and said, "Mercy, I didn't know our little summer festival was known all the way in Washington, D.C."

Ted floundered for a moment and then just smiled. Well, at least they now had a cover story of sorts. Small-town America is what readers want to know about.

Walking away from the counter, Ted said, "Hey, guys, we now have a cover story. There's some kind of summer festival here in town. Not that we need a cover story, but it's there if we want it. I got us a Ford Explorer. We can all fit in with comfort. We got a map, and the GPS will do the rest. Let's get something to eat before we descend on the ladies. I'm thinking we're going to get a blast of real heat from our two favorite people. Hell, Annie will probably fire me on the spot."

The boys trailed through the parking lot of the airport till they came to their rental. They all piled in, with Bert driving. He fiddled with the GPS, made sure everyone was buckled up, and suggested a sing-along, in which everyone declined to participate.

"What's our plan?" Jack asked.

"We don't have a plan," Espinosa barked. "And we aren't making one, either. Every time you mention the word *plan*, something goes haywire. I say we leave it to the ladies and their plan, whatever that may be, and we just do what they say unless they boot our asses all the way back to D.C., which is probably what is going to happen anyway. And if that's the case, we won't have to worry about our plan, their plan, or no plan."

"Well, damn, Espinosa, that little speech was like a dissertation, something I never heard from you before. I might add, you are a little snippy today, aren't you?" Jack exploded.

"Yeah," was Harry's contribution to the conversation.

"It needed to be said," Espinosa pointed out defiantly.

"He has a point," Harry volunteered again. "I have a very clear recollection of a pumpkin plan awhile back."

"Yeah, well, in the end it worked. You know what they say about the best-laid plans of mice and men, don't you?" Jack grumbled.

"No, I don't know that one. Why don't you enlighten us, Jack," Bert guffawed.

"I would, but I can't remember what it is," Jack grumbled again.

Ten minutes later, Bert pulled off the interstate, followed a road, and then another, which took them to the parking lot of a Cracker Barrel.

"You guys are going to love this place. Downhome cooking at its finest," Espinosa said, gleefully rubbing his hands together. "Just order one of everything on the menu, and you can't go wrong."

Inside the restaurant, the boys, who, with the exception of Espinosa, had never been to a Cracker Barrel, stood still and gawked at the sight that greeted their eyes.

"Told you!" Espinosa chortled in glee. "What a

concept, huh? You shop while you wait for your table. I'll sign us in, then we have to wait till they call our names. Shop it up, boys! There's something here for everyone!"

Jack looked at Harry, whose eyes were glazed over as he took in the mountains of merchandise. Jack had a fearful moment until he saw Harry start to shop. By the time the hostess called their names, each of the boys had a shopping bag filled to the top. Between the five of them, Bert estimated they'd dropped over $400 on stuff no one needed and probably wouldn't want when it was given out. Jack couldn't remember the last time he'd seen Harry this happy over mere shopping. In fact, to his knowledge, Harry had never seen the inside of a store, much less shopped. He wondered if he was looking at a miracle named Harry Wong.

Ninety minutes later, stuffed to the gills, and carrying takeout bags, the boys trotted out to the Explorer, packed their shopping bags in the back, and climbed aboard. "Now, wasn't that a pleasant way to do lunch?" Espinosa cackled.

"I loved every minute of it, Espinosa," Harry said sincerely. "I am so glad you had the foresight to bring us all here. You should be commended. The food was . . . well, the food was not too much to my liking, but I did eat it. Do not pay attention to these clods. They don't know a thing about what's good and what isn't."

The silence in the Explorer was louder than thunder.

Ten minutes later, Bert said, "We're two miles from our destination. We are driving through the main part of town now. Nice town. People milling about on a nice summer day. Lots of trees and flowers. Bet there are bumblebees in those flowers. Buildings look kept up. Yep, I'd say this is a nice place to live and raise a family. The flip side is this place just went through a hurricane. And yet it's like it never happened. Guess people care about their town and their neighbors. I don't know if I could live in a small town like this, though. But it is nice."

"And thank you for that little speech," Ted said. "Come on, we're all city boys, we'd stagnate here. But I agree, it appears to be a nice little town."

The robotic voice on the GPS came to life just as Bert shouted for all of them to pipe down so he could hear the directions.

Bert reduced the speed on the Explorer to a crawl. He pointed to the electronic keypad. "You guys got any bright ideas on how to get into this place?"

Harry craned his neck. He looked at the iron spikes on the six-foot-high fence and said, "I could vault over it, but that still won't help me to open the gate from inside. I say you blow the horn, lean on it, and see if you can rouse someone. If not, I'll tackle the fence and knock on the door."

Bert leaned on the horn for a full thirty seconds. They could all hear the dogs barking frantically inside the house. The moment Bert released his hand from the horn, they heard a voice asking them to identify themselves.

"Bert Navarro. I'm here to see Ms. Rutledge

and Ms. de Silva." He rolled his eyes for the guys' benefit just as the gate swung open.

"Man, I am not looking forward to this meeting," Ted said. "Annie is going to hand me my walking papers. I just know it. How in the hell did I let you guys talk me into this gig in the first place?"

"We didn't talk you into anything. This was all your idea," Jack said.

"Oh, yeah? Well that's not how I remember it. Oh, shit! Look at them standing up there on the porch—excuse me, *veranda*. And they look meaner than cat shit," Ted groaned.

Jack hopped out of the Explorer and, with as much cheerfulness as he could muster, said, "Well, hi there, ladies! It's really very good to see you. Charles sent us."

# Chapter 22

The boys trooped up the steps to the veranda, bright smiles on their faces, not sure what to expect from the two steely-eyed women standing next to another woman they had yet to meet.

Introductions were made with more bright smiles and a slight quiver to the voices of the newcomers. Julie looked at the five men and said, "Let me see if I can guess which one is which. Myra and Annie told me all about you." As she went down the line, she had each one pegged. She laughed, a sound of pure mirth. "Please, come in. We were just talking about you all, if you can believe that."

And then they were inside and headed to the

kitchen, the dogs yipping and yapping for attention. "I'm sorry for their bad manners. They love company. While you all get acquainted, I'll make coffee," Julie said as she bustled around the coffeepot.

An uneasy silence followed as Myra and Annie stared across the table at the five men both women considered the sons they'd never had. "Speaking strictly for myself, I'm glad you're here," Annie blurted. Annie's outburst was so unexpected, the boys could only gape at her.

"I feel the same way," Myra said. "Having said that, I'll deal with Charles on my return. He should have let us know you were coming. Neither Annie nor I deal with surprises very well."

Jack leaned across the table. "Tell us everything and don't leave anything out, no matter how unimportant you think it might be."

Myra and Annie did as instructed, as a sideshow started to unfold where Harry was sitting. Cooper sat on his haunches, eyeing Harry with adoration. Harry stroked the retriever's head as he listened to Annie and Myra and the plans they had come up with to take care of Darlene Wyatt. Suddenly, Cooper bolted from the room, only to return with one of his toys. He laid it at Harry's feet, then raced off for another. All told, he made eleven round-trips, to everyone's amusement. When the little pile of stuffed toys was up to his ankles, Harry looked to Julie, his gaze questioning.

"I don't know what it means other than I think he suddenly loves and adores you. Cooper doesn't share his toys with anyone. What's his is his. Seems to me like he's giving them to you. Cooper has separation anxiety, which we are working on. I have to say, though, I've never seen him interact with anyone like this. You should be flattered."

"I am," Harry said softly as he slid off his chair and dropped to his knees until he was eye level with Cooper.

"I think this is some kind of Zen thing or something. Harry can communicate in ways we only dream about," Jack whispered.

Man and dog stared at one another, neither blinking. Time passed, with neither moving, and the others went back to their discussion at the table. It was Cooper who made the first move. He placed both paws on Harry's shoulders, bent forward, and licked at his cheek before he moved off to join Gracie and Lola, who were waiting for him at the doggie door. Harry watched until Cooper was out of sight before he sat back on his chair. He looked around at the faces staring at him. "We are as one," he said by way of explanation.

Julie felt a chill wash over her. She didn't like the way that sounded, but she didn't say anything.

The discussion continued as she poured coffee, her gaze never far from Harry Wong.

Bert held up his hand for silence. "If I understand this correctly, we have the balance of today and all day tomorrow, until Monday, when you plan to strike. You chose Monday because the little girl starts school and will not be in the house, is that right?"

"Yes," Myra said.

"You said Darlene has webcams set up all over, so she can see anyone approaching her property from any angle, is that right?" Jack asked.

"That's right," Annie said.

"So how do you plan on getting in there?"

"We thought Julie would just go over and knock on the door. Darlene might or might not invite her in. We think she's going to want to make a deal with her, so more likely than not, she will invite her in. Once that garage door goes up, we all hotfoot it and follow her in. There's an entrance to the main house inside the garage. It leads down a hallway into the kitchen. Her webcams are set up in that hallway. We have been toying with the idea of calling Abner to see if he can disrupt the power in some way. If he can't do that, Julie will have to go to the front door. Same deal, but we can go in from the side because there is heavy foliage. Julie said none of Darlene's neighbors will do a thing to intervene. How does that sound?" Myra asked.

"Iffy," Ted said. "The lady has a cell phone, right? She could call the police."

Annie laughed. "I don't think so. She's already gone a few rounds with the local police, to her own detriment. Julie thinks this is the best way, unless you guys have a better idea. Do you?" Annie asked pointedly.

"Daylight is never good for infiltration. Darkness is your friend," Espinosa said.

"Whoa! Whoa!" Ted said, jumping up. "I have an idea! Sometimes I am so smart I can't stand myself. How about this? Espinosa and I are here to cover the summer festival. You know, small-town America, that kind of thing. The woman at the car-rental kiosk told me all about it. While we were here, we got downwind of this woman whose identity was stolen. As you all know, the *Post* has done numerous stories and articles on that very thing. It's all verifiable if Darlene wants to check. If she was as pissed as you say she was when that all went down, she's going to jump at a chance to spout off and get her jabs in about Julie, and blame her. Once she lets us in, I think Espinosa and I are capable of getting the rest of you in. Party time!"

"You know what? I think that might work, and I like it better than Julie's going in there cold turkey. From all you've said about this woman and her boyfriend, I wouldn't trust either one of them around her, since they have a bigger-than-life hate on for Julie. But I would like to go in Espinosa's place. Darlene won't know the difference," Harry said.

"Harry, you are so loquacious, and I am loving it. That is an absolutely brilliant idea. Let's all vote on Harry's idea," Jack said, happiness ringing in his voice.

All of them, even Julie, raised their hands in the air.

"Done!" Myra said happily. Harry beamed his pleasure.

"Then it's a go. What about the little girl?" Jack asked.

"The minute we get in the house, we have to have Darlene call the school and tell them my daughters will be picking Ollie up from now on," Julie said. "That child is going to be so happy. In fact, my girls are coming over shortly so that we can get Ollie's old room all ready. Actually, I think they're here now; the dogs are barking. I suspect you all want to . . . you know, get down to business. I will be okay with anything you all decide. It was nice meeting you all. Oh, where are my manners? Myra, Annie, when you're all finished with your business, will you show the gentlemen the bedrooms upstairs and let them pick out their rooms. I have more than enough room for you all to stay here. And I will be cooking dinner."

The beloved words, *Hey Mom, we're here,* made everyone smile as Julie scurried from the room to greet her daughters.

"More coffee, boys? A sandwich?"

"I'll take the coffee, but we stopped to eat before we got here," Bert said.

Annie walked over to the coffeepot. She listened as Harry voiced a concern. "Are we sure there will be no repercussions where the little girl is concerned? Like, all of a sudden, her aunts are picking her up. Won't the school ask questions about her mother? How are you prepared to handle that?"

Myra frowned. "We were discussing that before you got here. Darlene will have to write a letter, and it will have to be notarized. She's going to be signing off on everything. Going out of town for an extended period of time, going back to help her ailing parents, wherever they live. Something like that. Julie did say she knows someone who is a notary who will agree to stop over and witness Darlene's signing the papers. That's going to be really tricky, though. That's what we're all worried about."

"Then I suggest we talk it to death and come up with a solution that will work so that Julie will be able to live with no blowback," Jack said.

They fell to it, all of them starting to talk at once. Bert whistled through his teeth, an ear-piercing sound that silenced the group. "One at a time! Remember now, we're talking about a little girl's future life."

Annie rummaged through a pile of folders. "These came via fax last evening. Myra and I were on the phone with Lizzie till all hours. Here's the contract where Darlene gives Julie her power of attorney. This one is a release to the school for Julie and her authorized representatives to pick up the child from school. This blue folder is where Darlene signs off on custody of Olivia. This one is where she signs off on the house, and it is to be put into a trust for Ollie, with Julie and her daughters as trustees. This yellow folder is the one that will give us the most trouble. This says she admits to cheating and carrying on an affair with Adam Fortune while she was married to Julie's son. She also admits to negligence in her husband's death. She's going to balk at signing that."

"No she won't," Harry said quietly.

"And the guy, Adam?" Espinosa asked.

Myra smiled. "Annie and I will take care of Adam Fortune. He will pay for every mean-spirited thing he's ever done to Ollie, every abuse, every unkind word he ever uttered to that poor child."

Jack swallowed hard. He didn't think he'd ever seen such evil looks as he was seeing on Myra's and Annie's faces. He almost felt sorry for Darlene Wyatt and her boyfriend. Almost.

"Avery and some of his crew are flying in to Huntsville this evening. That's a lot of strangers in a small town all of a sudden, don't you think? Do these people keep up with things like that?" Jack asked, his tone worried.

"They do, according to Julie, but these people are Julie's friends. Once word gets out she has guests, there won't be any blowback, as Jack put it. I think we're okay," Annie said confidently.

"Did any of you tell the child what you're planning?" Jack asked.

"Julie said she told Ollie that in a few days everything would be okay. She said Ollie is very good at keeping secrets. If she told her anything else, she didn't tell us," Myra said.

"A lot can happen in a day and a half until the child goes off to school on Monday," Harry said glumly.

"You just had to go ahead and say that, didn't you?" Ted groused.

"I did have to say it. And if the rest of you aren't thinking the same thing, then there is something wrong with you."

Myra held up her hand for silence. "Even though she didn't like it, Julie was comfortable letting Ollie go back to the house. Ollie, according to Julie, knows how to make herself invisible. What that means is she hides out in her room. The twins, along with Julie, bought her a lot of stuff, so she'll have something to occupy her until school starts on Monday. It is a concern, Harry, but nothing major at this point." She hated the concern she was seeing on the others' faces, but she had to rely on Julie's opinion, since Julie knew the players and the situation better than all of them put together.

Harry's big toe poked around Cooper's pile of toys. "If you say so," was Harry's only comment.

Jack was so uneasy that he sidled up to Harry. "Talk to me, Harry. Tell me what is really bothering you. What are you feeling or seeing that we aren't?"

"She's just a kid, Jack. A little girl. She shouldn't have to make herself invisible. She should be with people who will love and take care of her. Thirty-six hours is a long time. I'm worried about that crazy-ass woman living in the house, a woman who seems to have that Fortune guy wrapped around her little finger and is calling the shots. The kid is a thorn in her side. She's blaming her, the kid, according to what Myra and Annie tell us they learned from Julie, for all their bad luck. And she kicked Fortune's kids out of the house. Didn't someone say one of the neighbors called Julie to tell her when that all went down? His kids versus Olivia. Do you want me to paint you a picture, Jack?"

"Hell no! What do you want to do, Harry?

You want to go in tomorrow? I'm okay with advancing it a day, but the girl will be there. How do we handle that?"

"I need to think about this. I'm going outside for a little while. You don't need me in here to beat this thing to death."

When the kitchen door closed behind Harry, the room went silent. "Harry pretty much goes along with the flow. He's feeling really strongly about this, as you can all tell. I'm okay with moving this gig up to tomorrow, but first I want to make sure that the kid is safe, and we can get her out of the house with nothing that will bite any of us on the butt. So, let's run it all up the flagpole and see if we can make tomorrow work for us."

"Shouldn't Julie and her girls be in on this, or at least Julie, before we make any major decisions?" Annie asked.

"Absolutely," Bert said. "You want to ask her? While you're doing that, we'll try and figure something out."

"The child comes first. Just remember that," Annie huffed as she made her way out of the kitchen and upstairs.

Jack smacked his hands together. "We need a plan."

The others groaned.

# Chapter 23

Annie stood in the doorway, staring at two miniversions of Julie Wyatt. They were all bustling about as they worked at turning their old bedroom into a little girl's fantasy room. Gossamer pastel butterflies hung from the ceiling, swaying in the draft from the air-conditioner vents. The twin beds the sisters had grown up with were gone, replaced with a double bed that had a lacy canopy matching the bedcovers. Sheer curtains, white as snow, covered the windows, which overlooked the backyard and the playhouse, where the twins and even Ollie had played for endless hours. The names on the colorful toy chest had been replaced with Ollie's name in bright gold script.

Bookshelves lined one whole wall and were filled with Ollie's old toys, the ones she had left behind when Darlene stopped allowing her to visit. Books, some belonging to the twins, others Ollie's books, which her real mother had read to her when she was little, filled the top two shelves. A white clothes rack stood in the corner, with brightly colored animals clinging to the spokes, which jutted out. A bright red jacket hung from the lowest spoke, along with shiny yellow rain gear. A pair of ladybug boots stood underneath.

The closet door was open, revealing ice skates, roller skates, and a skateboard just waiting for Ollie.

In the far corner was a pink nylon tent that was perfect for two giggling little girls to hide out in. Ollie and a friend on a sleepover. How wonderful.

Annie's eyes were wet as she stared around the room and at the happy faces of Julie and her daughters.

Julie cleared her throat. "We had all this stuff, we just didn't know when we would be able to . . . to fix the room for Ollie. I think she's going to like it, don't you, Annie?"

"Absolutely. Ah, Julie, I wonder if you could spare a few minutes; the boys and I need to talk to you about something."

"You girls can finish here, can't you?" The twins nodded.

"I was just about to come downstairs to start dinner. I was wondering, Annie, if I get it all ready, can you and Myra serve? Mr. Goldfeld called and wants to meet with me. He suggested dinner, and I agreed. I feel so terrible about Mace, and I've purposely put his . . . death and my . . . his will out of my mind with all this going on with Ollie. I have to go and meet with him. There are just some things in life you can't put off. You understand, don't you, Annie?"

Julie's voice was so sad, Annie wrapped her arms around her shoulders. "Of course I understand. You have to do what you have to do. We can take care of things while you do whatever it is that you need to do. Come along, dear, we need to talk. There's been a change in plans. Harry is not happy with our current plan. Harry is . . ."

"Different? I already sensed that. Cooper did, too. I guess we should pay attention to what he thinks and says, then," Julie said. "Oh, look, Annie!" Julie said as she peered out the window on the landing of the stairway.

Annie looked down into the yard and smiled. Harry was sitting in the middle of the yard in the bright sun, in a lotus position. Cooper was sitting next to him, still as a statue. Gracie and Lola were busy chasing squirrels at the far end of the yard, completely oblivious to Harry and Cooper.

Annie could feel Julie suddenly tense up. She reached for her hand, and together they walked down the stairs and into the kitchen.

In the kitchen, the boys and Myra were standing by the sliding doors in the sunroom, their eyes on Harry and Cooper.

"I know that means something. I just don't know what," Jack said fretfully.

"Figure it out later, boys. Julie is here, and she has to go out, so we need to cut to the chase and let her be on her way," Annie said.

They all gathered around the kitchen table again. Bert took the floor. "Harry seems to think waiting till Monday would be a mistake. He says thirty-six hours is too long to wait, and he believes—at least, I think he believes—that the child might be in danger. Do you think we could pull this off tomorrow morning, Julie? I know it's Sunday, and everyone in the neighborhood will be home, so that might pose a problem."

Julie drew a deep breath. "On the contrary. Everyone will be at church. Tomorrow morning should work fine. I know all of Darlene's neighbors, and they all belong to Saint Ann's Church. Services start at eight, Bible school is at nine, then there's a brunch at ten thirty. Everyone goes and helps out. The neighborhood will be pretty much empty."

Julie moved over to the kitchen counter, where she set to work preparing the dinner she'd promised. She could still hear and talk as she bustled about preparing a stew in her pressure cooker. Within twenty minutes, she had everything ready. She wiped her hands and looked at her guests. "I'm for whatever will work for Ollie. You don't need my approval. Just, please, make it work for us. I don't know how to thank you. Last week at this time, all of this was just a dream. Cooking dinner for you hardly seems enough."

"It's enough," Jack said. "We're good here. We'll fine-tune our plan, and by the time you get home, we should have all the kinks worked out."

Julie nodded, then raced off to her room, where she quickly washed her face, combed her hair, put on lipstick, and changed into a clean blouse. She was out the door in ten minutes flat, her thoughts all over the map. Cooper and Harry. Mace's death, her inheritance, Oliver Goldfeld. Darlene Wyatt and her punk boyfriend. Ollie and her new room. Her world was suddenly moving at the speed of light. She hoped she was up to all these changes in her life. Well, if she wasn't, she damned well better get on the stick and get ready for the blizzard that was heading her way. She was wired too tight just then and didn't like the feeling.

Fifteen minutes later, Julie stopped in front of the property that now belonged to Oliver Goldfeld. She stared up the slight incline to where the old house rested. She sighed. In real-estate terms, the house was a fixer-upper. All it would need, a cheerful broker would tell you, was a boatload of money, patience, and a dedicated construction crew working twenty-four/seven, and even then the outcome would be iffy. In Julie's opinion, a wrecking ball was what was required. But if this was what Mace had wanted and Oliver Goldfeld was prepared to do, who was she to even offer an opinion?

Julie climbed out of her truck and headed up the driveway to a cracked and broken slate path, which led to the ramshackle front door. It opened just as she set foot on the lopsided steps. She picked her way carefully, her fingers crossed that she wouldn't fall through the rotted wood.

Julie liked the smile she was seeing on Oliver's face. "Looks like you have your work cut out for you," she said.

"The Realtor put me in touch with some people who, for a ton of money, say they can turn this dump into a showplace." Julie laughed.

Oliver stood aside for her to enter the house. "They tell me there's a history to this old relic. I plan on reading up on it. The staircase, or I should say, dual staircase, is straight out of *Gone With the Wind*. It's in perfect condition, as are the floors. For the most part, the inside is in good condition. The floors are heart of pine and need to be sanded. Everything needs to be updated. The kitchen and bathrooms and the seven fireplaces have to be rebuilt. The major part of the work is outside. So I can live here while the work is going on. I think I see what Mace saw. I'm going to do it. That's the bottom line."

"It's a big piece of property, Oliver. You're going to need a full-time gardener."

"Nope. I'm going to do that myself. I went on the Internet last night and ordered every book ever written about gardening and the upkeep of yards such as this. First thing Monday morning, I'm heading to Burns Hardware so I can buy one of everything that I'll need. That was Mace's plan, and now it's mine."

"I love old houses. There's such character in them, such history. I'm all for a modern kitchen and bath, but I hope you don't tamper with the walls and doorways and such."

"Nope, they will stay the same. Coffee? Something cool to drink? I have some iced tea."

"Iced tea sounds good. Does the air-conditioning work?"

"Nope! Nothing really works," Oliver said cheerfully.

In spite of herself, Julie burst out laughing. Oliver laughed with her. She decided at that moment that she liked the man sitting across from her at the table.

"So where would you like to go to dinner, Julie Wyatt? You know the town, so you pick the place."

Julie thought about the question and decided she really didn't want to go out to eat. "Do you have any food here?"

"Cheese, crackers, eggs, muffins, that's about it. I have to find a grocery store, so I can buy . . . you know . . . real food."

"I could eat some scrambled eggs. I can even make them for us if you don't mind. Breakfast has always been a favorite meal of mine. More often than not, I have breakfast for dinner when I'm by myself. So, what do you say? You do have pots and pans, right?"

"One pot, one fry pan, one spatula. But I do have two forks. But only because I found them in a drawer. Don't worry, I washed them." Oliver chuckled. "Believe it or not, there is a raggedy garden out back. I think it was an herb garden at one time. Do you want to take a look and see if there's anything you can use if you're planning on an omelet? Hint, hint." He grinned as he opened the kitchen door and headed out to an overgrown garden.

Even from where she was standing, Julie could smell the rich scent of basil and parsley. If there was one thing she loved, it was an herb garden, be it one on her windowsill or one in an overgrown, uncultivated backyard.

She broke off stems as she walked along. "You should, if you have the time, Oliver, clear all the weeds away and try to save the herbs. You have everything here. You can harvest them in a few months and dry them out and put them in jars. Fresh is best, of course. Or you could root some and put them on the windowsill in a sunny spot and have fresh herbs all the time."

"That's assuming I learn how to cook. I was thinking of hiring a housekeeper."

"Oh."

Oliver looked sheepish. "I guess that 'oh' means I should take care of my own house like Mace was going to do. Learn as I go along, screw it up, then call someone in to fix it."

"Something like that," Julie said as she picked her way through the weed-choked yard back to the kitchen.

Oliver decided it was time to get a little huffy, and his tone showed it. "I don't see myself as Mr. Homemaker. I'm a lawyer."

Julie reacted to his words. "Uh-huh," Julie said as she rinsed off the herbs and diced them with a knife whose blade was so dull it couldn't cut through the wind. In the end, she tore the leafy herbs into tiny pieces and dropped them into the eggs she scrambled into the fry pan. God alone knew how these eggs were going to come out, she thought as she scraped the chunk of cheese with a fork. This whole visit was starting to irritate her. She was only as good as the tools she had to work with. And she said so.

"I offered to take you out to dinner," Oliver said. "This was your idea."

And it was all downhill from there.

"Yes, it was, and it was a stupid idea. I'm not even hungry." She turned off the stove to make her point. "I think I'll go home."

"You just got here," Oliver snapped.

"And now I'm leaving," Julie snapped back. "I have a lot of things on my mind, and I don't have time to hold your hand. No one helped me. I had to do it all myself. I learned from my mistakes; you can do the same thing. How do you even know Mace would want you to be doing what you're doing? You're doing this to make yourself feel better. And I do not want Mace Carlisle's estate, so take my name off whatever it's on," she snapped again. She stomped her way to the front door and out to the rotted front porch. "Don't send me anything in the mail, either, because I won't open it. Did you hear everything I just said, Mr. Goldfeld?"

"I did, and I imagine everyone in the next county also heard. I told you, it doesn't work like that. Man, was Mace ever wrong about you. He said you were the sweetest, kindest lady he had ever met. He said you were the real deal, all sugar and spice and everything nice. You snookered him, didn't you? And he was hurting and gullible, and he fell for it," Oliver shot back. "Not to mention he was dying. And to think I left his dog with you! Well, I want her back!" Stunned at his own tirade, Oliver couldn't believe he'd just said what he said. In the whole of his life, he had never spoken to a human being that way, much less a woman.

Julie stopped in her tracks. Her eyes glistening, she thought her heart was going to pound right out of her chest. "You are beyond hateful, Mr. Goldfeld. I considered Mace a good friend, even though he was pretending to be Oliver Goldfeld the whole time. I haven't even had time to mourn his death. Yet. I don't do well with . . . death. Not that it's any of your damned business. You just try to take that dog back, and you'll . . . be sorry. It's a fair trade—I keep the dog, and you keep the estate. Read my lips: I-do-not-want-it! Now go back inside and eat those shitty eggs I almost made for you. I hope you choke on them!" Julie screeched as she tore down the front steps. A chunk of wood from the bottom step fell off. Julie stopped, picked it up, and threw it in Oliver's direction. She didn't even wait to see if she hit her target or not. She whirled and ran to her truck.

Tears rolled down her cheeks as she headed for the highway. She drove aimlessly for a while as she swiped at the tears pooling from her eyes. Finally, she pulled to the right and entered the parking lot of a Walgreens drugstore. She drove around to the back of the lot and pressed the button to roll up the windows, then turned off the engine. Then she howled her misery. She banged on the steering wheel, kicked out at the gas and brake pedals, before she calmed down.

When she felt like she had herself under control, Julie turned the engine back on and lowered the windows. The heat and humidity slapped at her like a wet blanket. She really needed to get the air-conditioning fixed. Had she really done what she just did? What was wrong with her? Why had she wigged out? She needed to place some blame here. But where? If she wasn't on overload, she was on the fast track to getting there. She recognized the symptoms from way back when. She needed to get a grip on things, or she'd be sitting in a corner sucking on her thumb.

At that moment, though, she needed to get back home. She would grieve for Mace Carlisle when all her other affairs were taken care of. The most important thing was that she'd told Oliver Goldfeld she didn't want Mace's estate. *That,* he would have to deal with. What she had to deal with was the fact that Mace and their kiss didn't mean what she thought it had meant at the time. If he thought it meant more than it had, and left her his estate because of it, then Goldfeld was right; she'd deceived Mace. But at the moment it happened, it was what it was. On

Mace's return, she would have come to her senses and explained that they just got caught up in the moment before his departure.

She couldn't worry about any of that now. Now, she had to think of her granddaughter and what was going to go down in the coming hours. She was going to be raising a child again, something she was meant to do. She didn't have time for wills and probate and a lawyer who thought she was some kind of cheat. Sugar and spice and everything nice. Not. At least in Oliver Goldfeld's eyes. Like she was really going to return Lola to him. Not in this lifetime or the next. No way, no how. Lola was hers. Possession was nine points of the law. Wasn't it?

Back on the front porch of the dump he had just purchased, Oliver Goldfeld stared down the long driveway. "Sugar and spice and everything nice, my ass," he muttered as he tossed the chunk of wood from the broken step out into the yard. "Damn it, Mace, I told you it was a mistake. She's not who you thought she was. Did you listen to me? Hell, no, you didn't, and now I have to deal with *that woman*. Now I have to go in there and eat those shitty eggs your lady friend *almost* cooked for me."

Oliver wasn't sure, but he thought he could hear Mace laughing at him as he let the screen door smack him in the rear end.

# Chapter 24

The house was so quiet, Julie was frightened. Five men in her upstairs, and she felt fear. It didn't compute. She looked at the clock. It was ten minutes past one in the morning. She'd been sitting here for over an hour watching the clock count down the time. She stood up and looked through the kitchen cutout leading into the sunroom. Gracie and Lola were sleeping nose to nose. Cooper was nowhere in sight. That's what was bothering her more than the episode with Oliver Goldfeld. Cooper and his toys were in the bedroom where Harry Wong was sleeping. Her eyes burned. She knew as sure as she was sitting there that Cooper was lost to her. The lump in her throat was so huge, she could barely breathe.

Julie looked down into her teacup, wishing she could read tea leaves. How many cups had she consumed so far this evening? Four was the number she came up with. There was no way she was going to be able to sleep, so she poured another cup of tea, finishing the pot, and carried it out to the dark front veranda, where she settled herself in her favorite rocker. She turned on the paddle fans to stir the air. Even in the dark, she could see the fern fronds dancing in the breeze the fans created. She had so many memories here on this veranda, most of them good, a few bad.

She thought about Larry then, the way she always thought about Larry. And after Audrey had died, how many times had she sat out here with him and Ollie and had tea parties? Too many to count. They had taught Ollie how to play checkers out here on rainy days. Larry. Larry. Larry. It always came down to Larry. She cried at her failure, hoping Larry understood. Now, tomorrow, maybe the tide would turn, and she would really have Ollie back where she belonged, in a loving home. Maybe then Larry would forgive her. Maybe. But what if Larry didn't approve of her methods? Would the end justify the means? She sure hoped so.

Julie closed her eyes and let her mind wander. She'd wake up Ollie in the mornings, the way she always woke up her own kids. She'd make sure she had a pretty outfit for school, which she would lay out the night before. She'd

make sure she showered and washed her hair
with soap and shampoo befitting a little girl.
She'd have breakfast ready so they didn't have
to rush. Ollie loved pancakes and waffles cut
into star patterns. And she adored Julie's homemade syrup. She'd have her lunch money and
her book bag on the counter ready to go.

They'd never be late to school, because punc-
tuality was a trait of hers. They would talk about
her classes for the day, discuss her homework on
the ride to school. Then she'd drop her off, kiss
her good-bye, and pick her up again at two
o'clock. They'd come home, have a snack. Then
Ollie would play and romp with the dogs, play in
her newly decorated room. Then they would do
homework and have dinner. Dinner over, the
two of them would cuddle on the sofa so that
Ollie could begin the healing and bonding process.

There was not going to be any room in Julie's
life for lotteries or pharmaceutical companies,
and everything that went with that. Ollie had to
come first. She was going to need friends, activi-
ties, when she felt secure. That was going to take
some doing. But with the girls' help, she knew
she could make it all happen, and Ollie would
be right where her real mother and father would
have wanted her to be. Life would be so good.
So right.

Julie set her teacup on the floor, leaned her
head back, and closed her eyes. Was Ollie sleeping peacefully? What was she dreaming about?
Did she cry herself to sleep with no one to comfort her the way she'd told the twins she did?

\*   \*   \*

Three blocks away, in her darkened bedroom, Olivia Wyatt covered her ears so she wouldn't have to hear Adam and Darlene screaming at each other. She looked up at the little clock on her night table. The red letters said it was one o'clock in the morning. She crept from her bed on tiptoe and walked over to her closet and her hidey-hole, the feather from her Crayola box in her hand. She didn't have a pillow, so she used the blanket from her bed. She tried not to look at the pile of stuff Darlene had destroyed. Now her little corner was bare. She curled into a ball and whimpered, the feather held close to her chest. "Please, Daddy, help me. Grandma said she's going to get me out of here. Can you help her?"

*Shhh. I want you to listen to me, Ollie. And when I'm finished talking to you, I want you to go to sleep. I'll watch over you. Pretend you're sleeping on a pile of feathers. I'll take them from my wings and put them all around you to keep you safe. Is that okay, little one?*

"Oh, Daddy, you came. I miss you. I miss you so much. Is it true? Is Grandma going to come for me?"

*Ollie, remember what I said to you? When you need me, just call my name. Yes, it's true. When you wake up in the morning, your aunts will come and get you. You have to be ready. I always keep my promises, Ollie, you know that. I want to tell you something, and I want you to remember it so you can tell Grandma. Can you do that?*

"Daddy, I'm a big girl. I can remember. What is it you want me to remember?"

*You have to tell Grandma not to be sad, because Cooper is going to go away. Because he has a job to do. A very important job. It's important that Grandma not be sad. So, can you remember that?*

"Yes, I can remember. What kind of job, Daddy? What if Grandma asks me, and I don't have the answer?"

*Grandma will know, Ollie.*

"What will Adam and Darlene do when I go with Grandma?"

*I don't want you to worry about them, Ollie. They're going to go away, too. You won't see them for a long time. Will you be okay with not seeing them?*

"If I can stay with Grandma and Connie and Carrie, I'll be okay, Daddy. I can't tell you a lie. I won't miss Darlene. Where are they going, Daddy?"

*Far away, Ollie. I can't tell you a lie, either. You might never see them again. That's why I asked you if you would miss them. You have to tell me the truth, Ollie.*

"Okay, Daddy. Maybe I won't miss them. It's not nice to say bad things about people. Darlene never hugs me, Daddy. All she does is chase me away. Darlene is so mean to me, she makes me cry. I try not to cry, Daddy, but I do. She pulls my hair, slaps me, and makes fun of me. She calls me bad names. I don't like it here anymore."

*I know. That's why Grandma is coming for you in the morning. When you wake up, get dressed and wait for Connie and Carrie to come for you. I want you to go to sleep now, Ollie. I'll stay right here with you, so you'll be safe. Close your eyes now and dream about all the nice things that are going to happen tomorrow and the day after tomorrow and then all the tomorrows forevermore. Shhhh.*

Across the hall and down two doors, Darlene and her boyfriend were punching and jabbing each other as they cursed and bellowed.

"I told you that little snot ripped up the pillows and shoved them in her closet. Did you do anything? No! All you do is yell and scream at me. You're no man! You're a loser! I must have been out of my mind to get mixed up with someone like you."

"Shut up before the neighbors call the cops. The whole world can hear your screeching. *You* cut up those pillows. I know you did it. Why do you hate Olivia? She's just a kid, for God's sake."

"Because she looks like Larry's first wife, that's why. Every time I look at her, I see his wife. Pretty, perfect, prissy Audrey. The wife who did everything right. She ironed his shirts, loved him, cooked for him, gave him a daughter."

"But Larry couldn't give you what you wanted and got from me. You let him die because you're a greedy bitch. Well, look at you now! Just walk over to that mirror and take a good look at what a loser looks like. That's you, all right. Little Miss Perfect might be dead, but she beat you in the end. You got squat, hotshot. You're going to go back to your roots, that run-down tenement where you were spawned. Then again, you won't even be able to afford that; you'll be living in a damned tent and pissing in the gutter. Which is where you belong." Darlene ducked the blow coming her way and bolted from the room to run downstairs, Adam following her. Darlene locked herself in the downstairs bathroom.

Adam didn't feel like breaking down the door. *Let her sleep in the tub for all I care.* He opened the refrigerator and looked for a bottle of beer. There was none, so he made coffee. He sat at the table while the coffee dripped into the pot. He was forty-seven years old and had never, ever, been this miserable in his whole life. His whole life, what there was of it, was crashing down right in front of his very eyes. Thank you, Julie Wyatt.

Adam longed for a crystal ball, so he could see what the future held for him. Then again, did he really want to know? He was tempted to get on his motorcycle and ride until he ran out of gas.

His own ominous words ricocheted around inside his head. What he had said to Darlene applied to him as well. He was going to have to go back to tenement living, too. He cringed.

Hunkered down and cowering in the bathroom, Darlene thought then about the good life she'd had with Larry and how she had screwed it up. She was smart enough at that minute to know and realize she would never have that again, not ever again. She'd had the perfect life, and she alone had screwed it up. And for what? That degenerate she'd hooked up with? She thought about Olivia then and what a miserable mother she'd been to her ever since Larry's death. Guilty! Guilty! She hadn't done one damned thing right since Larry's death.

Adam poured coffee, even though he didn't really want it. He'd never be able to sleep if he drank it. What else was new? He hadn't really slept in days, not since Darlene had gone to Starbucks for coffee and her debit card had been declined. He laid his head down on the table and was asleep within minutes.

Adam woke when he heard the bathroom door open. He was too tired to care if Darlene came out of the bathroom or not. He squinted at the clock on the stove: 6:20. He couldn't believe he'd actually slept. Well, he needed to believe it, because his neck was stiff as a board. He felt like he was eighty years old when he started upstairs to take a shower. Every bone in his body ached.

As he walked down the hall, Adam noticed that the door to Olivia's room was open. He looked inside, expecting to see her fast asleep in her bed. He was only half right. She was on her bed, but she wasn't sleeping. She was dressed, her hair combed and her Little Mermaid suitcase with the handle sitting at her feet. He blinked. He positioned himself in the doorway so he could lean up against the frame to support his aching body. "You going somewhere, Olivia? It's only six thirty."

Olivia thought about the question. Her father hadn't told her it was a secret. And she'd learned in school that you should never tell lies to anyone. "I'm going to Grandma's house when Connie and Carrie come to pick me up."

"No, you're not going there. If those crazy aunts of yours told you that, then they lied to you. You're not going anywhere."

"I am, Adam. Connie and Carrie didn't tell me. Daddy told me. He said I had to get up early and be ready to go with them to Grandma's when they came to pick me up. There is something very important that I have to tell Grandma. I'm ready."

"That was a dream, Olivia. Now, unpack your bag. I'm going to take a shower; and then, if you're good, I'll take you and Darlene to Perkins for breakfast."

"I don't want to go to Perkins, and I don't want to ride on your motorcycle. You have to get ready, also. Daddy said you and Darlene are going away, too. He said you aren't going to come back. I'm never going to see you again. Well, maybe I will when I'm big like Connie and Carrie."

"You need to stop with this crap, Olivia. You just had a bad dream. I'm not going anywhere, and neither is Darlene."

"Yes you are, Adam. Daddy said so, and fathers don't lie to their children."

"Olivia, your father's dead. It was a dream. Now do what I tell you."

Olivia's face turned stubborn. "I have to do what Daddy said. If you don't believe me, look at this. He stayed with me last night. Darlene ripped up my pillows, and Daddy didn't want me to sleep on the bare floor, so he put all the feathers from his angel wings on the floor for a bed for me. See, Adam?"

Adam looked into the closet and almost blacked out. "Those are feathers from the pillows, Olivia. You had me going there for a minute."

"No, Adam, Darlene is allergic to feathers. She threw out all the old feather pillows and bought the foam ones, like the ones she ripped up. She said that feathers make her sneeze."

Adam grew light-headed. He did remember Darlene spending over $400 on new pillows.

Olivia skipped back to her bed, where she sat down primly, her hands folded in her lap. "Where are you and Darlene going, Adam?"

"I told you. We aren't going anywhere."

"Daddy said you are. He said you and Darlene are going to spend forever wishing you had been nice to me. If you send me a postcard, you have to send it to Grandma's house, because that's where I'll be living. But I don't want a postcard."

Adam clapped his hands over his ears. "Enough with this crap, Olivia. I am not going anywhere, and neither are you, so get that through your head."

"No, Adam. You have to get it through *your* head that what Daddy said is going to come true," Olivia said solemnly.

It sounded to Adam's ears like the child was reading from a written script.

"I am going to Grandma's house, Daddy said so. You should tell me where you're going, so I don't worry about you and Darlene. Daddy said I'll forget about you both really quick because I will be busy."

Adam stared at Olivia, then at the picture of

her mother and father on the bedside table. As he stared into the laughing faces of her parents, he knew in that instant that everything Olivia had just said was true. Shaking from head to toe, he left the room, slamming the door behind him, his eyes wild and unfocused.

"Did I do that right, Daddy?"

*You did, honey. I'm proud of you.*

"How much longer before Connie and Carrie come for me?"

*Not long. You have to be patient. We can talk about what the first thing is that you're going to do when you get to Grandma's. That will help pass the time, okay?*

"Okay. The first thing I have to do is tell Grandma about Cooper and the important job he has to do. Then I have to give her lots of hugs and kisses, so she won't be sad about Cooper."

*Good girl, Ollie, good girl.*

# Chapter 25

Standing on the veranda, Julie Wyatt and her seven guests looked like a small army ready to go into battle. All they were waiting for was Connie and Carrie Wyatt, who had just turned into the driveway. It was exactly seven fifty Sunday morning. Inside, behind closed doors, the dogs yapped their displeasure at being left behind.

At the bottom of the steps, in the driveway, cars were lined up, one of the three cars Annie and Myra had rented, which had yet to be driven, behind the lead vehicle, the SUV that Ted had rented at the airport. Bert, Jack, and Espinosa climbed into the car behind the SUV. Annie and Myra would drive in their own rental, followed by Julie in her Blazer. Connie and Carrie would be last in line. The plan was that Ted and Harry, who was posing as Joseph Espinosa, would go first. Harry had assured everyone that he would need no more than five minutes, if that, to incapacitate Darlene and Adam, if need be. The boys were scheduled to leave ten minutes after Ted and Harry did.

Ted turned on the engine and looked at Harry when it growled to life. Harry looked serene, almost like he was in a trance. They'd made six dry runs in the early hours of the previous evening. Ted felt confident enough to find the address with his eyes closed. Still, he clicked on the navigation system and waited for the greeting, which always set his teeth on edge. Not for the first time, he wondered if the reason the voice used was so grating was to prevent drivers from falling asleep.

He risked another glance at Harry out the corner of his eye. He wished he knew the secret to the man's serenity. He felt his insides quiver at the thought of just the two of them in the same closed-in vehicle. Harry Wong scared the living daylights out of him, and he didn't care who knew it.

Five minutes later, Ted pulled to a stop directly in front of Darlene Wyatt's house. Both men climbed out. They were dressed alike, in pressed khakis and white Izod shirts, their press card on lanyards, hanging around their necks. Neither said a word as they walked up to the door and rang the bell. When nothing happened,

Ted pressed his thumb on the bell and held it there. He looked at Harry and shrugged. "Here goes nothing," he hissed.

"Darlene Wyatt, if you're home, open the door. I'm here from the *Washington Post* to talk about your stolen identity," he bellowed at the top of his lungs, hoping Julie Wyatt was right, and the neighbors were all at church. He jabbed at the doorbell again and held his thumb in place. Harry pointed to his watch. Ted nodded.

Ted bellowed again, "The *Post* checks with the Social Security Administration every day. Your name came up. I don't have all day, so either open up and talk to us, or we're outta here. We also have to cover the summer festival." He jabbed at the doorbell one more time before turning to pretend to leave.

The door opened. Ted hoped he looked irritated. The truth was he was so scared he could barely breathe. He reached for the lanyard and practically shoved it into Darlene's face. Before Darlene could say anything, Ted said, "You want to tell me your story or not? If you do, let's get to it. This is Joe Espinosa. He's my photographer. Decide now, lady; I don't have all day."

The disbelief in Darlene's face was almost comical. "You came all the way here from Washington, D.C., for the Rosemont Summer Festival?"

"Yeah. My editor used to live here and has fond memories of the place. It sucks, but it pays the bills. They threw you in as an added incentive. You want to talk or not? I'm thinking you might be a whole hell of a lot more interesting than that hokey festival."

Adam pushed his way past Darlene to the door and looked at Ted and Harry. "Finally, someone wants to do something. Where are your manners, Darlene? Invite these gentlemen into the house." He looked at Harry and the camera bag hanging from his shoulder. "You will be taking pictures, right?" Harry nodded.

"Well then, Adam, make some coffee, and I'll freshen up. We want to look real nice for the pictures, so people will know we aren't someone's nightmare. Someone like my mother-in-law," she simpered.

Ted could hardly wait for the door to close behind him. He saw Harry looking at his watch. Ten seconds to spare. Jack should be arriving momentarily, along with the others.

"You guys want some coffee?" Adam said, leading the way to the kitchen.

"Yeah, sure. Didn't get a chance to get any yet this morning," Ted said, stepping aside so Harry could walk in front of him. Harry waited until Adam had the coffeepot going—in case Ted really did want coffee—before he stepped up to Adam, reached out, and pressed a spot on the back of his neck. Both men watched as Adam crumpled to the floor.

"You might as well have some coffee while we wait for Darlene and her transformation. I'll open the garage door for the others. The minute Darlene shows up, I'll put her to sleep, and you get the girl. We good on that, Ted?"

"Yeah. This is really shitty coffee. Tastes like colored water."

"You should drink tea, Ted."

It didn't sound like a suggestion. Coming from Harry, it sounded more like an order. Ted nodded. "Yeah, yeah, I think I will switch. Tea is good. My mother always drank tea. You know, in times of crisis and things like that. When you're sick, too," Ted babbled.

"Shut up, Ted. You're humoring me, and I hate it when people humor me."

Ted shut up immediately.

Darlene appeared out of nowhere. Harry and Ted stared at her. Ted wanted to ask her if she had used a trowel to put on her makeup. Harry wanted to ask her if she had to go through a car wash to remove it. She was dressed in an off-the-shoulder peasant blouse, her dyed hair frizzed on top of her head like a beehive. So far, she hadn't noticed her boyfriend lying on the floor. When she did notice him, she yelped in surprise, her hand flying to her mouth. Harry grimaced as his hand shot out. Darlene fell on top of Adam Fortune. Harry dusted his hands together dramatically.

"You do really good work, Harry."

"Stop sucking up to me, Ted. I know I do good work. What about the girl?"

"Well, I think that's up to the twins. They just pulled up in front of the house. I hope they don't come out here to the kitchen. Stay here, Harry, and I'll make sure they take Olivia to the front door."

A moment later, Ted blinked when he saw a whirlwind racing down the steps, a small pink suitcase hitting every step on the way. "I knew you would come! I knew you would come! Daddy said to get ready, and I'm ready. Can we go now? Daddy said I never have to come back here. Where's Grandma? I have to tell her something. Daddy made me promise not to forget. It's important. I have to tell her. I can't break a promise to Daddy."

The twins looked at each other, then down at Ollie. Connie licked at her lips and dropped to her knees. "Did you dream about your father last night, Ollie?"

"No! No! That's what Adam asked me, and I told him the same thing. Daddy told me what to do. He made me a bed with his angel wing feathers because Darlene ripped up my pillows." Tears pooled in the little girl's eyes. "Adam didn't believe me either till I showed him, then he looked sick and slammed my door."

"Show us," Carrie said.

The little girl galloped back up the steps and down the hall to her room. She pointed dramatically to her closet. The twins looked in, their faces draining of color. "Feather pillows?" Connie hissed.

Ollie heard her. "No, Connie, that's what Adam said. Darlene is allergic to feathers, so she bought all new pillows. Daddy put them there from his wings. I want to take them with me, but I don't have anything to put them in. Daddy might want them back when I get to Grandma's house. Can you get a bag, Connie?"

Connie was already out the door and running down the steps. She went into the kitchen and didn't bat an eye at what she saw. She headed straight for the pantry, where she assumed the trash bags would be. She was right. She grabbed one and raced back upstairs. Ollie was crying, saying over and over that her father wouldn't be able to fly without feathers on his angel wings. She perked up when Carrie told her that the feathers would grow back like magic.

"I really don't want to talk about this anymore, Carrie," Connie said, as she scooped the last of the feathers into the bag. As she was backing out of the closet, she thought she heard Larry's voice say, *Take care of my daughter, Connie.*

"Count on it," was the best Connie could say past the lump in her throat.

"You talking to yourself now?" Carrie asked as she shepherded Ollie to the door.

"No, she was talking to Daddy, Carrie. Daddy told her to take care of me. Didn't he, Connie?"

"Yes. Yes, he did, Ollie." Carrie could only gape at her twin as Connie's head bobbed up and down.

Carrie slid behind the wheel, Connie and Ollie in the backseat. As they rounded the corner, they saw the string of cars parked in Darlene Wyatt's driveway.

"Let's have a sing-along," Connie suggested. Anything, so she wouldn't have to think about what had just happened. "Let's sing all the way to wherever we go for breakfast."

"I like the itsy bitsy spider. Let's sing that one. That was Mommy's favorite," Ollie said as she broke out into song, the twins laughing and joining her. Everyone was off key, of course.

Back at the Darlene Wyatt household, the kitchen was overcrowded, not only with people but with *gear*.

"I can't believe I'm standing in Larry's kitchen. This is an abortion," Julie said, looking around. "This used to be such a pretty kitchen, the kind you just wanted to work in. Not this . . . this abomination." There was nothing for any of them to say to Julie's broken comment, so they remained silent.

Bert grabbed Adam Fortune by the feet and dragged him roughly toward the family room. Jack dragged Darlene.

"Don't worry about them, they won't wake up till you're ready for them," Harry said cheerfully.

"Who has the duct tape?" Ted asked.

Myra and Annie both held up their oversize purses. "Never leave home without it. Duct tape is a woman's best friend," Annie said.

"That's why we carry such big purses," Myra explained.

"I did not know that," Espinosa said.

"Well, now you do," Annie shot back. "Be afraid, be very afraid of women carrying big purses."

Espinosa wasn't sure if his chain was being yanked or not, so he simply nodded.

"We're ready when you ladies are," Jack said, plopping down in a burgundy recliner. "Has anyone noticed how dark and gloomy this house is? Are these people vampires or something?"

Julie swallowed hard. "I guess they wanted to erase all signs that my son had ever lived here.

This particular room used to have flowered furniture in it. The walls were white, not this deep gray color. Very few people have carpet in Alabama because of the humidity. The oak floors under this ugly carpet used to be polished and beautiful."

"Anytime you want these two to wake up, just say the word, ladies," Harry said.

"Let's tape them up first and sit them on chairs; and then you can work your magic, Harry. Who has the tape?"

Annie and Myra each tossed him a roll of tape. Jack handed one to Bert, who went to work on Darlene. Jack ripped off a strip of tape and slapped it around Adam Fortune's ankles. He looked around at Julie. "Your daughters did take the child, right? She's not in the house, is she? We don't want her seeing this."

"They're gone. We passed them on the way here. They're going to take Ollie out to church, then breakfast. This place will be just a bad memory for Ollie," Julie said.

Jack nodded. "Okay, Wizard Harry, do your thing."

"Your wish is my command, oh bearer of the torch," Harry replied. And Harry *did his thing*.

Just seconds before Darlene opened her eyes, Julie planted herself directly in her line of vision. She was the first person her ex-daughter-in-law saw when she opened her eyes.

"Hello, Darlene," Julie said, venom dripping from each word.

"What the hell are you doing in my house, and who are these people?"

"Whose house, Darlene? Let's be clear on that right now. This is Olivia's house. Not yours. Not those . . . those skanks you moved in here. Say it, say it right now. I want to hear you say out loud that this is Olivia's house."

"Go to hell! This is *my* house."

"I'm real sorry you feel that way. Okay, that was number one. Here's number two. Admit you let my son die so you could get all his money. Admit it right now."

"Kiss my ass; you know as well as I do that he just up and died. You can't blame me for that."

"Well, sure I do, Darlene. And my family and everyone else in this town believes it, too. Okay, here's number three. Admit right now that you cheated on my son with that . . . that . . . person sitting next to you."

"I'm not admitting anything to you. You and your whole damned family hate me; you're all crazy."

Julie laughed, a truly ugly sound. "Crazy enough to steal your identity and put you in the position you're in right now. Oh, well, I asked you nicely. You have no manners, Darlene. You never did. You're like one of those snake-oil saleswomen.

"Well, now, Ms. Wyatt, let's see what you have to say for yourself. I'm going to ask nice, and you would be wise to respond in kind. Let's hear your story."

"I don't have a story," Darlene said defiantly.

In a nanosecond, Julie was in her face. "Are you going to sit there and tell me you never hit my granddaughter, never whipped her, never made fun of her, never humiliated her, never made her do your bidding like some child slave while you and your . . . your weasel boyfriend and his delinquent kids availed yourselves of her house, her monies?"

"Yeah, that's what I'm telling you, and, no, I didn't cheat on your son with Adam. I knew it was you, you bitch. I told Adam you were the one who stole our identities, but he said you weren't smart enough to do that. He told me to give you back that snot-nosed kid, but I wouldn't listen."

Julie smiled and bowed. "Did my granddaughter's money pay for those breast implants you're packing around, the ones that make you look like you're about to topple over on your face with every step you take?"

"What? What are you talking about, you crazy bitch? What breast implants?"

"I'm more than capable of taking them out to show you exactly what I'm talking about. A slice here, a slice there, and out they pop, along with the serial numbers, which will let us determine who paid for them. You want to give it a shot, Miss I-Don't-Have-Breast-Implants?" Julie snapped.

For the first time since waking up, Darlene's face registered fear. "Okay, Adam paid for them. He didn't tell me where he got the money."

"Tell us what we want to know, and maybe we'll let you go, with your double false front. I'm saying *maybe*, because it depends on whether you're truthful or not."

"Why should I believe you?"

" 'Cause I'm the only game in town right

now," Julie said. "What about you, Mr. Adam Fortune? What do you have to say about all this?"

"She's a damned loser. She promised me the moon and the stars, said she'd buy me a big boat and a Cadillac Escalade. She said I could have whatever I wanted; we could get a housekeeper. She said we could shop at Neiman Marcus and Saks, because she was going to get all her dead husband's money. She even said the kid was going to be getting two grand a month in her Social Security until she was eighteen. She said we could live as high as we wanted, take trips all over the place. We didn't even make Disney. Yeah, right, I'm damned lucky if I can shop at Walmart. She is one sorry-assed loser," Adam said viciously.

"Tell me about the day my son died," Julie said quietly, so quietly the others had to strain to hear her words.

"I don't know anything about that."

"You're lying," Julie said.

Darlene clamped her lips tight. She looked over at Myra and Annie, then at the boys. Her eyes popped wide. She cowered back in her chair, her face a mask of fear. Then she looked at Adam and screeched at the top of her lungs. "I knew those two women looked familiar. They belong to the vigilantes. Those guys work for the vigilantes. You are beyond stupid, Adam. They're behind all this. What . . . what are you going to do to us?"

"Nothing you're going to like. Julie Wyatt here asked you questions, very nicely, I might add, and you both had attitude. So, unless you want to share your knowledge, we're going to have to use some rather unorthodox methods to get the answers we want. We don't like attitude unless it's *our* attitude. You disrespected us. We can't have that now, can we? But before we go that route, we need Ms. Darlene Wyatt here to sign some papers," Myra said.

Darlene started shaking her head so violently, it looked like it was going to spin right off her neck.

"I think all that shaking means Darlene is letting us know that she has no intention of signing anything," Annie observed.

"Want to bet?" Jack asked, firing up the acetylene torch.

"I'm not signing nothing," she spit.

"Yeah, you are," Jack said, advancing with the flaming torch. "That frizzy-assed hair of yours is going to go up like dry tinder. Your head will have third-degree burns on it. And if you still hold out, well, see that battery over there? I'm going to hook it up to your implants and watch this chair holding your body bounce all the way to the ceiling. Make your choice and do it quick."

"Do it! The bitch deserves every bit of it," Adam bellowed.

"It might be a good thing if you shut up right now, you gigolo, because you're next," Annie said. "I couldn't find a scalpel on such short notice, but this very dull-looking steak knife should work almost as well. You'll be a eunuch before you know it. Well, that depends on how much sawing is involved."

"Sign what?" Darlene asked.

"First, this paper giving guardianship of Olivia to me," Julie said. "The second set of papers is your admission that you did not give aid to my son when he was dying and never called EMS and that you were negligent in his death. This one says that you carried on an affair with that *thing* sitting next to you while you were married to my son. This set of papers says you relinquish any claim to this house and admit that it belongs totally to Olivia. This final set of papers is your admission that you squandered Olivia's Social Security money and need to reimburse her. Five years at two thousand dollars a month is a tidy sum. In case you can't do the numbers, it's one hundred and twenty thousand dollars."

"You bitch!" Adam screeched. "You told me the kid only got eight hundred dollars a month and that's why I had to get a second job. You said in a few years she'd be bringing in two grand. You lied! You bitch!"

Even as he was screaming at Darlene, Adam Fortune wasn't thinking about Olivia's Social Security or even the papers these people were talking about. He was thinking about what Olivia had told him earlier in her bedroom. "Where's Olivia?" he asked.

"That's really a stupid question for someone who thinks he's so smart. Olivia is with Connie and Carrie. They came here for her while you were taking a snooze on the kitchen floor. She will never come back to this house, and you will never come back to it, either, Adam. The good life is now officially over. You and your lady friend here are going on a long trip. The people of Rosemont, Alabama, will just have to live without your presence in this town," Julie said.

Adam felt his heart start to pound. Olivia had said he and Darlene were going away. The kid was right. Still, he blustered. "Darlene, do not sign anything. Go to hell."

"Sorry, Adam, you just earned yourself a bit of a haircut. Hit it, Jack!"

The little group cringed at the sound of Adam Fortune's hair crackling in the torch's blaze. His howl of pain and stunned surprise could be heard ricocheting all over the house.

"Oh, my God! Oh, my God! I am not going to sign those damned papers. You people are crazy."

A vision of her implants being ripped out of her chest flashed before Darlene's eyes.

"That wasn't nice, Darlene," Annie said as she gave the beehive hairdo a vicious yank. "Say you're sorry."

"Yeah, okay, I'm sorry," Darlene bleated, as she looked at Adam's blistered head, thankful that her own hair and implants were still in place.

"You ready to sign those papers now?" Myra asked.

"Go to hell, you bitch!"

"I'm going to take that as a no," Annie said cheerfully. "Get the battery ready, boys. Myra and I will strip her down."

The kitchen chair Darlene was strapped to with duct tape took on a life of its own. Ted and Espinosa literally flew across the room to steady it so the two women could peel off Darlene's clothes. With Harry's help, Bert stripped off Adam's clothes.

"Ain't much there, boys and girls," Jack said with clinical interest as he stared at Adam's private parts. "What that means is there isn't all that much to work with. And, I need some plastic gloves. Two pair, to be on the safe side." Myra whipped two pair of surgical gloves out of her oversize bag and held them up for everyone to see.

"I'll be happy to do it for you, Jack, if it's bothering you. Annie's going to do the implant removal, so I should do this. Fair is fair," Myra said, as though she were discussing whether it would rain or not.

Darlene Wyatt fainted.

Adam stopped screaming, his eyes rolling back in his head. Then, he, too, passed out. Jack's arms flapped in the air. "What? Is this break time? Cigarette break? What?"

"I thought you quit smoking," Ted said.

"I did, but this is stressful. I need a cigarette. I really do."

"Fortune smokes. I saw a pack of cigarettes in the kitchen," Ted said.

"Why don't all you boys go outside for a little break. Annie and I will have a little Come to Jesus meeting with these two after we revive them. My goodness, this skunk's head is really blistering. Reminds me of the time we skinned what's his name way back when. His whole body was *raw* and looked just like Adam's head."

"I really need a cigarette," Jack said in a strangled voice.

"I know you do, dear, and no one thinks any the less of you for it. Scoot along now and let us ladies tend to things."

Annie grinned as the boys bolted for the kitchen and the back door.

"We need to watch the time, Annie. We've been here a good while." Myra looked over at Julie and asked what time the neighbors would be returning from church.

"Not till around one o'clock. We have plenty of time. It's bothering me that we don't have a real notary, though."

"Bert's a notary, not to worry," Myra said. "In the end, it really isn't going to matter, because these two won't be around to contest it. We're good to go."

Julie heaved a huge sigh of relief. "Adam is coming around."

"So is the princess with the fake boobs," Annie said.

# Chapter 26

Julie towered over Adam Fortune. "The pain you're feeling right now is nothing compared to what else we're going to do to you. And you," she said, glaring at Darlene, "you, I am going to deal with personally. When you leave here, you're both going to wish you were dead. But death is too good for the likes of you." Julie continued to glare at Darlene, who was bawling her eyes out.

Between sobs, she managed to sniffle and wail that it was all Adam's fault, he'd gone after her. "He lied to me. Everything was a lie. He wouldn't leave me alone. He lusted after me like a tomcat after a bitch in heat. He said we would give the kid back to you when you coughed up Larry's money. Neither one of us wanted to be saddled with the kid. He promised me, and he lied. That kid hated me from day one. I hated her, too. Every chance he got, Adam threw your son in my face. He was this, he was that, he was handsome, he was rich, he was perfect. How do you think I liked hearing crap like that every day? Take your hate out on him. He's a loser scumbag weasel."

Julie stared at the woman as she spouted her venom. She very calmly walked out to the kitchen, looked around at the butcher block of knives, and saw a meat mallet jammed in among the knives. She picked it up and hefted it a few times to get the feel of it. Satisfied, she calmly walked back into the family room and once again looked down at Darlene Wyatt. Without a moment's hesitation, she raised up her arm and brought it down on top of Darlene's nose. Blood flew in all directions. Darlene's screams bounced off the family-room walls. Julie shrugged and moved over to Adam Fortune. "Give me one good reason, just one, why I shouldn't do the same thing to you? Are you going to encourage her to sign those papers or not?"

Adam struggled to take a deep breath. "She's not signing anything, you crazy bitch! You're insane! You need to be locked up somewhere with padded walls. So there!" he screamed. He could hardly think straight with the way his head was burning. He could actually feel blisters popping up all over his head.

*So there!* The heavy mallet found its mark. A sea of blood flew up and down and around the room. "*So there,* yourself!" Julie said, as calmly as if she were wishing him a pleasant day.

Annie and Myra looked at one another as if to say, *this lady has it going on.*

Julie walked back to Darlene and her bloody face. "I think you need to convince your boyfriend here we mean business before I knock those pricey veneers out of your mouth. Because then, he won't be able to understand a thing you say. Why do you even bother listening to him, anyway? It's not his decision, it's yours. One chance," Julie said, waving the mallet around.

"Adam, for God's sake, let me do what she wants. Don't you get it, you stupid ass? She won. The kid is gone. She just waltzed out of here with her two aunts. She was my only bargaining chip, and it's gone now, so I'm going to sign the goddamned papers."

"Shut up, Darlene. They can't keep the kid, you stupid jerk. That would be kidnapping. So they have to cough up some of that money the bitch got from Oprah. But if you sign those papers, that's all gone."

"Stuff it, Adam. We don't exist, or have you forgotten that? How can we bring any attention to Olivia's kidnapping if there is no record of our existing, much less having Olivia?"

Julie, who had momentarily been concerned about the possibility of a kidnapping charge, bounced back when she considered the obvious truth of what Darlene had just said. "Ah, true love! Isn't it wonderful? She's right, Adam. Ollie is gone. You will never set eyes on that child, or her money, again. So, how much longer do you want to play this game?" Adam spit in her general direction. Julie stepped back just in time to avoid the bloody discharge spewing from his mouth. In the blink of an eye, the mallet came down, and Adam's teeth flew from his mouth. In the second blink of an eye, Darlene's teeth sailed across the room. Both bound occupants blacked out.

"Do you think I overdid it?" Julie asked.

"Not one little bit," Annie said. Myra agreed. "It doesn't look like she's going to sign the papers, Julie."

"It does look like that, doesn't it? I wonder what she'd do if we threatened to pour vinegar over his burned head."

Myra shivered. So did Annie.

"I'm thinking the pain would be pretty unbearable," Julie said.

"We think that, too, don't we, Annie?"

"Uh-huh."

Adam stirred, his eyes wild and unfocused. "Yo, Adam. You ready to tell your bimbo girlfriend to sign those papers yet?" When there was no response, Julie trotted out to the kitchen and returned with a bottle of rice vinegar. She waved it around. Adam spit again. His eyes were focused now and spewing hatred.

"See, now this is how it's going to work. I'm saving the vinegar till last. I really hate stooping to your level, Adam, and talking the way you do, but this is what's next on the agenda. We're going to hook up your . . . ah . . . dick to that battery sitting on the coffee table, and we're going to charge you up. Right now, though, the only problem I seem to be facing is whether I should remove Darlene's implants while you watch, or should we charge you up and let her watch? Such a dilemma. Such a simple thing, signing one's name to a bunch of papers."

"Rot in hell, you bitch. No court is going to give you Olivia. Grandparents have no rights in this state. Darlene legally adopted that kid. The court system here bends over backward for the parent." At least, that's what the women thought he said without his teeth. They all started to laugh hysterically.

"What part of *Olivia is already gone* don't you get, Adam? Hey, worst-case scenario, we'll forge Darlene's name on those papers. Neither one of you exist in the eyes of the law, remember? What that means is you are suffering this torture—which, by the way, is only going to get worse—for nothing. So, you going to tell her to sign or not?"

"I told you to rot in hell, you bitch! You might have Olivia, but you didn't get her legally. One of these days, it will catch up with you, and you'll end up in jail."

"Yeah, maybe that will happen. But, by then, Olivia will be old enough to talk to a judge and tell her the way it was. You underestimated that child, Adam. And you underestimated Larry. You, too, Darlene."

"I have an idea," Annie said happily. "Let's do a twofer. We do the surgery on Darlene and hook up old Adam here at the same time. They can scream a duet together before we have them carted off."

"That's a splendiferous idea," Myra said. "Julie is definitely nodding, so I think she's agreeing with us."

"I'm all atwitter," Julie said.

"Adam, please, let me sign the damned papers. I don't want to die. They're going to kill us, and if they don't kill us outright, we'll bleed to death. For once in your stupid life, do the smart thing. I wish to hell I had never met you! God, I hate you!"

"The day I met you was the worst day of my life. You're the reason we're sitting here tied up like two chickens. I gave up my whole life for you, you skank."

Myra, Annie, and Julie stepped back and listened as the two lovebirds went at it tooth and nail.

The boys walked in at the tail end of the tirade. They looked around at the blood-splattered floor and walls, at Darlene's pricey veneers scattered all over the rug, and at Adam's squared-off oversize teeth. "You've been busy, I see," Jack said.

"Where's Avery?" Myra asked.

"Twenty minutes out," Bert said. "You want me to hook up the fire hose to the fire hydrant out front now or wait until Avery gets here?"

Myra looked at Annie. "What do you think? The pressure of the water could kill them. Should we chance it? If they pop, no one but us will know. Wanna flip a coin? But to answer your question,

Jack, hook it up and test it to make sure the pressure is what we want."

"What!" Darlene screamed. She screamed again when she saw Ted and Espinosa drag what looked like a six-inch canvas hose across the floor. The nozzle looked as big as a saucer. She continued to scream at Adam. "Look at it, you damned jerk, and pretend you're a three-alarm fire, and they're squirting that damned thing at you. It will turn your body black and blue. You'll get blood clots. Oh, my God! Look, I'm sorry. I'll do whatever you want, say whatever you want. I'll sign the papers no matter what he says. Just please don't turn that thing on me. Please," she wailed between her missing teeth.

"Shut the hell up, Darlene," Adam bellowed. The bellow came out as a hissing sound.

Julie sat down in front of the couple and assumed the lotus position. "I just cannot get over the love you two have for each other. You make my skin crawl." In a nanosecond, she bounded to her feet and pulled on the latex gloves. She looked at the boys and said, "Hook it up. Ladies, I'm ready when you are. Someone slap some duct tape on his mouth; I don't want him spitting on me again."

Annie obliged as the boys looked on, their expressions frightful, their complexions almost green. She wondered which car the battery was hooked up to. Then she decided she really didn't care as long as the juice flowed straight into Adam Fortune's penis.

"This is exciting. I have to say, Myra, the last time I was this excited was when we took on the national security advisor. By the way, Darlene, Mr. Woodley died, years later, in a vegetative state." Darlene screamed and screamed until Myra slapped a strip of duct tape across her mouth, but only after giving the beehive hairdo a vicious jerk.

Julie advanced to Adam's chair. She used her own knee to pry his legs apart. "Oooh, this is like looking for a needle in a haystack." She giggled. "Ah, here they are! Oh, Adam, I never thought you and I would get this up close and personal," she cried excitedly.

Julie hooked one clamp to Adam's balls, the other to his penis, then stood back. She called out, "Hit it!" Bert passed the word to Ted who passed it to Espinosa who was in the garage and shouted the same words to Jack at the wheel behind their rented SUV, "Hit it, Jack!"

Jack clenched his teeth and muttered to no one in particular, "You stupid, dumb son of a bitch. All you had to do was tell her to sign her name, and this wouldn't be happening." He stepped on the gas and clenched his teeth as he tried to imagine what Adam Fortune was feeling. He almost fainted with relief when he finally took his foot off the gas pedal.

Darlene tried not to look at her lover. *Tried* not to. But she couldn't force her eyes away from Adam, who was twitching and bouncing like a marionette whose strings were tangled up. She wanted to ask if he was dead, but the tape on her mouth prevented her from saying anything at all.

All this over some snot-nosed ten-year-old!

Julie sucked in her breath, removed the clamps, and winced at the burns on Adam's private parts. The hate she felt for him welled up in her, but she backed away. Adam's chin was resting on his chest, his eyes closed. It was hard to describe the color of his skin, which had once been tawny from the sun. Now it looked splotchy red and white. She wondered how that could be.

"This is just a guess on my part," Annie sing-songed, "but I don't think Mr. Fortune will be having sex anytime in the near future, if ever. Darlene, listen to the answer. Of course, I'm not a man, so maybe we should ask you fine gentlemen what you think."

Four heads bobbed from side to side.

"Sorry, Darlene," Myra said in a voice so gleeful, the boys scurried out to the garage to catch their breaths. Jack looked at them and forced a grin he didn't feel. "I told you guys more than once never to be in on the climax. Nikki was right the first time, when she said we couldn't handle the punishments the Sisters doled out. She was right, as usual."

"They're bloodthirsty," Ted said, almost in a whimper.

"They don't even blink," Bert said.

"They always look like they're enjoying it," Espinosa said.

"That's because they are," Jack said in a strangled voice.

The last to weigh in, Harry smiled. "And the world is a better place because of them." The boys gaped at Harry, but wisely refrained from commenting. Harry continued to smile as he checked the fire hose near his feet.

"I don't think we're going to need the hose," Bert said.

Harry just looked at him and laughed.

Inside, Myra was throwing ice water over Adam Fortune. He jerked upright in the chair, his eyes murderous. "You ready to tell her to sign these papers, Mr. Fortune?" she asked. "Just nod. Guess that means no. Okay, let's work Darlene over. Who among us has the steadiest hand?"

"That would be me," Annie said, holding out her hands for proof. Both hands were rock steady. Annie beamed. "I think I need a little sharper knife than this steak knife, though. It might take me a while to saw through the fatty breast tissue. There might be a lot of blood, too. Once we pop those babies, what do we do with them? Wait a minute, she said she was going to sign the papers regardless of what old Adam here said."

"Get the serial numbers as proof that Adam paid for them. Or proof that she paid for them with Olivia's Social Security money," Julie said. "Which one of them is lying?" she asked Darlene. "You want to tell us where the money came from for your implants?"

Darlene struggled to breathe. "All right, all right!" Darlene screamed. "I used her money. Now, are you happy, you bitch?"

"Use the dull knife, Annie," Julie said in a voice so cold it could have chilled milk.

"If you say so. Makes me no never mind." She turned and hissed to Myra, "Avery is going to have a doctor on board when he gets here, right? We don't want her bleeding to death. I'll just saw along the scar under her breasts. It's going to hurt, so slap that tape over her mouth." Darlene went limp as Myra ripped at her off-the-shoulder peasant blouse and bra. The boys, who had momentarily returned from the garage, bolted outside. Adam Fortune's head rolled from side to side.

"Before you start, let me check with Charles or the boys. Don't start till we know they're here, Annie. As much as we hate these two, we absolutely do not want to kill them. That would make it much too easy on them."

"Okay," Annie cheerfully agreed, looking over at Julie, whose eyes were glazed over.

"I didn't know I was capable of ... of ... something like this," Julie whispered.

"That's what we all said, way back when. You'll get over it. It's the outcome that matters," Annie trilled as she hopped from one foot to the other in anticipation of the impending surgery.

Julie drew Annie to the side. "I don't think she's going to sign the papers. She's afraid of us, but, for some reason, I think she's more afraid of Adam. She has to sign them, Annie, she just does. Otherwise, I can't live with this."

"She'll sign them, Julie. Trust me. We have one more arrow in our quiver if she holds up under the fire hose."

"What's that?"

"The inimitable, indomitable Harry Wong." Annie smiled.

# Chapter 27

Annie flexed the steak knife in her hands while the boys worked with the nozzle of the fire hose. "We're good to go here," Bert shouted so that his voice carried out to the garage, where Espinosa relayed his message to Jack, who was fiddling with the fire hydrant.

Bert looked at the women and said, "We tested this out on the street. Espinosa filled a wheelbarrow with bricks and put it in the middle of the road. The pressure sent that baby clear across the road to the neighbor's yard. What's this chick weigh, one hundred and twenty or so?" he asked curiously. "This is just my opinion now, but I think we should move this skank out to the driveway and let her fly in whatever direction the water takes her."

"So what you're saying is, if we do it in here, the pressure will put her through the wall or maybe even through the glass on the sliding doors?" Myra asked.

"Yeah, pretty much, not to mention a flood of water in here."

"I guess that makes sense," Annie said. "But, let's take a break; this is very intense. Coffee anyone?"

"Absolutely!" Julie said.

In the kitchen, with the door to the family room closed, Annie made coffee.

"Darlene isn't looking so good," Myra said. "And Adam looks even worse. I can't believe she's holding out. What do you think, Julie?"

"I'm as amazed as you are. I thought she would have caved in when we used the blow-torch on Adam. Guilt is a terrible thing, and she's up to her ears in it. I think she'll ride it out to the end. Like I said, this is the end of the road for her, and after we're gone, she *thinks* she is going to still be here with him. He's all she has left, so she's going to do what he says no matter how bad she wants to sign the papers. He has a hold on her."

"I'm thinking the same thing. But, here's my question—do we really want to remove Darlene's implants? I think she's told us everything she knows. Right now, she hates Adam Fortune, but by the same token, she's tied to him in some way. So, listen up. Tell me what you think of this. We bring Harry in as I prepare to start . . . you know, surgery. I nick her, just enough to pop some blood, then Harry puts her out cold with one of his magic touches. While we're doing that, the boys can play with Fortune, give him a couple of midrange squirts with the hose to blow him back and forth across the street a few times so he gets the feel of it. Then we bring Harry in to finish up the intimidation," Annie said.

"Do you think that will work?" Myra sounded skeptical.

"I do, Myra, I really do. Julie, what do you think?"

"I think whatever works for you guys will work for me. She has to sign the papers in her own hand. That's all I care about."

The coffee was ready, but no one wanted any.

"Harry!" Annie bellowed.

Harry came on the run. Annie outlined the plan, and Harry agreed without any hesitation. "Hold on one minute while I relay this to Jack and Bert. We have to drag the hose back outside. Ted and Espinosa can carry Fortune in his chair out to the garage." The women nodded.

Harry was back in minutes. The foursome headed to the family room in time to see Ted and Espinosa carrying Fortune out to the garage.

"Okay, break's over. Time to operate," Annie said as she whirled the dull-looking steak knife through the air. She looked down at Darlene, who was white as new-fallen snow. "I'm sorry we don't have any anesthetic for you, because this is going to hurt. Oh, damn, that's a lie—I'm not one bit sorry. Don't bite your tongue off now, because I refuse to be responsible for that. What size do you think these are, Myra?" Annie asked as she pulled up one breast, which was as big as a melon. She dug the knife in and sliced. Blood spurted just as Harry's fingers clamped down on Darlene's neck.

"Quick, where's the bandage?" Julie slapped it on and held it in place.

"There's not all that much blood. You just cut the surface."

"Well, guess my work here is done," Annie said as she peeled off her latex gloves. "How long will she be out, Harry?"

"As long as you want her to be out. At the moment, I'd say at least an hour."

"Is Avery here yet?" Myra asked.

"He's out there, just arrived when I went out to the garage. He pulled his van into the garage. Ted and Espinosa settled Fortune in among the oleander bushes. So, are we ready for the water show?"

The three women scurried out to the garage. "I sure hope you're right, Julie, and these neighbors are gone. I'd hate for them to report a man taped to a chair flying through the air in a waterfall."

In spite of herself, Julie laughed.

In the driveway, Adam Fortune stared at the men holding the hose. He knew what it was going to do to him. His body wracked with pain, his head burning unbearably, Adam knew it was all over, and yet he couldn't do what these crazy people wanted him to do. Worse than the pain, worse than his guilt, what bothered him was the kid's words up in the bedroom earlier. Larry Wyatt had definitely spoken to her. There was no doubt in his mind.

Adam tensed when he saw the fire hose being pointed in his direction. What if the water killed him? What if he really died, and he had to face Larry and Audrey? He worked his tongue around his broken teeth, and an ugly sound escaped his battered lips. Like he was really going to go where they were.

And then he was sailing through the air, drenched in water. He closed his eyes as he and the chair he was strapped to landed in a nest of azalea bushes.

"He's alive!" Bert called out dramatically. "His eyelids are fluttering."

"Enough!" Harry roared as he raced over to the bushes and jerked Fortune forward in his chair. "Listen, you worthless piece of shit. We've had enough of you, and we just ran out of time, so here's the deal.

"I'm going to stick my fingers up your nose and pull your tongue through, then I'm going to push your eyeballs down so they come out your ears. It will take me exactly nineteen seconds to do it. Tell your girlfriend to sign the goddamned paper *NOW*, or your tongue will be hanging from your nose and your eyeballs will be dangling from your ears."

Fortune looked into Harry's eyes, and whatever he saw there convinced him that the man would do exactly what he said he would. "Take me inside, and I'll tell Darlene to sign the papers," he croaked.

"Now, that's a wise man if I ever saw one," Harry chortled happily.

"And, once again, Wizard Wong saves the day," Jack said. "Hey, Harry," he hissed. "Can you really do that?" Harry laughed in reply.

The party of nine watched as Darlene Wyatt signed her name again and again and again. Twice, Jack had to steady her arm so that her signature wouldn't be shaky. Annie and Myra had to hold Julie upright. Bert did his notary thing, then pressed the seal onto each paper Darlene signed. When Ted handed Julie the signed papers, her sigh of relief could be heard by all. Her eyes thanked them.

They all watched as Avery Snowden and his men settled Darlene Wyatt and Adam Fortune into the back of the medical van, their destination unknown. No one waved good-bye.

The moment the back doors of the van closed, the rest of them scrambled to clear the garage and the house. The garage doors closed with a loud bang. It took only minutes to tidy up the family room and disconnect the coffeepot. Ted turned off the main water valve, and Espinosa flipped the circuit breakers. Myra turned the refrigerator off. "I think we're good to go, ladies and gentlemen."

"I just want to go upstairs and get some of Ollie's things. Want to help me, ladies?"

"Sure," Annie and Myra said in unison.

"We'll meet you back at the house," Jack said, sensing this was a private time for the ladies.

Upstairs, Julie walked through the rooms. "This . . . this was Larry's room," she said quietly.

"Larry and Darlene had separate bedrooms. This is Ollie's room. Kind of bare, eh? I wonder why she left this picture of her mother and father behind," Julie said, picking up the picture on the night table. "I'm going to take it, since Ollie won't be coming back here."

"This is just a guess on my part, Julie, but I think that little girl wanted to leave it behind so Darlene could see it every day. I'm not sure she understood clearly that she would be leaving this house," Myra said gently. Julie nodded as she slipped the framed photograph into her purse.

"I think we have everything, not that there's all that much," Annie said, anger ringing in her voice.

Julie bit down on her lip. "I think we can go now. This chapter of my life is finally over. Maybe now I can . . ."

"Of course you can. Now you have a little girl to take care of and to love. We'll meet you downstairs, Julie," Annie said.

Julie, her eyes misty, walked down the hall to the room where her son had slept. She squeezed her eyes shut, but the tears escaped. "Right or wrong, Larry, I did it. I made her pay, and her boyfriend, too. I can't say I'm proud of my actions, but I'm not sorry. I promised to make it right, and I think I did that. This would be a good time for you to let me know you understand, even if you don't approve of what I've done."

Julie looked around as she waited for a sign from the spirit of her son. When nothing hap-

pened, she trudged to the door and closed it behind her.

Out in the hallway, Julie leaned up against
the wall as she poked in her purse for a tissue to
wipe her eyes. Blinded with her tears, she pulled
what she thought was a tissue from her purse,
only to realize it was a white feather. She blinked
away her tears, and smiled. "Okayyyyy, kiddo!"

The last time there were this many people on
her veranda had been the twins' thirtieth birthday, Julie thought.

Knowing that her guests' leave-taking was going to be traumatic for their mother, Connie
and Carrie had opted to take Ollie to the Rosemont Summer Festival. Ollie, they said, didn't
need to see any more sad faces. Julie agreed.

Now it was time to say good-bye to her new
friends. Julie knew there would be tears, lots of
tears, but they would be happy tears—up to a
point.

The boys were self-conscious, uncertain if they
should hug this new friend of theirs or shake
her hand. Julie solved the problem by hugging
each of them so tightly, they winced. When she
got to Harry, she bit down on her lip, doing her
best not to cry. "Don't say anything, Harry. I
know it's what Cooper wants. Ollie explained it
to me. He has an *important job* to do with you.
That's what her father told her, and that's good
enough for me. I just wish I knew what that job
was. It might make it easier."

For the first time in his life, Harry Wong was

totally speechless. He hated it when he couldn't understand things. "If I ever find out, I'll call you."

Julie nodded, her eyes miserable. "I never asked, Harry. What is your little girl's name?"

Harry smiled. "Lily Rose Carter Wong. Want to see a picture?" Even before Julie could nod, Harry whipped out a picture of his daughter. "We call her Lotus Lily. Don't ask me why."

Julie turned white and had to reach out for Myra's hand to steady herself. "Carter . . . that was my son's middle name. Lawrence Carter Wyatt. I guess we have our answer," she said, when she was finally able to draw a deep breath. "That's Cooper's job now, to take care of Lily Rose Carter Wong. Larry was always my *wise* one. I guess being on the *other side*, one can see things we mortals can't."

Julie hugged Cooper, tears rolling down her cheeks. The big dog wrapped his paws around her neck and licked her cheek.

*Woof.*

"Woof yourself. You take good care of Lily Rose Carter Wong, you hear me?"

*Woof.*

There were special hugs and whispers between the three ladies and promises made. And then all her new friends were gone, and Julie was alone on her veranda. She sat down on one of the rockers, leaned her head back, and closed her eyes.

*I love you, Mom.*

"I love you, too, kiddo."

# Epilogue

*Two weeks later*

Julie Wyatt looked down into the picnic basket to make sure she had everything she would need for a mid-September picnic and an apology to go with it. Something she should have done weeks ago. Satisfied that she had everything, she closed the lid of the picnic hamper and headed for the door. Gracie and Lola looked at her, then went back to tugging a pull toy. If they missed Cooper, it was hard to tell.

Twenty minutes later, Julie brought her truck to a stop in the driveway that led to Oliver Goldfeld's new house. She looked around at the utility trucks, the construction trucks, and the pickup trucks of the workers. She could hear men shouting orders, the sound of buzz saws and nail guns. She recognized quite a few of the workers as well as the foreman and waved to them as she carried her picnic basket toward the front of the house.

"Do you know where Mr. Goldfeld is?" she called out. One of the workers pointed toward the back of the house. Julie walked around to the back, being careful not to step on the piles of rotten wood and the stacks of new lumber. She called out his name. Then she blinked when she saw the herb garden. Now, instead of a tangle of weeds, she could actually see the plants.

Oliver stood up, his eyes wary.

"I came to apologize for the last time I was here. That wasn't a good time for me, and I want to explain; that's if you have the time to listen to me. I brought a picnic lunch as a bribe, in case you want to run me off your property." In an instant, when Oliver merely nodded, Julie knew that he wasn't going to give her an inch. "So, do you want to hear my story or not?"

"Sure, why not?"

Why not, indeed. "Well, first things first. I have to retain you, and I forgot my purse. Guess I left it in the truck when I took out the picnic hamper." Julie fumbled in the pocket of her jeans and found twenty-nine cents. "Will this do for the moment?"

Oliver reached for the coins and shoved them in his pocket. "It'll do," he said gruffly.

Julie cleared her throat. "Just so you know, this isn't easy for me. I never talk about my personal feelings or my personal business to people. I did share some things with Mace, and somehow he managed to ferret out the rest. I'll try to keep it short, but you need to know everything there is to know about me. Somewhere, somehow, things always manage to leak out, and I don't want you to be blindsided or think I lied to you."

Julie licked at her lips and went into her story. She was like a runaway train, the words, the emotions, tumbling out faster than she could control them. When the words stopped pouring out, she summed it up by saying, "So you were right, I'm not sugar and spice and everything nice. I'm just a human being who felt like her soul had been ripped out of her body. Don't get the idea that I'm apologizing here, because I'm not. Now, do you want to share this picnic, or do you want me to leave?"

"You know, I'm actually pretty damned hungry. Did you bring anything good? But I need to know one thing. Is this something we don't ever talk about again, or is it up for discussion?"

"It's standard picnic fare—fried chicken, old family recipe; potato salad, old family recipe; hard-boiled eggs, fresh this morning. Crusty bread and sweet tea. For now, I'd like it that you know my story, and if it ever needs to be addressed in the future, we can run it up the flagpole and deal with it then."

"Works for me," Oliver said, reaching for a chicken leg.

In between chewing and swallowing, Oliver and Julie discussed the work being done on his house, when it might be completed, how he liked sleeping in such chaos, and, of course, the garden, which was already taking shape.

When the last of the food was gone and the picnic hamper packed, Oliver said, "So what's your game plan?"

"Well, on Friday I have to do the interview the lottery commission demands, then they pay me this whopping big check. Then, I expect you will tell me what I have to do concerning my inheritance from Mace. You know I never expected that, nor do I want it, but I understand the legalities of it all.

"I have three major missions once trust funds are set up for my kids and their kids, should any materialize. And, of course, Ollie. I'm going to donate a good portion to the town of Rosemont. I'd like you to oversee that, Oliver, if you can. I want us to have the best police department, the best fire department, the best EMS unit in the state—in the country, if possible. I want to donate money to our hospital; I want it to be state-of-the-art. Everything and anything they need. And I don't want any of our citizens ever to be turned away. I want to use Mace's money to make sure everyone in this town gets the medicines they need.

"Then, I want to do something about rights for grandparents, not just in the state of Alabama, but nationwide. Grandparents have few rights if any. I want to go to Capitol Hill and plead our case. I don't care what it costs, I want to do it. I know I can get a groundswell going. I'll go through AARP and get all those wonderful seniors on board. They'll have to listen to us. I'll need your help on that, too.

"Just yesterday, I put down a deposit on fifty acres of land so I can build an animal sanctuary. I want that to be state-of-the-art, also. Fully staffed. No more animals will be put to sleep in this state if I can help it. I want to make sure that the drugs continue to flow to Doctors Without Borders, as much as they need. That was such a wonderful thing Mace did.

"My boys will be returning in a few months, and they'll help. Connie and Carrie are going to hire someone to operate their art school and come on board. We'll have a lot of help. I won't have all that much time, because I have a grand-daughter to raise.

"This weekend, she's having a sleepover. She's made some new friends, sweet little girls, and I think she's going to be okay. I've got her set up for Girl Scouts, piano lessons, girls' softball in the spring, camp with her friends in the summer, and a host of other things. I have to try and give her back the parts of her childhood she was denied. There's only one thing missing."

"What's that?" Oliver asked curiously.

"A grandfather. Ollie never had a grand-father. Do you want to volunteer, Oliver?"

"Well, yeah, that sounds nice."

"That means you dress up as Santa at Christ-mastime, you take Ollie and her friends to the roller rink at times or pick them up. Sometimes you take them to the movies or fishing out at the lake. You take them sled riding in the moun-tains. You get to watch while they ride."

"Oh. Will you be there?"

Julie laughed. "Try and keep me away! So, do we have a deal? I'd like to tell Ollie about it when I pick her up from school."

"I'd be honored to be Ollie's stand-in grandfather."

"In that case, you're invited to supper so you can meet your new granddaughter."

"And I accept," Oliver said, reaching for Julie's hands to bring her to her feet.

*Told you she was sugar and spice and everything nice.*

Oliver whirled around, then burst out laughing. "So sue me, big guy. Just because I'm a lawyer doesn't mean I'm always right."

"Did you say something, Oliver?" Julie called over her shoulder.

"In a manner of speaking. Careful, there, so you don't fall."

"Guess I'll see you tonight, then?"

"What's for dinner?" he asked boldly.

"Meat loaf, Mace's favorite. Roasted potatoes, the last of the garden string beans, and strawberry rhubarb pie, another of Mace's favorites. We eat at six."

"I'll be there," Oliver said, settling the hamper in the backseat of Julie's Blazer. "Thanks for the picnic and thanks for the retainer."

Julie laughed as she slipped the truck into gear and backed out the long driveway.

Life was so good, Julie started to sing. Not perfect, but almost perfect.

## *Recipe for Julie's Alabama Stuffed Peppers*

Start with six peppers. Use either yellow, orange or red. The green ones tend to be bitter.

1 pound ground chuck
1 pound ground turkey
1 egg
Salt and pepper to your taste
Handful of flat-leaf parsley
2 medium-size cloves of garlic

The only other ingredient you need is a one-pound can of Glen Muir fire-roasted crushed tomatoes.

Cut bottoms and tops of peppers off so pepper sits upright in roasting pan. Set bottoms aside.

In a chopper or food processor add the egg, garlic, the parsley and the bottoms of the peppers. Puree. It's important that you use the bottoms of the peppers to give a full-flavored taste to this dish.

Mix chuck and turkey thoroughly, add contents from food processor, salt and pepper to mixture. Make sure that you blend it all the way for an even taste. You need to work it with your hands.

Fill peppers. If you have any of the mixture left over, depending on the size of your peppers, form into balls and freeze until the next time you are ready to make the peppers. What could be easier than setting the frozen ball into the pepper? Cover tops of peppers with the lids you cut off.

Pour the fire-roasted crushed tomatoes over peppers. Again, depending on size of peppers, the size of the pan and your personal taste for the tomato sauce, you can use it all or freeze the rest.

Bake at 350 degrees for one hour and thirty minutes. I cover mine for the first hour with tin-foil and remove it for the last 30 minutes.

For more of Fern's delicious recipes from *Gotcha!*, please go to www.kensingtonbooks.com/fernmichaels or www.fernmichaels.com.

**Fern Michaels talks about how she created the Sisterhood series, and the long road to publication . . .**

Dear Readers,

When I found out that my publisher, Kensington Publishing, was going to reissue *Weekend Warriors*, the very first Sisterhood book, I got a severe attack of melancholy as I thought back to the beginning when *Weekend Warriors* was just an idea in the back of my mind. The idea at that moment in time was like trying to catch a firefly during the heat of summer. One minute I almost had it and then it would elude me. I kept trying to catch and latch onto the idea and make it work, but like that little firefly I guess it just wasn't time for me to catch it. I struggled with the concept; women forming a union (that's how I thought of it at the time) and righting all the wrongs of the universe. I told myself if I was going to think big then I needed to think not just big, but *BIG*.

The whole world (at least the women of the world) knows women are strong and can do whatever they set their minds to, especially a mother. By pep talking, I convinced myself a group of women like that could do *anything* they set their minds to. That's when I had to define the word *anything* and how I could make it work with the book I wanted to write. The minute I did that, it was a whole new ball game. In other words, I caught the firefly. Once the idea was firmly planted in my head, I let the firefly go. I watched it flit about just the way the ideas were flitting around inside my head. The ideas came so fast and furious I had trouble keeping it all straight. When I thought I had it down pat, I put pen to paper and drew up an outline and sent it off to one publisher after another. The whole process took three years out of my life in the late '90s. I can truthfully say the publishers were so unkind and brutal in their rejection of my idea I sat down and cried. After which I drank a whole bottle of wine to numb me to the brutal rejections. Even my agent at the time told me to get over it and go back to writing my "normal" books. Well, that was exactly the wrong thing to say to me at that point in time. Remember what I said earlier, women can do anything. I set out to prove him wrong. Bear in mind it was a male agent. He went the way of the firefly because if he couldn't believe in me, what was the point of continuing the relationship?

I've belonged to a small club of five women for over twenty years now. You know, best friends forever, that kind of thing. We meet up once a week for dinner, usually at my house and talk ourselves out. We do a lot of moaning and groaning, grumbling and complaining about life, friends, what's going on in our lives, and how we wish we could wave a magic wand and make things right. We all have fertile imaginations, and at times we can go off the rails, saying if only we could do this or that, make this right, send this one to Outer Mongolia never to be seen or heard of again . . . if only. I can't be one hundred percent certain, but I think that's where the seed was planted to write about a group of women trying to right the wrongs of the world.

We all know what it's like to have to fall back and regroup, and that's what I did after all those rejections. Nine in all. The negative words ricocheted around and around in my head. *The reading world is not ready for this kind of book. Your regular readers will drop you and move on. Maybe sometime in the future the women who buy your books will be ready for something like this, but now is not the time.* Here's the one I liked the best, or should I say the least: *You will absolutely throw your career down the drain with this type of book.* I admit I was wounded to the quick, but then I remembered when I first started to write I sent one of my endeavors to the famous author Phillis Whitney, who was my idol at the time. She sent me back a note and told me not to quit my day job. I thought that was kind of funny since I didn't have a day job. I was just a wife and mother trying to be a writer at the time. I didn't quit then, and I wasn't about to quit now.

I told myself I needed to be smarter in presenting my idea, and enlist the aid of true professionals. And who better than my little dinner club, savvy women friends who would understand what I was trying to do and who would support my efforts. Remember now, women can do anything they put their minds to. So with that thought I called for dinner at my house, and a sleepover. The reason for the sleepover was the wine we were going to drink, which by the way we never drank because when I explained what I wanted we all agreed we needed clear heads. We were all so high on just the ideas we didn't need wine. But we did drink at least three gallons of coffee and never did go to sleep. I served breakfast. I have to say I never spent a more enjoyable, wonderful twelve hours in my life.

My own little sisterhood numbers five. Diane, Beverly, Susy, Stephanie, and myself. Back then, in the year 2000 when I seriously went tooth and nail trying to write the Sisterhood, we met up once a week, sometimes twice, at my house because I had more time to cook. Not that they couldn't cook, but they held outside jobs, whereas I worked at home and they would come straight here from work. We filled my dining room with charts, sticky notes hung from the chandelier, my fireplace was festooned with pictures and more sticky notes. There were corkboards everywhere. My dining room was where we plotted and schemed and wreaked vengeance as I struggled to bring to life the Sisterhood. Susy came up with the word vigilantes and we ran with it. It opened up a whole new stream of do's and don'ts. Female vigilantes! Boy, was that a whole new world to come to terms with, but I have to say, we were up to the task.

My day lady was very unhappy with what she called "the mess" in the dining room. She speaks fluent English, but when she's upset or excited she mumbles and mutters in Portuguese as she points to the mess in the dining room. Finally, I asked her what she was saying. She just looked at the mess, then at me, and pointed to the sticky notes decorating the dining room and said, "Kill the bastards!"

Whoa!

Another emergency meeting was called where we agreed that the vigilantes would not kill anyone. But, as Beverly put it, there's no reason you can't make the villain wish he or she was dead. That certainly worked for me and the girls, and my day lady was satisfied but not happy with that decision, or with the chaos in my dining room that wasn't going to go away any time soon. I'd chosen my dining room for our meetings, not that I don't have an office, I do, but the dining room is close to the kitchen where the food, the wine, and the coffeepot are. It was a question of priorities. The bottom line was anything goes, but the vigilantes stop at outright murder. Another sticky note on the chandelier.

I spent weeks and weeks developing the characters for the Sisterhood. Each one had to be just perfect for their continuing role that was to play out in what I thought at the time was going to be a series of seven books. Seven books, seven dedicated characters, and seven cases to bring to justice, vigilante style. Developing believable characters turned out to be harder to create than I thought. I called a meeting where we did a lot of snapping and snarling at one another. In the end I made my seven main characters composites of the five of us, with a few traits thrown in from other unsuspecting friends. For instance, Kathryn Lucas was patterned after Beverly. In the writing, I would find myself calling Beverly and asking if she would do this or that, or did she have a better idea. Her response was always the same: "Yes, I'd do that, and you nailed it." In case you're wondering who Myra and Annie are, that would be me, but you all probably already figured that out according to your many e-mails.

Isabelle Flanders resembles Stephanie. She (Isabelle) has visions, as does Stephanie. Actually, Stephanie scares me sometimes with the things she *sees*.

Nikki was patterned after my daughter Cynthia. Cynthia was not part of my little group because she said we were all nuts. She always showed up for dessert, however. Oh, my, did she come in for a lot of ribbing when the first book came out. Both Nikki and Cynthia are smart, savvy, and know how to stay focused.

Alexis turned out to be an extension of Diane. She's creative, and can make anything work given time. Always the voice of reason.

Yoko had me stumped for a while. I couldn't find a live person that had any of the traits I'd given Yoko, who I think grew and grew into the character she ultimately became. Finally one day when I was about to give up, I met my creation at my grandson's "Mother/Grandmother" day at his school. While we waited for the program to start, one of the other grandmothers and I talked. She told me what it was like growing up in China and how hard she had to work, how she learned martial arts, showed me the callouses on the bottoms of her feet and her hands. I don't know where I got the nerve, but I asked her if she'd ever killed anyone and she said, "many times." She did clarify that by saying she did it only in her quest for freedom. I thought about inviting her to the Barbed Wire to meet my friends, but I squelched that thought real quick. Yoko was born that day.

Cosmo Cricket was created from scratch, as was lawyer Lizzie Fox, or as the gals called her, The Silver Fox. Lizzie was also a pure creation. Beautiful, smart, sexy, witty, and she controls the courtroom, not the judge or the prosecution. And at heart she is a true vigilante. If I ever come back in another life, I want to be Lizzie Fox or my old dog Fred. Such a choice.

Introducing and creating the male characters proved a little more difficult. Mainly because they were introduced one at a time and over many books. Again, they turned out to be composites of our kids, our brothers, and just people we interact with on a daily basis. Take Harry Wong for instance, who is one of my personal favorite characters. My grandson went for martial arts instruction years ago and his Master was a real character, as was his assistant. Months and months of picking Master Choo's brain finally brought the comment, "Are you writing a book?" Well, yeah, I am. You okay with that? Like Harry, Master Choo is a man of few words. All he said was, "Okay, make me look good." I think I did that. Readers have written me tons of letters saying they love Harry. No more than I do. Jack Emery is almost one hundred percent my UPS delivery guy. Someday I'm going to tell him, but not yet.

Ted Robinson and Joseph Espinosa are products of my imagination and made up of whole cloth.

I cloned Maggie Spitzer from an American waitress at a Japanese restaurant I go to. Like Mr. Choo, I picked her brain over time. She also told me to make her look good.

With the character situation down pat it was time to move on to plots. I needed seven plots to fit each of the seven characters. Armed with the thought, and what we felt was the knowledge, that the woman hasn't been born who didn't want to get even with someone for something or other, I went at it. We kicked it around for WEEKS with each of us asking friends and acquaintances who they would like to get even with and what they would like to see as a satisfying punishment. I think it's safe to say that between us we spoke to over a thousand women. Right here and now I want to say that considering my age, I thought I had seen and heard it all, and there was nothing out there that could surprise me. Ha! Was I ever wrong, as were my friends. I will also admit a few times I turned a little green at what some of those women we spoke to wanted done. Bet you'll never guess who had the best punishment ever for one of the characters. Renata, my day lady who has been with me for twenty-eight years, that's who. Who knew? I ran with it. Several years later it was a best seller. Renata bought fourteen copies to give out to her friends. That's in addition to the dozen I gave her.

Now it was time to actually sit down and write

the book. And I wrote it on spec. That means
without a contract in the hopes of selling it.
Writing fiction (that means I make up stuff) is
like having a free Go Past Go card. You can write
pretty much whatever you want, burn down a
building, maim or kill a character, you can create love, hate, payback. You can create fictional
places that over time actually become real to
you the writer, and also to the reader. For exam-
ple, Pinewood, where the vigilantes hang out, is
a fictional farm in McLean, Virginia. You can
make people rich or poor. I can say Countess
Anna de Silva is one of the richest women in the
world simply because I say so between the pages
of a book. I can give a character a scorched
earth personality if I want, or I can make them
sweet as honey. It's great fun. But it's how you
tie it all together as a whole that makes the story
work.

Finally the day came when I was ready to type
the first page of *Weekend Warriors*. I wish I could
say something meaningful, like it was a dark and
stormy night, or it was a beach day with marshmallow clouds and blue skies. The truth is, all I
remember was it was a Monday morning, and I
know this because I always start a project, no
matter what it is, on Mondays. It took me a year
to write the book. I had one setback. My husband passed away in May of that year. I didn't
write for a while, but in the end it was the writing that got me back on track. I wrote and wrote
and wrote. Then I rewrote, at least a dozen different drafts that I printed out and passed

around to my friends for them to critique, and critique they did. When we were all satisfied that it was as good as it was going to get, I packaged it up and sent it to my publisher. We all went to the post office to mail it. I remember it cost $7.67 to mail it. Somewhere I still have the receipt, because I wanted that memory for some reason.

I took the gang to a place called the Barbed Wire where we ordered steaks and beer by the pitcher. I had to call my son to come and drive us home. My friends and I finally had our long overdue sleepover. *And* a hangover the next morning.

The next two weeks were two of the worst weeks of my life. All I did was answer the phone, calls from the gang asking if I'd heard anything. The answer was always the same, "No!"

Finally the call came. I was trying to unclog the garbage disposal and almost didn't answer it, but caught it on the sixth ring. It was my editor at the time who has since retired, telling me that Walter and she would be coming to Charleston the following week to discuss my submission. Walter was Walter Zacharius, the founder and owner of Kensington Publishing. Walter was my boss, and my friend. I want to say right here and now that I absolutely adored that man. He saw me through some bad times, the death of my husband, and then the death of my youngest daughter a few years later. Just talking to him made things right somehow. In my heart of hearts I knew I would have to abide by whatever his decision was because I respected his opinion. I'm sad to say he has since passed away and I miss him terribly.

I never did fix the garbage disposal. I had to call a plumber.

I called the girls. We went to the Barbed Wired again. We ate but passed on the beer this time around and got home under our own power. Talk about beating a dead horse. Why was Walter coming here? To tell me no way, no how would the book fly? To tell me he loved it and wanted to sign me up for all seven books? We were all a nervous wreck. The days crawled by. And then the day of the meeting finally arrived. I was early because I was about to crawl out of my skin.

Flash forward forty minutes, after the amenities, and Walter said, "It won't work. It's too over the top, too out of the box."

"It will work. Give it a chance. Can't you trust me when I tell you it will work? If you get behind it . . ."

We argued back and forth till I was about ready to cry. Then I looked at my editor who up to this point hadn't said a word. She winked at me. *WINKED?*

Walter the businessman, and not my friend at the moment, said, "Tone it down."

"NO! If I take out what you're referring to, it's not the same book. It will work."

"Tell me why it will work."

Ahhhh, I thought I had him right there. "Because, Walter, the woman hasn't been born yet who doesn't have someone she wants to get even with. That's why. The more daring, the more over the top, the more reason it will work. I know I'm right. I did my homework, I talked to hundreds of women. It will work. Just so you know, Walter, I'm not giving up."

"Okay. We'll do it." Well damn! Just like that, we'll do it! I was over the moon.

To be honest, I don't remember what happened after that. I remember what happened the next day, though. Walter came to Summerville where I live and we sat on my veranda and drank mint juleps. We talked for hours until it was time for him to leave for the airport. I walked him out to the car and he hugged me and said he'd snatch me bald-headed if it didn't work.

Ooooh.

But it did work. You know how I know that? Because I'm writing this and you're reading it.

Before I end this letter, I would like to share one more thing with you all. It is my opinion that most writers, if asked, will say there is one thing or another that lets them know what they're working on will either work or not work. It could be a whole chapter or perhaps just a scene or a scenario, it really doesn't matter. With me that thing is my dogs. I run everything by them. I have four dogs, two golden retrievers, Jam and Jelly (95 pounds each). Then there is Lucy Red (65 pounds) who is a rescue hound dog, and last but not least, there is Charlie, a Yorkie (12 pounds). He's the boss. I whistle, tell them all to line up and they do it. Then I read what I wrote. If they don't go to sleep, that means it works. If they lie down, I have to scratch what I wrote. I'm serious here; I'm not kidding. When they don't approve, they don't get a treat, so you can see they're spot on. My dogs are very smart. (Every dog owner says that, just so you know.) But, Jam and Jelly can buckle up their seat belts. Jelly knows how to lock the kitchen door. Jam is the bigger of the two, she knows how to ring the doorbell, which is too high for Jelly to reach. Lucy knows how to open the refrigerator. She does that four or five times a day. I think she just does that to feel the cold air on her face. That's her only trick. Charlie is so smart he doesn't have to do anything. He knows to the minute when it's time to eat. He knows to the second when it's time to go outside. He heads for the bedroom before I can get out of my chair at 10:57. He is never off by more than a minute. So, readers, when you read one of my books, know that four of the most important creatures in my life have given their seal of approval.

At this moment I would like to thank all you readers who bought the Sisterhood series, then wrote me to tell me how much you loved it. I want to thank my own vigilantes, my kids for encouraging me, and of course Walter, because without Walter and all his staff I wouldn't have published *Weekend Warriors*, let alone been given the opportunity to write and publish twenty more books in the series.

Thanks, Walter, and thanks to all the wonderful people at Kensington who were there for me every step of the way, believing in me and taking a chance on my ability to create the Sisterhood series and making it work.

Warmest wishes,

*Fern Michaels*

must face the Sisterhood and answer for her crimes.

## 6. Lethal Justice
Alexis Thorn spent a year behind bars for a crime she never committed, but the time has come for the Sisterhood to seek revenge on those truly responsible.

## 7. Free Fall
Things turn personal when the women of the Sisterhood set their sights on a brutish man who terrorized Yoko Akia's mother years ago.

## 8. Hide and Seek
The Sisterhood's last assignment almost landed them in jail, but even as fugitives with a bounty on their heads, they plan to take down a culprit who is no less than the assistant director of the FBI.

## 9. Hokus Pokus
Beseeched by Chief Justice of the Supreme Court Pearl Barnes into helping her combat a blackmail scheme, the exiled Sisterhood must find a way to sneak back into the United States undetected.

## 10. Fast Track
The Sisterhood's mentor, Charles Martin, aids the women in tackling the corrupt president of the World Bank in one of their most dangerous—and rewarding—missions to date.

### 11. *Collateral Damage*
The group is torn between accepting two different missions, one of which may come with a presidential pardon and the chance to emerge from hiding.

### 12. *Final Justice*
A close friend of Annie Sullivan and Myra's tasks them with finding her missing daughter, which brings them to Sin City and up against some of the most powerful people in Vegas.

### 13. *Under the Radar*
Myra and Charles are called away, leaving the remaining members of the Sisterhood to take down a sinister cult and rescue its exploited and pregnant teenage girls.

### 14. *Razor Sharp*
Attorney and valued friend of the Sisters, Lizzie Fox, has a new client being targeted by Washington power players, and the only way she can protect her is with the Sisterhood's help.

### 15. *Vanishing Act*
Yoko's husband, Harry Wong, becomes the victim of a ruthless identity-theft ring, but it will take all of the members of the group and their complete bag of tricks to set things right.

### 16. *Deadly Deals*
When adopted twins are snatched from their loving parents, Lizzie seeks the Sisterhood's help

in returning the children and punishing the evil "baby broker" lawyer responsible.

### 17. Game Over
The group's dear ally, Lizzie, is up for a spot on the Supreme Court but it will take a masterful plan to protect her from the nasty approval process and being tainted by her association with the Sisterhood.

### 18. Cross Roads
Nikki and Kathryn's private jet is hijacked, but their captors are actually Interpol agents with an exciting new assignment for the recently pardoned Sisterhood.

### 19. Déjà Vu
The Sisterhood is reunited in Las Vegas to celebrate Kathryn's birthday, but the president of the United States has other ideas: it's time to take down Public Enemy #1, a/k/a Hank Jellicoe.

### 20. Home Free
After years of successful missions, the president has formed a new organization allowing the Sisterhood to operate legally but secretly. More empowered than ever before, Myra, Annie, Kathryn, Alexis, Nikki, Yoko, and Isabelle once more answer the call for justice.

### 21. Gotcha!
The long-awaited return of the Sensational Sisterhood!

They're back!
The Godmothers return in Fern Michaels's
brand-new novel:


# CLASSIFIED.


Read on for a special excerpt.

A Kensington trade paperback on
sale in October 2013!

Having tossed and turned for the past hour, Abby finally rolled over and looked at the alarm clock. It was 3:00 AM, the witching hour. Chris had fallen asleep on the sofa downstairs in the formal dining room. She didn't have the heart to wake him. She knew by the time he walked upstairs and showered, he would be wide-awake, and it would take hours for him to get back to sleep. He'd spent fourteen hours today stripping the wood floor in the dining room—back-breaking and exhausting work. He was sitting on the sofa when Abby went to the kitchen for iced tea. When she returned, Chris was sound asleep. She covered him with a light throw and decided to go upstairs alone.

Unable to sleep without Chris by her side, she switched the lamp on. A swatch of fabrics for the new drapes she wanted to order was lying on the night table. She picked it up, felt the different textures, examined the colors, feeling unsure. While she didn't want something dark and heavy, she didn't want something so light you could see through it. What she needed was something in between, yet something that stayed true to the Clay Plantation decor. Her mother had advised her and had spent many, many hours with her, going over the long history of the plantation, for she, too, had lived here for a short period of time when she was married to Garland, Chris's father. There were old pictures of the many rooms, but they were so faded she could not even begin to guess what kind of fabric had been used to decorate them. One thing Abby knew for sure, she had to get rid of the heavy dark green velvet drapes. They reminded her of *The Carol Burnett Show* parody scene of Margaret Mitchell's *Gone With the Wind*, which she'd watched late one night on TV. Carol Burnett, playing Scarlett O'Hara, had ripped the heavy drapes from the window and worn them as her new dress, hoping to impress Rhett Butler, who had just returned from fighting in the Civil War. Abby had laughed until she cried, but the drapes had to go. They were just plain ugly.

Not seeing any fabric or color that caught her eye, she found the remote and channel-surfed for ten minutes. When none of the television programs captured her attention, she turned the TV off. She flipped through the latest edition of

*The Informer.* Josh was doing an excellent job, but the stories didn't capture her attention, as they once had. Frankly, she thought they were silly and a waste of time. Why the sudden change of heart? She'd almost died because of that paper and that total idiot, Rodwell Archibald Godfrey—behind his back, they referred to him as Rag. He'd kidnapped her, locked her in a tiny closet, tied to a chair, while he waited for his ransom money to be delivered. As it turned out, her mother was the owner of *The Informer,* something that was unknown to her at the time. Clearly, Rag was also unaware of that minor factoid. It had been a horrifying experience for everyone, as well as one of the principal reasons she and Chris had moved to Charleston.

Now, for the past month, she'd been having trouble sleeping, only to be completely wiped out during the day. She thought of going downstairs to the kitchen to warm up a glass of milk, but she didn't want to risk waking Chris. He'd worked so hard, and their new venture required his legal skills, making sure all their documents and contracts were legal. But he continued to tell her he wanted to be a farmer, and she now believed him. She remembered his telling her this when they had lived in Los Angeles, but she hadn't believed him then. Of course, they had only been friends at the time. And he was her stepbrother, but not in a gross way. Her mother and Garland were married for a short period of time; Chris had been away at college; she'd been a teenager, spending time with her girlfriends, shopping, going to the movies, gabbing. Before she knew it, Garland had passed away. She and her mother, whom everyone called Toots, had moved into the house, which her mother would share many years later with Abby's three godmothers.

Finally Abby started to get drowsy, and she turned out the light and curled up beneath the sheets. She drifted off to sleep quickly.

*Octavia knew her time was coming soon, but prayed she would have a few more weeks left before she had to tell Mr. Clayton. He'd been sending for her since she'd been thirteen years old. She's tired, so tired, and it ain't even half day gone. Her belly hurts, an' her feets swollen, but she cain't stop 'cause there's so much work to do. She hates workin' in the big house. Ever' day she tries to upset the Missus in hopes she'd send her back to the field with her momma and sisters, but she says she be a "special" girl, and Octavia doesn't know what she mean by that. She dropped a fancy china plate yesterday, an' the Missus just tell her to clean up the mess, but Octavia might only be fourteen and three months, but she know the Missus knows she's with child. She seen her lookin' at her belly, she watches her, an' Octavia is scared, but not so scared that she's gonna stop tryin' to get back to her home with Momma. The little cabin ain't too big, but it be better than some other plantations have. They got real wooden plank floors, an' their house is made of the same bricks Mr. Clayton's got. They got a real fireplace, too. The beds is straw, an' the coverin's plenty soft, 'cause Momma cleaned them an' rinsed them in hot water, an' she put dried magnolias in the straw so's they'd smell good, too. Her back is hurtin' real bad, and she knows this ain't suppose to happen now. Her belly ain't big enough yet. How she wishes she could slip away to see Momma. She'd know what was ailin' her, an' what to do.*

*Octavia is gonna go see her momma tonight. After the Missus and Mr. Clayton go to sleep, she'll slip out through the kitchen door. Soon as she finishes her duties, she'll go. She hopes Mr. Clayton doesn't want to visit her tonight. She hates him. He crawls on top of her like she's an animal. Them sounds he make scare her, too. His breath is hot, and smells of tobacco. No, he'd been to see her last night. Maybe Telly would get a visit tonight. Telly was only twelve and four months. Octavia felt sorry for her, but she couldn't stop Mr. Clayton from crawlin' on top o' her any more than she could stop him from crawlin' on herself. She prays every night that he would die. She knows it's wrong to pray for bad things, but Mr. Clayton is a mean, bad man. He likes to use the whip on the men workin' in the fields. Her daddy had thick, ropy scars on his back and arms from Mr. Clayton's whip. Momma would cry when she see them. She'd rub lard on his wounds an' make a poultice that stunk to high heaven, but Daddy said it helped the cuts heal faster. Octavia knows as soon as he be healed, Mr. Clayton will rip him open again. And Mr. Clayton will laugh. She hates him, an' she hates the baby in her belly. A sharp pain rips through her back. She grabs the kitchen chair to keep from keelin' over. She takes a deep breath, an' the pain eases up. As soon as the pain's gone, she turns to head upstairs to turn down the beds, an' another pain hits her in the belly. She falls to her knees, pressing her hands against her, thinkin' this will stop the pain. Sharp, searing pain in her back comes again. Tears fill her eyes, an' she bites the sides of her mouth to keep from screamin' out.*

*In the midst of her pain, she calls out, "Momma, I need you. Please, Momma, help me." Takin' a deep breath, she lets it out slowly, thinkin' her pain's all gone, when she feels another pain, this one worse than ever. She wants to push hard like she has to go to the bathroom, but she cain't. Rolling on her back, she puts both legs against the chair legs. She don't care no more. She pushes and screams. An' she pushes again. This time she feels like her woman part is tearin' in half. She screams again, not carin' if Mr. Clayton or the Missus hears her. She really hates him now and begs God to make him dead right now! She prays for his death and prays for her own as she gets hit with another sharp pain, hot like a kitchen knife got stuck in her belly. She bears down again, this time so hard she feels the veins in her head an' neck gettin' so big.*

*Another push, an' she feels something warm and damp between her legs. She tries to push herself up with her elbows so she can see. Another pain, and she screams and screams and screams. Again, she feels something warm and wet between her legs, something heavy. Her body gots sweat ever' place. She tries to push herself up, when she hears a soft sound, like a baby cryin'. She struggles to see what lies between her legs an' sees a baby, but it ain't right. It's got an arm missin'.*

*"The devil!" she cries out. She'd just given birth to Mr. Clayton's devil.*

*No!!!*

\*   \*   \*

Abby bolted upright in the bed. Trembling, she turned the light on. Chris ran into the room. "Are you okay?" He cradled her in his arms. "I heard you screaming."

"Oh, Chris, I had a terrible nightmare. My God, it seemed so real." Abby pushed herself up in the bed and leaned against the headboard.

Chris cradled her against his chest. "Want to tell me about it?"

Abby took a deep breath. "There was this girl, a young girl. She was . . . she was a slave. In the dream, she was scared and so alone. She kept calling for her mother. It was so sad."

She stopped. Something in the dream was so familiar, tugging at the back of her mind, but she couldn't place exactly what it was. "She was having a baby! Alone. She was all alone! Chris, there is something in the dream that I should know, something I've actually seen, but I can't pull it up." Abby wrapped her arm around Chris's waist. "Sorry I woke you."

"Hey, I'm glad you did. That sofa is not meant to sleep on. Why didn't you wake me up?"

"You looked exhausted, and I knew that if I woke you, once you showered, you'd be wide-awake, so I let you sleep."

"And here you are in bed without me for the first time since we've been married, and you had a nightmare. What does that tell you?"

"Not to go to bed without you?"

"Yep. Now, since I'm up anyway, I'm going to take a shower. You want to join me?" Chris nuzzled her ear.

She gave a half laugh. "Not now, sorry." She

glanced at the bedside clock. It was almost five o'clock. "I tell you what. Why don't you get your shower, and while you're doing that, I can make us some breakfast. I won't be able to go back to sleep anyway. If I get tired during the day, I'll have a nap."

Chris kissed her cheek and ruffled her hair. "You've got yourself a deal, Mrs. Clay."

As soon as Chris said "Mrs. Clay," she stopped midthought. "Chris, wait. Listen, I know this is . . . strange, but has this place always been called Clay Plantation?"

Standing at the chest of drawers, Chris pulled a pair of boxers out of the top drawer. "Good question. Why would you ask something like that?"

She didn't know, but she somehow knew it was important for her to find out. It was the dream. The man in the dream. The man the young woman hated, the man she wanted to die. "Just tell me, has the plantation always been referred to as the Clay Plantation?"

"To the best of my knowledge, it has, but then again, it's been around a few hundred years. It's possible that it had a different name at some point before the Clays owned it. Is it important?"

Abby's reporter instincts were at play. Instincts she'd scoffed at earlier. "I'm not sure. It's something in the dream. I don't know."

"Well, don't worry your pretty little head off. Now, woman, get your little rear end downstairs and fix that breakfast you promised me."

Abby grabbed her robe off the foot of the

bed, careful not to wake Chester, who was still sound asleep at the foot of the bed. "Some guard dog you are," she said as she walked out of the room.

Downstairs in the kitchen, Abby started a pot of coffee. Her mind kept straying back to her dream, and it was silly. *Damn, Abby, it was simply a dream. Weird? Yes. Strange? Yes.* She opened the refrigerator. "What to make?" she asked herself aloud.

"Ruff!" Chester gave his low-sounding morning growl.

"You want some grub, old boy?"

Chester walked over and stood by his dog bowl. Abby had chicken breasts left over. She chopped half of one, threw it in the microwave for a few seconds to get the chill off, then scooped the chunks of chicken into his bowl. Mavis had started doing this for Coco and Frankie. Chester had been over a few times and received the same meal. Now Abby had to bribe him with chicken breasts just to get him to eat his dog food. "You are so spoiled," Abby said, leaning over and rubbing him between the ears.

She grabbed a carton of eggs, a chunk of bacon, and a can of buttermilk biscuits out of the refrigerator. Usually, she loved the smell of coffee, but for some reason it gagged her now. She would swear she smelled a chemical smell coming from the pot. She lifted the carafe up to her nose. "Yuck." She took a chamomile tea bag out of the canister, filled a mug with water, and popped it in the microwave. She usually loved her coffee, but not today. She felt shitty, like she was coming down with the flu. The last thing she needed now. With all that she and Chris had going on, she didn't have time to get sick.

Hurrying now, she removed a skillet from the cupboard, turned on the stove, and tossed several strips of bacon in as soon as the skillet was hot. She cracked half-a-dozen eggs into a bowl, added a splash of milk, and then, with a wire whisk, beat the mixture until the yolks were no longer in evidence. She'd seen this technique used on some cooking show, with the chef saying that the eggs would be much fluffier. It worked, so she'd been using it ever since. She heated another skillet, dropping in a tiny bit of butter. She stared as it sizzled and turned a creamy light brown. She poured the egg mixture into the skillet, then remembered the biscuits. "Oh, the hell with it. We can have toast." She took the can of biscuits and put them back in the fridge.

Chester ran through the doggie door, scaring her. "Darn, boy, you scared the bejesus out of me." She hadn't even heard him go out.

"Hey, I thought you'd have the table all set with the fine china and cloth napkins. What's this?" Chris asked. He came up behind her, wrapping his arms around her waist.

"You smell good. And you're lucky I'm making your breakfast. Don't get used to it, either, because I promise not to make this a habit. If my memory serves me correctly, you used to exist on mint chocolate-chip ice cream."

Chris kissed her head, then poured a cup of

coffee for himself. "You're not having your coffee?"

"It smells weird to me. I'm having tea." She removed her mug from the microwave and dropped the tea bag in the hot water. "Does it taste okay?"

Chris took a sip. "Excellent."

"You can't smell that chemical smell? Like iron or something?" Abby asked as she stirred the eggs, then removed the bacon and placed it on a paper towel to drain.

"You're imagining things, Abs. This is perfectly fine. If it weren't, I wouldn't drink it."

She just nodded and set about finishing breakfast. She took two slices of wheat bread, put them in the toaster, then removed the eggs from the pan. She dabbed at the bacon with another paper towel, put four slices on Chris's plate, together with most of the eggs, just as the toast popped up. "Good timing, if I say so myself."

Abby put Chris's plate in front of him. "Remember, do not get used to this."

She took her mug of tea to the table and sat across from him. Chris dug into the food like he hadn't eaten in weeks. She smiled. She loved this man.

"How come you're not having anything?" he asked between bites. "You think the food smells weird, too?"

"No, I'm not hungry. Must be coming down with the flu or something. I can't seem to shake this."

"You need to rest."

"Yeah, well, tell that to . . ." She wanted to say "that poor girl in my dream," but she didn't. Still, she couldn't shake the dream. There was something about the man in the dream. The girl kept calling him something. . . . *Mr. Clayton!* She'd called him Mr. Clayton in the dream.

"Chris, are you sure this place didn't go by another name?" she asked again.

"Not that I can remember. When you live in one of these old places as a kid, it's almost an embarrassment. I remember thinking, when I was a kid, why couldn't I live in one of those McMansions that all my friends lived in? Of course, I was too stupid to realize the history, and too young to appreciate it. Why don't you ask your mother? She lived here, too. She might know."

Abby brightened. Of course. Why hadn't she thought of that? "You're a genius. Thanks." She took her tea into the living room. Her mother was an early riser. She glanced at the big grandfather clock. It was ten to six. Her mother was up. She grabbed the portable phone and took it back into the kitchen. They were going to get a phone installed in the kitchen, if it was the last thing she did. The house was old, but there had been many updates throughout the years. Unfortunately, a phone jack was not one of them.

She sat back down at the table. Chris took his plate, rinsed it, then put it in the dishwasher. He refilled his cup and came back to the table. "You going to call Tootsie?"

"Yes." She punched in her mother's number.

"Abby Simpson-Clay, what are you doing up so early?" her mother asked. No "hello."

*Caller ID is killing the pranksters,* Abby thought.

"Well, I just finished making breakfast for my adoring husband. I couldn't sleep, so I got up early, and Chris was up, so here we are. Mom, listen, I know this is going to sound odd, but do you recall the Clay Plantation being called something else? I'm talking way back in the day, when those slave quarters were in use."

"Let me think a minute. Hmm, I don't really know. I have some of Garland's papers stored away in a box somewhere. Seems like there were several documents that were connected to the plantation. Why do you want to know? You're not thinking of changing the name, are you?"

"No, nothing like that." Abby wasn't sure if she wanted to tell her mother about the dream just yet. It kept clinging to her; it was as though she were supposed to remember something from the dream for a reason. She just didn't know what it was.

"I can look for that box, if it will help."

"Thanks, Mom. Would you mind if Chester and I came over and looked through it with you? He's needing a doggie love fix anyway. And I'm sure Coco and Frankie could use a Chester fix."

"Come on over. We're on our third pot of coffee. I'll make a fresh pot for you."

"No, Mom, really, I'm drinking tea today. I think I have a bug, and coffee isn't agreeing with me right now. I'll be over in half an hour."

"Okay, dear."

"So, what did Tootsie have to say?"

"She didn't know, but she has a box of your

dad's things at her house. She said she thought there might be some papers in there connected to the plantation. I'm going to take a look and see if there is anything in there. Chester, do you want to take an early-morning walk to see Coco?" Hearing the magic word *Coco,* the shepherd rushed out through the doggie door.

"I take it that means yes," Abby said. "You want to come with us?"

"No, I better pass. I'm expecting an early phone call. You go on, tell everyone 'hi' for me. I'll see you when you return."

Abby wrapped her arms around him, then stood on her tiptoes in order to reach his mouth. She planted a sloppy kiss on his lips. "I've got to dress now, Mr. Clay. I told Mother I'd be there in thirty minutes. She probably started a stopwatch the second I hung up the phone."

"Go on, woman, I'll be here waiting with bated breath."

Abby raced upstairs and grabbed a pair of yoga pants and a T-shirt. She crammed her feet into her sneakers. In the master bath, she washed her face and brushed her teeth. She looked at the mass of curls and balled her hair into a knot, securing it with a couple of bobby pins.

She raced down the stairs and out the back door. Chester was waiting at the gate. If she hurried, her mother's house was a ten-minute walk. She needed the exercise. Her clothes were starting to feel a bit too tight. *It's all this Southern cooking,* she thought.

Chester raced ahead, then stopped, waiting

for her to catch up with him. "Smartest dog in the world, aren't you?"

Ten minutes later, she was at her mother's house. She tapped on the back door so as not to startle her or whoever was in the kitchen at this hour.

"Abby, Chester, I'm glad you came over. I needed a daughter fix."

Chester saw Coco and Frankie in their corner and took off. "He's happy, that's for sure. He needed a Coco fix, too. Did you find the box?"

"Right there." Toots pointed to a large plastic carton. "Some of those documents are very old. You should probably take them and have them preserved. The historical society will help you with it."

Abby dragged the box over to the table. Sitting in the chair, she removed the lid on the box. A musty odor assaulted her, and it was all she could do to keep from throwing up. Damn, she really hated feeling bad. She started removing papers, careful not to tear them. The documents were old and yellowed, stiff with age. Abby dug through the box and stopped when she pulled out a thick volume labeled THE CLAYTON PLANTATION.

"Oh, my God, Mom, now I know what's been bothering me about the dream I had this morning! Yes, that's what woke me up. There was this girl—she was young, in her early teens. In my dream, she was a slave, and there was something so familiar about the dream. You know, sort of like déjà vu? It's really been bothering me ever since. It was like there was something I was supposed to know, and now I think I remember. In the dream, there was a small brick house. It's where the girl lived before she was moved to the big house. It was one of the buildings at the plantation—I know it was. And in the dream, the girl kept saying something about a Mr. Clayton. She was pregnant, and the baby was his. Oh, my God, Mother, the dream was a nightmare."

# Books by Bestselling Author
# Fern Michaels

| | | |
|---|---|---|
| ___ **The Jury** | 0-8217-7878-1 | $6.99US/$9.99CAN |
| ___ **Sweet Revenge** | 0-8217-7879-X | $6.99US/$9.99CAN |
| ___ **Lethal Justice** | 0-8217-7880-3 | $6.99US/$9.99CAN |
| ___ **Free Fall** | 0-8217-7881-1 | $6.99US/$9.99CAN |
| ___ **Fool Me Once** | 0-8217-8071-9 | $7.99US/$10.99CAN |
| ___ **Vegas Rich** | 0-8217-8112-X | $7.99US/$10.99CAN |
| ___ **Hide and Seek** | 1-4201-0184-6 | $6.99US/$9.99CAN |
| ___ **Hokus Pokus** | 1-4201-0185-4 | $6.99US/$9.99CAN |
| ___ **Fast Track** | 1-4201-0186-2 | $6.99US/$9.99CAN |
| ___ **Collateral Damage** | 1-4201-0187-0 | $6.99US/$9.99CAN |
| ___ **Final Justice** | 1-4201-0188-9 | $6.99US/$9.99CAN |
| ___ **Up Close and Personal** | 0-8217-7956-7 | $7.99US/$9.99CAN |
| ___ **Under the Radar** | 1-4201-0683-X | $6.99US/$9.99CAN |
| ___ **Razor Sharp** | 1-4201-0684-8 | $7.99US/$10.99CAN |
| ___ **Yesterday** | 1-4201-1494-8 | $5.99US/$6.99CAN |
| ___ **Vanishing Act** | 1-4201-0685-6 | $7.99US/$10.99CAN |
| ___ **Sara's Song** | 1-4201-1493-X | $5.99US/$6.99CAN |
| ___ **Deadly Deals** | 1-4201-0686-4 | $7.99US/$10.99CAN |
| ___ **Game Over** | 1-4201-0687-2 | $7.99US/$10.99CAN |
| ___ **Sins of Omission** | 1-4201-1153-1 | $7.99US/$10.99CAN |
| ___ **Sins of the Flesh** | 1-4201-1154-X | $7.99US/$10.99CAN |
| ___ **Cross Roads** | 1-4201-1192-2 | $7.99US/$10.99CAN |

### *Available Wherever Books Are Sold!*
Check out our website at **www.kensingtonbooks.com**

# MEET FERN MICHAELS IN CHARLESTON!

*Are you one of Fern's biggest fans? Well, here's your chance to meet Fern and let her know in person!*

Enter the "Meet Fern Michaels in Charleston" contest; the winner and a friend will receive an exciting trip to Charleston, SC, to have lunch with #1 *New York Times* bestselling author Fern Michaels, tour the historic town, get a Fern Michaels tote bag filled with signed editions of *GOTCHA!* and the entire Sisterhood series, and go on a $500 shopping spree!

**AND a character will be named for the winning entrant in a future Fern Michaels novel!**

## IT'S EASY TO ENTER!

**On Facebook:**
Visit @OfficialFernMichaels or @KensingtonPublishing

**Online:** Visit fernmichaels.com or kensingtonbooks.com/Fern

**Via Mail:**
Send in the entry form in this copy of *GOTCHA!*, or download a copy at kensingtonbooks.com/Fern

Hurry—entries must be postmarked by **August 30, 2013!**

**For prize details and full contest rules, visit kensingtonbooks.com/Fern**

# MEET FERN MICHAELS
# IN CHARLESTON
# OFFICIAL ENTRY FORM

(No purchase necessary to enter or win)

Name (First/Last)

Street Address (P.O. boxes not accepted)

City

State

Zip Code/Postal Code

Phone

Mobile Phone

Email

Purchased at

**Mail this entry form to:**
Kensington Publishing Corp.
119 West 40th Street,
Dept. 21 FM Contest
New York, NY 10018

**To download a copy of this entry form,
visit www.kensingtonbooks.com/Fern**